Marrying Up

JACKIE ROSE

lives in Montreal, Quebec, with her husband, daughter and dog. After cutting her teeth in the publishing world editing a travel magazine, she decided to devote herself to writing full-time (and not just because she prefers to work in her pajamas). Jackie is the author of *Slim Chance,* also published by Red Dress Ink. *Marrying Up* is her second novel.

When she's not looking herself up on the Internet, Jackie likes to spend her time sleeping, shopping and musing about the meaning of it all. She's currently hard at work on her third book.

Marrying Up

Jackie Rose

**RED
DRESS
INK**
™

MARRYING UP

A Red Dress Ink novel

ISBN 0-373-89530-5

www.RedDressInk.com

Printed in U.S.A.

For Dan, the bookends of my love life.

Eternal thanks to…

My amazing editors: Sam Bell, for your kindness, calmness and can-do-ness (I'll miss you terribly!), and Farrin Jacobs, for your thoughtful, artful guidance in shaping this story. My devoted agent, Marcy Posner, for all your wisdom and patience. Superdesigners Margie Miller and Tara Kelly for another wonderful cover. Margaret Marbury and the rest of the brilliant group at Red Dress Ink for making it all happen so beautifully yet again.

A truly stellar team of baby-sitters—Sandy, Bubba, Rachel, Nelu and Allison Ouimet—for loving my kid as if she were your own. Galit, for letting me adopt and abuse your laptop (I hope it's still under warranty). Shoel, Issie, Rose, Ted, Dan, Darline, Selena, Dino, Keenan, Jordy and Sarah, and all the girls, near and far, for asking, caring and sharing.

Dan, most of all, for being my live-in motivational speaker. Your passionate sincerity, sympathetic soul and boundless enthusiasm for all things me remind me daily why I married you. And, of course, Abigail—the littlest, loveliest person I know.

prologue

The Last First Day of the Rest of My Life

Buzz buzz! "Looks like another scorcher today folks! Eighty-eight degrees and—" BUZZ BUZZ! "—rising fast! But we've got twelve uninterrupted minutes of cool tunes coming up—" BUZZ BUZZ! "—so stick around for some Culture Club, Metallica and Phil Collins—" BUZZ BUZZ! "—right after these—"

My first conscious thought is that I want very much to stab myself in the eardrums to make it stop. But I smack Snooze instead, the blessed silence returns, and I bury my aching head beneath the pillow.

Soon, instead of cursing Buffalo's Number One Home of the Eighties, Nineties and Beyond with all the fire and venom I can muster, I'm dreaming fitfully about Phil Collins. He's holding a crisp white bouquet of stephanotis and riding naked on a unicycle down the aisle at my brother's wedding....

BUZZ BUZZ! "—and the seventeenth K-HIT caller who can tell me Axl Rose's real name—" *BUZZ BUZZ!* "—will win a pair of tickets for tomorrow night to see November Rain—" *BUZZ BUZZ!* "—the rockingest tribute band Buffalo has ever—" *BUZZ BUZZ!*

Oh, for God's sake!

(SMACK!)

I lift the pillow and squint, one-eyed, at the glowing green numbers…. 8:10. *Crap.* But everything gets fuzzy and warm again and I drift off… Ahhh…there's Phil again, and he looks lovely—

BUZZ BUZZ!

Grrrr…

(SMACK!)

I squint again… 8:23? *Damn.* I squint harder… 8:28! *Shit!*

Painfully, excruciatingly, I open the other eye. A pack of Canadian cigarettes next to the alarm clock comes slowly into focus….

No. Please no. Oh God, NO! NOT AGAIN!!!

I wipe the sleep from my face, panicking now. On the floor, ripped spandex shorts, a bicycle seat and a muddy tire….

Maybe it's a dream. A bad, bad dream.

I pinch myself—hard—just in case, and wait.

Nothing.

Hoping against hope, I turn over….

Ugh. There he is—Jean-Jean. On my formerly very white Egyptian polished-cotton sateen jacquard sheets by Ralph Lauren. Still wearing that dirty baseball hat. Still sleeping. *Snoring,* even. The audacity.

Maybe he's just a hallucination.

Yes, that's it! A hallucination induced by alcohol poisoning!

But as last night's events bleed through my slowly waking mind like a spreading stain, I recall that I only drank two and a half martinis over a four-hour period. Barely enough to give me a hangover, let alone mental delusions or visual disturbances of any kind.

But wait... Hold on a second... I *did* have several olives, come to think of it, and hadn't I once read somewhere that gin-soaked olives have been known to cause, in some suggestible individuals, effects not unlike those of the storied tequila worm?

Perhaps not. But surely there was an explanation other than the obvious: That I'd slept with the idiotic French-Canadian bicycle messenger from work.

Again.

And yet here he is, all wrapped up in my fine 400-thread-count bedding like a birthday present from hell. *Happy 29th, Holly! Here you go—humiliation incarnate. Hope you like it!* What, pray tell, could I look forward to next year? A tumor?

But it isn't my birthday. Thank God at least for that. Nope, it's just a plain old Friday morning. Which means that last night's senseless debauchery was both desperate *and* stupid, completely devoid of any excuse—rational, alcoholic, depressive or otherwise. Understandable for a Saturday night maybe, when the symptoms of singlehood flare up and otherwise disgraceful hookups might be forgiven, but on a Thursday?

I should be ashamed of myself. *Beyond* ashamed, really. Why hadn't I just stayed home alone and watched an *E.R.* repeat with a cheap bottle of wine like all the other normal, hopeless, single women in Buffalo?

"*Excuse* me," I say, and nudge him with my heel. Hard.

He turns over, grunts and smiles.

"Ahem!" I say loudly, covering myself.

"Heh?"

"Please, Jean-Jean, wake up! *Allez vous!*" I don't know much French, but I can assure you my tone spoke volumes.

"Come hon now, *ma petite*. Believe me when I tell you I *know* you don't want dat! For sure I know dat!"

"Jean-Jean, it's like this, so please listen carefully. Last night was a mistake. I know I've said this before and I'm sorry, but this time I really mean it—I don't want to see you anymore! So please just go home, okay? *Please*. Just go…"

He grins and rolls his eyes at me. "Dat's what you said hlast week, 'Olly, and da week before dat! But you halways come back to Jean-Jean for more!"

"Well, I can promise you I'll be sticking to my word this time and—"

"Eh!" He puts a nicotine-stained finger to my lips. "Why say someting you regret? Jean-Jean, you know, is twice da fun! And to love 'im is to deserve 'im more dan once, *ma petite*. Many, many more time dan dat! So now dat you 'ad 'im, you can't forget. No *never!*"

With that, he hops out of bed and begins collecting the T-shirts and rags and rubber bands which comprise his work uniform.

"What does that even *mean?*" I moan to no one in particular, and fling his cigarettes toward the door. "*Please* hurry, will you? I'm late for work…."

"Jean-Jean is halways 'appy to oblige you, 'Olly. See you—layter!"

The cheeseball winks at me twice, in case I didn't catch it the first time. He stuffs his crap into a mud-splattered backpack and swaggers out the door, leaving me alone with a beer bottle full of cigarette butts and unwelcome memories of last night's awkward fumblings.

I pull the covers back up over my head for a few precious moments and vow to try and see the bright side of this latest romantic debacle. Like…at least I was getting some! That has to be worth something, right? And to be completely honest, Jean-Jean isn't such a bad guy, anyway—

he just needs to grow up a little. With some career counseling and maybe a *Queer Eye* makeover, he might even
make a nice boyfriend for someone someday. Just not for
me. In the meantime, what did it matter? Nobody would
ever have to know...

Except *moi,* that is.

Fortunately, my history with Jean-Jean taught me that
while the nausea and self-loathing born of my temporarily
misplaced affections may linger for a while, eventually they
dissipate along with most of the gory details. (Mother Nature is no fool—if the passage of time didn't take the edge
off our labor pains, our heartbreak, our bikini waxes, the
human race probably would have died out aeons ago!) And
thanks to a few modern amenities—namely condoms, soap
and water—potentially unwelcome reminders of such ill-ad-
vised trysting are practically a thing of the past.

The regret, though...well I suppose that's a little different.
It never fully disappears. It just sort of fades away until it be-
comes a tiny little pinprick of shame, part of the growing
list of things I wish I'd done differently, or not at all. Yes, the
regret is unfortunately quite permanent. Kind of like the new
grease spot on my pillowcase.

Two showers later—including a violent exfoliating session
that would have skinned a lesser woman alive—I am officially
late for work before I've even left my apartment.

No, the day has not begun well.

On difficult mornings such as these, I try to find solace in
a series of uplifting aphorisms I've collected over the years.
They help me salvage whatever shreds of optimism I can
from the wreckage of my life. So I try to tell myself that the
world is my oyster, that comedy is just tragedy plus time, that
today is the first day of the rest of my life.

Today is the first day of the rest of my life?

The perfect mantra for chronically regretful yet eternally

hopeful sorts like me. Most of the time, the simple, wonderful truth of it is enough to put the spring back in my step.

Only today the slate is not clean, the start is not fresh.

The start, in fact, stinks.

part one

Buffalo, New York*

*Home to the most millionaires in America
at the turn of the 19th century.

chapter 1

The Day I Died

It would probably go something like this:

Hastings, Holly. 1975–2060. Passed away of chronic liver disease on Friday, December 31, 2060, alone again on New Year's Eve, since she didn't have a date, and hadn't in many, many years. She was 85.

Miss Hastings, was born in Buffalo, the fourth child and only daughter of the late Louise McGillivray Hastings, a bookkeeper, and the late Lawrence Hastings, a schoolteacher, both also of Buffalo.

After completing a three-year degree in Journalism and Professional Writing in slightly more than five years at Erie County College, Miss Hastings took a job at this newspaper, which she believed would be an important stepping stone in her fabulous career as a writer. The single Miss Hastings quickly found her place among the many talentless hacks at the *Buffalo Bugle,* penning obituaries and taking classified ads for more than fifty years, until her forced retirement in 2052.

During college, Miss Hastings took up social drinking, which eventually evolved into full-blown alcoholism after a string of failed relationships. Due to her inability to write the Great American Novel, or even a Not So Great One, the mateless Miss Hastings never left the *Bugle,* as she had planned. In fact, she never left the Buffalo-Niagara Region. Hell, during the last five years of her life, she never even left her house!

Miss Hastings leaves behind nobody—not even a cat. The bulk of her meager estate will be divided among her many creditors, and her body will be donated to medical science, unless somebody claims it before noon tomorrow.

Well, that wasn't so bad, really. I've almost certainly—no, make that definitely—come across worse lives, *written* lamer obits for real, actual people. Haven't I?

Hmmm…

Okay, so even if I haven't, technically speaking, there's no cause for alarm just yet. The whole point of the exercise is to imagine the way things *might* turn out, you know, if everything stays the same. To see where my life is heading, worst-case scenario. But even if it all comes true, so what? Cats, after all, are pretty crappy compared to dogs, so if ever there were a pet *not* to have… And let's not underestimate the ultimate satisfaction of sticking it to the credit-card companies from beyond the grave.

I print my final draft, fold it up until it's a tiny little square and shove it way down into the bottom of my bag.

Okay, Holly. Back to work. No need to feel sorry for yourself.

Despite the fact that I hardly have a thing to do except sit around and wait for someone to call, I try to keep busy. I hone my pitch for a story about the Buffalo fashion scene (don't laugh—we can't all live in New York or London or Paris, no matter how much we might like to, but that doesn't mean the rest of us are oblivious to life's finer things) and color-code my files until at last the phone rings. Will it be a trumpet seller? A passport found? A grieving relative? My boss, Cy, telling me he finally needs my feature, A.S.A.P?

"Holly Hastings," I say into the receiver.

"Um, hi." A woman's voice. Very shrill. "I want to place an ad. In the personals."

"All right," I sigh. "Go ahead."

"Okay. It's for the 'Women Seeking Men' section."

Of course it is. "Yup. Go ahead."

"Will you tell me if you think this is okay?"

"Sure." Poor thing. I knew she didn't have a chance, and I hadn't even heard it yet.

"Okay," she exhales purposefully. "This is what I have. 'Cuddly thirty-five-year-old princess seeks knight in shining armor. I love babies, four-star restaurants and international travel. You're a gorgeous, tall, marriage-minded physician or lawyer, between thirty-three and forty. I'm five foot one, have brown hair and brown eyes.'"

"Oh, that's perfect," I say, taking it down.

"You think?"

"Definitely."

"Oh my God! I can't believe I'm doing this!" she shrieks. "I'm so excited! Can you get it in for tomorrow morning? Before tomorrow night, I mean? Can you? I have an extra ticket to *The Vagina Monologues* at Shea's!"

"Sure thing."

"Great!"

I take the details and hang up.

Women Seeking Men. As if. Had she ever taken the time to

actually read our little rag, she might have noticed that for every ten women seeking men via the services of the *Buffalo Bugle* there is only one man seeking woman.

It is all just so sad. Sad and funny. Sad that she dares to believe Dr. Right will call her by tomorrow night to begin with. Funny that she thinks a show about female sexuality and the c-word will make suitable first-date entertainment anyway. And sad again that *The Vagina Monologues* is not just a theatrical experience, but also a fairly accurate way to describe so many of our sex lives. Because only the rare, the proud, the few can claim to be involved in any coed, long-term, mutually respectful…er…*dialogue*.

And that's okay.

Just because it's sad doesn't mean it has to ruin your life.

You see, some women wallow in singlehood the way pigs wallow in shit. But that's just not me. There's no shortage of far worthier sources of anxiety and self-reproach, like bioterrorism and ozone depletion and flat-chestedness. I also find obvious desperation of any kind profoundly futile, since I know that men—even the most uninformed, unenlightened, uninspired of them—unerringly pick up on that scent a mile away. In theory, therefore, there's no point in being miserable simply because one happens to be flying solo, while broadcasting your panic at the thought of it will simply ensure that things stay that way.

So even though the prospect of dying alone and poor and completely catless might faze some, I will probably handle it quite well; as a person who's experienced near-epic singlehood, I don't even know what it's like to be in a meaningful relationship, save for one long-term mistake and a few flings here and there, all of which ended in varying degrees of disaster and confusion. Truthfully, it has never really bothered me before. I've always trusted that fate will bring me together with the man I'm designed for, some day, some way.

Until now, I suppose.

I reach back down into the bottom of my bag and feel around for the little square of paper. For the first time ever, as I reread my pitiful obituary, twinges of doubt make inroads into the romantic certainty that has served me so well for so long.

What if he never comes? What if he doesn't exist? What if we never meet, and just pass each other by in the street over and over again until we marry the wrong people, divorce, grow old, get senile and die? More likely still, what if I screw it all up when we finally do find each other, and all that lonely, crazy, catless stuff really, truly happens?

The seeds of self-pity had been sown that morning, when Jill, my roommate, whose life I'd always thought was at least a little bit worse than my own, threw some sympathy my way after she saw Jean-Jean exiting my room.

In the kitchen, she and her everpresent but vaguely mysterious boyfriend exchanged knowing glances across the table as I frantically ripped open a box of Pop-Tarts.

"There's fresh coffee," Jill offered. "Hazelnut-vanilla decaf. I just made it." I could tell that what she really meant was, *Holly, you poor, poor thing. What a horrible ordeal you've been through. Perhaps a hot beverage might distract you from the memory of it, if only for a few moments.*

"No time," I said, fighting with a silver package. "You'd think there was gold inside these bloody things...."

She looked at me with sad eyes. "You're so meticulous about everything, Holly. Except what you put in your body."

"Thanks, Jill. I know."

The girl is a health fiend. Yoga, soy, supplements—the whole package. How someone can go through life like that is beyond me. The way I see it, we only have five senses, and to squander one of them on the likes of kale and lentils is akin to blinding yourself voluntarily, no matter how much cumin is involved.

Somehow, though, she manages to make me feel like a child every time I order a pizza or sleep in on Sunday. Don't get me wrong—I love her to pieces. In some ways, Jill Etherington is like the mother I never had. Well, that's not exactly fair, since I do in fact have a perfectly serviceable mother, albeit one who never really minded if I ate Count Chocula for dinner in front of the TV or skipped phys ed in high school.

To save a few minutes, I decided to eat my Pop-Tart raw. She shook her head as I stuffed the broken pieces into my mouth.

"It's an acquired taste," I informed her.

"Why don't you at least sit down to eat?" she suggested.

"Why don't you stand up?" I snapped back.

Despite my impatience with her that morning, one of the things I admire most about Jill is how she's always ready and dressed for work two hours before she has to leave the house. Granted, she goes to bed at 9:00 p.m., but still—being early for anything is an excellent quality I hope one day to have. Maybe it has to do with being excited to get where you're going—work, date, spinning class, whatever—but since Jill is a clerk at a paper-processing plant, and I know for a fact that she despises her job, that theory couldn't possibly explain her rise-and-shine attitude.

Not to say that I'm late for things. Actually, I'm often on time, even if it's just barely. When I have to be somewhere, the digital clocks in my life govern my every move. In the morning, I know precisely how long it takes me to shower, to get dressed, to eat. A mere minute one way or the other might make the difference between panic and calm. I'll even blow a traffic light to save a few seconds on my way to work.

A therapist of mine (I no longer remember which one,

exactly) once suggested that my personal game of *Beat the Clock* has nothing to do with valuing punctuality, but rather that it's part of a need to inject drama and adventure into my daily life. While that may be true, I also know that waltzing in past your coworkers twenty minutes after nine makes a bad impression, no matter how late you stay to make up for it, and is definitely not a good way to get ahead.

Lately, though, despite knowing better, I seemed to be having an awful lot of trouble getting to the *Bugle* on time, and not just on those mornings after the night before. Since it was becoming clear that I was never going to get ahead there no matter how early I showed up, I suppose I was finding it a little hard to stay motivated.

"Don't be grumpy, sweetie," Jill said.

"Huh?"

"I said, don't be grumpy."

"I'm not grumpy. I'm late," I mumbled.

Boyfriend, who'd been uncharacteristically quiet until that point, slammed his mug down on the table. "No way! I hope that *dupa* with the bicycle seat isn't the father!"

"No, you idiot. Late for *work,*" I said.

Boyfriend was a bit of a moron, and a lot of an asshole, though Jill chose not to see it. His name, for the record, is not at all important. Although my dear roomie is quite taken with the idea of having a boyfriend in general, she doesn't seem to care all that much about who fills the position, and is content to overlook all manner of glaring biographical inconsistencies in order to enjoy the perks of coupledom. She hasn't been single for more than forty-eight hours since junior high, and this latest prize was simply one in a long line of subpar rebound guys who'd morphed into serious boyfriends.

"Seriously," Jill said. "What's going on with you and Jean-Jean?"

"Umm, we… I mean he and I were just… I was… I mean, he was…"

She waited patiently for me to finish, but there really wasn't much I could say in my own defense. It was a rotten, unholy lust whose name I dared not speak for fear of giving it any more power than it already had.

Boyfriend glanced up and offered, "Well, I think you two are perfect for each other."

"You don't have to be ashamed, Holly," Jill added kindly. "Your personal life is your business and I'm sure you have your reasons. And he's…not so bad, really. So why don't the two of you consider dating more seriously?"

"Are you joking? I can't tell…"

"Well, you obviously can't keep your hands off each other. I suppose you have chemistry or something. What's so terrible about that? It's…*nice.* Embrace it."

The girl was obviously insane. Served me right, answering an ad for a roommate from the bulletin board in my therapist's waiting room.

"I don't want your pity." I put my head down on the table and closed my eyes.

"There, there," she said, and began stroking my hair.

But Boyfriend would not be deterred. "I think Holly's hot-hot for Jean-Jean!"

Brilliant.

"Yeah, I think maybe she is," Jill agreed.

Walking in to work late was definitely better than this. "I think one of you's *extremely* jealous and *incredibly* hot for Jean-Jean, and the other one's crazy. And I think Jill's the one who's crazy."

"I suppose that makes me jealous," he deduced.

"Among other things." I got up and headed for the door. "And if you don't mind, keep your nose out of my business."

"She must be on the rag," he said loudly to Jill, who rolled her eyes and looked at me as if to say, *"I know he can be a little insensitive, but at least he's got a pulse."*

The beauty of my job is that I know, better than almost anyone, how even the most pathetic of existences usually reveal at least some merit when you simmer them down to a mere two hundred and fifty words. Vacuous socialites, crooked politicians, celebrity pornographers and yes, even old maids—all leave their mark in one way or another. Sometimes you just have to read between the lines.

Take the life of John Michael Whitney. Local boy, beloved son and brother, star of his high-school football team—that part was easy. Unfortunately for Johnny, though, his True Defining Moment—most every life has one, subtle or not, and the best obituarists can nose them out like bloodhounds—came a bit later on, when he ran over and killed the mayor of a small town on the Texas-Arkansas border while fleeing the scene of a botched liquor-store robbery in the mid-'80s.

Of course, poor Mrs. Whitney loved her son dearly despite his many vices, and requested that we gloss over the incident in his obituary. "He was so good at football," she told me plaintively over the phone, "and crafts, too." Turns out the guy was the Martha Stewart of Death Row, finding solace among his beeswax candles and Christmas wreaths, which he sold to the guards' wives for cigarette money. But the state wasn't nearly as impressed, and in the end, not even his God-given talent for macramé was enough to save him from Old Sparky. But I made sure to include it in his final tribute.

It may sound overly forgiving—what of the poor mayor (a bigot and a drunk!) and his grieving widow? (a two-timing tramp!)—but that's just part of what we obituarists sometimes have to do: rewrite people's less-than-stellar lives into pleasant little blurbs to help friends and relatives feel all warm and fuzzy about them. It's the ultimate final makeover, and I believe everyone deserves at least that.

Everyone except me, it seems.

There is nothing warm and fuzzy about my life lately, unless you count the chenille throw I'd taken to huddling beneath on the sofa, emerging only for work and a few hours of drunken weekend abandon, with the occasional booty call from an idiotic bicycle messenger thrown into the mix. If there is merit in there somewhere, damned if I can see it.

The upside of such a mundane existence is that I am left with plenty of time to wonder about the meaning of it all. Where is my life going? Will I ever have a real boyfriend? Do I have a destiny? And if I do, and it turns out to be a shitty one, will it be possible to change it?

Answering these questions has recently become Number One on my priority list, relegating to Number Two for the first time in three years my plan to save up enough money for a set of large but not huge breast implants. The tasteful kind.

As the waves of existential angst wash over me day after day, week after week, month after month, much as they had in high school (minus the haunting Bauhaus soundtrack), it has begun to dawn on me that there might be more to it all than an okay job and a rundown two-bedroom flat over Marg's Olde-Tyme Medieval Shoppe.

Which brings me back to why I really spent the better part of this morning writing my own obituary and cursing the cats I didn't have. It's not as morbid as it seems, actually. Plenty of obituarists while away the hours in between jobs perfecting their own final tributes, as well as those of friends and loved ones, or even, if the mood for vengeance strikes, those of enemies, bosses, ex-lovers and so on.

Of course, I usually while away those very same hours taking classified ads for free puppies and used cars, since I wear many different hats at the *Bugle*. Many ugly, unflattering hats, including one Get-Me-A-Coffee-Will-Ya-Holly fedora, ungraciously bestowed upon me most mornings by the Life & Style Editor, Virginia Holt. Not that I even work for her, but what can I say—no? I don't think so. Not if I want her to accept one of my story pitches before the end of time. One day, I hope she and her enormous crocodile Hermès Birkin bag—which I would bet a year's salary was the only one in the entire city—will be kissing my arse, but until then, my lips are glued to hers.

Anyway, maybe it's because I'm superstitious, but I have never been able to shake the feeling that if I wrote my own obit, there would suddenly be occasion to use it, like the second I left the building a giant anvil would fall on my head and pound me into the pavement à la Wile E. Coyote. The same reasoning prevents me from signing the organ-donor spot on the back of my driver's license, something which I believe is tantamount to suicide. It's like saying, "Hey! Whoever's up there—I'm ready! Take me now and feel free to use my parts!"

I explained all this to Dr. Martindale last week after he suggested the exercise as a way to pinpoint the source of my growing anxiety, but he wasn't buying it.

"Nope. It's a bad idea," I told him. "Definitely a bad idea. Hits too close to home."

"What are you afraid of?" he asked.

"Ummm, dying?"

"That's original."

"I'm in no position to be taunting the gods, Doctor M. No way."

"It'll help you learn a little bit about yourself. Writing one's own obituary is a fantastic impetus for action. I recommend all my patients do it—even the ones who don't happen to write them for a living."

"Ha, ha. But seriously…I can't do it."

"Sure you can."

"I don't want to."

"Why not?"

I thought for a moment. "Maybe I don't want to confront my own mortality?"

That sounded good.

"No, I don't think so," he said. "But maybe…just maybe…you're afraid of confronting your own *vitality*." He pronounced the last word slowly, as if I needed help figuring out how very witty he was. Utterly spent, he leaned back in his big leather chair and folded his hands triumphantly over his belly.

I squirmed on the couch. "Are you going to put that in your next book?" I asked. "It's pretty cheesy, if you don't mind me saying so. Oh, but that reminds me—I've been meaning to tell you this—since it doesn't look like I'll be writing *my* book any time soon, I thought maybe *you* could immortalize me by using me as one of your case studies. Whaddya think?"

"I think you're using humor to avoid a difficult topic."

"…maybe something like, 'Holly H., moderately insane twenty-eight-year-old brunette with flat hair and obsessive-compulsive tendencies including but not limited to a fear of free-falling anvils and severe stove-checkitis?' That would be fine with me, if you want. And maybe you could also mention that I'm cute and not currently seeing anyone."

He smiled broadly. "Is it really any wonder why?"

Even my own shrink didn't think I was relationship material.

"Careful…" I told him. "I know you have a son, and I know he's single. You don't want me looking him up now, do you?"

"He doesn't go for pretend-crazy, Holly. He prefers the real thing," he said without skipping a beat. "And if you want me to use you as a case study, you're going to have to give me a little more than just garden-variety phobias and general wishy-washiness. Not if it's going to be a page-turner."

"I'm sorry my misery bores you, Doctor M."

"Not always. Have you had any more poodle fantasies lately?"

"Huh?"

"Oh…sorry," he said, flipping back through his pad. "That was my eleven o'clock."

Nice. How could I beat that?

"I do have a recurring nightmare about Phil Collins. I think it might be sexual. Does that help?"

"Not so much, no."

"Well, I'll see what I can do."

Dr. David Martindale is a very well-respected and widely published psychologist on the self-help circuit, and I was lucky to count myself among his patients. Still, I wasn't so sure it was going to work out between us. The butterflies were gone, so to speak.

Yeah, yeah, so I'm a therapy junkie. I've been to twelve different psychologists and psychiatrists over the past five years and I'll make no apologies for it. I see the entire mental health profession as a sort of sanity buffet from which I can pick and choose what I like and pass over the rest. The breadth of my phobias and anxieties demands a holistic approach.

Hmmm…

Okay. So maybe I'm making it sound a *little* worse than it actually is. I am in fact quite a normal person. A normal person who simply has no luck with men, feels underappreciated at work and whose self-esteem just so happens to be in free fall at the moment. That's the problem, I guess. I figure if I keep digging a little deeper, I'll find something fascinating behind my averageness. Something less mundane than the truth, which is that growing up being relentlessly teased by my three older brothers and for the most part ignored by my beaten-down parents has turned me into one of those self-deprecating panicky types looking for love and appreciation in all the wrong places.

I know it may seem self-indulgent on the surface, since I don't have any *real* problems to speak of, but therapy has changed my life. It has helped me learn who I am—privately quirky, a little bit dark, but ultimately hopeful—and imparted to me the gift of self-awareness. You see, monitoring my own thoughts and feelings saves me from the thing I fear the most: Limping through life like a mindless automaton. The woman in the gray flannel suit. The lovesick puppy dog. The enthusiastic imbiber of cyanide-spiked Kool-Aid.

The problem, I'm beginning to realize, is that all this heightened consciousness comes at a price. When you finally start to see yourself as the universe sees you—one of roughly six billion ants living beneath a perpetually upraised foot—desperation and apathy cannot be far behind. So, to take the sting off the inexorable march to the grave, I sometimes enlist the services of other ants with medical prefixes to help me turn my frown upside down.

I'm currently involved with two therapists. They don't know about each other, but I'm thinking of telling Berenice about Doctor M., just to spice things up. Since she sees all psychiatrists and even most psychologists as pill-pushing whores in cahoots with evil pharmaceutical conglomerates, it'll give her some incentive to come up with something a little more inspired than Saint-John's-wort and a bubble bath, those panaceas of the antiProzac set.

Despite my misgivings about Martindale's commitment to the seriousness of my complaints—I had to admit that his obituary exercise sounded a lot more promising than Berenice's solution (which involved some sort of birth reenactment), so I decided to throw caution to the wind and give the obituary thing a shot. There was just too much junk swirling around in my mind, and it seemed like a decent way to start clearing it out.

As I reread the news of my passing, one possible path laid out before me, I have to wonder: What would it take to rewrite this life? Defined by one horrible crime and faced with years of boredom and loneliness and regret on death row, John Michael Whitney clung hopefully to his pine cones and glitter glue. I'm sure, in his own mind, he saw himself not only as a murderer, but as an artist, with something positive to offer the world. But what about me? Is there anything out there to redeem *my* existence, before it's too late?

The prospect of emerging from Berenice's giant plastic womb a brand-new person suddenly sounds a whole lot easier than figuring that out.

chapter 2

Writer's Block

Even though I knew George was probably busy—Fridays being the day she rips the covers off mercifully unsold fantasy novels at the Book Cauldron and sends them back to the publishers—I called and asked her to meet me for an emergency lunch. I calmly explained that if she didn't come and rescue me from myself, I was bound to dash immediately across the street and buy seventeen cartons of cigarettes, after which I would be only too happy to ditch work and spend the rest of the afternoon in the park, smoking one after the other until there was nothing left of me but a bit of charred lung and one diamond earring. (I'd lost the other last week, and was hoping that the remaining stud, in its loneliness, might magnetically guide me to its partner's hiding place.)

"Why all the doom and gloom?" George asks as she plops down into the booth.

"Look, you know me," I say. "I'm an optimist."

"Mmm, I wouldn't say that. You're too superstitious."

"Fine. Then I'm a *guarded* optimist…."

"More of a fatalist, I'd say. But a cheery fatalist."

"George! Just listen. The point is, I think I'm losing my grip on happy thoughts. Something's got to be done." I pull the tattered obituary out of my purse and slide it across the table.

"What's this?"

"Just read it," I tell her, exhaling dramatically.

As she does, I signal the waitress. "I'll have a bacon cheese-burger, a double order of fries, and a Jack and Coke."

She looks up from her pad and pushes her sliding glasses back up her nose with her pencil. "We don't have a liquor license here, ma'am."

Nice. The one day when I could really use a bit of liquid lunch.

"Fine. Make it a milkshake, then. Chocolate."

"I'll have the Nicoise salad," George says. "With the dressing on the side, and no potatoes. Oh, and are there anchovies on the salad?"

The waitress nods.

"Were they packed in oil?"

"I would say so, miss."

"Hey!" I interrupt. "Why is she a miss and I'm a ma'am?" The nerve.

They stare at me blankly, then return to the business at hand. "Well, then forget the anchovies," George tells her. "No, wait. Keep them. No wait! It depends on the tuna. Was that packed in oil?"

"I don't know, *miss.*"

George is utterly confounded. "What should I do?" she asks me.

I shrug.

"How about I just bring you a nice green salad?" The waitress suggests.

"Okay," George smiles, relieved. "Oh, and a Diet Coke. With a wedge of lime."

The waitress shakes her head and shuffles off in her sensible orthopedic shoes.

"Dressing on the side!" George calls after her. "God. That was close. Which do you think are worse—carbs or saturated fats?"

"Are you kidding? I have no idea," I say impatiently, motioning for her to keep on reading. In the meantime, I snack on my fingernails.

As soon as she finishes, she reads it again, then ponders for a minute or two. "I think you're nuts. Why did you write this? Didn't you say you'd never do your own?"

"Yeah, but Doctor M. said it would help me see where my life is going, give a voice to my hidden fears and then identify new goals for myself."

"And the problem is…what exactly? You're afraid you'll never have a cat? 'Cause if that's it, we can get you a cat. I think there might even be a sign up at the store. Black kittens or something…"

"Ha, ha," I manage weakly.

"Look, Holly. If you're for real about this…"

"I am. I *so* am. Help me."

George nods seriously. "Okay. Where to begin? Well, I guess everyone's afraid of dying…"

"I'm not afraid of dying," I tell her. "I'm afraid of dying *alone*. I'm afraid my life will have meant nothing to anybody."

"I get it, I get it." She thinks about it for a second, then adds, "Look. It's okay to want to change your life, to write a book or whatever. It's okay to want a better job. Work on that. Fine. But you're afraid of being single? Come on. That's so…mundane."

"I know. But all of a sudden I can't help it. I just never thought my life would turn out like that. And looking back over my eighty-five years—what did I really contribute? *Nothing!* God, what a waste! And I had so much love to give...*so much love to give...!*"

My throat tightens and my ears begin to ache. I flash back to Dr. Pink, a self-styled "lacrimal therapist" from a few years back whose clinical methodology involved systematically reducing her patients to tears. She believed that public crying was not a sign of weakness and emotional instability, but rather a healthy purging of inner turmoil and a sacred statement of communal trust to be celebrated by anyone fortunate enough to witness it. But I hated crying—here, there, anywhere. No wonder Pink only lasted three sessions.

I gulp back the tears, but George is unimpressed. "Okay, first of all, Holly, you're still alive. All right? You didn't die single. You didn't even die. For God's sake, you're only twenty-eight. So it's not like you can say your life 'turned out' like anything, because you haven't even lived it yet."

"Exactly," I whimper.

"Huh?"

"I've got to *do* something, G. Before it's too late."

"So do something. Take action, girl!"

"But what? That's the problem."

"Why don't you just try to write something?"

Just what I need to hear. "You write," I snap, a little too cruelly. It's a sore point for her. George has been working on the same *Star Trek* screenplay since our second year at Erie. By the time she gets around to finishing it, the actors who play the characters will all have boldly gone into retirement.

She twirls a dark and frizzy curl around her finger and stares down at the table.

"I'm sorry," I say. "You're absolutely right. I should try. I really should. But...but you know how hard it can be. It's like,

I work all day, and I finally get home and the last thing I want to do is stare all night at another screen."

She snorts.

"TV doesn't count." Just try and come between me and my set.

The waitress delivers our meals and leaves before I can complain.

"This is wrong," I whisper, knowing George will forgive me if I can make her laugh. "Didn't I ask for chocolate? What's the point of vanilla? Who would want a vanilla shake? It's the complete antithesis of chocolate—it's the absence of flavor!"

The waitress glances over at me from the cash with a dour look.

"You want me to get her back?" George giggles as she wrings every last drop of flavor from the lime wedge into her Diet Coke.

"Don't you dare!" She knows I am deathly afraid of incurring the wrath of food-service persons. They have so much power. Complain one too many times and God only knows what might find its way into your tuna-salad sandwich.

"You've seen too many *Datelines,*" she informs me as I sullenly drink my shake.

"Hidden cameras will be America's new conscience in the twenty-first century," I say between slurps. Vanilla isn't so bad, really.

"Now *there's* a topic worth exploring…."

I've spent the past five years trying to come up with a great idea for my book, and George is always trying to help.

"Naw, it's already been done."

Since September 11th, countless writers have taken fear and ignorance to the bank, but I feel that people are ready for happier thoughts, instead of just another paranoid title like *The Osama Next Door,* or *Nine Legal Ways to Watch Your*

Nanny, or *Why Vegetables Cause Cancer*. Unfortunately, though, thoughtful critiques of consumer-health alerts and diatribes decrying the end of privacy have also been done to death. But what if I incorporated those themes into a novel? *Hmmm*… It just might be crazy enough to work.

"Holly?"

…a sort of *Bridget Jones's Diary* meets *1984* meets *Dr. Atkins' New Diet Revolution*…

"Holly? Hello?" George snaps her fingers.

"Sorry," I mumble, and promptly lose my train of thought. Ideas for my book are so exquisitely rare and delicate that the mere act of remembering them crushes their goodness into oblivion. I've all but resigned myself to the impossibility of writing a single word.

"You just need a little inspiration."

"How can I get inspired when all I do is work, come home, watch TV and boink the bike messenger?"

Oops.

"Aw, tell me you're kidding! You *didn't!* Not again! Ew!"

"I did," I reluctantly admit.

"But he's so…he's so…"

"Gross? It's okay. You can say it. I know he is."

"I knew I should have come over last night. You're not to be trusted. How many times do I have to tell you? Holly Hastings *good*. Bicycle boy *bad*."

"I was working late, and he was there picking something up…."

"Mmm-hmm…"

"Look, I finally finished the piece about that new parking lot on Broadway and I wanted to celebrate! Is that so wrong?" Very occasionally, when they tired of my constant begging for assignments or felt a hint of guilt after turning down yet another one of my story proposals, one of the editors will ask me to fill a few very unimportant inches, usually sandwiched on some back page between the calls to tender and the previous day's corrections.

She peers at me skeptically. By now, George has long since inhaled her salad and has moved on to eating her dressing-on-the-side with a spoon.

"Well, I was home alone, and would have been delighted to go out for a drink."

"Umm…didn't you have that coven thing with your mom last night?" As the product of a mixed lesbian marriage, George was half Wiccan, half Jewish.

"Oh please, Holly."

It was worth a shot. I knew full well that the next Wiccan day of worship wasn't until the fall equinox.

"Okay, so maybe I just needed to be held."

"But by Jean-Jean?"

"What can I say? I'm pathetic," I groan. "What's wrong with me?"

"You're just a lonely, lonely woman. You know, I bet if you found a job you liked better, everything else would fall into place. And one that uses FedEx instead of that shitty messenger service."

Oh, if only it were that simple.

"There's nothing really wrong with my job. I can think of at least a half dozen people who would kill to work there. It's me, G. I know it is! It's like all of a sudden, I'm so bloody bored and frustrated and negative about it that I don't know what to do with myself. And it's not like I'd be able to find something better in Buffalo, anyway… I'd have to move to New York for that, and God knows that would be a little more than I could handle right now! Besides, I'd rather be at the *Bugle* even if there's no chance of me ever getting promoted to anything, *ever,* than at some boring software company or bank writing internal newsletters. My job's fine. It's me that isn't!"

"Well, that's a relief. Because frankly, just being bored at work isn't a good enough reason to drive you into the arms of Jean-Jean."

"I'm teetering on the brink!" I shriek. "I'm playing Russian roulette with my love life.... God! I must be *insane.* Who knows what else I'm capable of!?"

She nods sympathetically and glances around to see if my ranting is disturbing any of the other patrons. "I know, Holly. It sucks."

But there's no stopping me. "You know, up until a couple of years ago, everything was fine.... I liked work. I was proud of my job. Yeah, I was! I learned something new every day, even if it was just useless stuff like how much Sabres tickets were going for, or how to spell the names of rare diseases. And you know what else? I was even able to write. Not that I always did, mind you, because usually I didn't, but I could, you know? When I wanted to..."

"Calm down. I remember. There was that short story about the big empty house with all the locked doors and the kid with the key-shaped fingers. It was very *Twilight Zone.* You could have submitted that somewhere, you know. It was good. *Really* good."

"You think?"

"Oh yeah."

"Maybe I should have written a whole book of short stories," I sigh. "It was totally my genre."

"Still could be."

"Don't you ever just feel like things used to be better in general? Like weekends. Weekends used to be so much fun, remember? Clubbing Fridays *and* Saturdays. Sometimes even Thursdays. Waiting in line at Blaze all night. Who cares if we even got in? That was fun! Why don't we ever do that anymore?"

"Blaze burned down. And I think you might be romanticizing things a little…. We mostly just got drunk at McGinty's. There was never any lineup there."

I laugh. "Probably because there were no doors on the stalls in the bathroom. What a dive! Still, it was great, wasn't it? But now whenever we go somewhere, I feel like everyone's five years younger than me and five times hotter and has better clothes and better jobs. Don't you find?"

"Um, this is still Buffalo we're talking about. You may very well have one of the best jobs in town," she points out. "And *nobody* has good clothes."

I raise an eyebrow at her.

"Except you," she corrects herself.

"Thanks. But I have to buy everything over the Internet because you can't find so much as a Louis Vuitton key fob in this town, not that I can afford one, anyway. I *hate* Buffalo, I feel like I'm over the hill at twenty-eight and…oh, screw it—I'm just going to say it. I want a boyfriend! I know it's wrong, but I want a boyfriend. I want to be in love. *So* badly. It's pathetic, I know, but I'm ready for my man. I really am. I'm tired of being above it all."

George stares at me blankly. I've broken a sacred secret contract, and admitted That Which Should Never be Admitted by enlightened twenty-first-century women.

"Don't look at me like that."

"Sorry. I was just wondering what a key fob is."

"I guess I thought that once I truly stopped caring about being alone, I wouldn't have to be."

"Like attaining nirvana the moment you shed all of your worldly concerns?"

"Exactly."

The waitress, who has been listening in on most of our conversation, pops over to strike while the iron is hot. "Dessert, ladies?"

"Cheesecake," I manage faintly.

"And two forks," George adds. "You *will* find him, Holly. You're both just doing your thing until you're ready to meet, remember? And when you do, it'll be forever. Isn't that your theory?"

It is, but the whole Someday-My-Prince-Will-Come thing just isn't working for me anymore. What I need is a warm body. With a heart. And a head. And a… Hell, who am I kidding? I want the whole damn package.

"All these years…" I moan weakly. "All these years, and I've just been sitting on the shelf, like an unwanted carton of milk about to expire." The painful truth is that I've only had one long-term relationship, and that was back during my first year at Erie.

"That's not exactly true…"

"Jim doesn't count. Our relationship was based on a lie."

After the crushing disappointment of graduating from high school still a virgin (I was pretty enough in a plain sort of way, just ridiculously shy around guys), I allowed myself to be tricked into a relationship with one of my brother Bradley's loser friends. Jim was four years older than me, something that impressed me to no end, and still a virgin, too. I would later discover that as part of Bradley's continuing efforts to get poor Jim laid, he and his friends decided I would make the perfect sacrificial lamb, since apparently none of the girls his own age would have anything to do with him and my thoughtful brother had overheard me crying to a friend about the humiliating prospect of entering college never having gotten any myself.

Bradley told me Jim liked me, and I eagerly fell in love with him before our first date. Things really blossomed from there. Jim and I were both glad to finally be having sex, so much so that he was even willing to endure the constant ribbing from his friends at not kicking me to the curb the morning after I gave it up, precisely seventy-two hours into our courtship. For my part, I was happy to overlook his dubious career goals—any job that allowed him to collect a paycheck while still being able to smoke pot all day long, a plan that came to glorious fruition in a part-time gig he landed driving one of those mini sidewalk-snow-removal buggies. Naive young thing that I was, and because Jim wasn't exactly an evil person, I was also able to overlook those defects in his hygiene and intellect that had likely offended every other woman he'd met prior to me in order to experience the joys of couplehood for the first time.

Alas, the beautiful thing that was us casually dropped dead at a New Year's Eve party about a year and a half into our romance, when Jim's beer-soaked buddy Wojack marveled aloud at how much money had changed hands over the consummation of our relationship. I dumped Jim on the spot, after he high-fived Bradley instead of trying to lie his way out of it. And if I could have dumped Bradley that night, you can bet your life I would have. Making book on the Sabres was one thing, but your sister's virginity? It's no wonder my self-esteem's a little shaky when it comes to men.

"The years are flying by, G. By the time someone wants me, I'll be rotten and lumpy."

"Lumpy's not so bad," George says. "I'm already lumpy."

"But you're *good* lumpy."

My best friend's waist-to-hip ratio is fairly generous, though it certainly doesn't seem to bother anybody except her. When we walk down the street together, George's jiggles and curves and curls garner far more lustful stares than my straight lines do. Still, she's pretty timid when it comes to men, and almost completely oblivious to her effect on them. Her "sort of" boyfriend—one of our old creative-writing profs, a serial student-dater who's been toying with her for years—isn't helping *her* self-esteem much, either.

"Good lumpy? I wouldn't go that far." She snorts at the

suggestion that such a thing might actually be possible. "I'd take an A-cup any day. You don't know how lucky you are."

"So why hasn't it happened for me yet?"

The closest I'd ever come to a relationship since Jim (and now Jean-Jean, I suppose) was a string of three one-night stands with the same guy. Over the course of two semesters. He was a fairly cute bartender at a popular club just off campus—quite a coup, but I could never shake the feeling that Freddie thought I was a different person each time.

"Just give it time, Holly. It will. I promise. For both of us. And we're in it together till then…"

At least I have that. With George around, I know I will never really be alone. We sit in silence for a bit, finishing the cheesecake. Good old cheesecake. How can you be sad when it's giving you a great big hug from the inside?

"Maybe I just need to regroup," I say finally. "Get a handle on things. Figure out where my life is going."

"That's the spirit!"

We pay the bill and head outside. It's late August, and very, very hot. Three blocks away, the mirrored windows of the *Buffalo Bugle* tower shine brightly before the mostly older buildings of the city skyline. Inside, I know exactly what's going on: absolutely nothing of any interest whatsoever. Today is exactly the same as yesterday, which was exactly the same as the day before that, and the day before that. I want to walk in the other direction.

"I haven't taken a holiday since Christmas, you know."

"Nobody could fault your work ethic."

"It's not doing me any good. Nobody notices. I'm there late all the time, working on all kinds of things that aren't even part of my job description."

"They notice, Holly. You're really good at what you do. Look, call me later and we'll figure it out. Just promise me you won't start smoking again! At least not today…"

"Smoking, drinking, snorting—what's the difference?" I laugh. "Remember, I know how it's all going to end, anyway, so I may as well have a good time now. In fact, we should probably go out tonight and toast my long, lonely life. Like a premortem wake!"

"Oh, yeah!" She grins. "Now, *that's* my girl!"

We part ways and George heads back toward the dingy bookshop and her own lame job, which is just as boring and futile as my own, although, it suddenly occurs to me, she never really seems to complain about it.

Fortified by diner food and the promise of a good night out, my optimism surges. And thinking about John Michael Whitney reminds me that my life—even the sad and lonely one I'd envisioned for myself that morning—reads like an absolute fairy tale. My obituary will be a call to arms; things are going to change.

Cy will have to understand. Though ground down by years of unpaid overtime, he rarely takes a day off, opting instead to live and eat and sleep in his office and take it all way too seriously. It's not that Cy's nasty, or even sexist—something I'd heard implied more than once by my oft-overlooked female coworkers—but he just doesn't seem to get that not everybody can give one hundred and ten percent for $24,500 a year and no dental benefits.

"I need to take some personal time," I tell him as soon as I get back from lunch.

Personal time, I am fully aware, does not count toward employees' vacation time, of which I still have one week left and am hesitant to squander before Christmas. Though a right guaranteed by law, taking personal time usually imparts a faint whiff of mental instability, unless of course there's been a death in the family. If Cy perceives my asking for it now as crazy or, even worse, frivolous or lazy, it might move me down a notch in his books, and I need him on my side if I am ever to get ahead at the *Bugle*.

"I see," he says without looking up from his screen. "How much?"

"A week."

"When?"

"Starting Monday?"

He glances at me. "That's soon. Everything okay?"

"Yeah," I sigh. "But I'm a bit...burned out."

That oughta work.

Most of the senior reporters and editors I know seem to regard journalism as a sort of religion, with cynicism standing in where faith should be. It's their lives, twenty-four/seven, and it's easy to become weary under the weight of it all, whether you're reporting live from the trenches of a war-torn Iraq like Christiane Amanpour or penning "The Buffalo Entertainment Beat" like the *Bugle's* own Bucky Jones. In theory, it should be no different for me. Invoking a burnout, like losing the faith, is a serious admission, and one not to be taken lightly. Plus, it might even have the added benefit of suggesting to him that I take my job more seriously than I actually do.

"Okay," Cy says. "Just get that intern whatsisname to cover you."

"That's all?"

"Yup. Have fun. And shut the door on your way out—I can't seem to get a fucking moment's peace today."

So that's it. I am so easily replaceable that an unpaid intern whose area of expertise is photocopying his ass is able to do my job on a moment's notice.

I back out of his office and shut the door. His name, stenciled in stout black capitals, stares me square in the face: CY THURRELL, SENIOR ASSOCIATE EDITOR. Cy had finished school nearly two years after I did, though he was only one year younger. He'd started at the *Bugle* as a lowly free-lancer three years ago and moved up the ranks at the speed of light.

It has actually turned out to be a pretty big news day for Buffalo—a small warehouse fire and a hit-and-run involving a monster truck and a traffic light downtown—so the frenzied comings and goings of my coworkers are more than enough to distract me. The prospect of an accidental death or two has whipped me into stand-by mode, and I await intelligence of any fatalities with my usual combination of concerned journalistic professionalism and detached personal curiosity.

Now I suppose I should ask anyone who might find my anticipation of tragedy distasteful or inappropriate to please keep in mind that this is what I do, day in day out, and am no more eager for news of someone's death than a garbageman is eager to see the can on the curb. But I will admit that five years at this gig may have hardened me a little to the whole concept of death and dying, to the point where I can probably think of it and speak of it with more ease than most. I consider this a blessing of sorts, since it has freed me from the usual hang-ups and sentimentality associated with the whole mess, provided the death in question is not my own, of course.

The key, in my line of work, is to strive for balance. And what could be more life-affirming than someone who makes you thank heaven you're alive? Jesse, a reporter for the City Desk and deliverer of a crush that comes and goes, scoots over on his chair to apprise me of the situation.

"Fire's not too bad. Team's there now," he says, with a crack of his gum. Normally, that sort of terse sexiness would be enough to send me into a tizzy of stuttered responses and imagined wedding-planning, but today I'm not up for it, even though he is in Abercrombie & Fitch from head to toe.

"What about the monster truck?"

"No word on any casualties yet, Hastings."

"Except for the light, of course."

"Ha! Except for the light, yeah."

I'm always my bravest around Jesse when the crush is in its dormant phase. Nevertheless, I half hope my sympathy for defenseless city property and humor in the face of senseless tragedy might awaken him to all the many wonders of me, but instead of asking me out, he just grins and propels himself backward down the corridor on his squeaky old office chair, quads bulging suggestively through perfectly worn-out khakis.

I long ago dismissed the possibility of anything ever happening between us, owing in equal parts to his gorgeous girlfriend and the fact that he rarely gets my jokes, which I know make me come off as an absolute idiot. Still, I can't resist, meaning the better part of my interaction with Jesse consists of awkward explanations. So the traffic light quip was a significant achievement, and by the end of the day, I've decided that we're going to have exactly four children: two boys and two girls, all black-haired and blue-eyed like him, but the girls would have my adorable freckles.

In the end, the monster truck claimed no human victims, so I have no subjects today other than the usual cancer-stricken and myocardially infarcted—and myself.

chapter 3

Goodbye, Norma Jean

Saturday afternoon and it's Madison's sixth birthday party. I have spent the past week trying to change my future and this is my reward. I brought George along to dull the pain, since I've already spent three out of the last five weekends watching my various nieces and nephews blow out candles and tear through stacks of gifts like tornadoes. Don't get me wrong— I love each and every one of the little brats dearly (except for maybe the twins), but they do try the patience. To complicate matters further, I am seriously considering hooking up with the usual entertainment: the guy in the furry purple Barney suit. Not that I've ever seen his face, but that's part of what intrigues me about him.

In addition to the possibility of seeing my mystery man, I am also hoping the party will give me a chance to talk to my brother about his job. Cole works at a car-parts factory in a depressed little rust-belt town northeast of the city.

"If I'd known there was going to be so much food, I would have stayed home," George complains sullenly as we settle into lawnchairs as far removed from the mayhem as possible. "I've resolved to lose ten pounds by Thanksgiving or else."

"Or else what?"

"Or else I'm blaming you."

"Auntie Holly! Auntie Holly!" My niece Savannah comes squealing around the corner and jumps onto my lap. "Save me! AAAAHHH!!! Don't let them get MEEEEEE!!!" Two boys I don't know and one of the twins—Harrison, I think—are close on her tail, brandishing neon plastic weapons of some sort.

"Stop right there," I demand. "What are those?"

"Thuper Thoakers!" Harrison growls.

"What?"

"Super Soakers," George explains. "They're water guns."

"Oh, don't even think it…" I tell them as I try to pry Savannah's sticky fingers from around my neck.

"She said we were worm barf," one of the boys explains matter-of-factly. "And now she must die."

With that, they all open fire. Savannah takes off shrieking, but we're already soaked.

"Fuck," George says as she stands up to shake herself off. "I think it's lemonade."

I try to use the hose to wash off, but there's no water.

"We turned it off this time," Olivia, my sister-in-law, explains as she dashes by with a tray of hamburgers. "They kept spraying into the house last time."

"Great." As I go inside to wash up, I can't help but notice that Cole and Olivia's house might benefit from a spray or two. The decor, courtesy of their three small kids and two large dogs, is suburban eclectic: broken plastic toys in primary colors, couch-pillow forts, Elmo paraphernalia as far as the eye can see and fur-covered wall-to-wall carpeting, which thanks to a little foresight on Olivia's part, is roughly the same shade as the dogs. At four-year-old hand level, black splotches of what might once have been grape juice provide a lovely focal point for the room.

When I finally make my way outside again, George is talking to my parents. Well, just my mother really, because my dad doesn't talk so much. He just sort of stands there next to my mom thinking about other things. Or maybe he's just standing there not thinking anything. It's impossible to tell.

"George just mentioned you took the week off?" Mom says while trying to untangle the chains from the three pairs of glasses dangling around her neck. "Do anything fun?"

I glare at George. "Nope."

"That's too bad. Did you have any cake, dear?"

"Yes."

"And did you see the kids?" she asks, looking past me toward the sandbox where Madison is hitting another little girl in the face with a plastic shovel.

"What kids?"

"Well, we're going to go on over and say hi to the birthday girl. C'mon, Larry." She makes a beeline for the sandbox and my dad shuffles off behind her.

We lie around in the sun for a while drinking beer, waiting for the entertainment to arrive. Alas, my furry purple hunk of burning love is a no-show, or maybe this particular group of kids has just seen enough of Barney for one summer, and so we are left with an adolescent acne-scarred magician. The kids, of course, are more interested in trying to steal his wallet than any of the handkerchief tricks he's performing.

George, who's been scanning the scene of frenzied, foaming six-year-olds and their wasted Stepford parents with as much interest as she can muster, turns to me languidly and slurs, "I don't think I want kids."

"Oh, come on—don't base your maternal future on one six-year-old's party."

She waves me off. "I just don't think I'm the breeding type. It's too much responsibility, raising a kid."

The thought of remaining childless by choice seems odd to me. "But what will you leave behind? It's our duty as human beings to make sure our genetic material continues its evolutionary march toward perfection."

"Big deal. There are plenty of others willing to carry that torch."

"I suppose."

"And you could choose to be single too," she adds. "Imagine the freedom. To actually *try* to stay single forever."

"That's warped."

"Think about it, Holly—it sure would take the pressure off. Men do it all the time. And it's not like either of us will have to deal with any backlash from our parents or anything like that…."

George's mothers, while perhaps overly involved in their daughter's life, would never dream of pressuring her into couplehood or marriage. The possibility that a woman's happiness or self-esteem might be dependent on anyone with a penis was simply beyond their sphere of comprehension. And my parents are more like spectators in my world, instead of active participants. They're pretty old (I was a fortieth birthday surprise package for my mom) and besides, their urge for grandkids has already been filled eight times over by my brothers. So my mother isn't all that interested in my social life, while my dad is so obsessed with model trains that he's hardly come up from the basement since he retired and probably wouldn't notice if I brought Marilyn Manson home for dinner.

"…although, since I am so truly fabulous it would be a crime…no, a *sin*—a sin of omission!—to deprive the world of my offspring. Hey, I know! Maybe I could just be an egg donor instead!"

George always gets a little cocky and grrl-powerish when she's drunk, and the Perlman-MacNeill family values come flooding through, unrestrained by her usual mild-mannered self-deprecation.

"Sounds great," I tell her.

"They pay you, like, a couple thousand bucks a shot for that, you know. And it would be a real mitzvah, helping an infertile couple get pregnant...."

The thought of George in stirrups with some mad gynecologist harvesting her eggs was a little far-fetched. "This from somebody who's afraid of tampons."

"Yeah, but I still use them," she giggles, propping herself up on a plump elbow. "I'm sorry, but if you *really* think about it, the idea is just totally gross. Admit it!"

After debating internal vs. external feminine hygiene products for a good twenty minutes, I'm ready to go bug my brother for a job. By the time I make my way over to the patio, Cole is a bit drunk and bleary-eyed himself, and his face is smudged and sweaty from standing over their old barbecue all afternoon.

"Aw, come on, Holly. You don't want to work with me. You're a writer, not a drill-press operator...aw, *shit*...would ya look at that? Mackenzie! *Mackenzie!*"

Three little girls turn their heads.

"But Cole—"

"Mackenzie go inside if you have to go potty! Sorry Holly, what did you say? Goddamit, like the dogs don't do enough damage to the grass...." Fluffy glances over at him from his spot in the shade and growls. Cole shakes his head and tosses him a hot dog that has been charred beyond recognition.

"Look, the truth is my job is totally dead-end, anyway. I've got to make better money so that I can save up and then take a year off to write a book." Not a bad plan. I'd come up with it during a *Roseanne* rerun—one of the episodes after the Connors win the lottery and we find out that Roseanne the writer had been imagining the windfall all along (a dreadful ending to a perfectly good sitcom, but inspirational for my purposes nonetheless). Since I couldn't count on winning the lottery, I needed to find a way to make good money fast.

"I don't know…"

"*Please!* I *need* you to get me in."

"Olivia! *Olivia,* goddammit! Skyler's playing with dog poop again!"

"Come on, Cole—you're union. You make tons of cash and you get amazing benefits."

"Yeah, compared to you, maybe, but I have all this to pay for." He makes a vast sweeping gesture with his spatula, indicating the yellowing sliver of lawn and modest house owned, for all intents and purposes, by the bank. "You don't want to work on the line, Holly. And you'd suck at it, anyway."

"No, I wouldn't."

"Yes, you would. It would kill you. Shit. It's killing *me.* You think this is what I wanted to do with my economics degree?"

Before I can respond, the back of my mom's red helmet of hair blocks my field of vision. "Cole, your brother wants another cheeseburger," she says, holding out a paper plate.

"Mike, you lazy bastard!" Cole yells. "Come and get it yourself! You're ten feet away! Ma, he's ten feet away…"

Mike, who'd been dozing in a lawnchair for three hours, flips him the bird, inspiring a hard punch from his wife, Lindsey.

Cole shakes his head and puts another burger on the plate for my mom to bring him.

"That's his fourth one," Cole says. "No wonder he looks more pregnant than Lindsey."

My three older brothers are nothing if not virile. Cole has three, Mike's waiting on his fourth (as if the twins weren't enough), and Bradley, who lives in Detroit, has two, but his wife Bonnie is also pregnant.

"Cole, you're not listening to me."

"Why should I? It's a stupid idea."

"Hey—I think it's a great idea!" Mike pipes in from behind.

"Shut up, Mike. No one's talking to you."

I've learned the hard way not to expect any genuine support from Mike. (My brothers really are a bunch of jerks—until the age of thirteen, I honestly believed my mother was planning to sell me to the circus when I was born, but that my father had discovered her plan at the last possible moment and intervened, saving me from a life of shoveling elephant shit.) Cole's the only one of them who takes any responsibility for the endless teasing and torturing they subjected me to while growing up, and I'm pretty sure that's because Olivia talked some sense into him over the years (she's like the older sister I never had). Mike and Bradley *still* snap my bra strap, and sometimes even practice wrestling moves on me when my parents leave the room.

But old habits die hard, and Cole feigns intrigue. "So tell me, bro—why should I get her a job?"

"Well, she has skinny fingers, so she might be useful for fixing the machinery…"

"True. Go on…"

I can see *exactly* where this is going. "Shut up, Mike! Cole, don't listen to him," I beg.

"…and she wouldn't be a distraction to the other guys, that's for sure."

"She wouldn't? Why not? Because I was kinda thinking she would…"

"Naw…no boobage!"

Cole stifles a laugh and elbows me playfully in the ribs, while Mike endures two more punches from Lindsey.

"Fuck off. Both of you." I grab another beer and make my way back to George.

"What was that about?"

When I tell her, she laughs. "Great idea, Norma Rae. So this is what you've come up with after a week on the couch?"

"Could it be any worse than what I'm doing now?"

"Uhhh, yeah."

"At least I wouldn't be broke."

"Please. You would not last a single day working on an assembly line," she says between bites of an empty hot dog bun. Apparently, she's decided that fat is indeed worse than carbs. "Your brain would revolt."

"I'll adapt. I'll write my book in my mind while I work," I inform her. (I'd thought it all through very carefully.) "The blue-collar experience will also contribute to my growth as an artist. And what doesn't kill you makes you stronger, you know."

"Maybe, but it also hurts a hell of a lot." She shakes her head and starts in on another bun.

"G, I am so sick and tired of being broke. And I'm tired of saving up for months to buy a proper pair of black boots."

I'll admit that it took me quite a while to realize that just because I had a real job didn't mean I could actually *be* Cosmo Girl and go out and buy all the pretty things I saw in *In Style* magazine. It required more than three years of scrimping and saving for me to pay down the unholy credit-card debt accrued during my first six months at the *Bugle*—something George will never let me live down. Despite that initial lapse in judgment, however, I remain a proud member of the Spend-a-Lot-on-Your-Bag-and-Shoes school of fashion. A true classic never goes out of style, and expensive accessories have the power to redeem the rest of a lackluster wardrobe.

"Well, no one said they had to be Jimmy Choos," she says coolly.

They were my one splurge this year; an investment certain to yield years of pointy-toed pleasure.

"Yeah? Well, I'm even *more* sick of having to shop online. I can't believe I live in a city that doesn't even have a Prada store…."

"As if you'd be able to shop there, anyway! You can't even afford the Saks outlet!"

"Maybe not, but I bet just knowing a Prada's around is a damn good feeling."

"If you want to move to New York, just do it already, Holly! You've been talking about it for years. But if you decide to stay, then we can probably both agree it doesn't really matter if Buffalo has a Prada store or not because unless their spectator pumps come in a steel-toe version, I highly doubt they'd pass the safety codes at the factory. And if they did, it would spoil your plan to save up enough money to take a year off, anyway!"

She's right. I am afraid. Afraid of New York—where real writers live, where rent exceeds my current annual income, where people toss last season's Jimmy Choos out with the trash. Why did it all have to be so damn hard? Why couldn't I just be one of those lucky people who has everything she wants, from guys to Gucci and back again? I quietly eat the icing off my third slice of birthday cake.

"This party sucks," I conclude.

"No available men."

We survey the scene. Aside from my brothers, my dad and a few other bored-looking fathers, the magician appears to be the only unattached postpubescent male.

As if she could tell what I was thinking, George shoots a dark look my way. "I think he might be a bit young for you."

"Maybe, but I bet he has a few tricks up his sleeve…."

"Cute. Very cute. At least you can still joke about it."

"I don't want to be a sad singleton," I sigh.

"Better a sad singleton than a happy breeder."

"Enough with the Camille Paglia. Tomorrow you'll be begging Professor Bales for a booty call."

"Yeah? Well the day *after* tomorrow you'll be back at work."

"Oh, that was cruel." I clutch at my heart. "So, so cruel."

She shrugs. What can she say? I'm trapped and we both know it.

We sip warm beer from sticky cups for the rest of the afternoon.

"So?"

George is demanding an answer. It's Sunday, the last day of my "vacation."

"Well, as you know, I've been doing some thinking…."

"Mmmm. Come up with anything since yesterday?"

"Well, I can admit you were right about the whole factory idea. I wouldn't want Cole to be my boss, and he'd probably just make fun of me all day long and I'd end up pushing him into some sort of giant turbine or whatever they have there and that wouldn't really be fair to Olivia or the kids."

"Obviously not."

"So I guess I'm still sort of mulling things over. Trying to see the big picture…"

"And?"

"These things take time, George. There's no telling when my epiphany might come. Could be tomorrow. Could be next month. Could be next year."

"Could be never."

"You can't force it."

"Enough's enough, already, Holly. I'm coming over."

"Knock yourself out. But I'm warning you—I'm *profoundly* depressed, and in no mood for company."

"Whatever," she says, and hangs up.

I am, of course, feeling fine. Things are much better now that I've had a full week to catch up on *The Young and the Restless*. Something about having a peek at the problems of others—especially the rich and fictional—always makes my concerns seem almost trivial. Who cares if a single Burberry scarf is enough to throw me into debt for six months? I have a job and a roof over my head. Does it really matter that my cup size is an A while my grades were always Cs, instead of the other way around? I can't change the past, but one day I might get the boobs I've always wanted. And so what if I don't have a boyfriend? At least I'll be spared the pain of him cheating on me with my devious stepmother and then developing amnesia after being thrown overboard from his twin brother's private yacht while fleeing to the Cayman Islands to escape some dark secret of his nefarious past. Plus, I don't have to worry about anyone leaving the toilet seat up.

By the time George shows up it's after eight and I'm starving. Not only is George incredibly slow-moving to begin with, but she still lives at home with her mothers out in Williamsville, so for her to shlep her ass into the city by bus takes forever. I've been on her case for years to get her own place, but with her salary, she'd need at least two roommates to make it work.

"Sorry," she says when she finally arrives. "There was an accident on the Kensington."

"You at least need to get a car if you're going to live out there."

"I know, I know. But then I'd have to get my driver's license, too."

Even though George claims to still be full from too much birthday cake and hot dog buns the day before, we order an extralarge pizza and wait for it to arrive.

"How's Jill?" George asked. "I never see her anymore. Where is she?"

"Oh, she's pretty much always out."

"That's good for you. It's like having the place to yourself."

"I guess." Truth is, I'd rather have someone around to talk to. "She'll probably be home soon. I think she does an underwater bicycling class on Wednesday nights. Or is it Pilates in a steam room? Something like that."

"Does she stay at whatsisname's a lot?"

"No. He usually stays here. I doubt if he even has a fixed address. He's such a weirdo. I caught him going through the Dumpster out back yesterday."

"What? Why?"

"He said he threw out some important paperwork by accident or something. Not that he has a job, so I have no idea what he was even talking about."

"Yikes."

"Yeah, plus I'm pretty sure I saw him on *America's Most Wanted*."

George's big green eyes widen in horror. "Tell me you're joking."

"Well, the actor sure looked an awful lot like him."

"Who are they looking for? What did he do?"

"Some guy from Wisconsin who disappeared from a halfway house about six months ago. He apparently slips in and out of a violent state without knowing it, and he's already responsible for three murders in the Midwest—"

"No!"

"Yes. But the really creepy part is that all of his victims look exactly like his mother—"

"Get out!"

"Yeah, and first he stalks them and then he lures them into this creepy van and then he—"

We both jump as we hear the key in the door.

"God! Oh my God!" George whispers frantically.

But it's just Jill.

"Is this pizza boy yours?" she asks. "I found him in the lobby."

"Yup!" I say, jumping up to get my wallet.

"Hi Jill," George says as I pay for dinner. The pizza boy ignores my attempt at a flirty smile and I consider taking part of his tip back.

"Hey," Jill answers, tucking a blondish strand behind her ear. "Long time no see."

"I brought a movie over, if you want to watch with us."

"Thanks, but I'm exhausted. I'm going to try and go to bed early. Don't let Holly stay up too late, 'kay?"

"I won't," George said. "She has a big day of doing nothing tomorrow."

"I hear you!" I yell from the kitchen.

"Yeah, well, get a life!" Jill yells back. "I'm not complaining," she continues to George. "Holly's been doing a lot of things around the house."

Since Saturday, I've reorganized the pantry, installed three new coat hooks in the hallway, laminated a list of emergency phone numbers to put on the fridge *and* found time to watch at least six hours of TV every day. All in all, time well spent.

After Jill watches us eat (she grabbed a sprout sandwich earlier), she retreats to her bedroom to talk on the phone. Boyfriend, apparently, is away on "business," and missing her terribly.

"Well at least she has someone to make her happy," I conclude sadly after we've torn apart his many flaws as quietly as we could.

"That's no excuse," George says. "She can do better."

"Do you have a pash on her or something?"

"What's that?"

"A girl crush."

"Oh," George giggles. "As if."

"Anyway, you're a fine one to talk about standards."

She sits up abruptly. "What's that supposed to mean?"

"Just that maybe you should try taking your own advice for a change."

"Oh, really."

"Don't be annoyed. You know you can do better than Professor Bales, but I don't see you turning him down when he invites you over for a quickie every once in a while."

"Would you stop calling him that already? And for your information, what I have with Stuart is totally different. I consider myself single. I'm still in the game. Jill's not. And I don't just drop everything and run whenever he calls me, by the way. I go only if and when I want to."

"When was the last time you didn't go?"

"I'm not a teenager," she frowns. "I don't keep track of things like that."

"Oh, admit it—if he wanted to get serious, you would in a second, even though he's a total player."

"We've agreed to keep it casual. It's worked for us for this long."

"You mean it's worked for *him*. Because casual or not, it sucks for you and you know it. You're afraid to call him. The sex is lousy, I'm sure. How could it not be? He's, like, at least fifty. And he won't even bring you out in public…"

"Umm, hello? It's, like, totally inappropriate for us to be seen together."

"Come on! I can't believe you're still buying into his bullshit. He's not your teacher anymore, G. No one gives a crap if you're together. I bet he's just afraid one of the dozen or so students he's probably sleeping with will see you."

She pouts for a while and stomps off to the bathroom. I put the pizza away and file what's left of my nails while I wait. After about five minutes, she returns with a dour look and puts the movie in the DVD player. As it's about to start, she lets out a big sigh and gets up to pause it.

"Not that I have to defend myself to you, Holly, but I still like him, okay? And I'm using him as much as he's using me. No more, no less. So until I find someone better, I see no reason to call off a perfectly good thing."

Poor George. She really believes what she's saying.

"Just as long as you keep your options open," I tell her. "Because he's never going to change."

"Why does everyone say that about him? He might. Stuart's very sweet when he wants to be."

"Don't confuse sweet with charming," I warn her. Although she tries to put on a feminist front, George is incredibly naive about men. Maybe it's because she had virtually no exposure to straight men growing up or maybe it's because she's just overly trusting in general. In any case, her instincts are notoriously off when it comes to the unfairer sex.

"You don't really know him, Holly."

"Well, I know that he gave me a D in 'Journalling for Profit, Part II' and that was enough for me. As if I needed Humbert Humbert to tell me my memoirs wouldn't sell a million…"

George rolls her eyes.

"What?"

"Don't even go there," she says.

"Fine. All I'm gonna say is that I can tell you for an absolute fact that that man will never change. How do I know for sure? Well, let me enlighten you, G—it's because *he* doesn't want any more out of the relationship. And he can tell that *you* do. That's why he only calls every couple of months—he doesn't want to give you the wrong idea. Because then the whole thing would be more trouble than it's worth."

I've tried to explain to George many times this most basic

of all dating truths: that neediness is like new-relationship poison. This fact is one of the few things I know for certain about men. In much the same way that sharks can smell a drop of blood in the water from miles away, men can pick up on even the slightest whiff of neediness. A more sporting type might circle your lifeboat for a while, letting you think you have a chance of surviving, but don't kid yourself: He's just playing with you. He knows you're wounded in there, and he's smacking his lips. If, on the other hand, you put out the ice queen vibe right away—let him think *he* wants you more than *you* want him—then you've got some breathing room. And I'm not just talking about sex. Getting a man into bed is easy, no matter how desperate you may appear. The hard part is sustaining your desirability. The hard part is convincing him that he wants to stick around long enough to fall in love with you. Once you figure out how to do that, you're in business.

"Yeah? Well maybe the reason you're single is because you never let anybody know you're actually interested in them," George suggests. "Did you ever think of that? All you do is go on like a *million* first dates, and then reject every one of them before he has a chance to reject you!"

"Well, duh." It isn't anything that hasn't occurred to me or a half dozen of my therapists before. But at least I'm reasonably confident that once I find a worthy prospect, I'll be able to keep him. In the meantime, I'll protect my heart from any further damage.

"Not all men are Jims, Holly. They're not perfect, God knows, but they don't have to be. Because neither are we."

"How perfect is your professor?"

"Let's just watch the damn movie," she grumbles.

"Fine," I say and press Play. "What is it, anyway?"

"*How to Marry a Millionaire.* It's with Marilyn. And I don't care if you hate it."

"Wasn't there anything with Brad Pitt?"

"I don't know. Who cares? This is *so* much better… God, Holly. You're, like, totally boy-crazy these days."

George loves Marilyn Monroe because she was sexy and powerful and vulnerable all at once, and also because she was a size 12 and the whole world loved her for it. She's seen all of her movies a thousand times. For me, though, Marilyn's sadness fills every frame of every film she made. I imagine I would have liked her better before, when she was just Norma Jean Baker. Plain and simple.

"There must have been *something* with Brad Pitt…"

"There wasn't."

"Not even an old one?"

"Just shut up and watch."

Purple moonlight filters through the gauze panels covering the open window, giving my bedroom an almost fluorescent glow. I glance at the clock— 4:15 a.m. Everything is perfectly still.

Since insomnia is one of the few anxiety-related problems I don't normally suffer from, I'm a bit confused. After thinking for a while, the image of Marilyn Monroe sneaking her glasses onto her face playing on a constant loop, a memory of Dr. Zukowski surfaces from among the usual places my mind goes when it wanders. She's a behavioral therapist who once berated me ferociously in the middle of Pearl Street during an exercise to get me to step on sidewalk cracks. Something she said, lost on me then, flashes into my mind.

"Life isn't really about luck or coincidence, Holly. Nor is it about destiny or kismet or any of that other stuff. You won't win a Pulitzer just by sitting around collecting good karma and then waiting for your fingers to accidentally strike the right keys. And if your mother ever breaks her back—"

"Bite your tongue!" I'd interrupted.

She ignored me and went on. "…and if your mother ever breaks her back, it'll probably be because she tripped over something. *Not* because you walked down the sidewalk like a healthy, well-adjusted person. The world just doesn't work that way."

"Doesn't every action have a reaction?"

"No."

"But I've always thought that life is like the game of pool…"

"It isn't."

"Pinball?"

"Nope… Well, maybe. But only if you think of yourself as the flippers and not the ball, see? Remember, Holly—you were the one who told me you want to be an actor, and not a *re*-actor."

"Look," I sighed. "I *know* you're right. I *want* to be the flippers. And I *know* that my mom's probably going be okay if I step on that crack, and that her health isn't something I have any control over—but it *feels* wrong to do it. It seems so… I don't know…reckless. Like, why take the chance?" It was lunchtime, a weekday, and pedestrians swarmed around us, irritated by our lack of motion.

Zukowski shook her head. "It only feels that way because you've been avoiding the cracks for so long. This problem isn't something I can just turn off inside your head. To overcome it you're going to have to actually *do* it. Over and over again until it doesn't feel wrong. Until it just feels normal. And soon it won't feel like anything at all. Okay?"

I nodded.

"So let's start with our deep breathing…good…good… and now we can try visualizing it, just like we did upstairs in my office…"

Bravely, brazenly, I took a step in my mind. And another. And then another, letting my feet fall where they might. It wasn't so hard.

"Now do it," she prodded.

I raised my foot and started to move forward, but an image of my mother in traction weaseled its way into my brain. My chest tightened and my palms began to sweat. I retreated.

"Holly," she sighed. "How do you expect to move forward if you can't take one simple step?"

She could barely conceal her exasperation, even though my insurance company was paying her $115 an hour.

"I've been getting along fine for years," I informed her. "You were the one who seized on this whole thing. I just mentioned it in passing, and jeez, look at us now."

"Let me put it in perspective for you. I have patients who can't leave their houses. Patients who can't work or eat or sleep. People who are so paralyzed with fear that their lives are barely lives at all. I can help you through this, Holly, but you have to be willing to move."

"I'm pretty happy, you know," I said. "I just want to be *more* happy. I want to be able to write my book."

And this is what she said: "*The difference between a dream and reality is the difference between a goal and a plan.* If you want to write a book, then commit yourself to doing whatever it takes to make that happen, because things will never change unless *you* change them."

Now, two years later, Zukowski's words resonate within my very empty bedroom as loudly as if someone had struck a gong. If I ever want my dreams to become reality, I know what has to be done.

The goal? To free myself from the bonds of serfdom and write my book, the subject of which was now also plainly evident.

The plan? To marry a millionaire. Or at least date one seriously.

chapter 4

A Room of One's Own

The cursor blinks hopefully. *Chapter One*, I type. *Finding a Mark*. How hard can it be?

I dial George's number at work. "Can you get out early?"

"I guess so."

"Meet me at Taylor's at six."

"Why? That place sucks."

Taylor's is an upscale-ish piano bar in the business district. The only reason I even know about it is because it happens to be next door to the only place in town to get decent Chinese takeout after 11:00 p.m., probably thanks to all the late-working lawyers and financial types in the neighborhood.

"I know, G." I tell her. "Just indulge me."

It's Friday, the end to a fairly crappy week. I've spent pretty much the whole of it tied up on a comprehensive 2500-word piece on the best fall getaways in upstate New York—

a rare and pleasant change from the usual bland tasks I'm entrusted with.

Maybe they really are beginning to value me here, I dared to dream as I handed it over to Cy just before deadline yesterday afternoon. I was actually quite pleased with how the story turned out, especially the cute little sidebar on the haunted inns of the Finger Lakes district. After thanking him for the opportunity for the umpteenth time (even though it was actually Mark Axelrod, Travel Editor, who okayed the pitch in the first place), Cy cleared his throat and informed me he'd decided to bank the story indefinitely and reprint something similar he'd seen that morning in the *Times*'s travel section instead. "Maybe we'll run it next fall, Holly, although you'd have to update it. No big deal."

Not to him, maybe. But at that very moment I knew for sure that I didn't want to be at the *Bugle* next month, let alone next fall. And although it was just one silly story on chintz-stuffed country inns and pick-your-own-pumpkin patches, and Cy hadn't even read it (which meant he couldn't possibly hate it), panic set in. The proverbial coffin was being nailed shut—I could *feel* it in my bones.

I had to compose myself in the ladies' room before I could go back to my desk and begin inputting the ads I'd been neglecting all week. Getting through the stack would surely take me the rest of the afternoon…

"Holly?"

I spun around. Virginia Holt, Life & Style Editor, tapping her tweed-wrapped toes like she'd been waiting there all day.

"Oh. Hi, Virginia."

"Did I interrupt you?"

"Uh…"

"Not working on anything important, then?" Her nostrils flared in anticipation while she smoothed back her brassy red bob.

*You know perfectly well that I rarely work on anything impor-
tant, Virginia, thanks in large part to you turning down every story
idea I've ever had.*

"Well, actually—"

"Good. Because I need you to run these down to accounting *immediately*. It's the contributors list for last month,
and the check numbers don't match up with the invoice
numbers on *any* of them. Wait there for those halfwits to
redo each and every one of them and then bring them back
up to me *personally*. Do *not* give them to my assistant—she's
been completely unfocused since she came back from mat
leave and this *absolutely* has to be fixed before the end of the
day, 'kay?"

She threw a pile of envelopes and papers down onto my
keyboard and clicked away before I could refuse. Apparently,
the fact that my desk happened to be within fifteen feet of
her office automatically cast me as her backup lackey.

But I couldn't. Not today. I opened my top drawer and slid
Virginia's papers inside, knowing the blast of shit I'd catch
for not doing exactly what she'd asked, but somehow unable
to stop myself, either. Through bleary eyes, I entered one ad
after the other, vowing with each new garage sale and adorable puppy giveaway to set my new plan into motion the following day, the first day of the rest of my life.

The *real* first day of the rest of my life.

I meant it this time.

In Buffalo, where ninety percent of the bars cater to either
the college crowd or career beer drinkers, Taylor's is probably the best place I know of to meet an eligible young bach-
elor of generous means. Even if nothing happens tonight, I
figure it would be a good chance to explain The Plan to
George while scoping out the scene for future reference.

I see my best friend bobbing up the street from a distance.

I can tell it's her because she looks like Stevie Nicks with brown hair, all flowing scarves and bohemian bangles. A curious splash of color in a sea of gray suits.

When she notices me she smiles. "I almost couldn't make it. The new *Mists of Avalon* limited-edition DVD/illustrated-hardback combo boxed set came in early and I had to call everyone on the list—"

I pull her into the alley around the corner. "My God, George. What on earth are you wearing? Do you mind if we tone this down a bit?" I giggle, tugging at a sparkly purple fringe. "We should probably try and maintain a minimum level of professionalism here, for appearance's sake."

That morning, I'd dug deep, deep into the back of my closet for the sleek charcoal suit purchased for my grandfather's funeral two years ago. I thought it helped highlight some of my better assets—small waist, decent backside, well-turned ankles. Being cleavage-challenged is definitely a plus when it comes to professional wear, so I decided to forgo the more obvious choice of a crisp white blouse in favor of a lacy black camisole instead. I even punched it up with some lipstick and blush, a ton of black mascara to bring out the hazel flecks that rescued my eyes from coffee-brown, and tied my too-long dark hair back into a chignon for a change.

More than a few heads turned when I showed up at work. "Got a job interview, Holly?" Cy shouted out as I passed by his office. He was kidding, of course, but he didn't sound overly concerned at the thought of it, either. Virginia just growled at me without looking up when I brought her the files from accounting that she'd wanted yesterday, and to add insult to injury, Jesse never even got the chance to see me in all my gussied-up glory; he was out of the office all day working on assignment.

George twists free of my grasp. "What? What are you talking about? It's too dark in there to see anything, anyway.

And besides, who gives a damn? I like what I'm wearing today."

"Look. Let's just go in. I have a lot to tell you."

"You are such a weirdo," she says, and sashays past me into the bar.

I suppose now would be an excellent time to explain how my decision to try and be…well…less poor and single doesn't make me shallow or evil or a victim or ignorant of sexual politics or anything like that. Okay, maybe it makes me a teeny, tiny bit shallow—I can admit it!—but the honest and sincere way in which I intend to go about the whole thing will infuse that shallowness with a certain depth. I promise.

Because The Plan was not born out of greed, envy, lust or any other deadly sin, but rather from a genuine desire for self-actualization, I know I'm going to have no problem justifying it to myself or others. And I can also tell you that like all great romantic adventures, it's about a whole lot more than just having a warm body to sleep next to or being able to buy Creme De La Mer moisturizer at $110 an ounce without thinking twice. It's not like I've been sitting around for years, crying and wishing I'd simply been born rich, or anything as ugly or unenlightened as that. Yes, this is going to be a love story of my own creation, inspired by my need to write something vital and necessary, and fuelled by my desire to grow and change into the person I want to become.

I will achieve everything I've been working toward in therapy in one fell swoop.

And there's one other thing…one other reason. Marilyn Monroe and her merry band of husband-hunters aside, I've seen the glorious effects of the marriage between love and wealth first-hand. Which is why I also had Asher and Zoe to thank for planting the idea of The Plan within me, at least subconsciously. Our lunch earlier in the summer had sparked a bit of a self-pity fest, so it should come as no great surprise to anyone that, in my weakened condition, I ended up indulging in one of those singlehood meltdowns I'd always felt so immune to. Only *my* meltdown was different, because from it, great change would soon be born.

Zoe and Asher were old high school friends, and I hadn't seen them in ages. Back in the day, the three of us were thick as thieves. Sure, we were big losers—boys who wear black eyeliner and girls who wear combat boots fall somewhere between band geeks and the janitor on the popularity spectrum in suburban American high schools—but we didn't give a shit. Cheerleaders mocked us and football players spat on us, and we loved every single minute of it.

Asher was supersmart and received a partial scholarship to Brown. His parents, though stunningly cheap, were so terrified he was gay that they liquidated their 401(k) plans to pay for the rest of their wayward son's Ivy League education, hoping that four years at what they assumed was a nice, conservative East Coast campus might be enough to straighten him out.

Although Asher wasn't even remotely into guys, he truly enjoyed letting his parents think he was, so he was more than a little peeved when he could no longer avoid telling them he and Zoe were getting married ("It worked!" Mr. and Mrs. Blake had apparently shouted to each other when he gave them the news). I was a bit surprised myself when I learned that they were together, since none of us had ever hooked up in high school, except for the time Zoe and I got drunk at a Pearl Jam concert and made out just to see what it would be like. After Asher left for school, Zoe says she just sort of realized he was The One, and so she eventually followed him out to Rhode Island. I suppose two years of soul-crushing, booze-blurred bar-hopping with me and George was enough to give shy little Zoe the courage she needed to profess her undying love to an old friend.

★ ★ ★

Happily, the feeling was quite mutual. Now they live in Philadelphia, where Asher works as a lawyer for the A.C.L.U. and Zoe has a dog-grooming business. These days, they're quite wealthy, too, courtesy of Zoe's generous dad, who had recently come into more money than he could ever spend, due to a substantial patent payout on some computer-chip thingie he'd dreamed up years ago. That's basically it. We still keep in touch, though not as often as we should.

When the two of them walked into the restaurant, they were as luminous as the last time I'd seen them, at their wedding almost a year earlier. Asher and Zoe were one of those couples who were completely unaware of how wonderful they were together. You know the type, I'm sure—that they didn't make you sick is almost enough to make you sick.

After the usual catching up, complete with mutual berating for not visiting more often, I could see that they were anxious to tell me something. Naturally, I figured they were pregnant.

"Are you kidding? *Me?* Pregnant? No way!" said Zoe.

Asher rolled his eyes.

"Why not?" I asked. "What's so crazy about that?"

"She tells me we're not even close to ready yet," he sighed.

"But you're the only married friends I have," I pleaded. "You're also the only normal people I know who are married. I *need* you to have kids. You've got to restore my faith in the whole process." Thinking of my nieces and nephews, I figured it would be nice to know there was such a thing as a non-obnoxious child before having one myself.

"Have your own damn kids," Zoe laughed, pushing her long blond bangs out of her eyes.

"Maybe later," I said.

"I've told her I'm ready to plant my seed," Asher said, grinning.

"My field needs to lie fallow for a while. But you can plant your seed in the shower, if you like."

"Mock me, hun, I don't mind," he said as he turned to face her. "But the simple truth is, I want to decorate the earth with as many beautiful babies as you'll let me give you. It's the only thing I know to do to keep from sliding into the abyss, to make it all mean something. Otherwise, it'll be like we were never here at all."

Zoe stared at him quietly for a moment. If a guy ever said anything like that to me, I'd be on my back with my legs in the air praying for fertilization before the waitress even noticed we were gone.

"Sorry." She sniffed a little and tried to smile.

"Don't worry," I told her. "He can wait until you're ready."

"It's not that…" Asher said as he squeezed her hand. "It's her dad. He's not well."

"What?" My heart tightened. Douglas Watts was a true sweetheart—a hardworking single dad who'd raised Zoe and her sisters into three strong, self-assured women.

He leaned in and said quietly, "They found a spot on his liver. He's having a biopsy tomorrow, but it doesn't look good. That's why we came home for a bit."

Zoe looked at the wall behind me and blinked back tears.

And I'd thought they were pregnant. I knew there wasn't much I could say to reassure her.

"I'm here if you need me."

That was more than three months ago—when all this started, I suppose.

In a typical addition to the Bad-Things-That-Happen-To-Good-People file, Mr. Watts's spot did turn out to be cancer. He had surgery, followed by a round of chemo, and he's doing okay for the time being, but there's really no way of knowing for sure. On the plus side, Zoe and Asher visited as often as they could throughout the summer, so at least

I was able to see them a bit more than usual. And there's nothing like the heady combination of hanging out with a great couple and a reminder that death can knock on your door at any moment to make you sit up and reassess your own life.

The more I saw of my two old friends—truly in love, free from money trouble, oozing career satisfaction, leaning on each other in a time of crisis—the more I wanted what they have for myself. If that makes me a pathetic throwback to the 1950s, unable to feel complete without a man on my arm, then so be it. I can live with that.

But I also began to see how Zoe's substantial cash flow likely has a lot to do with their overall happiness, their success, both as a couple and professionally. It's what has allowed each of them to be living exactly the lives they want to be living, which in turn frees them from ninety percent of the stresses the rest of us have to deal with every single day— the little things, like mortgage payments and business trips and mean bosses, which, in turn, all too often lead to the bigger things, like bankruptcy and divorce and broken dreams. Zoe and Asher are blessed with the freedom to put into their relationship the tremendous effort it requires to sustain a happy one, no matter how perfect or loving, while the rest of us are left bickering over bills, too exhausted by the end of the day to do anything but watch TV and not have sex.

Yes, the money really does seem to be a crucial part of the equation. And if actively looking for a partner who has some makes me materialistic, shallow, whatever…then I can live with that, too, provided he's there by my side to lovingly fib to me and tell me it isn't at all true, that I'm not like that, while we toast each other's successes in the hot tub.

"Virginia Woolf said that a woman can't write without a room of her own."

"But Holly, you already *have* a room of your own," George

points out. We are well into our second drinks, huddled in a dark booth at the back of the bar. So far, she isn't overly impressed with The Plan. Bringing her onside isn't going to be easy.

"And I spend fifty hours a week at work so that I can have that room! How can I be expected to write if I work fifty hours a week?"

"I don't know," she says. "But you rarely work fifty hours a week, Holly, and if I'm correctly remembering the bedtime stories of my youth, Woolf was talking about the dearth of women writers throughout history and how the root cause wasn't that women were inferior to men, obviously, but rather how having the physical space in which to write and the time to devote to it are necessary prerequisites to sustaining any kind of artistic endeavor. She was bemoaning the fact that most women didn't have that luxury, as well as the fact that even the wealthier ones who did also had to contend with meddling husbands and demanding children and a spate of oppressive sociocultural expectations that stifled their creativity beneath the endless, mindless minutiae of everyday existence. I don't think she was urging women to marry rich so they don't have to work. Quite the opposite, actually. Woolf believed that—"

"George!" I interrupt. "Never mind all that right now. I was just trying to make a point."

"And that point would be…"

"Well, basically, that if you want to turn your dreams into reality, you need more than a goal, G. You need a *plan*. And in order to execute that plan, you need a time line. And this…" I gesture expansively to include the entire bar, from the shiny black piano at one end to the velvet-draped windows at the other, "…*this* is the first step in the process."

"Huh? What process?"

"It makes perfect sense."

Still, a blank stare.

I sigh. "We're here to find rich men."

George practically chokes on the honey-roasted peanuts she's been inhaling. "*Oh… My… God…* Did you really just say that? How completely *disgusting.* What a *disgusting* concept." She shakes her head and stares at me in disbelief. "What happened? What's going on with you? How did you get sucked into this whole Must-Find-A-Man syndrome all of a sudden? And a rich one? Even worse…"

"Don't you see, George? It has nothing to do with that, it's about the big picture, although I have been feeling a little down and out these days, as you know. First with the whole Jean-Jean thing…" I shake it off. Better not to think about that anymore. Those days are behind me. "Look. It's not just about 'finding a man.' That's just a secondary perk."

"I suppose the money's the primary reason, then?"

"No, no. Of course not. The writing is the reason. The motivation. The call to arms! G, you know I've been crazy lately, with work, with my love life, with Zoe. But something's finally changed. It's like I've been trying to read the writing on the wall for years and just now it's coming into focus for the first time."

George raises a skeptical eyebrow. "So what does it say?"

"It says, 'You've got to *do* something, Holly Hastings, before it's too late!'"

"I see. And tell me, how exactly do you plan to justify this scheme of yours?"

"Because ultimately, The Plan is to realize my own potential and make positive life changes—to write my book. The Plan is not just to hook up or get rich. Those are just parts of the process. Fringe benefits, if you will."

"I don't know, Holly. Those are pretty small distinctions."

"Not to me! Nothing's changed, except that I've finally figured out a way to do what I've always wanted to do. Besides, I've pretty much lost my faith when it comes to finding Mr. Right. And what sense does it make to wait around forever for someone I don't really believe exists anymore? So I figure I might as well start looking for Mr. Financial Stability instead." As I explained it to her, the whole thing was beginning to make even *more* sense than it had at the outset.

"Mr. Financial Stability? Sounds romantic…"

"For the first time, I feel empowered, George, actually *empowered*. Like something great is about to happen. I am no longer going to accept being a leaf blown about by the breeze. I will be the mistress of my own destiny! I will do what I want with my life, and what I want is to be a writer. A *real* writer. Not an obituarist at a small paper or a drill-press operator who writes on the weekends…a real writer. Full-time. And the only way I can think to make it all happen is to find a sweet but wealthy guy who believes in me just a little bit. Is that so wrong?"

"I don't know. Is it?" She seems genuinely confused.

"And I'll tell you something else…" I pause just long enough to prepare her for the enormity of what I am about to say.

"What?"

"I can now see that my existence makes very little difference to the vast majority of people on this planet. Whether I like it or not, I don't matter much in the grand scheme of things. And quite frankly, I want to change that."

"Well, Holly, we can't all be Ghandi or Oprah," she intones seriously.

"Can't we, though? I've been thinking…"

"Haven't you done enough of that lately? Maybe you should just take it down a notch for a while and—"

"Bear with me please. A big part of what I've realized is that I want to help people. I want to make a difference in real people's lives. I want to be a philanthropist. A writer-philanthropist. And since I don't have any money, and I can't make any money writing until I actually write something, and I can't write something until I don't have to worry about making money, marrying rich—no, wait. That sounds so ugly, doesn't it? Let's call it 'actualizing financial freedom.' Yeah, so actualizing financial freedom is the perfect solution. It's like killing two birds with one stone, see? Because once I'm a successful author, I will not only be deliriously happy and personally fulfilled, but I will able to use my various sources of wealth to do some good on a much larger scale!"

George, by now completely stunned, shakes her head in amazement. "You're being manic, Holly. Are you okay? Do you want me to call Dr. Martindale?"

"I just want to make a difference, G. That's all. It doesn't have to be a big deal."

"God help me for even getting into this with you, because you're obviously *beyond* out of control with this, but I don't think being a philanthropist qualifies as a real aspiration. With all due respect to Grace Kelly, it's like saying you want to be a princess when you grow up. It's ridiculous."

"Well of course it sounds ridiculous when you put it like that, but it isn't. It's complicated, and it may be hard to justify in some ways, but it makes perfect sense to me. I'm sure of it. This is what I want."

"Do you really think you need a man to get what you want out of life?"

"A valid question, George. But look at it this way instead. I want a man so I can get what I need out of life."

"That's very cute."

I pull out my notebook and write it down so I won't forget.

George looks at me wearily. "What's this about, now?"

I scooch over so that we're right next to each other. "So this is where it gets *really* good," I whisper.

She begins rubbing her temples with her thumbs. "I don't know if I can take any more of this."

"I can admit that on the surface it might seem like I'm just some run-of-the-mill gold digger. But as you now know, nothing could be further from the truth. Because even though my motivations may be personal, they're also political. And *that's* where my book ties in…"

"Ah. Here it comes."

"Okay, so this is the thing… *I'm going to write a book detailing the entire process…*"

"Ha!" she practically shouts. "The process of selling out and setting the women's movement back about one hundred and fifty years?"

"Shhhhh! Keep your voice down, would you?"

"Why? If it's such a great idea you should shout it from the rooftops!"

"That's very funny, George. And you're a fine one to talk about the women's movement—you're sleeping with the original Doctor of Misogyny! Professor Bales could write his own book on how to convince big-boobed undergrads that sleeping with him was their idea!"

"Don't make this about me and Stuart. You're the one planning to completely prostitute herself."

"It's not prostitution. Technically, it's emancipation."

"You say tomato, I say tomahto."

"Cute. Don't you want to hear about the book?"

"Go ahead," she sighs. "Why stop now?"

"Okay, so on the surface, it's going to be a step-by-step guide on how to marry a millionaire, complete with informational boxes, exercises, worksheets, all that stuff. A blueprint for my weary, downtrodden, working-for-the-man sisters around the world. That alone should make it sell a million copies."

"Can't argue with that. Go on."

Her curiosity is getting the better of her. A good sign.

"But when you read between the lines," I continue, "it'll be an ironic commentary on male-female relationships, the history of the women's movement, and the plight facing the modern woman/artist." The idea is as close to brilliant as I can probably ever expect to come. "Tell me I'm wrong, G, but I think this book might have a little something in it for everyone!"

George twirls a curl around her finger. "I see what you're saying, but what if the subtleties of sexual politics are lost on the average girl next door who buys your little manual or manifesto or whatever. It'll just come off as an endorsement for gold digging."

"It'll be plainly obvious to anyone looking to debunk it. Trust me—*How to Marry a Millionaire (And Still Love Yourself in the Morning!)* will be immune from criticism. I do tongue-in-cheek very well, you know."

"So I've heard."

"The irony, of course, is that I don't know how to marry a millionaire, so I'll have to find a rich guy in order to write this puppy. For realism's sake."

"I got that already, thanks. What a happy coincidence for you, by the way. And I don't mean to nitpick, but if you ever read the *New York Times* or even *Vanity Fair* once in a while, you'd know that irony is dead. Been that way since 9/11…"

"Romance is what's dead!" I slam my fist down on the table for emphasis. "This is not a quest for romantic love. It's a quest for self-love, a pursuit of knowledge and insight and creativity which *on the surface* might seem like a grab for cash. But this *is* a search for something real. You've got to understand that."

"Okay, now you're just making me sad."

"I'm sorry…I didn't mean that romance is *dead* dead. Just that it seems that way to me lately." Losing one's faith is contagious, and I certainly don't want George suffering as I had. All I need to do is convince her there are plenty of other good reasons to come along for the ride. "Look, George. Maybe romance and love and chivalry are just hibernating for a while. Maybe in a few years, it'll be trendy again to commit to an honest, monogamous relationship and all the men who've been holding out will come back from the dark side and flood the market. Who knows? But for now, my writerly persona will have to assume a detached skepticism when it comes to matters of the heart, or how else will I be able to push the pursuit of cold, hard cash over holding out for true love?"

"I guess it all sounds okay," she says, scratching her head with a swizzle stick.

I lean in and hug her. "If you want, the *real* real irony could be that I actually *do* fall head over heels along the way. I mean, hey—I'm only flesh and blood! I'm *definitely* hoping to live happily every after when all's said and done here."

The more I explain it, the better it sounds. I would be free from a senseless job, perhaps even madly in love, artistically productive and obscenely wealthy—at first by association, but then, as the critically acclaimed author of a runaway best-seller, by my own merits.

Before I can prove to George why it's in her best interest to be my partner every step of the way, a waitress interrupts. "Excuse me, ladies. Those gentlemen over there thought you might like these." She plops two fruity-looking concoctions down on the table in front of us.

A couple of middle-aged suits a few booths over raise their martini glasses and smile. One of them has badly crooked teeth and neither has much hair to speak of.

"I… I… I don't think so," George stammers. I can't tell if it's the calorie count or our shiny-skulled suitors that has her spooked.

"Oh, come on," I say. "It's just one drink. They seem okay. Don't they seem okay?" I ask the waitress.

She shrugs. "They're in here an awful lot, so they're either single, unhappily married or alcoholics."

"Umm…yeah…well, thanks for clearing that up for us. Would you please just ask them if they'd like to join us?" She takes off for their table, shaking her head.

"Don't say a word, G. This is just a trial run. And I think this place has just the right demographics, so let's put our husband-catching hats on, just for fun, and—"

"Our *whats*? And did you just say *we*? So now it's *we*? I don't think—"

They slide in beside us before she has a chance to object any further.

"Hi guys! Thanks for the drinks," I say to the better-looking one sitting next to George.

"Yeah, thanks," she grumbles.

"You're welcome," he say. "I'm Trevor. And this is Ron."

"Hi," says Ron.

"I'm Holly, and this is George."

George half smiles and looks down.

"George?" Trevor says. "Bit of a funny name for a pretty lady like you, isn't it?"

"Maybe that's, you know, like her work name or something," Ron says to Trevor out of the side of his mouth.

"Her *work* name. I get it," he nods.

George and I exchange glances. Who knows? Maybe they're into names or something. "Well, even though I'm a Holly, I wasn't born in December or named after Christmas or anything silly like that, though people often assume that I am. I guess my parents just thought it was a nice name, you know?"

But Ron and Trevor just stare at George as she proceeds to deskewer her sword of maraschino cherries with her teeth.

"Yeah, that'll do it," Ron says. "That'll do it."

Trevor apparently agrees. "Let's get to it, then! I assume you ladies are working tonight?"

"Huh?" I am utterly confused.

For a change, George is not. "They think we're hookers, Holly."

The burgundy leather banquette squeaks as the offending parties shift uncomfortably.

"What?! Are you joking?" Three drinks have not dulled my capacity for righteous indignation.

"Wait! It's okay if you're not!" Ron suggests frantically.

"Yeah, that's totally fine, too. We just thought—"

"You just thought what?!"

"Holly, let's get out of here…"

"No, G! I want to know why they would think we're hookers!"

"Maybe it's her hair," Ron points at George. "And her… her…wow. Those right there. And your lipstick! I don't think bright red is the way to go at happy hour."

Trevor shoots him a nervous look. "What the hell are you talking about?"

"My sister works for Avon," he explains.

"Man, you're so queer…"

"You can go now," I tell them.

I whip my compact out of my purse while George slumps down as far as she can without completely disappearing under the table. True, I am a little more made-up than usual, but I figured the occasion called for a touch of sophistication. As for George's hair, it is undeniably large.

Scanning the room, I suppose we're a bit out of place. The only other women in Taylor's are the waitresses and a few frumpy accountant types. I am definitely the only one with an attempt at an updo, while George's cleavage apparently speaks a thousand words.

"Can we get out of here, Holly? *Please?*"

"Fine. But don't look so glum. This is going to make a great 'What Not to Do' appendix for the book."

George reluctantly agrees to give my tactics some more thought as we scarf down Chinese takeout in the cab on the way back to my place. If it were easy, I reason, then everyone would be doing it. Chapter One will just have to wait until we are a little further into the game.

chapter 5

The Mind of the Moneyed Man

"Just look into the camera and relax, sweetie."

It sounds like a line from a bad afterschool special.

I take a deep breath and begin: "Hi everyone! Okay, so I may not be a blond bombshell like Marilyn Monroe, but there must be at least one fabulous, semidecent-looking rich guy out there who's seriously into flat-chested brunettes."

I can see George shaking her head in my peripheral vision.

Violet Chase, the ageless madam behind the Buffalo branch of the Moneyed Mates franchise, is similarly unimpressed. "That was appalling, Ms. Hastings," she says as she comes over to flick a speck off my shoulder.

"Just needed to break the tension, I guess."

"We'll pretend it never happened. Let's do a few more takes. Just try and relax. And remember the guidelines we talked about. And for heaven's sake, *don't* mention money!

It's incredibly inelegant," she says as she stalks off the "set" to take her place beside the cameraman.

"Okay," I agree. "But it's kinda hard to relax when this is, like, the *one* impression they're going to have of me."

"Would you like half a Valium?" she offers.

I look hopefully to George, whose wrinkled forehead and downturned eyebrows relay a stern "No."

"No, thank you," I tell Ms. Chase. "But it was nice of you to ask."

After the whole hooker fiasco, George and I tried to be more discriminating in our choice of both evening wear and hunting grounds. We'd staked out a few hotel bars—most notably, the Mansion on Delaware Avenue, the only place in town where I could imagine a really wealthy person might stay—but we just ended up getting to know the bartender better than we wanted to and drinking away half a paycheck's worth of Harvey's Bristol Cream in about a month. Plus, George gained nearly five pounds from the nuts at the bar (I'm sure the alcohol had nothing to do with it). On Saturdays and Sundays, we walked Linus, her fat beagle, in circles around the Mercedes dealership on Main Street near her mothers' house. Once, we even skipped work and snuck into a hedge-fund conference at the Hilton in Niagara Falls, where we learned that most professional financial planners work with other people's money, not their own—a fact confirmed by their willingness to embrace the most revolting assortment of cold salads in lunch-buffet history.

All this work and nary a nibble at the line, yet alone a dinner invitation. It seems Buffalo just doesn't have rich men growing on trees, if you can believe that. We needed a way to kick things up a notch. And that was where Moneyed Mates came in.

George had stumbled across a scathing indictment of their

operations in an article Mrs. Perlman had suggested she read in *The Advocate* regarding the appalling state of contemporary American heterosexual mating habits. I was surprised George had even mentioned it, frankly, since she'd made it clear on numerous occasions that she was just chaperoning me on my little husband-hunting excursions. But it didn't take long for the truth to come out.

Professor Bales had dumped her. Or she had dumped him. (Whatever.)

"You were *so* right," she'd sobbed into the phone a week before we found ourselves at Moneyed Mates for our preliminary interview. George doesn't break down often, but when she does, there's no mistaking it.

"I was? About what?"

"I wanted to prove you wrong about Stuart, so I asked him outright, 'How many other women are you seeing?' and he was like, 'I don't know' and I was like, 'Don't you have any feelings for me after all this time?' and he was like, 'Of course I do,' and I was like, 'Feelings that originate above the waist?' and he was like, get this, 'Don't worry—*I respect you as a person.*'"

"Whoa, slow down…"

"That's what he said—'I respect you as person!' And I thought, what the hell's that supposed to mean? *I respect you as a person?*"

It sounded like she'd already had a few drinks. Otherwise, I would have suggested going out for one. "Jeez… So what do you think he meant?"

"Well, that's what I wondered," she continued. "So I said, 'I've been taking it for granted that you respect me as a person, Stuart, so thanks for nothing. But if you're bothering to mention it, are you trying to imply that you don't respect me as a woman?' and then he was all quiet for like the longest time and then he said, 'Well, since you never asked me before, I assumed you didn't want to know the answer, but now that you're asking I guess you want to know so I'm not going to lie to you,' and I was like oh God, do I want to hear this? But he just kept talking and he said, 'I guess you should know that I'm never going to want any more from our *situation* here because if I'm going to share my life with only one person, then I need that person to be on *par* with me."

"What kind of prick would say something like that?" I wondered aloud, silently amazed that she had never actually asked him where they stood before this.

"Exactly what I was thinking! Like, he doesn't even consider what we had a relationship. He called it a *situation.* Can you believe that?"

"No, I meant about you not being on par with him."

"I'm getting to that, Holly. So I was like, 'What do you mean?' and he said, 'You'll never be a great writer, George. There's skill, and there's talent, and you don't have enough of either, although if I had to choose, I'd say you have more skill than talent. In any case, that's something I would definitely need from a life partner, and I'm sure you can respect that.'"

"Oh my God."

"Yeah, so of course I was like completely stunned. But you know what I said? I said, 'Not only do I have more talent than skill, but I have enough of both!' and I hung up and I haven't called him back and I never will again and I hate him and he's an asshole and I just feel like I wasted so much bloody time on him! I'm such an idiot, Holly. God, I'm so embarrassed. I want to crawl under the covers and die. What was I thinking? How come I didn't see it? No—you know what? I'm not embarrassed. I'm *angry.* Yeah, angry! I deserve better than that…don't I? Oh God! Would you listen to me? Of course I deserve better. But I'm still such an idiot…"

And so on and so forth.

I comforted her the best I could, considering she'd skipped work and had been crying in bed alone all day, drunk on Manishevitz, the only booze her mothers ever kept around the house.

"First of all, you're not an idiot," I told her. "You're human and I love you. And even though I admit I may have teased you about him a little—"

"A little?"

"Okay, a lot… But I also hope you know that I know you wouldn't have been with him unless you were getting something positive out of the relationship, too. And there's nothing wrong with that provided you move on as soon as you see things aren't going in the direction you want them to. Which is exactly what's happening right now. So, that's all this is, okay? You're making the right decision at the right time for you. You have absolutely nothing to feel bad about."

I couldn't help but wonder at what it finally took for George to dump this guy. Not the fact that he was a lecherous old coot. It didn't bug her that he treated her like crap, that he'd stepped out on her countless times, that they'd done nothing but order in pizza and screw in his shitty old "loft," which was really just a one-bedroom near the water with the walls knocked out. No, it took him dissing her as a writer. Never mind that he'd been dissing her as a woman every time he failed to show her the respect she deserved.

"I know you're right, Holly. Thanks. I just wish I'd figured that out sooner, you know?" she sniffed once she'd regained her composure. "I feel like I need to make up for lost time."

"Don't beat yourself up. You're starting fresh now and that's what's important."

"I mean I really feel like I need to do something."

"You do?"

"Yup. What was it we swore in Creative Writing 101?"

She knew exactly what it was we'd sworn. "That we'd both be famous writers by the time we're thirty."

"And how old are we?"

"Twenty-eight."

"I've been unwilling to rock the boat," she said with a hiccup. "I can see that now."

"Are you sure you're ready for this, G? Can you handle it?"

Was that the theme from *Rocky* drifting in through the open living-room window?

"I'm ready."

"It is possible the rumors are true, you know—that money may *not* buy happiness. We need to be prepared for that contingency…"

She exhaled slowly, deliberately. "I know. But maybe we owe it to ourselves to find out for sure."

"Well, you know *I* think we do."

I didn't want to pressure her before she was ready, but the thought of having a partner in crime made my heart leap with anticipation and joy.

"As the *girlfriends* of millionaires," she slurred, "…not wives, but girlfriends, okay?—it sounds less evil to me—so as the girlfriends of millionaires maybe we could finally evolve beyond the mundane fiscal responsibilities that have been drying up our dreams…"

"Now you're getting it!" This was the drunk, reckless George I knew and loved.

"And if it doesn't work out, so what!? We'll just chalk it up to experience, which we like so totally need anyway in order to be good writers!"

"You go girl!"

"Because any life worth living is packed with one ginormous mistake after another!"

"Well, let's not get carried away…"

Jill, who'd been sitting next to me on the couch, watching *Nova* and eating barbecue soybeans, raised an eyebrow at this point. "What on earth are you talking about?"

I put my hand over the mouthpiece. "George's professor dumped her."

"I can hear you," she wailed. "Tell her *I* dumped *him!*"

Jill grabbed the receiver. "The best way to win him back is to ignore him. Don't call him, no matter what. He'll be *burning* for you within two weeks. Then all you have to do is—"

"Give me that!" I wrestled the phone from her hand. "Ignore her, George. She's completely insane when it comes to men. She'd rather date a complete jackass than spend a single Saturday night alone."

Jill stuck her tongue out at me and got up to leave. "Is that any worse than stalking delivery boys and bicycle messengers?"

"I'll deal with you later," I told her. "Now, George, listen to me. You know you're better off without him and all that crap. I'm not going to waste my breath going over every single reason why, because I've been doing that for years and you haven't listened to a word I've said—"

"Don't worry, Holly. You don't have to convince me. I'm bruised and I'm hurt and I'm mad at myself, but I'm also so totally over him. I just need to take a day or two to cry the whole thing out of my system, you know? But I'm fine with it. Really, I am. In fact, I even have an idea that might help speed along my recovery."

"Oh yeah?"

"Yeah. It's this weird dating service I read about…"

We arrived precisely on time for our preliminary interview with Ms. Chase. Of course, I'd done a little online research into Moneyed Mates beforehand, just to make sure it was a legitimate dating service and not some sort of escort service or prostitution ring. Happily, it appeared to be a successful international franchise—there was a Moneyed Mates branch in virtually every major city in the United States, Canada and Europe. Granted, it did seem a little odd that rich guys were apparently having as hard a time finding us as we were finding them, but I was willing to take the chance.

Before George could commit to the process, however, she needed to make sure that the most politically incorrect business operation either of us had ever come across was undiscriminating in its treatment of women.

"Ms. Chase, why is your corporate slogan *'Wealthy Men for Willing Ladies'*? Don't you have any Wealthy Ladies for Willing Men? And what exactly do you mean by 'willing'?"

But it would take more than George Perlman-MacNeill's vacillating brand of feminism to throw a professional like Violet Chase for a loop. "In all my years in this business, I can honestly say that I've never had a single wealthy woman come to me looking for a less well-to-do mate. You can infer from that what you will. Oh, and by 'willing,' we mean 'willing' to settle only for the very best."

George shifted in her chair, unsure what to make of this new information. "Why don't rich people just date each other? Why would they want to date normal people?"

I turned to Ms. Chase. It was a valid question.

She looked out past us into the hallway, uncrossed her perfect legs and leaned forward across her big glass desk. In a low whisper, she said, "The truth is, many wealthy men find wealthy women intimidating, in exactly the same way that many men of modest means find a lady who earns more than them an almost *unattractive* quality."

"That's awful," George groaned. "And completely outdated, sexist and totally offensive."

"Don't be naive," I told her. "Not all guys are as enlightened as we wish they were. It's actually kind of sad that so many of them still don't feel like real men unless they're the ones bringing home the bacon."

Ms. Chase nodded in agreement. "We're here to provide a service for those men who enjoy deriving power from their paychecks and are self-aware enough to know it. The beauty is, nobody's taking advantage of anybody when it's all out in the open like it is here at Moneyed Mates. There's no game-playing, no deception, just an arrangement beneficial to both parties. And for those who prefer a partner of similar means, there's Mutually Moneyed Mates in the suite next door. You might have seen it as you came in. So, have we answered all your questions?

"I have one. Why come here if they can probably have their pick of gorgeous babes?"

"She's very self-conscious about her chest," George explained. "It's bordering on insane obsession, actually…"

Ms. Chase glanced at my torso and zeroed in on the hard sell. "First of all, our clients know that many of the women who come to us are extremely attractive, such as yourselves. Plus, it's overly simple to think all wealthy men want is some trophy wife or blond-bimbo type with large breasts. Granted, some of our clients have gone that route in the past, but now they've come to realize they want a lasting relationship with more substance."

"Someone they can bring home to mother?" George suggested.

"In a manner of speaking, yes. And to be completely honest, very few of our clients come from old money. Most are businessmen, shrewd investors or savers…we've also had a few lottery winners, that sort of thing. And these men, these 'millionaires next door,' as I like to call them, often come from modest backgrounds and want to share their lives with someone whom they feel they can relate to on an essential level."

George seemed pleased. "So Playboy bunnies are out, then."

"Our clients are wise enough to understand that once

wealth enters the equation, nobody just likes them for them anymore, perhaps with the exception of the people they knew before. The money is always there, prejudicing people in their favor. It would be the height of egotism to believe otherwise."

I looked up from my pad. She was giving me great stuff here, and damned if I was going to miss a single word of it.

"What are you doing?"

"Taking notes," I told her.

"She's writing a book," George added.

"You're not going to quote me, I hope," she said sternly, adjusting the flaccid bow at the collar of her silk blouse and tugging down her smartly tailored jacket. Apparently, Ms. Chase thought she was the only one who'd figured out a way to turn the workings of the male mind into a moneymaking venture, and she didn't want the secret getting out.

"Don't worry," I assured her. "This is just a bit of preliminary research."

She leaned back and continued. "So ladies, why do you think these wealthy men come to Moneyed Mates?"

"Sex?" George offered.

Ms. Chase shook her head. "They can get that at the local singles bar, Ms. Perlman-MacNeill. Or yacht club, for that matter."

"Privacy?"

"No."

"Desperation?"

"No."

"Coupons?"

"Certainly not."

"We give up."

"I'll tell you."

"Promise?"

"Your curtness is unbecoming, Ms. Hastings, as is your sarcasm."

"She's very moody," George explained. "It's her cycle."

"Sorry," I said, stifling a laugh. "I'm just anxious to hear what you have to say."

Ms. Chase smoothed back her too-black hair and continued. "What drives them here is the one quality they all have in common—pragmatism. They assume that most women will be after their money, anyway, so they just want to be in control of the game. They're lonely, they work long hours and they have neither the time nor the inclination to play the dating game."

We nodded. It all made perfect sense. There was just one more question left to ask.

"So…does this really work?"

"If you don't get a date within two months, we'll refund your membership dues minus the video sitting fee of two hundred and fifty dollars."

"That seems fair, I guess. George—what do you think?"

"I don't know…"

"We've had thirty-three marriages since we opened eight years ago, and plenty of serious relationships," Ms. Chase added, sealing the deal. "Our receptionist Florence will provide you with a preparation packet on your way out."

"Well, I guess we don't have much to lose," George concluded.

Exactly what I was thinking.

After handing over our credit cards at the front desk and scheduling our next appointment, Ms. Chase popped her immaculately groomed head out of her office.

"Ms. Hastings? Ms. Perlman-MacNeill? Before you come in to tape your personal profiles, I'll remind you both to give some serious thought as to what you bring to the table. Be prepared to articulate exactly what sets you apart from the crowd if you want to catch a wealthy gentleman's eye. Remember, ladies, everyone wants to date *him*...but what would make *him* want to date *you?*"

I'm still unsure what my angle should be. How can you possibly convince someone—especially someone so highly sought after—that you're the one for him in under two minutes of bad lighting and a background of fall foliage? I imagine it would take a whole lot longer than that, especially in my case.

What didn't take long was for Ms. Chase's patience with me to run thin. "Are you sure you wouldn't like a Valium?" she asks again after the seventeenth take.

Our little afterschool special is quickly degenerating into *Valley of the Dolls.*

"Why? Is seventeen takes a lot?"

"Yes, Ms. Hastings. The most we've ever had."

At least that's something. "I don't know what to say—everything that comes out of my mouth sounds so...I don't know...desperate?"

"Just be yourself, for heaven's sake. Maybe your voice won't shake so much if you pretend you're having a conversation with an old friend. And don't say anything snarky this time. Coyness is one thing, but rudeness is quite another. Bob—get ready."

"How come she didn't have to do hers over seventeen times?" I ask, pointing to George. She flew through her profile in no time. Ms. Chase and Bob the cameraman both agreed the first take was perfect.

"It must be the twins," George says, squeezing her boobs together with her arms and making a kissy face.

"Fine. Just give me a few minutes to prepare this time, okay?"

Ms. Chase makes a big show of looking at her watch, and Bob drags himself over to the coffee machine.

Hmmm… What do I bring to the table?

What do I, Holly Marie Hastings—bitching obituarist, fallen optimist, aspiring philanthropist—bring to the table?

Well, the table itself, for one thing, if you included my chest.

But so what if I did? I don't know too many men who would kick Debra Messing or Kate Hudson out of bed, and they're not exactly stacked.

Always attuned to my state of my mind, George pops over to help me work it through.

"You may not be busty, but you are tall and willowy," she offers. "And believe me—that's a *good* thing."

"I wouldn't exactly say willowy. I'm barely five-six." With heels, though…

"Holly, compared to a five-foot-one bonsai like me, you're a willow. Trust me."

"Yeah?"

"Of course. And lots of guys love that."

"I guess. But what about my hair?"

"Have you tried a volumizing shampoo?"

"I meant the cut. It's so blah. I was thinking of getting one of those choppy bobs…"

With that, Ms. Chase clickety-clicks out from behind the backdrop. "Don't cut your hair. Men like it long. Ninety-two percent of husbands who cheat do so with women who have longer hair than their wives."

"An interesting statistic, Ms. Chase, but somehow, I don't really care," I say.

"Just trying to help," she says curtly and withdraws.

George heads over to inspect the box of Krispy Kremes next to the coffee machine, while I prepare by mentally reciting my Calming and Focusing mantra. An oldie but a goodie, it's one of the many helpful exercises gleaned from Sandeep, an Ayurvedic mental health practitioner I'd found in the Yellow Pages. The principle? Clearing one's mind readies it for inspiration and understanding. The practice: Repeating gibberish until nothing eventually means something...

Umbalabumbum... Umbalabumbum... Umbalabumbum... Umbalabumbum... Umbalabumbum... Umbalabumbum... Umbalabumbum... Umbalabumbum... Umbalabumbum...

The source of my tension isn't my haircut or my bra size. So what is it? Why am I so nervous? Why can't I come up with anything good to say?

Umbalabumbum... Umbalabumbum... Umbalabumbum... Umbalabumbum... Umbalabumbum... Umbalabumbum... Umbalabumbum... Umbalabumbum... Umbalabumbum...

Am I afraid of failure? Afraid of success? Am I sabotaging myself?

...Umbalabumbum... Umbalabumbum... Umbalabumbum... Umbalabumbum...

"Are we ready yet, Ms. Hastings? I have another appointment in fifteen minutes."

"Umbalabumbum! For $995, you'd think you could cut me some slack! I'm trying to figure out exactly who I am, and how to get that across to anybody who might remotely care."

She shoots me a dark look and motions for Bob to return to his post. "Ms. Hastings, remember when I told you to just be yourself for the camera?"

"Yeah?"

"Well, maybe you should try something else."

Eureka!

"Why, Ms. Chase! You've just given me a wonderful idea..."

I clear my throat and open the top button on my blouse, exposing more of what obviously isn't there.

"Any time you're ready," I say to Bob.

My instinct, understandably, had been to cover up all my insecurities and flaws, as we all tend to do when the stakes are so high. But I'd forgotten my own cardinal rule: Need-

iness bad, confidence good. And nothing leads to desperation and self-doubt more than having to sustain a bunch of
whopping lies about yourself. This is too important to be
playing games. If any guy, rich or poor, is ever going to be
interested in me, and stay that way long enough to fall madly
in love, he'll need to see exactly who I am. The real me. Not
the public Holly, but the private Holly. No bullshit.

I look straight into the camera.

"Hi out there! I'm Holly. My age isn't important, because
I'm still young. My height isn't important, because I'm not
too short or too tall, and my weight isn't important because
I'm thin enough. I'll admit that I may be a bit shy in the boob
department, but hopefully that won't be a deal-breaker for
you. And if it is, then you should probably just move on to
the next profile. Or give me implants for our first anniversary. Whatever. So what else can I say about me? Well, I don't
like walks on the beach, because the only beach I really
know fronts on the lake and you have to step over dead fish
and used condoms about every three feet. I don't like eating
in fancy restaurants, because I prefer a burger and fries. I don't
smoke, but I used to, and can't promise that I never will again.
I do indulge in the occasional cocktail and I hope you do,
too. I don't really like my job anymore, but I do enjoy lots
of other things, like writing and Halloween and the smell of
gasoline."

I pause to take a breath, and glance off to the side. Ms.
Chase's eyes are wide with horror.

"Oh! I almost forgot—I'm in therapy, and proud of it! Not
that I'm balls-out crazy or anything, but I am a teensy bit
neurotic. Most of my shrinks seem to agree that my problems stem from being an overthinker, except for one wannabe
Freudian who thought I was mired in some sort of unre-
solved Electra complex, which I doubt, frankly, and you
would too, if you'd ever met my dad, which hopefully you

will one day! But that's another story. Where was I again? Oh yeah—therapy. Anyway, ideally, you're in therapy too, because I strongly believe that getting to know yourself from the inside out is one of the most important parts of life's long and lovely journey. Okay! So as for what I'm looking for in a man, here's the deal…. Since I've only been in one committed relationship, and that was ages ago, I pretty much have no clue. I suppose the most important thing about you for now is that you like me. And yourself. But not too much. Because I find narcissism totally unattractive. That's about it. Oh, and no cat people, please. I am not fond of cats, either. Or people who like them."

I close my laptop and put it aside. I've decided to write my introduction at the very end, after all is said and done and I have the benefit of hindsight, but I am already well into my first chapter. Even though it's just a rough point-form outline of what will eventually become the first draft, *How to Marry a Millionaire (And Still Love Yourself in the Morning!)* is practically going to write itself. All I have to do is stay attuned to any potential research opportunities, wait and see if the Moneyed Mates thing pans out, and incorporate it all into the manuscript in the meantime.

Although I am still frustrated by the soul-crushing banality of my workaday world—Jill and Boyfriend's bedroom giggles have been driving me nuts all night; my job completely sucks, day in day out; my brothers seem in constant need of my babysitting services—I can sense that things are starting to change. First of all, I am writing at home, or at least trying to, which is something I haven't done in years. My life feels less out of control. Most importantly, though, hope is gleaming again on the horizon.

chapter 6

Love Lives, Past and Present

As the crisp and colorful autumn days fade into a cold and dreary November, I grow increasingly weary of Martindale's constant mocking. He is extremely opposed to The Plan, and never tires of sharing with me the many reasons why. Even Berenice has failed to see things my way, and couldn't, in good conscience, lend her approval. Though they've made some valid points—Martindale felt intentionally marrying rich would undermine any subsequent success I might have as a writer, while perpetually, deliberately impoverished Berenice wouldn't wish a million dollars on her worst enemy—I know the time has come to make a clean break and find me another shrink.

According to the rumors bouncing off the walls of the *Bugle* at the speed of sound, a therapist by the name of Lacy Goldenblatt was the genius who'd helped Virginia Holt through her extremely messy divorce and subsequent Vicodin addiction last year. Frankly, I was just as surprised to hear that retail therapy had failed her as I was that Virginia had turned to past-life regression as a solution.

Happily, when I called to inquire about the possibility of making an appointment, there had been a cancellation. "Lucky for you, Dr. Goldenblatt had another breakthrough this week!" The receptionist was apparently a true believer. "The 6:00 p.m. spot on Tuesdays is now available. Just so you know, the session fees are $80 each, plus $120 for the doctor's initial 'Getting to Know You' meeting."

"I could really use a breakthrough," I told her. "Fast."

"The doctor works quickly. Don't worry."

I'd long since committed the slim volume known as Bluebird Group Health's *"What's Covered"* pamphlet to memory, and I knew there was no way this would fly, seeing as how Dr. Goldenblatt's medical prefix came courtesy of a Ph.D. in Multicultural Studies from Walla Walla University, most likely mail-order to boot (I'd looked her up on the Internet to make sure she was a certified regression therapist). Still, I had the feeling there were lessons to be learned here.

"Could you put half on my MasterCard and half on my Visa?"

"If you like, we have a new installment plan with a preferred interest rate."

"How thoughtful."

"Dr. Goldenblatt doesn't want financial considerations to prevent anyone from attaining Realization."

"Of course she doesn't. So maybe I could just settle up with her in my next life?" Die now, pay later?

"She's in with a patient now, but if you hold on, I'll ask her…"

"No, wait! It's okay. I'll take the payment plan."

"Good thinking. Money might be tighter the next time around."

★ ★ ★

As usual, George's lusty good looks landed her one step ahead of the game.

Less than a week after we'd taped our personal introduction, Ms. Chase called with some good news: It seemed a well-to-do young fellow (her words, not mine) had been extremely impressed by George's tape and was already champing at the bit. After viewing his profile, George agreed and a date was set for Saturday night.

"But was he good-looking? You haven't really answered my question."

"For the tenth time, Holly, I told you I don't know," George moans as the cab pulls up to the restaurant. "It's hard to tell just from watching a tape. He seemed okay, I guess. Ms. Chase has met him a bunch of times and she said he was all right."

"Exactly what did she say? What were her words?"

"That he was 'not unhandsome' or something like that. Look, we're going to find out for ourselves in about ten minutes so let's just go over the signals before he gets here."

George insisted on my being a secret chaperone for her first date with Bobby Garrett, despite Ms. Chase's assurances that he was a perfect gentleman. But if I were in George's shoes (which I soon hope to be), I would want someone there to keep an eye out, too, just in case things got weird, especially since we'd each signed a waiver releasing Moneyed Mates from any moral or legal responsibility should one of their clients attack, harm, deceive or offend our persons in any way.

And what did we really know about this guy, anyway? That he was from Carson City, Nevada. That he liked sushi. That he was some sort of self-made shipping magnate at the tender age of thirty-four. For all we or Ms. Chase knew, he was also a bigamist with rage-control issues and a crotch full of pubic lice.

Since neither George nor I was exactly, ahem, the best judge of character (not by a long shot), we decided to play it extra safe with Bobby Garrett. Because it's one of those lessons best learned before it's too late, I was also planning to insist—in either a full chapter complete with cautionary tales or, at the very least, an important appendix—that my readers take all the necessary security precautions on early dates, as well, and possibly hire a private investigator to follow up with a thorough background check when and if things get serious. But before we could find out if Mr. Garrett had any outstanding arrest warrants or restraining orders in effect, we'd have to see if he was second-date material.

George is tucked into a booth at Trattoria Casa Linga by ten to seven. I take my place at the bar, glance over and give her the thumbs-up. She looks great—a tight but not *too* tight red faux cashmere V-neck, tall black boots that give her almost three extra inches and a demure charcoal DKNY pencil skirt we found on sale at Kaufmann's in the Walden Galleria just in time for the big date. Her layers of dark curls are pulled back into a low ponytail, with a few errant strands to complete the I-Hardly-Bother look. A bit of lip gloss, a bit of blush and easy on the eye makeup. All in all, pretty, pulled-together, but very relaxed.

At precisely seven, Bobby Garrett appears in the doorway. I can tell it's him because George's face flushes bright red the moment she looks up and sees him. He smiles as soon as he notices her and makes his way over to the booth, where he shakes her hand and slides in across from her, his back to me.

Though I only see him head-on for a moment or two, he seems fine. A bit on the short side maybe, but other than that, the basics are in place. Hair, clothes, face, body—all come together in a way that isn't altogether unattractive.

My God! This might actually work...

We'd been to the restaurant for lunch earlier in the week to case the joint and choose seats that would allow me to both see and hear what was going on. George needed to know that I had her back in case she felt the need to suddenly excuse herself and not return.

But she needn't have worried, because shortly into George's first real date in more than four years, it is becoming painfully obvious that Bobby Garrett is the one who wants to chew off his own leg in order to get away. George hasn't stopped blabbing since he sat down, barely giving him the chance to get a word in edgewise. By the time the calamari arrives, she's told him the entire story of her conception and birth, from insemination to placental abruption; by the time the salads show up, Bobby has heard all about what an asshole her professor was. Although I can't see his face, the poor guy has been nodding for almost forty minutes straight. Whether he is falling asleep or simply being polite I cannot tell, but either way it's a bad sign.

The third time he looks down at his watch, just as George is launching into an explanation of why Trekker and not Trekkie is the preferred term, I catch her eye and give her the emergency bathroom signal.

"What? What is it?" she asks as soon as the door closes behind us.

"Ummm... How's it going?"

"You've heard everything. It's going fine," she says impatiently as she reapplies her lip gloss. "I like him. He's cute."

"Well, I think you better slow down."

"Slow down? What do you mean?"

"George, you've been talking nonstop."

"I have?"

"Yes. You've hardly asked him a thing about himself."

"I haven't?"

"No."

"Really?" She puts her gloss back in her purse and glares at her reflection.

I shake my head. "Aren't you curious about him? Who he is?"

"Who he is…?" she asks cautiously, turning to me.

"God, George, this is like basic dating etiquette."

"Tell me, quick."

"Well, maybe you should be asking him stuff like if he's close with his family, where he went to school or if he has any pets, you know? Or how he got into the shipping business, considering he's from a land-locked desert state. That sort of thing. I mean, you say you like him, but you don't know anything about him. Oh, and by the way, most men don't respond well to *Star Trek* trivia on the first date, G. Or even the hundredth date, for that matter. It's not sexy. At all."

She plops down in an overstuffed chaise, devastated. "God. You're right. Did I fuck it all up?"

"Not yet, but when you go back out there, take a breath, have a bite of food and listen to him for a bit. Give him a chance."

"I guess I'm not used to this. Maybe I'm trying too hard."

"You're just nervous. And out of practice. You have to take it easy. Be patient, you know? Who you are is going to come out in time. Let him get to know you, but *slowly*."

"I see what you're saying, but whatever happened to letting it all hang out? You're the one who thought psycho-analysis and boob jobs were worth mentioning in your personal introduction, need I remind you."

"Exactly. And who's the one with the date tonight?"

"But I thought honesty was always the best policy…"

"Of course it is, *in general,* but this is your first date, so a little bit of restraint is also called for. Otherwise, how are you supposed to build an aura of mystery? You need him to be wondering who you are, wanting to know more about you. You don't have to beat him over the head with it."

She stands up and smoothes her skirt. "You're right. You're really good at this, Holly. Maybe you should be a dating advisor or something. That would be a great business—or wait!—a great reality show, following pathetic women around on dates and pointing out what they're doing wrong…"

"I'll have to include a chapter on that in my book," I interrupt. "For now, let's focus on the task at hand," I say as I guide her toward the door.

"What's that?"

"Well, you like him, so try and score a second date."

"Yeah!"

"And easy on the Chianti! You know how you get when you're drunk, and you don't want to scare him off with all that girl power just yet. Remember where we found him— he has a fragile ego and dubious self-esteem, so go easy. Let him take the lead."

She exhales deliberately, gathers herself up, and pushes through the door.

When we return to the dining room, Bobby is already gone. He's left two $100 bills on the table, and a message with the waiter about a family emergency.

George puts on a brave face, smiles even, but turns to me with the saddest eyes. "He had a cold sore, anyway. Who needs that?"

"Holly, I like to begin each session by devoting a few minutes to *pranayama,* or yogic breathing. This will help to not only relax us physically, but also to prime our minds and ready them for any impressions or fragments that might rise to the surface later. I assume you're familiar with the *ujjayi* technique?"

"Of course," I reply, and turn my palms upward.

"Okay, so let's shut our eyes…relax…and *breeeeaaathe…*" Lacy Goldenblatt closes her eyes, snorts in loudly through her nose and growls out from somewhere deep within her abdomen. I tense the proper muscles accordingly and try to follow suit, though I can't help but peek.

We are seated—Lacy in full lotus; me barely managing half—on a lovely antique Persian rug.

After we've breathed enough, Lacy instructs me to open my eyes.

"The fundamental principles behind past-life regression therapy are similar to those of Buddhism," she begins. "We accumulate psychic baggage, much like karma, both good and bad, over the course of many lifetimes. In Buddhism, the ultimate goal is to end the cycle of rebirth and misery by attaining nirvana. In P.L.R., we take it one step further and try to identify exactly who we were in the past in the hopes of understanding who we are today. Once we can see our former selves clearly, we can function better on a daily basis in this life, unencumbered by what I call the 'supraconscious' guilt and trauma accumulated over millennia of lives lived." She pauses to take a sip of something whose odor proves too much for the good scientists as Sharper Image. "Licorice bark and wormwood. Pungent isn't it?"

I can only nod.

"So I like to call what we're doing here 'Checking our Baggage.' Once we see what we've been holding on to, we can store it neatly away in the backs of our minds so that it doesn't bother us anymore. Got it?"

"Got it."

"Good."

"So…how does this work? How do we—I mean, I—get to that point?"

"Well, what I use is basically a form of hypnosis. Have you ever been hypnotized before?"

"Oh yeah. I'm as suggestible as they come." I'd once admitted to having a crush on Pat Sajak in front of two hundred and fifty people in a Las Vegas dinner club.

"Excellent. So why don't you just lean back onto some of those floor cushions there and make yourself comfortable. As soon as you're ready I'm going to start counting back from one hundred."

"Ready."

Lacy lies down right next to me. "Just listen to the sound of my voice. I want you to relax and think about nothing. Just the sound of my voice…" Despite the distracting whiff of wormwood on her breath, I ease into the cushions beneath my shoulders and try to get with the program. "…my voice is all that you hear, all that you're aware of, all that you're thinking about. The sound of your own lungs filling with air and the swish of your beating heart are fading into nothingness, fading into the background, fading into the past…"

"What are you doing in there?" Jill asks.

"I can't find my mittens," I grumble, digging around in the back of the hall closet. "You know—those cute pink ones I got on sale at the end of last winter…"

"Maybe they're in your room."

"No, I'm sure they're in here somewhere… Why are you hovering?"

"I'm not, I'm just…"

"Wait a sec…do you smell something?"

She sniffs the air and shrugs. "Nope."

"How can you not smell that?" I ask, struggling to pull a

big green garbage bag out from the back of the closet. "It totally reeks in here…"

Jill makes a beeline for the kitchen as I untie the bag. Inside is something quite different from the tangle of musty scarves and gloves I was expecting.

Holy crap! This can't be what I think it is…

"Jill!"

No answer.

"JILL!!!!!"

She peeks around the corner.

"Come here!" I yell, waving violently. "You gotta see this! You're not gonna believe what's *in* here!"

Slowly, she approaches the bag and looks down.

"So?"

"So?" I shriek. "*So?* You know whose this is, don't you? You know what this means, right?"

Jill rolls her eyes. "Come on, Holly. It's just a little pot. Don't be such a goody-two-shoes."

"What?"

"You heard me…"

Of course, I naturally assumed that Jill would be as shocked and as furious as I am to discover what Boyfriend meant when he said he was self-employed. But now I see that she knew exactly what he's been doing all along.

God, I am so naive.

"Are…are you serious?" I stammer.

"Come on. It's not like you've never smoked."

"Not since college. And I didn't inhale."

"Yeah, right."

"That's not the point, Jill—he's a *drug* dealer. A fucking drug dealer! Do you understand what that means? Do you *know* what that is? You have to dump him…get him out of your life! And get *this* out of our house!" I try to lift the bag for emphasis, but it's too heavy.

"You're totally overreacting," she says coolly, walking away. "It's not like he's a crack dealer. Marijuana should be legal, anyway."

I follow her into the kitchen. "He could be dealing Tylenol for all I care! But if I found fifty pounds of it in a giant Hefty bag hidden in the hall closet, I'd dump his ass, anyway!"

She slams her coffee cup down on the counter. "Dammit, Holly! You don't know him, okay? He's just doing this to make enough money to start his business."

I can't resist. "What kind of business?"

"Paintball. All he needs is to get enough money together for a down payment on a few wooded acres and some insurance. It's his dream."

"Yeah? Well my dream is to live in peace without worrying about the vice squad breaking down our door."

"Now wait a second—he'd *never* deal out of our place."

A string of brief visits from Boyfriend's no-good "buddies" springs to mind.

"Jill, Jill, Jill…" I say, pounding my head against the refrigerator.

"I can promise you it'll never happen again, okay? This was just a one-time thing."

"You *knew* about this? That he was storing this stuff here?"

"What difference does it make?"

"Oh, I don't know…maybe the difference between you getting off with a warning and going to jail? Wow, Jill…I hardly know what to say. He's really done a number on you."

"You've never been in love, Holly. You can't understand. And I don't want to talk about this anymore!" she yells, heading towards her room.

Maybe she's right. Maybe I can't understand. But if love means completely subjugating your common sense in order to hang on to a go-nowhere criminal loser, I don't think I want to understand.

I follow her, grabbing her by the arm. "Jill, please. You have to listen to me. You need to get away from him. A joint here or there is one thing, but this isn't a joke."

She twists out of my grasp and begins to cry. "You've always hated him. I don't know why. What did he ever do to you?"

I step away, amazed. "Hello? I was, like, completely, 100-percent right about him! What kind of asshole would get you involved in something like this?"

"God! He *didn't* involve me. He's not like that." She pushes me out of her room and slams the door in my face.

"Go ahead!" I yell. "Waste your life with this loser! But tell him he better get that shit outta here tonight or else! And I swear, Jill, if I ever see his face in here again, I'm calling the police!"

And I would, too.

The cracks in the office ceiling come slowly into focus.

"How long was I out?"

"We've been working for almost an hour and a half." Lacy is now seated behind her desk, her cheeks flushed. "Everything's fine, Holly. Just fine."

Maybe the wormwood has gone to her head. I check my buttons and bra hook, just to make sure nobody has been molested.

"And?" I rise up onto my elbow.

"Very exciting. *Very* exciting." She readies her notepad. "Tell me what you remember, even if it doesn't seem to make any sense."

"I don't really remember anything."

"Think. I want to see what floats to the surface here."

"Ummm…let's see. I don't know. A guitar, maybe? No…a violin."

Lacy's eyes widen. "Excellent."

"Oh, I get it. Is this like free association? I can do that."
During my short-lived stint with Dr. Chenkoff, the closest I
ever came to real psychoanalysis, I made it from my father
to cigars in four words flat. And my dad never smoked a day
in his life.

"Sort of. Keep going. But close your eyes. What do you
see? Close your eyes, please, Holly."

"Okay, umm… Okay… A very old woman in a cornfield.
With a…a barking dog?"

"Keep going. What kind of dog was it, Holly?"

"It was white and small. Maybe some kind of terrier…"
I peek a bit, just long enough to see her scribbling furiously.

"Could it have been a Corgi? A Welsh Corgi?"

"A Corgi? No, I don't think so."

"Oh."

"I guess that's it. What does it mean, Dr. Goldenblatt?"

"Please, call me Lacy. It's too early to tell, of course, but I
will say that I found our session here today very interesting.
Very interesting, both professionally and personally." Personally? My hands instinctively flew up to my chest to verify that
my Bounciful Bosom gel brassiere inserts were still neatly
tucked in place. "There's lots to uncover about you, Holly.
Are you willing to go the distance to find out?"

"I think so, Lacy, but can I, um, ask you something first?"
I get up and make my way over to one of the wicker chairs
in front of her desk.

"Of course."

"Now, I don't want you to take this the wrong way, because I'm not saying I don't buy into this whole thing—actually, I kind of feel like I already do—but I can't go forward
in good conscience until you answer one question for me.
The reason I haven't tried P.L.R. before is because I've never
heard a valid explanation for why people who've been
through it always claim to have been someone famous or im-

portant in a past life. The odds are pretty slim, wouldn't you say?" I may be a therapy addict, but I'm no fool. Spending my hard-earned dollars on a sham is something I can't afford to do.

"That's an *excellent* question, Holly, and I completely agree with you. You've actually stumbled across the number-one pet peeve of all certified P.L.R. therapists. There's no surer sign that someone's been to a quack than hearing something like that, and of course they're the ones who get all the press. Believe me—if I had a rupee for every guy who's been told he was King Louis XIV or Rasputin or a passenger on the *Titanic*... Look, Holly. I'm going to give it to you straight. I've been doing this for almost twenty years, and false memories aside, the closest *any* of my patients has ever come to anything like that was the one who I'd lay dollars to donuts was the lover of Napoleon's illegitimate half brother."

"Damn. I really wanted to be Cleopatra or Mata Hari or someone fabulous like that."

"Well, you never know..." She sighs, and leans in a bit closer. "I probably shouldn't be telling you this, because, like I said, there are never any guarantees, but I can already sense that you're a great candidate for this kind of therapy, and frankly I'd be quite surprised if we didn't learn *exactly* who you've been at least once or twice."

"Really? Wow." What made her think that? "So, uh, what exactly happened today? While I was...you know..."

"Since this is our introductory session, my goal was simply to get a feel for who you are today, with maybe just a smidge of who you might have been. Basically, I asked you some standard questions, about your childhood, your job, your dreams, your fantasies, that sort of thing. You see, the beauty of hypnosis is that it leaves your responses completely unrestricted and unedited. It's how I begin the process of opening your mind to energy imprints that are older than you are. And I also need to get to know you well enough so that you can be completely uninhibited in a way that your conscious mind would never allow. Does that sound okay?"

"Oh, what the hell. Knock yourself out," I tell her. "I hope you enjoy the Johnny Depp dreams as much as I do."

She smiles knowingly and leads me to the door.

In a generous leap of faith, I sign up for four more sessions over the next month. For all I know, the woman slipped some sort of barbiturate into my chamomile and spent the last ninety minutes filing her nails while I snored on the floor. But I do feel quite rested, which definitely counts for something. That and the subtle suggestion, however unlikely, that I might have been someone wonderful, like a Vanderbilt or an Astor or a Getty. Or Jane Austen or William Blake or Sylvia Plath. Or Genghis Khan or Catherine the Great or Mary Magdalene. It sure would put things in a new light.

Chances are, nothing interesting has *ever* happened to me, in this lifetime or any other. But my ego is no different from anyone else's—I'm hoping to learn something wild and amazing about myself nonetheless. If I turn out to be someone as cool as Napoleon's illegitimate half brother's lover, I'm more than willing to engage in the temporary suspension of disbelief to find out.

chapter 7

Where Have All the Magnates Gone?

"Ms. Hastings? Violet Chase here. Please call me back as soon as you get this message. I assume you still have my number."

At last, the call I've been waiting for. And seeing as it's December 18th, there's plenty of time to get a date in before Christmas.

Since it isn't the sort of conversation I want to have at my desk, I sneak into the bathroom (one of the private ones, so there'll be no chance of anyone overhearing) and call her back from my cell.

"Hi. It's Holly Hastings."

"Ms. Hastings! How are you?"

"Fine," I say, nearly jumping out of my skin with anticipation. "So who have you got for me?" *Please, oh pretty please, let it be somebody halfway decent. I'm not asking for anyone great, just good. Good would be great.*

"Whom have I got for you? What do you mean...?

Oooohhh. You thought… No. *Heavens,* no. I mean, nobody. I'm calling to remind you that it's been sixty days and it's time to renew your membership."

Umm… I don't think so.

"Ms. Hastings? You still there, dear?"

I am lonely, randy, poor and about to head into two weeks of holiday festivities flying solo. In fact, I would say I was on the verge of angry. Sure, I'm willing to settle for less—hairless, feckless, even penniless—but certainly not *this* much less, this phantom Millionaire and his empty promises, the continued shame of every day passing without an invitation to the ball. My self-esteem has plummeted as I envision guy after guy squirming uncomfortably in the luxuriously appointed viewing room at Moneyed Mates, possibly even snickering out loud as he watches me bare my soul for his amusement, or worse still, skipping immediately to the next gold digger's tape on the shelf upon seeing my listless hair and modest endowments….

"Hello? Ms. Hastings?"

God, I'm sick of feeling this way.

"Ms. Hastings?"

You know what? *Screw 'em*. Screw 'em all! Who are they to judge me? They don't even know me! And who is this Violet Chase but a harpy in Halston, a Heidi Fleiss in Herrera? And who am I but a complete idiot, paying her to auction me off like some sway-backed old nag in a last-ditch effort to avoid the glue factory?

I channel the sternest voice I know, the one Granny Hastings used to admonish my mother's skill as a laundress whenever she noticed a spot on my dad's tie or a dimness to his whites. (Granny may not have been the nicest lady, but nobody could say she was cheap with the bleach.)

"Actually, Ms. Chase, it's been more than two months, and I still haven't been contacted for a date yet. I am not satisfied with your service, so I think it would be best if we terminate our arrangement. At least for the time being."

"Well, I beg to differ, Ms. Hastings," she replies without skipping a beat.

Unfortunately, I'm miserable at terminating arrangements. I'm afraid to make a fuss, send a meal back, return defective merchandise, point out mistakes on the bill. It hadn't taken Anna Padgett—one of my first therapists, and below-average in every way—too long to figure out that my phobia of being judged by servicepersons could be traced back to the end of my senior year, when my mother insisted I keep the tags on my prom dress ("$217 dollars for something you'll only wear once? It's a *sin!* Your brothers never spent even *close* to this much!") and made a huge, public scene the day after the dance when the saleslady at the fancy store where we bought it refused to take it back.

"No returns on evening wear, ma'am. Says so right there on the bill," she'd said, louder than was necessary.

"But she didn't even wear it!" Mom shrieked, while I pretended to be dead, invisible and not hungover at the same time. I was also still reeling from the fact that I hadn't lost my virginity, despite my best-laid plans. By the time I'd finally peeled it off my aching, poisoned body at six-thirty that morning, the dress I'd insisted I'd die without—a sand-colored Calvin Klein knockoff, barely more than a shiny slip, really—already made me want to forget that the whole night had ever happened.

"Are you saying my daughter's *lying?*"

The salesgirl raised an overly plucked eyebrow.

Mom snatched the dress, stuffed it into the bag and stomped out of the store, pushing several other mothers and their nondrunk, nonlying, proud-to-be-a-virgin daughters out of the way.

On the way home, I threw up in the bag.

Of course, my mother refused to have the dress dry-cleaned ("Your father's not spending one more *penny* on that thing!") so it ended up snagged and ruined and four-and-a-half sizes too small after she ran it through our old Maytag. The textile embodiment of all this pain hung in the back of my closet until the day I moved into my first apartment, where, in a small ashtray during a simple ceremony, I burned the silk of my adolescent shame in effigy.

All this to say Ms. Violet Chase was not going to get the better of me. Not without a fight. Not today.

"But it's been over two months," I remind her, "and I believe you said I could get my money back if nothing happened."

"Minus the sitting fee."

"Yeah, minus that. I know."

"Ms. Hastings, I'm going to be frank with you."

"Please do."

"It would be a shame to let your membership slide now, sweetie. New Year's is coming up and it's a very busy time for us. I would be remiss if I didn't tell you I think you should give it another month."

I can only assume she's suggesting the Moneyed Mates who'd already passed me up once might be getting desperate enough to choke back their revulsion and take me for a spin around the block. In the bathroom mirror, beneath the stark fluorescent lighting, my pores seem deep and dirty as potholes. Tears I hadn't noticed welling up begin to slide down my cheeks. *A date for New Year's would be nice, and maybe with the proper facial…*

Slowly, my resolve slips away.

"Well…how much is it again? Just for another month?"

An exasperated groan escapes from Ms. Chase, whose tight white face I imagine contorting in agony at my utter stupidity. "Didn't you read the contract you signed?"

A second ago I was her sweetie, but now that she has me on the hook again, I'm just another idiot taking up her valuable time. "Refresh my memory."

"The special introductory offer was $995 for sixty days, *including* initial setup fee and including membership dues. Each month thereafter, we charge $150 to your credit card unless you cancel. That's why I'm calling. We tried to put the charge through and it was declined."

A knock at the door.

"Sorry—I'm in here!" I call out.

"You gonna be much longer?" It sounds like Cy.

"Yes… No… I mean, hold on." How incredibly rude to pressure a woman to come out of the washroom. "Can't you use the one down the hall?"

"Sorry," he grumbles.

Is there anything more nerve-racking than someone lurking on the other side of the bathroom door, sighing audibly? *Especially* when there's no good reason for it. It's not like we're on an airplane or in a nightclub. There are three other freaking toilets on this floor alone.

"Oh. I think it expired," I lie to Ms. Chase, silently praising myself for having the foresight to decline that last limit increase tendered by Visa. (If you cough up those minimum monthly payments like a good girl, they "reward" you with all kinds of nice offers and upgrades and points, but ask yourself this: Whose interest is served, exactly, by all that interest you're paying? Hint: Not yours.) But $2000 of credit card debt is my absolute cutoff. Any more than that, and it's impossible to ignore.

"Yes, yes. The new number, please, Ms. Hastings." I might as well have told her my dog ate my paycheck, because she clearly doesn't believe me, nor could she care less, so long as I ante up.

Shamed into submission yet again, I read out my Master-

Card number, wish her a Merry Christmas, even, and hang up. But it just doesn't seem right.

I straighten my collar, blow my nose and step back out into the hallway, where Cy is picking his teeth with a matchbook.

"I thought you'd left. Sorry," I mumble in the unsorriest way possible and push past him.

"What were you doing in there? Are you okay?" he calls out after me, but I pretend not to hear.

I toss and turn for hours, trying to imagine what I'm doing wrong, where I'm failing in my plan, in my life. Certainly, I'm open to the possibility of meeting someone; George and I both are. We have been diligently hanging out in grocery stores and coffee shops in the best parts of town. We've been doing happy hour in the financial district and brunch at the Hyatt downtown, for lack of anywhere better to go. And as for Moneyed Mates and my scandalous personal introduction, I'm not about to change it—not on your life. Even though George and I are both beyond broke from months of $10 cocktails and $20 omelettes, my reluctance has nothing to do with the $250 Ms. Chase would probably charge me to redo my tape. I am who I am, and if a guy doesn't want to date me because I dare to speak the truth, *my* truth, then I would rather not be with him, anyway.

I suppose.

So I'm not going to regret the tape. And I'm not going to beat myself up over letting that meanie talk me into parting with another one hundred and fifty hard-earned dollars. Maybe she's right—maybe the optimism (or desperation) of a New Year would lead to a date from a Moneyed Mate. I'm just going to have to be patient, give it a little longer…

But in the morning, I am still bothered. Bothered by my failure, not by my still-singleness, I realize as I pump gas into my Tercel in the freezing cold. (*Dammit!* 8:56—I'm going to be late. Again.) The fact that I will most likely spend New Year's Eve with George and her mothers watching *Pretty in Pink* and eating kosher Chinese food doesn't faze me. The fact that I never seem to make good on any of my resolutions does.

No matter how hard I try, things never seem to change.

When I pull into the parking lot at work, I grab some cash and my phone, and leave my coat and purse in the car to make it seem as if I haven't just arrived—*Who, me? I've been in since dawn. You?*—and try to not look cold and rushed as I walk past Cy's office and the desks of all my coworkers. Of course, the message light on my phone flashes tellingly when I finally slip behind my desk at 9:20ish. And of course, I spend the entire morning calling back proud suburban mommies wanting to submit head-shots of their offspring at $65 a pop for our "Babies of the Year" section before the deadline of noon today.

After a nice long lunch with Jesse, during which he tells me in excruciating detail how he plans to propose to whateverherdamnnameis at "exactly midnight" on New Year's Eve, I decide to devote the rest of the day to consoling myself with peanut M&M's from the machine in the lobby and figuring out why George and I are having so much trouble landing Moneyed Mates.

But first, I think I'll read the paper.

You might assume that I always read the paper, but you'd be wrong. Although I'm technically supposed to check over the ads and obits every day, I find the legion of overeager copyediting interns remarkably adept at making sure all the *i*'s are dotted and *t*'s are crossed. (Save for that one time Mrs. Millicent Beasley's grieving friends and family were politely requested to make donations to the American Dung Association in lieu of flowers.)

While skimming the *Bugle*'s front section, a little wire story picked up from the Associated Press catches my eye. The headline reads, "Buffalo Rated Least Desirable City For Dogs."

That seems a little harsh, I think, and proceed to read about how bad the canine set seems to have it here in the Queen City, which ranks dead last on a list compiled from such generally well-regarded indicators as mean annual temperature, square acreage of urban green space, veterinarians *per dogita* and the average income of pet owners.

Average income?

Hmmm…

Wait a second…

Could it be?

Frantically, I Google "Buffalo Millionaires."

Oh my.

It hadn't occurred to me that the problem wasn't me. Or George. Or our boobs or brains or posture or personality or hair or hearts or any of the other innumerable things we're taught to believe make us either attractive or abhorrent to the opposite sex. Yet there it is, plain as day, spelled out in detailed census information over the last one hundred years. The problem is Buffalo! *The problem is Buffalo!*

After an hour of research and two packs of M&M's, I have discovered four crucial facts:

1. In the year 1900, Buffalo, NY, was home to the most millionaires per capita in the United States.

By the turn of that century, you apparently couldn't throw a croquet mallet in these parts without hitting a titan of industry or future president. Buffalo's location at the terminus of the Erie Canal and near the burgeoning hydroelectric potential of Niagara Falls attracted prospective East Coast shipping magnates and bankers and businessmen, and here they founded their empires. Pretty soon, their wealth was expanding faster than the railway tracks they laid to connect their city's bustling port with the rest of the country.

2. There are between three-and-a-half and- five *million* millionaires currently living *throughout* the United States.

Although I can't find any statistics related to their marital status, it's pretty much safe to assume that several hundred thousand of them are still single and in the market for the love of their life.

3. In the year 2000, Seattle, WA, was home to the most millionaires in the United States.

By the turn of this century, however, Buffalo had become synonymous with chicken wings, while on the other side of the country, those teenage alchemists at Microsoft had spun software into gold during the '80s and '90s. Stock options made thousands of employees a part of the Millionaire club. Legions of nerds were rolling down their mansions' driveways in Bentleys and bling-bling.

4. Naples, Florida, currently boasts more millionaires per capita than any other city in the United States.

Millionaire-hunting in a small town probably has its perks—it's likely much easier to identify the men of means, because odds are almost everyone there is rich, anyway. Plus, the weather is certainly better in Naples than in Seattle.

Seattle definitely isn't the best spot for a warm winter getaway, but it might be worth our while to head down south for a few weeks and scope out the scene in Naples, just to see what it's like….

"George, we're taking a trip!"

She glares at me, tapping her watch. "You're late. The movie started five minutes ago. You know I like to see the previews."

"Forget about the movie. This is important! Wait till you hear what I found out today!"

"It's freezing. Can we just go in, please?"

I pull her into the doorway. Teenagers in jean jackets cheerily ignoring the ten-degree chill stream past us through the double doors of the multiplex, stomping out cigarettes with their Skechers. "You're not going to believe this, G, but Buffalo is so totally the wrong place to meet millionaires! The odds are stacked against us here!"

"God, Holly. Can we please give all that a rest for a bit? Just for tonight? I really *really* wanted to see this movie. Fulvia from my book club said it was the best documentary to hit the big screen since *Fahrenheit 9/11,* only not as cute, obviously, and with more Zapatistas."

"What? Hold on a sec—I thought we were going to see the one with Johnny Depp."

George's puppy-dog eyes grew wide as saucers. "But you said—"

"Fine, fine. Whatever. But we're going to talk about this later."

"There's nothing to talk about," she sniffs as she pays for her ticket. "I can barely afford popcorn, let alone a trip."

"Well, the price of popcorn here is absolutely ridiculous. I'll give you that. But it doesn't mean we can't take a vacation with our Christmas bonuses," I tell her. "Somewhere warm." A blast of frigid air blows in from an opened door and whips George's hair into a tangled mess. She struggles to smooth it down, dropping one Nepalese woollen mitt and her wallet in the process. "You definitely need it, my friend. We both do."

"Yeah, I need it," she snaps. "No shit I need it! But I also need to finish paying my student loans and move out of my mothers' house before I'm thirty. And let me remind you, my bonus is never quite what yours is."

I forgot that while most of us Buglers could look forward

to an entire extra paycheck come holiday season, the seven employees of the Book Cauldron had last year been graced with tickets to a free feng shui seminar, and leftover *Lord of the Rings* posters the Christmas before that.

"Word is, we're getting crystals for our keychains this year," she adds hopefully.

Of course, she's right. Spending money she doesn't have is probably not the best way for George to achieve the financial independence that has eluded her her entire adult life. But where there's a will, there's a way, and I am determined to make it happen for both of us—even if that means convincing my fiscally challenged best friend to spend a bit of money she doesn't have now in order to cash in on potentially huge returns later.

"Okay, George, well the popcorn's on me, tonight! Just promise me you'll think about it."

"Whatever."

As soon as I wake up, I call Ms. Chase. Even though it's Saturday morning, the receptionist informs me she is indeed in the office today, and transfers me immediately.

"Hello, Ms. Chase. This is Holly Hastings and I want to exercise my right to a refund!"

"Let's not be rash, Ms. Hastings…"

I push down the panic in my chest and remind myself that I could be mean here if I had to. This woman isn't about to serve me a booger-topped pizza or humiliate me in front of strangers in a dress shop. She isn't going pee in my tea or announce my bank account balance to the lineup behind me. The only card Violet Chase has to play is my fear of being single. And I'm apparently *already* afraid of that….

"It is no longer up for discussion, Ms. Chase! I expect you

to live up to your end of the Moneyed Mates guarantee in a courteous and timely manner."

"If you'd just let me—"

"No, I will not! The only thing I will let you do is offer me my refund."

Silence.

"Well?"

"Well, Ms. Hastings you may have your refund, I suppose. Minus the $250 sitting fee, of course."

"Of course."

I am woman, hear me roar! I never knew asserting myself could be so…so…*thrilling.* Maybe I could even take it a step farther…

"And I also want you to refund George her money, too."

A snort. "Out of the question. Ms. Perlman-MacNeill is not eligible."

"Why? She deserves it more than I do. Frankly, the way she was treated by one of *your* clients…"

"What? Who?"

"That Bobby Garrett creep who dumped her in a restaurant without so much as a good-night! His behavior was *so* abominable that you and your outfit over there should consider yourselves very fortunate to get out of this situation without any litigation on her part."

"Stop right there, Ms. Hastings! I'll remind you that you both signed waivers should this sort of thing happen, as it very rarely does. Now I'm very sorry, but we've never had *any* complaints about Mr. Garrett before. In fact, we've sent him out on over a dozen dates…"

"Great—so he's a serial dater! Is that supposed to make George feel any better? She's been *extremely* damaged by his callous disregard for her feelings on a variety of different personal levels, and, to make matters worse, publicly humiliated—and I mean *humiliated!*—by his reprehensible conduct. So I'm asking you again, please, to consider at least a partial refund for her."

"Listen here! She is *not* entitled to a refund. Especially since..." she pauses.

"Since what?"

"Well, it's not my intention to betray a confidence, since I'm normally very discreet in these matters, but your friend has turned down three other requests for dates over the past two months."

"What?"

"She didn't even come in to view the gentlemen's profiles. She just said no outright."

Poor thing. She was so damaged by that hell date that she couldn't bear the thought of a repeat occurrence.

It was one thing to be dismissed right off the bat for my looks (or was it my personality?) and be quietly rejected by all of Ms. Chase's so-called gentlemen, as I had been, but I imagine it was probably quite another to have the raised expectations of an actual date and subsequent relationship dashed by an asshole who was too dim to see through George's excited ramblings and too much of a prick to have the courtesy to finish the evening. And to make matters worse, I had virtually forced her into the whole thing. No wonder she didn't tell me about the other guys. She was too afraid to go, and too afraid to tell me she was afraid.

I had to make it up to her.

"Just refund my credit card, please," I say and hang up.

So what if we have no money? So what if we have no mates? So what if we seem no better off than before? At least I know what the next step is.

Three business days later, when the $745 shows up on my Visa statement, I immediately put it toward two last-minute plane tickets to Southwest Florida International Airport in Fort Myers, as close as I could get us to Naples on such short notice.

part two

Naples, Florida*

*The city currently home to the most millionaires
per capita in the United States.

chapter 8

Turbulence and Toothlessness

It's the day after Christmas, which was uncharacteristically ugly, and we're on our way.

"Louise and Larry sure seemed a little, um, tense, didn't you find?" George asks as she leans her seat back as far as it will go. "I don't think I've ever seen him snap at her like that."

But I'm still in the middle of practicing my deep breathing. "Just because the pilot turns off that damn light doesn't mean you should undo your seat belt, George! What about air pockets? We've all heard the story about the flight attendant who broke her neck when the plane dropped, like, one thousand feet in half a second!"

"Jeez! I'm *sorry,* okay? You don't have to get all up in my face like that...."

The only thing that makes me more uncomfortable than the thought of my parents fighting is flying, and now I have to contend with both at the same time.

"I'm sorry, G. Don't be mad at me. I need your support right now."

She grabs my hand. "If you get scared, just squeeze."

"Thanks," I say, grateful for the offer. "I just don't like being in the last row. It's so damn loud back here. All the engines and weird noises and as soon as you get used to a sound it cuts out all of a sudden, which is worse than it being noisy in the first place because you're sure an engine has died and the next thing you know—"

"Stop it! You're making yourself crazy. And we're not in the last row. There's one behind us."

Bravely, I turn around. Three flight attendants with decidedly unbroken necks glare back at me with icy grins.

After two fear-of-flying courses, you'd think I'd know better than to be afraid, but I can't help it—it just isn't right, us being up here, thumbing our noses at the natural order of things. I know all about the physics of lift, about the odds of double-engine failure, the negligible risks of lightning strikes, of terrorist attacks, of electrical problems, of pilot error, but still, the only image that ever comes to mind during my in-flight attempts at positive visualization are of jets plunging into stormy oceans or, variously, turning fiery cartwheels off the ends of slick runways. Sure I've flown before and obviously everything worked out fine. But I can never shake the feeling that every time I tempt fate by flying without dying, I'm just one step closer to hitting all the numbers in a lottery I don't want to win.

George is yammering on and on, presumably trying to distract me from the turbulence. To make matters worse, I haven't flown in almost two years, when I went to meet Zoe and Asher for a weekend in Atlantic City, and so the anticipated horror of the whole experience has been compounding, with interest, since then. That, and the fact that two planes have recently crashed (plane crashes always happen in threes, in case you didn't know). And there was also that funny feeling in my gut as we boarded the flight….

"I always wait for that feeling," I tell George, interrupting her play-by-play of every single thing that had happened at the Book Cauldron that week. "That feeling that says, 'Don't get on the plane!' You know the one…"

"Actually, I don't."

"It's that little voice that tells some people who have seats booked on doomed flights not to get on the plane."

"What?"

"Something just stops them from boarding the plane, and so they live and then tell the story for the rest of their lives about the miraculous sixth sense that saved them from certain death. Well, I think I might have felt something this time."

"You really are crazy. What you felt was all that Christmas pudding you ate last night."

"The reason I ate so much was because I couldn't take listening to them argue," I explain, ready to get my mind off the flight for a while.

"Did you see Mike almost choke on his eggnog when your dad said the roast was too dry?"

"Yeah. I think all my brothers were pretty surprised. My dad usually doesn't say much of anything. Especially not anything nasty." Aside from birthdays and holidays, my brothers rarely interact with our parents. I, on the other hand, have been fielding increasingly more frequent Just-Wanted-to-See-How-You-Were-Doing calls from my mom of late, and often heard them bitching at each other on the other end. "It's probably because he's been around a lot more lately. It's an adjustment."

"It might be more than that."

"I don't think so."

"You know, I think you idealize your parents' marriage. Every couple goes through rough patches. Especially when they've been married nearly forty years."

"Not my parents. They don't have any rough patches. All they have is the same exact day, which they live over and over again. It's like Groundhog Day. It doesn't change. If they're fighting, then they probably always have. Maybe we just never knew about it. That's all."

George stares out at the clouds for a bit. "Didn't you walk in on them doing it once?"

"Okay, now you're pushing it… And could you close the window shade? It's making me nervous."

"I bet they don't do it anymore," she muses.

"It's taken me fifteen years to get over that," I snarl, "as well as thousands of dollars in therapy. So I'm telling you to drop it. Now."

"All I'm saying is, I'm not feeling the love anymore."

"Drop it. Please just drop it."

"Why? It's okay to talk about it, Holly. You have to start seeing your parents as real people, with wants and needs of their own. You're not a kid anymore."

"I have an idea. Let's talk about *your* mothers and *their* sex life for a while." I'm starting to hope the plane will crash, just to get her to shut up.

"Oh, come on. Don't be such a prude."

"Don't push me, George…."

After an hour-long layover in Atlanta, a particularly bumpy landing in Fort Myers and a forty-five-minute drive to Naples in a tin-can rental car, we are still squabbling. Once we finally turn onto the palm-lined drive leading to our hotel, though, we are stunned into silence.

I hadn't told George all the details of our trip; I guess I sort of wanted to surprise her. But even though I was the one who'd made all the reservations, I had to admit I wasn't exactly expecting *this*—an oceanfront ivory palace, fifteen stories high, dressed in climbing bougainvillea, flowering fuchsia and orange and flanked by acres and acres of landscaped greenery, complete with stone fountains, ivy-covered gazebos and free-roaming flamingos.

"My God, Holly. How much is this costing us?" George whispers nervously as we pull up to the main entrance.

"One hundred and twelve dollars a night."

"Each?"

"Uh… No. What are we, made of money? So it's, like, fifty-six dollars each, I guess. It was a little more than I figured we wanted to spend, but it was all I could get last-minute."

Two valets in Bermuda shorts pop out from behind the fronds of a potted bird of paradise to open our doors.

"I don't know, Holly…this seems a little too good to be true," she insists suspiciously as we get out of the car.

"You think maybe there's another Naples Ritz-Carlton?" I double-check the receipt I'd printed of our reservation confirmation. "I'm pretty sure this is the right place…."

"Be careful with this, hun." She winks to the bellhop, passing him her beat-up old backpack. He smiles back broadly, his head cocked to one side in an expression of what could only be described as bemused lust.

"It's José, ma'am."

"It's *miss,* José."

George mouths "he's so hot!" as we stagger into the grandest lobby either of us has ever seen.

"We're not here to fraternize with the help," I remind her, half-joking. That bellhop *is* hot.

"Would you look at that!"

We crane our necks to take it all in—shiny marble floors and columns in the palest shade of pink; antiques and oil paintings everywhere; a tiered chandelier dripping with crystals; towering palms decorated in thousands of tiny white Christmas lights. Palm trees. *Inside.*

"Toto, I've a feeling we're not in Kansas anymore!"

"I don't think anyone from Kansas has ever even *been* here," George whispers as a lady with a tanned, stretched face and a poodle under her arm clicks past us over the polished floor and into a waiting limo. I try not to giggle, but George pushes me over the top when she points out our reflection in a large gilt-framed mirror. Bedraggled and travel-weary, we are nearly as pale as the ivory wallpaper behind us. The humidity has made my hair even limper, while George's frizzy curls are practically standing on end.

"I look like a young Albert Einstein with tits."

"Hello! Hello!" something squawks.

Not five feet from us, on a golden stand, a huge white parrot shifts rapidly from foot to foot. George shrieks as quietly as she can and jumps back.

"Next, please!"

A clerk taps her nails impatiently at her post behind the front desk, barely able to contain her contempt. We can already tell she's far less friendly than José the hunky luggage lugger.

"Uh, we're here to check in."

"Name."

"Hastings, Holly."

"Perlman-MacNeill, George," George adds.

"*You're* George Perlman-MacNeill?"

"The one and only."

"I wouldn't be at all surprised if you were," she says with a fuck-you smile. "But I'll need to see a passport or driver's license from each of you, please. I assume George is short for something else. Let me guess—Georgette? Georgina?"

"No," says George, a little miffed. "I'm just George."

"Is there some sort of problem?" I ask as we slide our IDs across the marble.

"No. But we take security here at the Naples Ritz-Carlton very seriously, especially as we have a number of high-profile guests staying with us this week and—"

George isn't about to let that go. "Who? Who? Oh my God—imagine we saw someone famous! Would that not be *the* coolest thing ever?!"

"—and we have a responsibility to make sure everyone is...who they say they are. It's for your own protection as well. I'm sure you understand."

"We completely understand. Ms. Perlman-MacNeill and I will try and refrain from stalking anyone while we're here." Buoyed by my successful negotiations with Violet Chase, my new life attitude is going to be all kick-ass and take-no-crap. "And thank you very much for your concern."

I'm sure it physically pains the smarmy wench to pass over our keys, especially when she prints up the bill and sees what we paid.

"Tell me again how it is that we're here?" George asks once we get up to our room, which more than makes up for what it lacks in largeness with over-the-top luxe.

"Priceline. I bid one hundred and twelve dollars for a five-star resort, just to see what would happen, and it was accepted right away!"

"Huh?"

"It's a Web site. Never mind. Let's just call it a computer glitch."

George nods and picks up a small white card on the bed-side table. "What are Frette linens?"

"You'll find out tonight when you get into bed," I tell her as I throw back the curtains dramatically. The sun is setting over the Gulf of Mexico, and the water glows like gold as it melts into the blazing horizon.

We take one look at each other and burst out laughing.

After a seriously caloric breakfast in bed that costs almost as much as our room, we venture out for our first day. According to the brochures we found in the lobby, Fifth Avenue South is the place to see and be seen, so we jump into our car and head over there ASAP.

To get a feel for the place, we cruise the strip before looking for a place to park. "Wow…this really *is* upscale," I muse aloud as George deftly maneuvers our little subcompact between luxury cars as big as buses. "Kind of old-ladyish, though…resort wear, that kind of stuff."

"Ugh. There's one of those stores that only sells white clothes…."

"Well, I think you'd look lovely in white, *dahling!*"

"You don't say! Well, let me just find a place to valet this and we'll pop in. Heavens to Betsy! I can't believe I've gone this long without a white linen suit!"

"I need something too," I say, playing along. "The gala's only a week away and I haven't a *thing* to wear!"

"You could borrow my pink Versace, if you like, or my silver Roberto Cavalli!"

"Why, George—I didn't know you knew about Roberto Cavalli," I say, breaking character.

"Give me *some* credit, Holly. I may shop at Urban Outfitters, but I haven't been living under a rock my whole life. And I've been doing a little research of my own. Ever since you came up with this whole crazy idea."

"You have?"

"Yeah. I got a subscription to *In Style* and *The Robb Report*. By the way, did you know you can lease a luxury yacht for only $17,000 a month? That's downright affordable, wouldn't you say?"

"You're kidding, right?!"

"Why would I kid about a thing like that, *dahling?* How else do you expect me to get from Palm Beach to the Bahamas when the jet's in the shop? Carnival Cruise Lines? I don't *think* so."

"Okay, Zsa Zsa. Just promise me you won't forget about the little people."

"Oh, I plan to forget about nearly everybody back home. I'm looking forward to it," she says as she checks her gloss in the rearview. "Now let's get out there and find us some sugar daddies!"

The sea air is apparently getting to her brain, but I like it.

We window-shop till we nearly drop, pop into a gallery or two, then stop for dinner (gazpacho and lobster rolls!) at the cutest little bistro in the heart of all the action. We ask for a table outside on the terrace, just in case any eligible young hotties walking by are tempted to chat us up.

"My feet are killing," I complain as the waiter brings us our soup. I'm sporting a sexy new pair of strappy sandals I bought on sale at the end of the summer. "Shit. I already have two blisters."

"What about those guys over there?" George points at two shirtless teenagers getting into a beat-up pickup truck filled with gardening equipment parked across the street.

"Um, they're like eighteen years old. We're not here to get our groove back, Stella. We're here to…"

"To what?"

"To scope things out."

"Oh. I thought we were here to meet the men of our dreams."

"We are. But that might not happen in six days and seven nights."

George tugs at her halter top for the umpteenth time.

"Don't do that," I tell her. "Just leave them be."

"So what happens if we don't meet anyone?"

Good question.

"What happened to all that sugar-daddy talk from this morning? Have you lost your optimism already? Let's just wait and see, okay?"

"Seriously. What'll we do?"

"We've barely been here for twenty-four hours!" I polish off the rest of my frozen lychee daiquiri and prepare to rally the troops. "Look. If we don't meet anyone this trip, then at least we had some fun in the sun. And if we like the town, then we might consider a…how should I put this…a *longer* visit."

"Like move here?"

"Sure. Why not? Look at us. Look at *this*," I say, gesturing grandly to include everything within a three-hundred-mile radius. "A day ago, we were tripping over our winter boots and fighting traffic in two feet of snow, and now we're in a tropical paradise scoping out *real* moneyed mates."

"Those teenagers were the first guys I've seen under the age of sixty-five," she says.

"Don't be ridiculous. There's…José. And our waiter right here, for example," I say and smile at him. Though obviously gay, he was quite adorable.

"Would you like another daiquiri, miss?"

"Do you mind?" I ask George.

"Go ahead. I'll drive."

"I think I will, then. And could you please make it a double?"

"And I'll have a piece of Key lime pie."

"And two forks," I call out after him.

"With the exception of guys in the hospitality or food-service industries—who are therefore *P-O-O-R*—I haven't seen any prospects at all," she says sullenly. "Not a single one."

"Well, technically that's not true. There were those kids across the street."

She pouts and shakes her head.

"What the matter, G?"

"I guess I'm just tired. We've been out in the sun all day."

"You should have bought that cute straw hat. It looked amazing on you."

"Yeah, but it was sixty-five dollars, and I don't think the cost-per-wear ratio would be respectable, considering we live in a city with only two seasons—winter and July."

"Well, tomorrow we'll just go to the beach and sit under an umbrella all day."

"That sounds good. I brought three books."

"And the beach is probably the best place to meet guys around here, anyway."

"Since it's the weekend, maybe they'll be out in droves?" she suggests.

"That's the spirit!"

On our way up to our room, the cute bellhop from the day before is in the elevator with a cart full of Louis Vuitton luggage.

"Hi," George says. "José, right?"

He nods at her bosom.

"Remember us?" she asks.

"Of course. How could I forget?"

She smiles. "Well, I was wondering…maybe you could help us out with something. You seem to know your way around, and, well, like I said, we were wondering, exactly what is there to do around here?"

Sometimes it's hard to tell if George even knows she's being a flirt, since she comes by it so naturally. Most of the time I think no, but since she'd been dumped by her professor, I've noticed she's a little more outgoing. Which is no doubt a good thing, since I on my own rarely attract much attention from the opposite sex.

"Well, miss, there are three bars in the hotel, and two pools, and the gym is on the—"

She giggles. "No, silly! I mean, what do people around here do for fun?"

"Like the locals?"

"Yeah," I say. "Like the locals."

"Well…there are exactly two things to do in Naples—shopping and golfing."

"Golfing," George repeats, as if it's the first time she's ever heard the word.

Sensing he's losing her interest, José adds cautiously, "And there's the staff bar in the back of the hotel, if you were, you know, looking for something a little more laid-back…"

The doors open onto our floor. "Thank you, but no," I say, pulling George out of the elevator.

"Thanks, José! You're a sweetie!"

After two divinely serene but boyless days at the beach, it's becoming clear that José was right. Naples isn't exactly the hotbed of singles activity I hoped it would be. George and I found the hotel bars to be pretty stodgy, while the nightclub in town recommended by the concierge wasn't really our scene. (Picture *Cocoon* meets *Cocktail*, only with more Don Ameche and less Tom Cruise.) Fortunately, the weather has been wonderful, so George and I are having a blast just relaxing, sleeping in and enjoying the general opulence that surrounds us.

On our fourth day, I make an executive decision—we're going to get some action.

"We have to start being serious, here, G," I say as I finish off another eight-dollar blueberry scone by the pool. "We didn't just come here to work on our tans, you know."

She rolls over onto her back and puts her hands up to shield her eyes from the sun. "Let's not push it. I'm having fun just doing nothing."

"But we have to be open to the possibilities. Maybe we should expand our horizons a little."

"I'm afraid to even ask."

"New Year's Eve is the day after tomorrow, right?"

"Right…" she says cautiously.

"And we haven't met anyone yet."

"So? I can't see how that's our fault. The only eligible men around here are triple our age."

"Don't exaggerate."

"I'm not! Did you see that old guy at the buffet this morning? He smiled at me and he had no teeth. No *teeth,* Holly!"

"All the better to eat his prunes with?"

"No! I don't care what you say. I'm not Anna Nicole Smith. I can't do that. Not even for a million dollars."

"Of course not! That's not what I mean at all…her husband was like ninety-four or something. And that's obviously pushing the boundaries of good taste. But within reason, a big age difference might not be so bad. Lots of women do it."

"Like who?"

"Like Calista Flockhart, that's who!"

"Han Solo is not now, nor will he ever be, a senior citizen."

"Technically, I think he is."

"Apologize immediately or this conversation is over."

"I'm sorry. You're right—Han Solo doesn't count. What about Annette Bening?"

She shakes her head. "Warren Beatty's still got a little bit of hotness left in him. He's not old yet."

"Catherine Zeta-Jones?"

"Michael Douglas is one thing, Kirk Douglas is what you're suggesting."

"I am not."

"Look around here, Holly. There's a lot more Kirk than Michael."

I scan the pool area. She has a point. But I'm not giving up. "Oh, lighten up. You've been halfway to old and back with your professor, so what's the big deal?"

"Stuart is fourteen years older than me. It's hardly the same thing."

"Look, George—I'm not suggesting you have a romp in the old Craftmatic with Methuselah over there." I motion towards the lone swimmer in the pool, whose diaper is peeking out from the back of his swim trunks. "All I'm saying is I don't think it would be so bad, dating a distinguished older gentleman. Think Jack Nicholson or Robert Redford or someone like that."

"Well, I guess they're not so bad. I did see a guy who looked like George Hamilton at the beach the other day. He was okay, I guess."

"He sure was!"

She glares at me suspiciously. "I don't know what you have in mind, Holly, just promise me you won't go getting all…"

"All what?"

"All, you know…*crazy*."

"Crazy works well for me," I say, slipping my newly pedicured feet into my flip-flops. "I'll be back in twenty minutes."

When I return to the pool an hour later, George hasn't moved.

"I hope you put some more cream on."

"Tan is the new pale," she groans and flips over to get away from me.

"Wake up."

Silence.

"Okay, fine. Be that way. But I'm going up to change."

"Change? For what?"

"Our 1:30 golf lesson."

George sits up. "Golf lesson?"

"Yup. I figured we better get busy or else we're gonna look like complete idiots tomorrow."

"Tomorrow?"

"We have a 9:00 a.m. tee time"

"Tee time?"

"Yes, George. Tee time."

She stretches lazily. "I don't think I like that idea."

"Technically, I think it was José's idea."

"Jose," she says dreamily.

"Come on. We don't want to be late."

A cute little shuttle bus picks us up by the hotel's side entrance and drops us off fifteen minutes later at the Ritz-Carlton Golf Resort. By the time we find the golf school, buy a couple bottles of iced tea and rent our clubs, I notice that George is looking more than a little flushed.

"I don't feel well, Holly."

"You probably have sunstroke and I'm not at all surprised. You've been baking yourself silly for three days. And you're definitely not drinking enough water so you might be dehydrated, too."

"Ms. Hastings?"

"Yes?" I spin around.

"Hi. I'm Mateo."

A dark, sexy Spaniard with bulging forearms reaches out to shake my hand.

"Nice grip," I say to him.

"Well, I do get a lot of practice."

"I bet you do...."

He's a bit older than the type of guy I normally fall for—forty, maybe forty-five.

I sigh. You could drown in those eyes—dark, black almost, and fringed with a double row of lashes any supermodel would envy. He smiles back at me warmly.

Hmm...

Maybe this is a good way to ease into an attraction for older men. A little experiment. Just to see what would happen. Nobody would get hurt. Quite the opposite, hopefully...

"Holly?" George says weakly.

"Okay, ladies. So what do we have here?" He claps his hands together, takes a step back and looks us up and down. "First of all, halter tops are not permitted on the course. Collared shirts only. But since we're going to be on the driving range today, I'm sure nobody will mind."

Although she already resembles a lobster in a wig, George blushes even redder and attempts a smile.

"Come," he instructs us. "This way."

"This is the thing, Mateo…" I say as we struggle to keep up. He's tall, and for each stride he takes, I take two. George is at a full jog and fading fast. "We have no idea—and I mean absolutely no idea—what this whole golf thing is about and we need to learn fast."

"I've been playing for twenty years and sometimes *I* still feel like an amateur, so don't get your hopes up. We'll start with the basics, yes? Grip, stance, swing… And in a few weeks and a few more lessons—"

"Sorry," I interrupt. "Maybe I didn't make myself clear. We need to look like we know what we're doing by tomorrow morning."

He stops in his tracks. "This is impossible! Surely, you must be joking, yes?"

It's going to take some encouragement to get him to see things our way.

"I think I need to sit down," says George.

"Look, Mateo. You're a professional. We both know that. And you're also a very experienced teacher. So just teach us what we need to know in order to properly, um…handle the balls…and we'll be all set!"

George's lashes flutter as her eyes roll back into her head. I can't tell if it's a reaction to my painful attempt at flirtatious double entendres or the sunstroke.

Mateo's dark eyes twinkle. "There's more to this game than balls, Ms. Hastings."

"Please, call me Holly."

"Holly, then. But like I said, there's more to it than balls."

"Really?"

"Oh, yes. There's the stroke to consider as well," he says as he hands me a club.

"The stroke?"

"Yes, the stroke."

"As in, how many strokes does it take to...finish?"

He steps behind me and puts his hands on my hips. "Spread your legs a bit wider. There, that's it. How many strokes it takes to finish, Holly, depends on if it curves to the left or the right."

"Excuse me?"

"The holes. Some dogleg to the left, others to the right." Mateo bends down and places a ball on the tee. "Now let me see you swing, yes?"

I swing as gracefully as I can, trying to visualize what Tiger Woods looked like in that Nike commercial. Of course, I completely miss the ball, lose my balance and end up on my duff.

"Holly?" George calls out. She's sitting cross-legged on the grass about three yards away. I'm trying very hard to pretend that she's okay.

"Hang on, George! Have some more iced tea!"

"That was appalling," Mateo whispers in my ear as he helps me up.

"But this is my first time—isn't it *supposed* to hurt?"

"My first time, I got a hole in one."

"Impressive...though I bet you had a titanium driver."

"Well, there aren't many clubs like mine," he agrees with a wink. "Forty-five inches."

And on it goes, until George actually faints and we have to call it a day.

Despite my teacher's best efforts, I only managed to make contact with the ball once, and even then, it didn't go very far. Golf is definitely not my game. But at least I managed to write my room number down on a chit and slip it into Mateo's pocket as he helped George board the shuttle back to our hotel.

chapter 9

Gentlemen Only, Ladies Forbidden

"Are you sure you're okay?"

"Yes. I'm fine."

"We don't have to go."

"I feel fine. I slept for thirteen hours, Holly."

"Are you sure?"

"Yes."

"'Cause we can just stay here and rest if you want to."

"I want to go."

"Really?"

"Yeah. It'll be fun."

Good ol' George. She really is a trouper.

Within an hour, we are back at the golf resort, waiting to tee off. The day before, the concierge had explained they would pair us up with two other players to make a foursome, and that the Executive Course—an easier par-3 with only nine holes—allowed mixed play. I took that to mean we had a very good chance of being matched up with two guys.

"I have no idea how to play this game," George marvels as she examines the golf clubs we'd rented. "It's absurd, really."

"It doesn't matter."

"Easy for you to say—Mateo probably showed you a thing or two so you won't embarrass yourself."

"I can guarantee you I'm just as terrible as you are, if not worse. While you were drifting in and out of consciousness yesterday, I was busy proving that. But it doesn't matter. They told me this course isn't really for competitive players. We'll be paired up with people just as bad as we are, or who don't care anyway."

"But I don't want to be embarrassed. Especially if they're cute…."

"I wouldn't go getting my hopes up for a love match just yet. This is a real long shot, remember."

"I know." She sits down on a wooden bench and sighs. "But didn't you say this was the best place in town to meet guys?"

"Yeah, but…"

"Oh, for heaven's sake! What's the point, then?"

"To have fun, remember? You said it yourself. And to try something new!"

"Yeah, well I didn't mean it," she grumbles. "I thought we were here for the boys."

"It's a golf course, G. Not a singles bar."

"Maybe we should skip right to the end, then, and head straight for the 19th hole. Have a few drinks and wait for a couple of cuties to come in after their games are over."

"You have to play to get in there."

"The green fees alone are more than a day's work for me. If there were some boys, that's one thing, but—"

"Don't worry so much! We have to stay optimistic. It's gonna happen for us, one way or the other."

"Yeah, right." She kicks a pebble, following it till it disappears into the edge of the grass.

I don't mean to take all the fun out of it for her. After all, I'm hoping for the exact same thing she is.

"Maybe our partners *will* be cute," I concede.

"Really?"

"Sure—why not? And rich, too. You know, Naples is not only the millionaire capital of America, but the golf capital, also."

"It is?"

"Yup. There are more courses here per capita than anywhere else. So I naturally take that to mean millionaires like golf."

"I hope so." George turns to look out across the course. The sky is a wash of blue, and out past the seventh hole, there is the ocean—an almost unexpected sight, bottle-green and fierce, its waves pushing the surf up into a periodic curtain of spray. "I'm sorry, Holly. I'm just being a baby. It doesn't really matter if we meet anyone. I mean, look at where we are. This is beautiful. Heaven. I bet they're digging out from a storm back home...."

"Ahem."

We spin around.

"I think we're with you today, ladies."

The hum of a lawn mower off in the distance isn't nearly enough to temper the awkward silence.

"Are you sure?" George asks.

"9:00 a.m.?"

"Uhh...yeah. I think so," I say, and George shoots me a panicked look. But there's no use lying.

"How's that?" one of them ask.

"Yes!" I shout. "We're at nine!"

"Shall we, then?" The other one grins and extends an arm, presumably for me to take.

And that's how George and I end up playing our very first

round of golf with two of the three oldest living male triplets in the United States.

Before we left for Florida, I saw Lacy one last time. I tried to stick it out with her. Really, I did. But past-life regression was definitely not for me, and I was in no position, financially speaking, to be dabbling in therapy my insurance provider considers "beyond the sphere of reputable and recognized psychological practice." So I resolved simply to play it out until the last of my prebooked appointments, right before Christmas.

"Does the name Clifford Boyer mean anything to you?" Lacy asked me at the end of our final session. Not that she knew it was our last session, since I'd decided just to leave her a message with the news over the holidays instead of telling her in person. I couldn't afford to be convinced otherwise, and didn't want to hurt her feelings. Of all the therapists and practitioners I'd encountered in my quest for sanity and self-acceptance, Lacy Goldenblatt was by far the most personally invested in her belief system.

"Clifford Boyer?"

"I don't think you've ever mentioned him to me before," she said.

I wanted to say, "Maybe that's because I'm asleep, entranced, unconscious, whatever, during forty-seven of our sixty minutes together each week!" But I didn't. Instead, I lied.

"I have no idea who that is. Why?"

"Oh—just thought I'd ask," she shrugged. "He's probably just a fragment from someone else."

"Another patient?"

"No, silly. Another you."

"Oh."

But Clifford Boyer was no fragment. He was an odious little troll, the first boy I ever kissed. He'd cleverly wooed me by chanting "Tall-y Hall-y! Creepy Crawly!" throughout all of seventh grade. The event I'd been waiting for my whole life unfolded behind the garden shed during Marcy Drell's annual Fourth of July pool party. I was expecting something along the lines of what I'd seen on *General Hospital*—basically, people pressing their faces against one another—so when he shoved his tongue in my mouth, I was so shocked and repulsed that I bit down. Hard.

Of course, he ran off screaming and bleeding, and Mrs. Drell had to call his mother to come and get him. The subsequent fallout branded me as a sexual pariah for the remainder of Junior High. When we returned to school in September, Clifford told everyone I was a hermaphrodite who'd had his breasts surgically removed. And so I was left alone to hold up the walls during the Homecoming Dances, Valentine's Day Socials and Spring Flings, while my friends bumped up against boys on the dance floor and snuck out behind the gymnasium to get felt up. I still get nauseated when I hear *Stairway to Heaven*, or *Dream On* by Aerosmith.

It wasn't something I was fond of rehashing with just anyone. In fact, I'd barely touched on it with any of my therapists.

"Hey! You there!"

I pretend not to hear, and keep walking toward the sand trap, but Milt just shouts louder.

"You know what golf stands for?"

"How should I know?"

We are only on the third hole, but we've already figured out that the easiest way to get through this game as painlessly as possible is to play along. (And, in my case, when it comes to the actual golf part, sticking to a fifteen-stroke maximum per hole, then giving up and moving on to the next one.)

Milt raises a bony finger in the air and pronounces, "Gentlemen Only, Ladies Forbidden!"

"Is that true?" George asks. The slightest whiff of misogyny and she's on guard.

Morrie takes a step closer to her and grabs her hand.

"Holly…" George whimpers.

I slip in between them. "Morrie, you're going to have to back off a little. George here is very shy."

Milt rolls his eyes. "Leave the nice girl alone and get back in the cart!"

"I didn't fart!" Morrie protests.

George has had enough. "Don't you think you're a little old for me, Morrie? I'm twenty-eight. You could be my grandfather."

"My second wife was twenty-eight when I married her in 1947," Morrie informs us.

George slices a ball off into the distance. "Did you see that? I'm not bad!"

"Marvin—he's our other brother. He's the oldest, by three minutes, and he's been married for—"

"Oy, he never lets you forget those three minutes."

"Like I was saying, he's still married, Marvin is. Coming up on sixty years."

"Sure, sure. Sixty years," Milt grumbles. "But his Beverly had a stroke in '82, so it hardly counts."

"I'm sorry to hear that," I say.

"Can we get back to the game, please?" George suggests. Turns out she's a natural. I'm not surprised—her hand-eye coordination is beyond reproach, which basically means that she tends to excel at the video-game versions of real sports.

She really doesn't know what to make of these two funny old men, but I can't get enough. To me, they are pure gold. By the sixth hole, when Milt and Morrie's debate on mutual funds versus treasury bills has reached a fever pitch, I decide to devote an entire chapter of my book to dating the elderly. Although not everybody could handle it, myself included, there are obviously certain benefits. Frankly, I wish I had the constitution for it, but the likelihood of genital liver spots puts me off the population entirely.

"I'd like to take you out dancing," Milt says to me as we wait for the shuttle.

Morrie nods his approval. "He's a good dancer, my brother."

"That's not all I'm good at…"

"I think I see the shuttle," George prays aloud.

"Ach! She doesn't know what you're talking about, Milt. He means he's got the little blue pills, Dollface!"

George shuts her eyes tight and, I'm sure, pretends she is somewhere else.

"Thanks," I tell them. "I get it. But we're not really interested."

"Not at *all* interested," George clarifies, without looking at either one.

"Ach," hacks Morrie. "Let's go."

Milt reluctantly agrees, and hobbles off after his brother. Pretty good for someone with two artificial hips, I can't help but think.

"We had a lovely time!" I call after them. "And thanks for the pointers!"

"Oh, thank God," George says when they are finally out of earshot (about five feet, just to be safe).

"I thought they were cute," I say.

"Puhlease."

"You, my friend, need to learn a thing or two about respect for your elders."

Milt turns around and waves.

I smile and wave back.

I check my e-mail at the hotel business center and find two new messages in my in-box.

To: hhastings@thebugle.com
From: zoewatts@doggietails.com
Subject: Hi!
hi beach bunny! hope yer havin' fun. I think there's something wrong with your voice mail. call me when you get home. have to tell you something…
luv, z

To: hhastings@thebugle.com
From: jill1281@buffalonet.com
Subject: Good news
Dear Holly,
I hope you're having a good time. But I have to tell you something and I thought this would be the best way so that you're not surprised when you come back home and see all my stuff gone. You've made it very clear how you feel about Barry, so I've decided to move out. I know you said the things you did because you care about me, but you just don't know him the way I do.
Barry and I are going to get married in the spring. I love him very much, Holly, and I need to be with him, so I don't think that it would be very healthy for us to keep being roommates. I know that it would be impossible for you to be happy for me, so all I can do is wish you the best.
I hope you find what you're looking for, as I have.
Love, Jill
P.S. I've switched the phone and gas bills to your name and had the landlord take me off the lease.
P.P.S. There's a gluten-free banana loaf for you in the freezer.

"I can't believe we're going home tomorrow," I say. "I can't believe the week's almost over."

"I can't believe this is how we're spending New Year's Eve," George says, waving her hand to indicate Chip's Supper Club, where "midnight" starts at precisely 9 p.m. "And yet somehow, I'm loving it! I'm having a blast even though it sucks!"

"It does not!"

"Except for the weather, it does."

"And the hotel," I remind her.

"And the shopping." She slurps piña colada out of a pineapple before continuing. "Neiman Marcus Last Call was truly an experience. And although this top makes me look like a hooker, who could turn down a twelve-dollar Vivienne Westwood bustier with only one hook missing? Not that I have a clue who Vivienne Westwood is, but it sure sounds good...."

"Oh, it is," I assure her. "And he seems to like it, too." A slick old guy in a leisure suit and a combover leers drunkenly at George's cleavage.

"Scram," she says.

"That could have been Mr. Right."

"I'm nowhere near drunk enough to laugh at that." She slurps up the remainder of her drink. "Do they put any alcohol in these things?"

"So it would seem."

"I'm a deap chate. What can I say?"

"Apparently, not much!"

"Haw, haw. You're killing me."

George's admirer waves at her from across the table.

"But as much fun as we're having here, Holly, I think I'm almost ready to go home."

"Me too," I says. "It's been a real education, and great material for my book, but I'm ready."

"If I see one more bony sixty-five-year-old ass with 'Juicy' written across it, I'll puke."

"Or one more Louis Vuitton Murakami bag..."

"Or one more white Cadillac...

"Or palm tree..."

"Oh yeah, they're the *worst*."

"Let's go back to the hotel and see if José's working," I say. "I bet we could sneak into the staff bar…"

"Really?"

"Of course! You deserve a prize for agreeing to this trip!"

"Oh, Holly, don't say that! I had so much fun!" she says, and hugs me. "Thank you so much for my ticket!"

Three octogenarians seated at the next table hoot and clap.

"Do guys ever grow up?" I ask the gray-haired waitress as we settle up the bill.

"Sorry, dear," she says. "They just get shorter and shorter till eventually they disappear and all that's left is a closetful of white shoes and a life-insurance policy. And that's if you're lucky!"

Just because Florida happened to be a complete bust doesn't mean I'm giving up.

While George sleeps off her New Year's hangover, I sneak down to the hotel business center. A few minutes of intense Googling reveal that I may have jumped the gun a little with the whole Naples thing. In fact, it turns out we were on the wrong coast altogether.

Yes, I have discovered a fifth and final fact:

In the Year 2000, the San Francisco-Bay Area was home to more Millionaires under the age of 50 than any other urban center in the country.

Again, thanks to the dot-com dorks and their love of microchips and circuit boards. And just to sweeten the pot, the City by the Bay sounds like a pretty nice place to be. Even the so-called Silicon Valley seems to have its good points, according to the San Jose Convention and Visitors Bureau Web site. Sure, there's endless urban sprawl and hundreds of miles of fault lines, but next to the inclement weather of Seattle, strip malls and the occasional earthquake might be easier to live with on a day-to-day basis. (Who am I to be picky, anyway? I live in a place where the mean annual temperature has been deemed unfit for dogs.)

Shit. How could I have missed this?

On my way back up to the room, I alternate between cursing myself out for choosing the wrong city to lay our groundwork in and praying that George will be willing to give The Plan another go on the other side of the continent. Neither of us can afford a vacation again any time soon, but one way or the other, I'm going to make this plan work.

No matter what.

Of course, Mateo calls as we're packing our bags. He wants to know what I'm doing tonight. "Digging my car out of a snowbank at an airport parking lot in Buffalo," I tell him. "Then going home to an empty apartment."

A day late and a dollar short is the way my dad always puts it. Typical.

"At least one of us got some action while we were here," I say to George after hanging up.

"Oh, I wouldn't say action, really. It was more like canoodling."

"Well, I personally witnessed you get to second base on the dance floor last night, so that's got to count for something. And by the way, canoodling sounds like something Morrie would say."

"Come on—we're going to be late."

The plane blessedly climbs into the sky without incident as I press George for more details.

"José's very special. He plans to go to med school one day. He's only working at the hotel to save up enough money for tuition. The tips are awesome."

"What a line," I say, pulling down the window shade to avoid the sight of bouncing wings. "That's exactly what strippers say to rich guys. Men just love thinking that the women they're treating like slot machines are up there degrading themselves for a higher cause."

"You think José's a gold digger?"

"Sure. Why not? He's probably just looking to meet some leathery-faced old sugar mama who'll feed him grapes all day and roll around with him in the pool house."

"Do you think he thought *I* was rich?" George marvels.

"Probably."

"Wow! I like that!" she says, snuggling down in her seat.

"You're not insulted by that?"

"No."

"Doesn't it bother you to think that someone would like you just for your money?"

She thinks about it for a minute or two. "Actually, no. I guess it doesn't. At least in some circumstances, anyway."

"Interesting. I take that to mean you're okay with The Plan, with what we're doing…."

"You mean, what we *wish* we were doing? Because in case you haven't noticed, we're having a little trouble putting the puck in the net."

"Yeah, yeah."

"Well, even though engaging in this sort of behavior promotes the worst kind of stereotype about women, I guess I am okay with it. Mostly because we're having fun and I honestly don't think it's actually going to happen."

"You think The Plan is going to fail."

"Don't be so sad, sweetie."

"Easy for you to say."

"Cheer up—the movie's starting. I think it's *Love Actually.*"

I slip on the headphones and try to watch. Normally, two hours of Hugh Grant's fumbling sexiness would be enough to distract me from anything—even the fact that I'm thirty-six thousand feet higher than I'm supposed to be— but I can't really concentrate. My mind races off in other directions....

"George. *George*—wake up!"

"Wha? Are we there yet?"

"Almost."

"What's wrong?"

"I've been thinking. It's going to take about two-and-a-half months of living without Jill's half of the rent and bills before I'm flat broke. And where am I supposed to find another roomie on such short notice?"

"I can't afford your place, otherwise you know I'd move in a heartbeat."

"I know, I know. Don't worry about that now... My point is, this trip was our best chance, now it seems like probably our *last* chance, to find us some Moneyed Mates. And we failed... No, make that me—*I've* failed.... It was all my fault, G, and I'm sorry. If I'd paid closer attention to all that research I was doing, I would have chosen a better vacation destination for us than Naples. Like San Francisco, for example! The San Francisco Bay Area has more Millionaires *under the age of fifty* than any other urban center in the country! Did you know that?"

She shakes her head.

"Well, neither did I until this morning! I am such an idiot! A complete idiot! Naples? What was I *thinking*? We should have at least gone to Seattle. There's a ton of them there, too, and I bet they don't have pacemakers...."

"It's okay, Holly. Calm down. You didn't know. It's not your fault. We had fun, anyway, right?"

"I know," I sob. "But I want to change. I don't just want a vacation. I want a new life."

"I know, sweetie. So do I."

"That was the spirit behind The Plan. Not just to kid around. I don't want to live in a city that's unfit for dogs." I wipe my nose with a cocktail napkin.

"Of course you don't, Holly, and neither do I, but we have to be realistic, too. We have to make small changes, one thing at a time. And we've made a good start. Things are going to look up for us soon. We just have to be patient. Okay?"

My ears pop as I blow my nose again. We've begun our descent.

Damn it. George is right. I *know* she's right. But I don't want to go back to the *Bugle.* And I don't want her to squander her talents for another six years at that shitty bookstore. She deserves better than that. We both do. Before we know it, we'll be forty…fifty…sixty…and still in exactly the same place we are today. *I don't want my obituary to come true.*

So I turn to face her. "We have to go for it, George. Really go for it."

"Put your seat up, Holly."

"Your work sucks. My work sucks. I'm not happy."

"Yeah, I know, but I can coast on the José thing for months before it fades away. Maybe we can go back next winter. Wouldn't that be great?"

"George. We're moving."

"Okay, Holly. Sure we are. Where to? Monte Carlo? Las Vegas? Peru?"

"I'm serious."

"I can't move."

"Yes, you can."

She reaches across me to lift up the window shade. The plane shudders as we descend haltingly through the clouds, through the darkness. Buffalo twinkles beneath us and slowly comes into focus. We pass over highways and neighborhoods we know. Pretty from the sky, but we both can tell how cold it really is down there, how bleak, how familiar.

"Funny how the snow makes everything look so white from up here, but when you actually see it up close, it's all dirty and slushy and brown."

"How true," I say.

"I'm not happy, either, Holly."

"I know."

She sighs.

"I know you'd never agree to Seattle," I say, sensing a change of heart.

"No way. It's far too rainy for people whose hair tends to frizz."

"So…San Francisco, here we come?"

The ground approaches outside my window, and anticipating my fear, George grabs my hand. But for a change, it's a pretty smooth landing.

chapter 10

Queen of the Sea

The bushy little patch of hair on Cy's forehead is dangerously close to becoming an island. The causeway that connects the patch with the mainland is no more than an inch wide, and in the unkind overhead fluorescence of his office, it appears the link is eroding fast.

I've always thought bald guys are kinda cute; a completely overlooked team of swimmers in the dating pool. Of the many physical traits that can relegate men to overall B-list status—short, chubby, flaccid, bald—bald is arguably best. At least, that's the way I see it. Those men whose confidence or personality can outshine their gleaming pates are definitely worth a second look, for who among us has not also been stung by the cruelty of nature or heredity? And if you happen to be one of those fortunate women whose bodies are unblemished by familial saddlebags or cankles, and whose facial features formed into pleasing, symmetrical arrangements, just wait—gravity and time will have their way with you, too. Only by then, when the playing field is finally level, all the good men—the bald, the bellied, the humble, the humorous—will be gone.

In the meantime, those of us prescient enough to date guys with more character than hair or height or abdominal musculature will be laughing all the way to deliriously happy eternal coupledom. Yes, ladies, though you may prefer the look of a six-pack now, a spare tire is definitely a better bet in the long run—it'll get you where you need to go in case of emergency, and the guys who own one are more likely to have their egos and commitment issues in check. Besides, men suffer at the hands of time, too, though perhaps not as cruelly as we do. Once-glorious hairlines recede, bulging biceps atrophy, Levi's don't fit quite like they used to. With gorgeous guys, the fall from grace is the most striking, because all that's left behind is a series of personality flaws gleaned from a lifetime of coasting on their looks.

Well, that's one way of seeing things. (I'm looking for something altogether different these days, anyway.) It's pretty much the same philosophy behind my burgeoning "Two-Thirds Theory" of dating, what was to be one of the central thematic concepts in my book. Basically, the idea is this: The holy trinity of looks, money and personality cannot possibly coexist in a single vessel at any one point in time, and so we must be willing to prioritize (on a case-by-case basis, of course), accept two out of the three and move on. It's the reason why dating the elderly seems to work so well for so many women. It's the reason why pairings like Marilyn Monroe and Joe DiMaggio, and Julia Roberts and Lyle Lovett, *technically* could have lasted. It's the reason why I've always been sure not to overlook bald men, rich or poor.

At least, until today. Because now I fear the follicle-free—or at least those sporting Cy's particular capillary configuration—will forever be associated for me with pain, humiliation and rage.

Yes, rage.

It's an emotion I'm not entirely familiar with, so when my boss informs me that not only is yet another one of my story pitches being turned down, but that Virginia Holt herself has commandeered my idea and will be "tweaking" it into a story of her own, it takes me a while to realize that the burning sensation in my gut is actually anger and not cheeseburger.

"But what about me?" I ask him, trembling.

"What about you?"

"It's my idea. Shouldn't I get to write it?"

The story in question was inspired by our trip to Naples. "Grandmother Chic: Life's a Beach" would be a perfect fit for the Life & Style section, a how-to guide to looking sexy over sixty when the weather turns warm. But Virginia wanted to take the elderly angle out completely and turn it into a boring pictorial about resort wear. Like the world needs another look at models in sarongs.

"Well, technically, it's not your idea anymore, anyway. And I guess Virginia feels she's the best one to write it."

God forbid she should tell me this herself, instead of getting Cy to do her dirty work for her....

My scowl must give me away, because Cy feels compelled to add, "Virginia thought it would be best if I told you. She mentioned that you seemed a little on edge lately. And also that she's been having trouble communicating with you."

I can't look him in the eyes, so I focus instead on that little bush on his forehead while I fight back the tears.

"She never liked me."

"Oh, she's not so bad. Did you ever make an effort to get to know her?"

"Sure," I grumble. "I know she takes her coffee with two milks and one Sweet & Low."

Cy throws his pen down on the desk and sighs. "Don't be upset, Holly. This is just how things go sometimes. It's not that big a deal. Really."

Dammit. I hate that I'm being such a girl about this. Real reporters are tough. Real reporters don't cry when things don't go their way or when their story gets spiked. Real reporters just take what's theirs and make no apologies. Maybe that's why I can't seem to get ahead here—because I'm too damn conflict-avoidant, too much of a doormat, too polite to insist on anything.

Or too afraid to take charge. Maybe I'm just not cut out for this after all.

"It may not be a big deal to you, Cy, but it is to me. This is *my* piece. *I* did the research. It's just the same damn thing, over and over again. Haven't I proven myself yet? Tell me—exactly what does a girl have to do to get noticed around here?"

A sheen of perspiration glistens on his brow. Although it wasn't really my intention to hint that the men seem to move up through the ranks around here a lot faster than the women do, I realize after I've said the words that that's exactly how it sounded. I wouldn't be the first female employee to suggest the possibility. Unspoken accusations of sexism and harassment bristle beneath the surface at the *Bugle*, which is still pretty much an old-boys' club. But that's not what this is about for me, so I ease back a bit.

"What I'm trying to say, I guess, is that I feel unappreciated, and I'm no longer sure what's holding me back here. If it's a lack of talent, fine—but then somebody should come out and tell me. I'm tired of the excuses. I've been here longer than you have, you know, and all I do is write obituaries and take ads for lost dogs and passports. When I was hired I was told there'd be room for advancement."

If he thinks I've crossed the line, he doesn't let on. "You're good at what you do, Holly. We appreciate that."

But I am in no mood for generic placations. "Who exactly are 'we'?"

"Uhh…the senior staff."

"Cy, I don't think it's fair and I don't think it's right. This piece was my idea."

"It may not be fair, but it is right," he insists. "It's Virginia's section so it's her call. She knows best what works and what doesn't, so we'll have to defer to her on this one."

"That's bullshit!"

He leans back and gives me a long hard look. "Just give it some more time. When the time is right and the story is right for you, you'll get your chance."

"I don't believe you," I say quietly. "I've queried Virginia over and over again and she nixes every idea I have. Sometimes, she assigns the exact same piece I suggested weeks before to another writer. It's happened at least half a dozen times, and I've never bothered saying anything before, but it really pisses me off!"

"I get it, I get it. What can I tell you? She's been here for a long time, Holly. The publishers are really happy with Life & Style—"

"I just don't see why a personality conflict should stand in my way here. She's, like, the *only* person I've ever had trouble getting along with in my entire life! But I've accepted it and tried to move on, even though I think I've had a lot of great ideas for that section. So what do I do?"

"What can I tell you? That's just the way things go sometimes."

"Well, I don't think I can wait around here forever." My chest tightens, and I can scarcely believe the words coming out of my own mouth. "My opportunity for advancement here isn't what I'd hoped it would be."

"Aw, come on, Holly. Don't be rash…"

"I'm not being rash. But I *am* angry. *Really* angry. And after this whole thing, I know my heart will never really be in it again." I adjust my gaze from the tuft on his forehead to his eyes. "I just don't think it's right to stay under these circumstances. I'm sorry."

As I say it, my rage dissipates. I know it's crazy, completely crazy, but it's also the right thing to do.

Cy stands up as I do, and extends his hand. "We'll all be really sorry to see you go."

"Have you spoken to your mother since you got back from Florida?" Zoe asks after a few minutes of chitchat.

"No. Things have been a little hectic around here. You're the first one I've called. Why? What's up? I thought you had something to tell me."

The annoying Christmas scene at my parents' house is still pretty fresh, so I'm in no hurry to speak to either of them. And I've barely had the chance to get my thoughts together after quitting the *Bugle*, something I need to do if I'm to have any hope of properly justifying it. To my parents, leaving a job voluntarily is something normal people don't do. Concepts of vague unrest, professional dissatisfaction and the desire to self-actualize are definitely beyond them. They're still having trouble coming to terms with the '60s, for God's sake, and they were *there*.

"I do," Zoe says. "You should call her."

"Okay, now you're freaking me out!"

"No, no—don't worry. Your mom's fine—"

"Oh my God! My dad?"

"He's fine… They're both fine! Sorry—didn't mean to scare you." She pauses to gather her thoughts. "But she did call me while you were away."

"She called you? You're kidding, right? How on earth did she manage to find your number?" I would have bet one hundred bucks that my mother couldn't remember any of my friends' last names, let alone track down their phone numbers.

"She spoke to Asher's dad. They went to high school together, remember?"

"Oh yeah."

My mother's resourcefulness is beyond alarming. Certainly, the end of the world is nigh.

"She couldn't remember the name of your hotel in Florida, and your voice mail was down. She…umm…wanted me to let you know where she's staying, in case you're looking for her."

It's almost 10:00 p.m. by the time the cab drops me off at my aunt Deb's house, where my mother has apparently moved in pending the divorce.

She comes down the stairs in her curlers and nightcap and greets me coolly.

"I didn't know where you were," she says. "And you didn't call me when you got back. If I was dead, you wouldn't have known."

"Mom, the guilt thing doesn't really work with me. You can't start pulling that now after a lifetime of not minding what I did or where I went. So please, don't even go there."

"You think I don't care?" She tears up. "I care. I've *always* cared. I just wanted to give you your space. Your brothers always wanted their space, so I did the same with you. And I think it worked out very well. Look at you now—with a degree and such a good job. But don't I deserve to know where you are when you're out of state?"

"I told you where I was staying, Mom. You just forgot."

Aunt Deb hurries in from the kitchen. She looks a lot like my mother, only older, shorter and with an even bigger helmet of red hair. "Holly dear, don't just stand there in the hallway—come in, come in. Take your boots off and throw your coat over there. It'll be a few minutes for the tea. Louise, go sit down. You'll catch your death."

Mom tightens her twenty-year-old floral housecoat around her waist and pads off into the living room.

"Where's Dad? He hasn't been answering the phone."

"Your father is at Cole's," she all but growls. "I told him, 'Larry, if I have to leave the house, then so should you! It isn't fair that one of us gets to stay,' I said. And between you and me, your father would die of starvation before he'd turn on the oven, anyway. He needs someone to cook for him! I just hope Cole and Olivia have the good sense not to take his side. He'll try and win them over, I'm sure…."

As my mother plays out each and every possible machination and plot against her, I collapse into Deb's enormous overstuffed couch. Cole and Mike and Brad used to use its big square pillows to construct a fort whose sole purpose was to keep me out. "I don't know if I have the energy for this," I say to no one in particular.

"…and it's not my fault! Any of this! Because if your father were more assertive, we all might have been spared this agony!"

The poor man had been listening to her drone on and on for decades, and she's faulting him for his patience? "Dad's just introverted. He has a lot going on inside. A rich inner life."

"He's weak," she says. "Weak and broken. How can a marriage stay fresh when only one party shows signs of life? Marriage is more than a wedding, Holly—it's a sincere commitment you make to each other every single day, not just a life sentence under house arrest."

Odd words, coming from her.

"I can't say I care for your tone, Mom. You can be very demanding of him, you know. And Dad's not weak—he's just very…tolerant. That's why you guys work so well together. So Dad loves you, and you love him, okay? Oh, and by the way, I quit my job."

"Do you know what it's like to be married to a man without a tongue?"

"What do you care?" I mumble. "You don't seem to have any ears, anyway."

Deb brings in the tea on a tray and sets it down on an aluminum TV table. "I'll leave you two to talk. I'm going up to bed. Uncle Herbie needs his pills."

"What would I do without her?" Mom says after Deb leaves the room. "She says I can stay as long as I want."

"That's great, Mom, but do you really think you're going to stay for long? I mean, this is all going to blow over, right?"

She snuggles up beside me and pulls my head down onto her shoulder. Normally, I would have resisted—physical displays of affection aren't exactly the norm for us—but I need her to tell me that everything is going to be all right.

Instead, all I get is, "No, I don't think so this time."

I pull away and look at her. "This time?"

"This is the third time your father and I have separated since you left the house, dear."

"What?"

"Things aren't always as they appear."

"Yes they *are,*" I insist. "Especially when it comes to parents. If they manage to make it through their kids' teenage years without divorcing or killing each other, then they should automatically get to skip to happily-ever-after."

"You'd think so, but that's just not how things are. You're old enough to know that."

"No I'm not."

"Holly, I just want to live my best life."

Her best life?

"What?"

"I've been watching *Oprah*. I tape it at three o'clock and then I watch it from five to six every morning before your father wakes up."

"You do?"

"Yes. And I think I finally understand what she's been getting at. At first I was really confused, let me tell you! But you see, we're all here for a reason, Holly. And at last I've found mine."

"You have?"

"Yes."

"Oh."

She takes a big slurp of tea. "Aren't you going to ask me what it is?"

"I'm still trying to figure out how you learned to work the VCR."

"Did you ever see that show *Flipper*?"

"The one with the whale?"

"Actually, it was a dolphin. Well, when I was younger, just before I got married, I wanted to be a marine biologist or a park ranger, like Porter Ricks on *Flipper*. Deb and I used to watch that show every Friday night. We'd sit together on Grandma's comfy old couch and she'd make us grilled-cheese sandwiches and tomato soup—Grandpa hated tomato soup, by the way—and we got to watch in front of the TV…"

"Mom, weren't you, like, in your twenties when that show was on?"

"I was working at the bank, then, but I was so happy to finally find something that interested me. Even after I married your father, I came home to watch every week. I collected anything and everything from the show—lunchboxes, posters, dolls, you name it. And it's all been sitting in boxes in the attic ever since."

"Sounds pretty weird to me…"

"Well, your Aunt Deb didn't marry until she was in her

midthirties, so she lived at home until then," she says, then adds in a whisper, "She was lucky she found someone at that age. I was considered way over-the-hill when I married and I was only twenty-nine! That's why I had your brothers one after the other—because I was so behind."

"Am I on *Candid Camera?*"

"And then I had to quit working after your dad and I got married, anyway."

"Why?"

"Why? I don't know why, Holly. Because that was the way things were done back then. I had to look after the house. And soon I was pregnant with your brother and, well, you pretty much know the rest."

"You lived happily ever after."

"Not exactly."

"So…let me see if I get this. Now you're going to be a marine biologist?"

"Don't be ridiculous, Holly. That would take years of school, and I don't have the time or the money."

"So…"

"So I've decided I need to see him. That would be enough."

"See who?"

"Flipper!"

"He's still alive?"

"Yes. He lives at the Miami Seaquarium. They gave him his own show there!"

"It must be a different dolphin, Mom."

"They call him Flipper, Flipper, faster than lightning… No one, you see, is smarter than he… They call him Flipper, Flipper, King of the Sea…."

My mind reels with the insanity of it all. "Let me get this straight… You're divorcing dad and making a pilgrimage to Florida to see a famous fish? And that's going to fix what's wrong with your life?"

"Yes. After Flipper, everything in my life went all crazy and haywire. If it wasn't for your father and his seductive ways, maybe I could've made something of myself. I could have gone back to school…."

"Mom, don't say that—you *have* made something of your life! And believe me when I tell you that even though I haven't seen *Oprah* lately, I think you may be missing the point. Running away isn't going to help."

"It's not running away. It's doing something I need to do. For *me*."

"Fair enough. I can understand that. But—"

"She had this guest on…a psychologist or someone—a life manager, I think she called herself—and she said that all you have to do to be happy is to find something you like to do and turn it into your job. Oh! And then there was this man, a man who loved macaroons, and so one day he decided to devote his life to making macaroons. And now he's a *millionaire!*"

"I'm still confused…."

"Well, I wasn't finished explaining it to you. This is actually the best part," she says, taking a deep breath and exhaling dramatically. "I'm going to start collecting again!"

"*Flipper* memorabilia?"

"Yes! I want to be the world's foremost authority! And there's tons of it on eBay, so add that to the great stuff I already have, which is all in mint condition—"

"eBay?"

"Stop repeating everything I say!"

"Mom, do you have a computer?"

"Yes! I took some money out of your father's retirement fund and used it to buy a laptop."

I pick at a spot on the threadbare upholstery and look out at the falling snow while I let it all sink in. "I don't know what to say, Mom. I honestly don't know what to say."

My mother deflates a little. "You think I'm very silly. I can tell."

Only I don't think she's silly at all. Okay, well maybe a little with all that Flipper stuff, but I also can't help but admire her. There is clearly a method to her madness, and in her own warped way, in the context of her life, it actually makes a lot of sense.

"Actually, Mom, I think it's great…I just don't understand why Dad can't be a part of it."

She squeezes my hand. "This is *my* dream. Your father has been living his dream his whole life—the kids, the house in the suburbs, the retirement, the toy trains. It's *my* turn now."

chapter 11

Going for Broke

My dad is the first one I tell.

"I think it's great, Holly," he says, bouncing a grandkid on each knee.

"Tell me I'm not crazy, Dad."

"You're not."

Olivia comes in from the kitchen, wiping her hands on her pants. "I agree, Holly. Get outta here while you still can!"

With three kids clinging to her skirt by the time she turned thirty and a string of dead-end beauty salon jobs behind her, my sister-in-law likes to joke that she's the poster child for higher education. But she also adores those three kids and is still totally in love with Cole, and my brother, despite all his teasing, practically worships her.

"I could have been a ballerina, you know," she sighs as she bends over to pick up chunks of hardened Play-Doh off the carpet.

"Let me get those, dear. You sit down," my dad says, plac-ing Skyler and Mackenzie back on their feet. Instantly, they drop to all fours and begin chasing each other around the living room, trying to pull each others' socks off.

"I didn't know you wanted to be a dancer," I say.

"Yeah, well, you know how things go."

"Maybe you still could…do something like that…some-how…" I venture.

She lifts up her sweatshirt and grabs a fistful of her soft tummy. "Ya think?"

"You're pretty light on your feet, considering," my dad of-fers helpfully.

"Thanks for the vote of confidence, guys, but I think my professional dancing days are behind me…"

"Mummy, Mummy!"

"Yes, Mackenzie."

"I have an ouchee." She holds up a rug-burned knee and Olivia lifts her up and carries her upstairs.

While Skyler takes advantage of his sister's absence and plays quietly in the corner with her dollhouse, my dad tries to explain to me what's going on.

"Your mother just needs a little time, Holly. She'll come around. And you don't have to worry about me—I'm fine. Enjoying spending some time with the kids. And I still sneak home to my trains every couple of days," he winks.

I imagine my dad at home alone in our basement wear-ing his conductor's hat, playing with toys, no one upstairs to fix him lunch….

"You're killing me here, Dad. You gotta throw me a bone. *Please.*"

He musters a smile and gives me a *there-there dear* pat on the knee. "Don't worry. Your mother and I will work it out. We always do."

"I know," I say, though I'm not convinced. It's hard to tell if he's lying or not; I've never known my dad to be dishonest with me, so I have no idea what it might look like.

"The important thing now is for you to stop worrying about us old farts. Don't get stuck here in all this garbage—leave for a while, get some perspective. It's a good idea." His watery gray eyes turn to meet mine, and he seems to choose his next words carefully. "Find something you love to do, Holly, before you get…tied down. We have enough grandkids for now."

"But I *want* to have kids…."

"Of course you do, dear. All I'm saying is I'm in no rush for you. And neither is your mother. I never want you to feel pressured. Not by anyone or anything."

"I don't, Daddy."

"Your brothers—Cole especially—they all…well… I guess they let their lives get away from them. But you're different, sweetie. At least, we've always thought you were. Your mother and I both worry that you may be holding yourself back…."

They worry about me? They talk about me? It's odd to imagine my parents discussing me, my life, who I am, what they want for me. My brothers, the Hastings boys, were so popular and so wild when we were growing up; they seemed to take up so much of the air in our house, provide so much of the noise and energy, that I always felt like I was just born to be their sister, their punching bag. A familial afterthought. Someone to wear their hand-me-downs. (Which probably accounted for my early reputation as a tomboy and later, with no chest to fill out those navy blue rugby shirts, a hermaphrodite lesbian.)

"…you've always had big plans. We don't want you to forget about that."

"Mom thinks that, too?"

"Of course she does."

"I figured she'd think I was nuts to quit the *Bugle*. I thought you both would."

"Not at all! Did she give you that impression?"

"I guess not…she didn't really say anything when I told her."

"Silence is definitely approval where your mother is concerned. You know that."

He has a point. "And you?"

"I'm pleased, provided you use this opportunity wisely. It's a risk, that's for sure, but when you dream of big things, you have to take big chances. And if not now, then when? You're still young—it's still relatively easy for you to make changes in your life. Look at your mother. She's so unhappy, *so* unhappy. And there's nothing I can do about it now. Had I known, maybe…"

"Don't you dare blame yourself for this! She's been hiding her feelings for a long time."

"Yes, so it seems…" He pulls his reading glasses out of his shirt pocket and reaches across me for the paper, signaling the end of the conversation. "But we used to want the same things, your mother and I."

I nod, but secretly I wonder if that had ever really been true.

The more I think about my parents' floundering marriage, the more it amazes me. Is it really possible that my dad thinks everything is fine, even though my mom has apparently been leaving him for years? Why hadn't he ever noticed anything was wrong? And why hadn't she *made* him see, or simply told him what she was going through? I imagine they probably weren't in the habit of sharing their dreams and goals and regrets and all the other sorts of things that to me seem so basic and obvious for the proper functioning of a couple of people who've chosen to forsake all others—legally, physically and spiritually—and bind their lives to one another's *forever.*

But maybe it simply isn't fair to hold them to that standard. Many mothers and fathers of our parents' generation are likely still oblivious to the relationship rhetoric we've been virtually bombarded with since opening our very first *Seventeen* magazine, those mighty principles gleaned from self-styled relationship experts and talk-show gurus that have become so deeply ingrained within us that we don't even question them anymore....

Mutual Respect. Communication is Key. Love Yourself First. Sex is Better than Chocolate. Men Are From Mars, Women Are From Venus.

Don't get me wrong—I'm glad for all that stuff. I *believe* in the trite dogma of modern love. But consider also that I was—that *we* were—indoctrinated from youth, so it feels pretty natural to demand open communication from our partners. How confusing it must be, though, coming to all that later in life, *after* you've spent decades dealing with your demons in silence, or simply seeing marriage as a convenient but necessary social arrangement in which each partner gives something and gets something in return, and I don't mean love.

In many ways, the expectations our mothers and fathers had for their lives were probably higher than our own. By the time *That Girl* and *The Mary Tyler Moore Show* came around, it was too late—they had already imprinted on the Cleavers and the Nelsons, with their insidious portrayals of middle-American nirvana. The families I grew up watching on TV—which, let's face it, is the greatest social barometer the world has ever known—were flawed. The Keatons, the Connors, even the Huxtables, had to contend with *real* problems, everything from their kids' sex lives and drug dabblings to their own midlife crises and the deaths of their parents. June and Ward, meanwhile, spent half an hour each week helping the Beav with his paper route and getting the cat out of that darn tree.

Those of us who choose to walk down the aisle these days do so *knowing* half of all marriages fail, while my parents probably expected their union to be as delightful as Ozzie and Harriet's, as pleasant as their own parents' marriages seemed to be. How disillusioning it would have been to admit they actually had to work at their relationship. And so they didn't. Otherwise, how could things so fundamentally important to each other's happiness have gone unnoticed or overlooked for so long?

To make matters worse, my mother turns on the TV one day and instead of escaping to the world of crime-solving dolphins and Barbara Eden in genie pants, there's Oprah telling her she has a right to expect more. But Mom's no fool. She knows her marriage was never perfect, that she gave something up in order to toe the line, only now she's beginning to understand that it was never really her job to serve up perfection in the first place. No wonder she has no desire to sit on an empty nest—she's ready to stretch her wings. And no wonder my father's in denial—he got the suburban bliss he always wanted, but to admit that he had it at his wife's expense would take all the joy out of it.

Maybe my parents loved each other and got married for all the right reasons. But maybe—and I wish with every fiber of my being that this wasn't the case—they willfully deluded themselves as to who the other one was from day one, just to fulfill other people's expectations of them. Still, is it fair of my mom to resent my dad if she's never been honest with him? And is it fair of him to expect her to never change just because he himself hasn't? And what if…

…and what if I just stopped trying so hard to figure it all out?

My head is pounding, aching with the possibilities, the explanations, the analysis. An automatic habit of mine, I know, and one I've come by honestly through years of addiction to recreational therapy. I continually pick apart the motivations behind my own thoughts and actions, deconstructing every feeling and exploring every potential path in order to come to the best possible decisions in my life. But Martindale once pointed out that attempting to apply my personal logic system to other people's hearts and minds assumes facts not in evidence.

The end result? Frustration and disappointment for everyone, especially me. Martindale showed unusual insight when he suggested that when people don't live up to my expectations, or behave differently than I would if I were in their shoes, I tend to believe they're making a mistake. Which is, of course, ridiculously unfair and not at all true since everyone's different and I don't have the full picture.

So I silently vow to let my parents work it out for themselves from here on in, and to support them in whatever decision they come to. Even if that decision is one I hate with all my heart.

"How's your dad doing?" George asks.

We've been meeting at the diner every day for lunch since my last day at the *Bugle*, almost two weeks ago.

"He's okay, I guess. I think I've spoken to him more since all this started than in the rest of my life combined."

"So at least something good's come of it."

"I suppose."

"When God closes a door, she opens a window. You just have to be patient."

"Okay, George. I get it."

"Same thing with your job. I think quitting will really give you the impetus you need to get back into your book. Desperate times, you know. Are you gonna eat that bun?"

"Go ahead."

At first, I thought the exact same thing. That without the whole nine-to-five thing to distract me, I'd be able to whiz through my first few chapters, no problem. After all, I've been gathering information, researching, taking notes for almost four months—there's a ton of material to go through. But still, something wasn't right. I've begun to wonder how many copies a book tentatively titled *How to Marry A Millionaire (And Still Love Yourself in the Morning!)* would actually sell if the author is single and living at the YMCA. Or, worse, in her old room at her parents' house.

It was a generous offer, made separately by both my mom and my dad, who weren't using the house, anyway, but the implications were so horrible that it had spurred me to action.

George slathers the bun with butter and puts it down in about three bites.

"Don't look at me like that," she says, wiping the crumbs from her chest.

"Like what?"

"Like I shouldn't have eaten that."

"Are you insane? Do you think I care what you eat?"

"I know I probably seem ridiculous to you, Holly. I've been trying to lose fifteen pounds for ten years. God, even if I'd lost one pound a *year…*" her gaze hovers dreamily on something behind me, presumably the glass-and-chrome tower stacked high with cheesecakes and pies. "But in all this time, all the calorie-counting and fat-counting and cabbage-soup crap obviously isn't working."

"You look great the way you are, G."

"So!" she claps her hands together and straightens up. "I've decided to try something different. Tell me if you think this'll work. When I feel chubby, like I did this morning, I put on my tightest jeans and then eat, like, the *hugest* breakfast and lunch. The idea is, the pain I'm forced to endure all day as a reminder of my gluttony will inspire me to new levels of self-disgust, which in turn will fuel my resolve! Whaddya think?"

"Sounds good," I giggle. "Very progressive."

She leans back, undoes her top button and tries to breathe. "When I get home tonight, I'm going to get completely naked. Then I'm going to take one of those big black permanent markers and trace all the ugly red lines these jeans will have left on my stomach, and then just stare at myself in the mirror beneath bright lights for fifteen minutes. After a few days of that, I think I'll be ready to hit the gym."

"Health by humiliation—I love it!"

By this point, we're laughing so loudly, people have begun to stare.

"Who needs Atkins? The Perlman-MacNeill Way will be the next big thing!" George shrieks.

"That's just about enough, ladies," our waitress says as she passes by with a tray of burgers for the next table, stopping long enough to toss our bill down.

"Sorry," George apologizes. "We don't get out much."

"Lunch is on me."

She grabs for the bill. "No way—you're unemployed. Let me get it."

"I'll be rolling in it soon enough, my friend."

"Oh yeah? And how's that? You find a job? Sell your book?"

We haven't talked about it since the flight home from Florida. Presumably, George is happy to pretend it never happened, that she hadn't agreed—or at least sort of agreed—to leave town with me in search of greener pastures. But I can't let it go. It is potentially the best idea I've ever had.

I brace myself and launch into the conversation I've been practicing in my head for the past week. "No, silly—I'm going to marry rich! My parents married for love, or so I thought…and well, whatever it was, *that* didn't work out so well. So I might as well be practical about the whole thing."

George rolls her eyes. "Not this again."

"There's nothing for me here but an empty apartment and

in a month or two, being forced to take some job I really don't want. I've got nothing to lose, so why stay?"

She sighs dramatically and picks at what remains of my fries as I continue.

"…and what better place to find a nice, rich, *young* guy than San Francisco? I tell ya—all those delicious dot-com millionaires are out there, George, just waiting to be plucked out of Silicon Valley. Can you see it? Can you? They're wealthy, lonely, sexy…"

"And geeky!" she interrupts. "I thought you were kidding about all that San Francisco stuff."

I exhale slowly. Time is running out, and I've been putting off telling her for too long.

"I leave in ten days."

George drops her fork.

"What?"

"I bought a one-way ticket."

Her eyes widen with panic and disbelief. "No you didn't."

"The moving company's booked. And I've sold my car."

"I don't believe you."

"I found an apartment online. It looks pretty great, actually."

She pushes my plate away in disgust. "I can't believe you're doing this to me. Don't *leave* me, Holly, *please!* You have to cancel your ticket!"

"You know I can't do that!" I'm far too superstitious to cancel travel plans. Once you're booked, you're booked. (Unless, of course, you get That Feeling when you're boarding the plane, something I was actually hoping *wouldn't* happen for a change.) "But don't worry—I made sure to get us a place with two rooms. I would never leave you behind, G! You're coming, too!"

"No! No, I can't!" she says, pressing the corners of her eyes to try and stop the tears.

"Yes, you can! *We* can. We can try it for a while. Nobody's saying we can't come home if we don't like it. Think of it as an adventure—an amazing, crazy adventure you'll remember for the rest of your life…."

"No, you don't understand. I have no money…and my moms will *never* let me go…"

"Don't worry about money. My dad's going to help us out for a bit, just until we get set up."

"He said that?" she sniffs.

"Uh-huh."

"He thinks I'm going? And he doesn't mind?"

"Of course not! He loves you. You're part of my family." I squeeze her hand. My dad knows how much it means to me to have George along, and he's more than willing to help out for as long as we need it. "He's going to float me for a while, anyway, whether you come or not, so there's really no reason for you to feel bad about it."

"But…" She hesitates. "But…can he afford it?"

"Yes. Absolutely." If there's any chance of convincing her, I know I have to be firm on this point. "My mom's been so totally cheap for the both of them their whole lives. And now that she's taking her little hiatus, I think he's feeling the need to loosen the purse strings a little, you know?"

Before I agreed to accept his offer, my dad had shared the details of their financial situation. It turns out my parents have a nice little nest egg socked away, a respectable 401(k) and two really good pension plans, not to mention social security and, apparently, a decent inheritance from my father's parents. I had no idea they were so comfortable, but I suppose I should have expected it—my mom's a pretty good bookkeeper, after all, and I knew my dad would rather die than ever be a burden on his children. "All any decent father wants is to be able to help his kids," he'd said. "Make things as easy for them as possible. And you didn't have it easy, Holly. Your brothers put you through a lot. I can see that now, and

I'm sorry I didn't do more to get a handle on them." And here all these years I'd thought he was just oblivious.

George nods. "I can understand that."

"He's *really* happy to do it, George. And he completely offered, by the way. I didn't ask. In fact, I already had my ticket booked when he suggested it."

"Yeah?"

"Honest to God."

"You didn't tell him about The Plan, did you?"

I shake my head. "It's *our* plan."

She turns to stare out the window just as a woman across the street slips on the ice and falls. Two men walk by before a third stops to help her up. Silently, George breathes out onto the cold glass, fogging it up. With her index finger, she traces the letters *O.K.*

A wave of relief washes over me and I jump up to hug her from across the table. "You won't regret this! I promise!"

"But we'll pay your dad back once we get jobs, right?"

"We could think of it as a long-term loan, if that makes you feel better."

"It does."

"Then we'll pay him back as soon as we can."

"Maybe my moms could help, too," she suggests.

"You could always ask…"

But George's mothers won't help.

Quite the opposite, in fact. They've screwed things up entirely.

After extracting the whole story from their beloved only child—who'd been too nervous to tell them she was going anywhere until the very last minute, the day before we were scheduled to leave—they forbid her from getting on the plane. *Forbid* it entirely. I knew it wasn't because they couldn't afford to help her. Dr. Perlman is a dentist with a very successful practice, but I highly doubt either she or her wife would have been willing to support, financially or otherwise, any scheme that put twenty-three hundred miles in between them and their daughter. Especially one that involved hunting rich men.

None of it comes as any surprise to me, but George, for some reason, is shocked and devastated.

"I…" *Sniff.* "I…" *Sniff.* "They…" *Sniff.* "I…" *Sniff.*

"George, you should have told them sooner. So they would have had a chance to get used to the idea."

"But…" *Sniff.* "But…" *Sniff.*

I try to contain my frustration. "But what?"

"But…but why don't they want me to be happy?"

"It's not that," I sigh, annoyed that I'm forced to defend them to her. "It's because they don't want to lose you. And telling them *everything* just made it worse."

George's relationship with her parents was stalled in adolescence. Dr. Perlman and Mrs. MacNeill were beyond overprotective, probably because some of their daughter's more suspect decisions as a teenager had, in their minds, warranted her close supervision. Her inability to lie without getting caught didn't help matters. Apparently, they nailed her every time she skipped school, got drunk or smoked pot. Once, when George was about fifteen, they came home early from a movie to find her wrapped around their twenty-one-year-old gardener in the sauna.

"Ricky was so cute," George used to sigh. "If only he hadn't been so old. I think my mothers would have liked him."

"They're so mean," she sniffs now, just as she had then.

"What the hell did you think was going to happen?" I snap. "That you'd say 'Oh, by the way Moms, I'm moving across the country tomorrow to go and stalk millionaires,' and they'd be *happy* about it? That they'd throw you a bon voyage party?"

"Now you're being mean."

"You would have had an easier time telling them you were eloping with Milt!"

"Mine was Morrie. Yours was Milt."

"Whatever, George."

"You're right, though. At least Milt is Jewish."

"God, I'm sure they blame me for all this, too," I say, more to myself than to her.

"They do," she concurs. "For putting the idea into my head. They think you might be a bad influence."

"Well, you didn't have to tell them everything!" I growl into the receiver, pissed that the mothers didn't like me anymore, because I still liked them. I can't help it. They've always been super to me. "I can't believe you. I could have told you this is exactly what was going to happen."

"I'm sorry. I just didn't think, I guess."

But the dream is slipping away and I am furious. "They're so hypocritical. Who are they to say what we're doing is bad? Feminists my ass…."

Mrs. MacNeill is a suburban housewife like any other. Always has been. She cooks and cleans and irons and sends her spouse to work every day with a nice healthy lunch packed in a brown paper bag. The only difference being, of course, that unlike the rest of the kids on the block, her daughter had two mommies.

"I've been dealing with this my whole life," George says.

"Oh, for God's sake. Just tell me exactly what they said. Maybe we can convince them. Do you want me to come over so we can try together?"

"No! That'll just make it worse!"

"Fine. So what do you plan to do to fix all this?"

"Nothing," she moans into the receiver. "We've been arguing about it for six hours and they won't budge. There's no hope."

"I hate to point out the obvious, but you could just come, anyway."

Silence.

"I mean, you are technically a grown-up," I continue. "You don't have to do what they tell you. They can't *forbid* you from doing anything."

"I know that, Holly. But you don't understand."

"What don't I understand?"

"I can't go without their blessing. I don't want to disappoint them." Her voice is small and tinny, like she's on the other side of the world. "I'm all they have."

What can I say to that?

"What about your job? Are you going to get your job back and just pretend everything's okay? You're going to just pretend you're happy and live the rest of your life the way you're living it now?"

"I, uh, didn't quit yet, Holly."

Of course she hadn't. Except for a brief moment or two when I'd pumped her up, George was probably never really planning on coming with me anywhere, and caused this whole stir with her parents at the last minute so that she'd be able to back out and blame it on them without losing face. She's happy enough with the way things are. And what kind of monster am I to convince her that her life sucks? Just because *mine* does, just because *I* want out, doesn't give me the right to manipulate my best friend into doing something drastic that she isn't ready for.

"I'm sorry, George. I feel awful now. I didn't mean to put so much pressure on you. I've been horrible. Absolutely horrible…"

"No, *I'm* sorry, Holly. I'm sorry I'm backing out like this."

"You don't have to apologize to me. You *never* have to apologize to me. Just promise me you'll make this decision on your own. Stay here if that's what feels right for you, but if you do want to come—if you really do want to come, George—then there's still time to change your mind. The plane leaves tomorrow at ten. And I'm going to be on it."

"I know, Holly. But I just can't."

"So…this is goodbye?"

"I guess so."

A little part of me thinks she might actually show up at the last minute.

As I wait in line at the metal detector, and as I wait in line again to board the flight, I keep glancing over my shoulder to see if she's here.

But she isn't.

Even after I buckle my seat belt as tightly as I can and the plane is careening down the runway like a runaway train, I half expect her to slip into the seat beside me.

part three

San Francisco, California*

*Currently home to the most millionaires
in America…**

** or so I thought.

chapter 12

The City by the Bay

San Francisco International Airport has seventeen bars and I am beginning to fear I won't be able to find a single one. I'm still in a daze from almost fifteen hours of delays, layovers, weather warnings, rubbery chicken with asparagus, sleeplessness and a small nervous breakdown at thirty-six thousand feet, so the jumble of multicolored signage isn't going over too well. Still, despite my physical and emotional fragility, I figure a celebratory drink is in order—not only am I on solid ground again, but this is my first time ever on the West Coast.

The *real* first day of the rest of my life. *Finally.*

Bleary-eyed and unable to locate alcohol in the immediate vicinity, I ditch the bar plan and shuffle toward the next best thing: food.

The moment the first bite hits my belly, I realize how famished I am. And with the food, the fog and monotony of the day begin to lift, replaced by that sort of hyperreality you usually only notice at times of either great stress or complete boredom. Moments of being and nonbeing, Virginia Woolf called them. At least, I think that's what she called them, if I'm remembering my Modernism 101 class correctly.

I pull out my notepad and jot that down. Peppering my manuscript/memoir (as it was quickly becoming) with literary allusions might guard me from accusations of frivolity later, although I'm not exactly sure how that particular quip might fit in, or how Virginia herself would have felt about her inclusion in a project she'd likely consider anathema to her life's work. From the beginning, I've known the hardest part about writing my book would be finding a way to elevate it beyond the obvious—that it was nothing more than a poison-filled how-to guide for morally bereft gold diggers—and convincing intelligent women that the end sometimes justifies the means, provided the ending is of the fairy-tale variety and the means not too mean.

I tuck the notebook back into my bag. Moral semantics aside, I'm also pretty sure Woolf was a big proponent of stopping to smell the roses, and that's exactly what I'm planning to do every chance I get from here on in. She'd certainly agree with that, wouldn't she?

"I can't believe I'm actually here!" I whisper to myself as I look around. Although it's dark out, about 10:00 p.m. local time, this unknown city where I will make my new home reveals a tiny suburban bit of itself through the food court's floor-to-ceiling windows. Beyond the hangars and rows of jets are hills and highways, twinkling amber lights and nary a snowbank in sight.

It's all almost too good to be true.

I scarf down my second Nathan's hot dog and wonder if it's cool to ring my new landlord's doorbell at midnight. Probably not. Pissing him off before I've even moved in isn't a good idea, seeing as how I have no backup living arrangements. Then again, he did sound pretty young when I spoke to him on the phone earlier this week, so maybe he wouldn't mind.

Just as I'm resolving to err on the side of caution—book a hotel room near the airport for tonight and pick up my keys in the morning—a cute young businessman in a two-thousand-dollar suit floats by, speaking Japanese into the tiniest cell phone I've ever seen. The airport is far from crowded, and the guy stands out brightly among the few straggling tourists and cleaning staff. He's walking quickly towards the International Terminal on the other side of the building, a black Tumi carry-on trailing behind him.

Hmmm…

How amazing would it be if I found the love of my life the instant I stepped off the plane? I frantically wipe the mustard from my fingers, hop down from the stool and turn to follow him, imagining a luxurious life of silk and sushi in Tokyo….

"What took you so long, Holly?"

I spin around on my heel.

A headful of brown curls, big boobs, a nose ring…

The most beautiful sight I've ever seen!

"George!" I shriek, and practically collapse into her arms. "What the hell!? I mean, how did you…? What are you *doing* here?!"

"I should have known I'd find you in the food court…. Come on—I've been waiting around this bloody airport for four hours. They changed your arrival gate three times, you know, and by the time I found the right one, well, I must have missed you getting off the plane. Let's get your bags."

"No way! Not until you tell me what's going on!"

She smiles mischievously. "I guess I just got a better flight than you. Cost me an arm and a leg, though. Man, they really gouge you when you book last-minute!"

"George!" I jump up and down impatiently.

"Okay, okay! Let me see… Well, I couldn't sleep after everything that happened yesterday—my God, was that yesterday? It seems like a million years ago!—anyway, I suppose it just finally hit me, what was really at stake. I know my moms love me, and I certainly don't want to give them any *tsouris,* but—"

"Sorry, George. My Yiddish is a little rusty…"

"Oh. Sorry. Umm…*tsouris* is like aggravation, heartache, that sort of thing. You know, what pain-in-the-ass kids give their parents. So after I tossed and turned on it for, like, five hours, I guess I realized I really *did* want to do this, and the only reason I was backing out was because of them. 'Cause I didn't want to hurt them, blah blah blah. And the more I thought about it, the more that seemed like not really such a good reason. So I told myself, why the hell not? I know they love me, and eventually, they'll get over it and forgive me."

"Of course they will!" I should have known the tough-as-nails, matter-of-fact George would shine through in the end. "You know, I was kind of expecting you to show up at the last minute this morning."

"I tried! By the time I realized I was being a chicken-shit and packed up whatever I could carry and lugged it all on the bus and train to the airport, I'd missed the flight! So I just grabbed the next one I could. I take it yours wasn't direct?"

"We stopped in Chicago for three hours. And we hit a *huge* storm going over the Rockies so we made an unscheduled stop in Denver. The plane was shaking and rolling almost the whole time!" I explain, as we walk over to the baggage claim area, arm in arm. "Wow! I really can't believe you're here."

"Jeez! I'm just glad I wasn't on that flight with you."

"Ha, ha. Actually, I was fine, for your information. A nice lady sitting next to me gave me a few of her Valiums."

"That's great, Holly. I bet if the plane actually *had* crashed, you'd have been the only one too drugged to find her way to the emergency exits."

I stop so I can hug her again. "I'll never forget this, George."

"I'm not doing this for you, silly. I'm doing it for me."

"And I'm doing it for me. But I'm glad we're doing it together."

"So am I. Now tell me—where the hell do we live, exactly?"

"Tonight, the Best Western! Tomorrow, the Western Addition!"

By the time we check in, we're both too exhausted to even think about hitting the bar. I make sure to pull the heavy blinds together as tightly as I can, in case any hint of sunlight dare wake me in the morning. I hang the Do Not Disturb sign on the door, take a shower, then crash.

When I wake up, George is already watching CNN. I stretch and realize it was the best sleep I'd had in months.

No dreams. That's the key—no dreams.

"Are you sure this is it?"

"This is Pierce Street, lady. Take it or leave it."

I look down at the scrap of paper I'd scribbled the address on. This had to be the right place.

"No, this is fine," I tell the cabbie as George and I exchange glances. "Thank you. You can keep the change."

We get out of the cab and grab our bags from the trunk. The car screeches off down the street, dipping out of view almost instantly.

George blows out a sigh and drops her backpack down on the curb. "Whoa. It's…quite something."

I shield my eyes from the midday sun and look up at the tall, narrow house. It's perfect.

To my left, a dozen steps lined with potted purple flowers dissect a tiny front yard and lead up into a small front porch with carved columns at each corner. Above the impressive double doors, which are painted a cool steel-blue, a pitched overhang drips gingerbread trim in different shades of gray and blue. Two stories of rectilinear bay windows framed in teal woodwork are stacked one on top of the other on the right side of the house, jutting out from indigo horizontal wooden strips covering the facade. Beneath them, at street level, a smaller steel-blue door next to a quaintly shuttered window stands where there had probably once been a garage door, and leads into what I am by this point desperately praying is our apartment. Way up high, oversize brackets are tucked beneath the eaves of a gabled, gray-and-purple shingled roof capped with ornate millwork and, at the very top, an iron weather vane.

"I think it's a Victorian," George whispers.

"Really? Ya think?"

She shoots me a look. "Don't tell me you rented this on Priceline."

"You don't have to whisper!" I laugh. "It's not going to disappear. At least, I hope not!"

"Seriously, Holly. How'd you find this place?"

"Craig's List. It's a great Web site for finding rentals. There were no pictures of this one, though, so I'm just as surprised as you are."

"Well, what did it say?"

"I don't remember… I guess something like, 'Renovated two-bedroom in Western Addition. Appliances, utilities included.'"

"Uh-huh. And exactly how much is this costing us?"

"$700 a month!" I beam. "Do I have a horseshoe up my ass, or what?"

She looks up at the house again, then back at me skeptically. "What's the catch?"

"Why does there have to be a catch?"

"Is this some sort of crack neighborhood or something?"

"Not that I'm aware of…"

We look left and right. More houses like this one, some a little run-down, maybe, but all of them old beauties just the same. On a wrought-iron bench across the street, in as quaint an urban patch of green space as you are ever likely to see, a pair of young mothers in Madonna-inspired tracksuits chat and clutch Starbucks cups while their bundled babies snooze in matching Italian strollers. There isn't much traffic, but the smattering of parked Volvos and BMWs hints at affluence. Unless, of course, that guy walking the King Charles spaniel with the Burberry booties is a drug dealer.

Probably not.

"You ring the bell," George says.

"No, you."

"I'm shy."

"So am I!"

She crosses her arms. "Well, I'm not going to do it."

"Fine."

I push through the little wrought-iron gate and walk up the stairs. George is right behind me. A wood-framed stained-glass square bearing the house's address hangs beside the door. I put down my bags, shoo away the fat tabby cat curled up on the welcome mat and ring the bell.

Nothing.

George nudges me. I ring it again.

Still nothing.

"What's this guy's name, anyway?"

"Remy something. Wakefield, I think." I check my paper. "Yeah—Remy Wakefield."

"Sounds like the hero of one of those cheesy romance

novels with Fabio on the cover. I used to buy them secretly with my allowance money, from the 99-cent bin at the library."

"My grandmother read those. The large-print kind. Before she died, we spent a month every summer at her house in Saratoga Springs, and I used to sneak her books and read them under the covers at night with a flashlight. It was years before I finally figured out what all that throbbing and groaning was about."

"Still, you knew enough to know you shouldn't be reading them!"

"Why do you think I loved them so much?"

George sighs and goes to sit down on the top step. "My mothers found my stash when I was thirteen. They bought me a leather-bound Anaïs Nin collection for my birthday that year—to try and counteract the effects, I guess—but it was already too late. They say that's why I turned out straight. So, you think maybe he's not home?"

I shrug.

"Try the knocker."

I knock as loudly as I can. "Maybe we should have called first."

"He's probably just out. We could wait for him across the street...."

Just as we're about to leave, we hear the creak of floorboards. They get louder and louder until they stop behind the door.

"Who is it?"

"It's, um, Holly and George. From Buffalo...."

The door swings open.

"Oh my God!" George whispers, louder than she probably wanted to.

The guy standing in the entrance laughs. "Don't tell me you've never seen a wet, naked guy before!"

Not like you, that's for sure!

In my peripheral vision, I notice George's face flush pink at the speed of light. "S-sorry," she stammers. "I just wasn't expecting…"

What she wasn't expecting was for our new landlord to be, well, for lack of a more mature way of putting it, super hot. And wearing only a towel.

"No, I'm the one who's sorry. I was just in the shower. Didn't mean to freak you out. I'm Remy, by the way. Nice to meet you. Which one of you's Holly?"

I smile.

"So that makes you George." He grins at her. *Teeth: Just the tiniest bit crooked. Charming.* "I'd, uh, shake your hand, but I don't want to lose my towel. Come in, already—it's freezing."

"Freezing is where we just came from," I say as we step inside. "This is positively balmy for us."

"Yeah, well, I'm from San Diego, where it's seventy-five degrees in the winter and seventy-six degrees in the summer. I've been here almost ten years and I still can't get used to it."

The tabby cat from the porch darts into the narrow vestibule and begins rubbing his face ferociously against my shin in an apparent effort to rid himself of eye crust. "Uh, is this guy yours?" I asked, hoping it isn't.

"Yeah. That's Fleabiscuit. He moved in last summer. You like cats?"

"Oh, yeah. Can't get enough of 'em," I lie. *For you, I'd swim across a sea of whiskers, climb a mountain of hairballs…*

He squeezes past us to push the door shut, and I notice he has some sort of tattoo on his chest, though I can't tell exactly what it is because I am way too shy to let him catch me looking at it.

"Just leave your bags in the front there and I'll help you downstairs with them later."

"Thanks," I say. *And he's a gentleman, too!*

"So! Welcome to San Francisco. Your first time here?"

We nod like idiots, following him into the front hallway. His back is perfect—toned and smooth, with really nice skin. And his legs! Oh, his legs…what I can see of them, anyway…are muscular and well proportioned, from his flip-flopped feet to just above the backs of his knees.

The gods must have heard my prayers for a change, because his towel snags briefly on something sticking out of the door frame and starts to fall away. Of course, he catches it before it drops, but I might later convince myself I'd seen some upper cheekage. I hear George suck in her breath as she smacks me from behind.

"Almost saw a little more than you bargained for, huh, ladies? I really oughta fix that…. Wow, so it's your first time in San Francisco! Don't call it Frisco, by the way—the locals hate that. God, I remember my first time here. State soccer finals junior year of high school. Sacramento creamed us, those bastards, but I swore I'd live here someday, and now I do!"

"And you like it?"

"Love it! You will, too. There's no place like it. So when's your truck coming?"

"Tomorrow morning," I say. "I guess we'll have to sleep on the floor tonight."

Remy pauses, running his fingers back through his wet hair. "I'd offer you the couch, but as you can see, I don't have one."

I'd been so overwhelmed by the unexpected gorgeousness of our new landlord that I hadn't even noticed that the inside of his home is a little less awe-inspiring than the outside. Apart from an antique coatrack, there isn't a stick of furniture to be seen. Actually, there isn't much of *anything* to be seen.

The entire first floor is almost completely empty, save for a few kitchen appliances lined up at the far end of the house. There are no rooms, no walls, no ceiling—just a huge stack of gyprock and two-by-fours piled up in one corner, an old toilet in another, partial framing around the perimeter, and what looks like an original but severely worn mantelpiece in what is presumably the living room. Even the bay windows, so magnificent from the outside, are considerably less impressive set into a wall of dusty, crumbling brickwork.

"Give me a minute, will ya? I think I should probably slip into something a little less comfortable…."

With that, Remy bounds up the stairs, calf muscles bulging, and disappears out of sight.

As if she knows exactly what I'd been wondering, George looks to me and says, "He's gay. He *must* be."

"I don't think so."

"Trust me, Holly. I know. I can tell. This is San Francisco!"

"So? I'm just not getting that vibe from him."

"What vibe? How would you know? You don't know any gay guys. You don't even watch *Queer Eye.*"

"I watch *Will & Grace,* for your information. *Religiously.*"

George waves me off. "That actor's not even gay in real life."

Before I can protest, Remy appears at the top of the stairs in a pair of paint-splattered gray sweatpants, pulling a Stanford T-shirt over his muscled midsection.

"Tight shirt," George whispers. "See?"

"I'm not convinced," I whisper back.

"You have a beautiful home, Mr. Wakefield," she says to him as he reaches the bottom.

He smiles again. "I'm well under forty, and I don't have a job, so I think it would be okay if you just called me Remy."

George blushes once more and manages to squeak out an "Okay!"

"C'mon—I'll give you a tour…. As you can see, she's a work in progress. I decided to restore the outside first, in case I ran out of money before it was done."

"Sure," I say.

"I'm joking. But it was a *huge* pain in the ass—the city restoration committee is insane about permits. They freak out over even the smallest details with these old places. Took 'em two months just to approve the damn paint colors, if you can believe that!"

George and I shake our heads sympathetically.

"Anyway, I have a buddy who's an architect and he finished up the plans about six months ago, then they went to the committee, of course, and then there was the demolition, so I'm only just now getting started on the inside."

"Are you doing all the work yourself?" I ask.

"Yup!"

Gorgeous, courteous *and* carpenterly?

"Wow," George says. "You must really be good with your hands."

I pinch her, just for fun, to let her know I know she's flirting.

"Ow!" she whines. "Whyd'ya do that?"

"Do what? Please, go on," I say to Remy.

"Well, the kitchen's going to be in the back, there, with a huge porch. The backyard's pretty pathetic and it gets no sun, so eventually I want to put some sort of Asian rock garden back there or something like that, but until then, I thought I might as well take advantage of the space…."

Remy walks us through his plans for the ground floor and tells us all about his search for period moldings and woodwork and windows frames; how he won't rest until he scores a set of eighteen brass doorknobs, circa 1880; how the right wallpaper is going to be *really* hard to come by, and so on and so forth. By the time we've made it up to level two half an hour later, I am almost convinced that he *is* gay—none of the guys I knew back home have ever waxed poetic about antique fixtures or knew the politics of auction houses or scoured flea markets on the weekend.

When we finally get to what appears to be the only room with finished walls on the second floor, which is in even more disarray than the first, I think George and I are both heartened to realize we're standing in his bedroom. Aside from the mattress on the floor, it seems more like an office—a computer that could land the Space Shuttle is set up on a desk, and there are a few filing cabinets and a bookshelf. Almost the entirety of one wall is covered with drawings and plans and swatches tacked to bulletin boards.

I get a little closer to examine the details. "Did you do these?"

He flops down on the mattress. "Not the blueprints, Dave did those, but the sketches, yeah."

"They're incredible…" I say. "You're *really* talented. And the detail's amazing. I can totally see what it's going to be like when it's done."

George, who's been staring out the window, walks over for a cursory glance. "Wow…I'm sure you and your partner are going to be very happy here."

Subtlety was never her strong suit, God bless her.

Remy stares at her, an eyebrow arched in bemusement. "If you want to know if I'm gay, just ask."

"Are you?" George blurts, then steps back behind me.

I lean in anxiously for the answer.

"Ha! You girls—you're here in this wonderful city not twenty-four hours and you're already catting around! You should be ashamed of yourselves! Why don't you go to a museum or something? Take a tour. See the sights."

"That's not fair!" I say, proving I'm just about as immature as he's making us sound. "You told her to ask!"

"Gay, straight, bi, whatever—they're all mere labels by which I choose not to define myself."

"Gay," George says. "Definitely gay."

He laughs and pushes up off his bed. "Come on—I'll

show you to your place. Oh, and maybe grab some pillows
and take this top blanket. It can get pretty cold down there
at night."

I roll my eyes and follow him back downstairs.

After we've settled in and looked around a bit, George calls
her mothers from her cell phone. Apparently, she hasn't been
through enough in the past two days.

"Hi, Ma, how are you?"

Long pause.

"No, we don't have a land line yet."

Pause.

"Yes, Ma. I'll call as soon as I have the number."

Pause.

"Yeah—it's clean. It's big, too. And in a great neighborhood.
We each have our own bedroom, and there's a living area and
the cutest little galley kitchen. And it's all freshly painted."

Pause.

"Yes, it's really clean. The owner just renovated it. We're
his first tenants, I think."

Pause.

"No… I mean, yes. I mean…well, yes there's a fridge and
a stove, but technically there's no washer or dryer. The landlord said we could just use his."

Long pause.

"Ma! It's fine! Don't worry—he seems like a nice guy and
not at all creepy or weird or—"

Pause.

"Remy Wakefield."

Pause.

"His phone number? Holly—do you have his number?"

I pass her the paper with the details.

"It's 415-555-9594. But don't worry! It's fine. He's a
nice guy!"

Pause.

"No, Ma, I haven't seen *Pacific Heights.*"

Long pause. She puts her finger over the microphone and whispers, "She's nuts!"

"Look, Ma. I think you're being really silly about this. I'm *sure* he's not a homicidal maniac…"

Pause.

"No! Don't put her on! I don't want to talk to—"

Pause.

"Hi, Mom, how are you?"

Long pause.

"No, Mom. I'm not coming home."

Long, long pause…

George flips her phone closed. "She hung up on me."

"You're a glutton for punishment."

"I just wanted to let them know we were okay. Aren't you going to call your folks?"

"You think I should?"

"Yes," she says and passes me her phone.

"I'll call them tomorrow. It's been such a long day already and—"

"No. Call them now."

Even though the kids are probably already asleep at Cole's, George is right—I should at least call my dad.

"Fine," I grumble and begin dialing. "I just hope I don't wake anyone."

My dad picks up on the first ring.

"Hi, Dad, it's me!"

"Holly, sweetie! You got there okay? Everything's fine?"

"Yeah. Sorry I didn't call last night, but it was late by the time we got in."

"Of course, of course."

"I'm having fun. It's a beautiful city."

"It sure is," he agrees, then yawns.

I can just see him there, in his robe and plaid pajamas, nodding off on the couch in front of *Law & Order*.

"Anyway, I'd better go 'cuz I'm on George's cell. The phone guy's coming tomorrow so I'll call you with the new number."

"Okay, dear. Bye!"

"Bye, Dad!"

I shut the phone and hand it to her. "And that's how it's done!"

She passes it right back to me. "Now, your mother."

"No way."

"Holly…"

"Grrr…"

I dial Aunt Deb's house.

"Helloooo?"

"Hi Deb, it's Holly."

"Holly! Good to hear your voice. Are you settled in okay?"

"Yeah."

"Hold on—I'll get your mum. *LOUISE!!! LOUISE!!! HOLLY'S ON THE PHONE!!! LOUISE!!!*"

I cross my eyes and George laughs.

"Hello?"

"Hi, Mom."

"Hello, dear. I can't talk right now. I have an eBay auction ending in six and half minutes."

"Okay."

"You're okay?"

"Yes."

"Good. E-mail me a picture of your new place."

"Okay."

"Bye! Miss you!" she says, and hangs up before I have the chance to say anything else.

George puts the phone back in the charger. "Now that wasn't so bad, was it?"

"I suppose not. But she's so—"

She puts her finger up to interrupt me. "Was that a knock?"

"I think so." I walk over to our back door, the one that leads to the laundry room and the stairs up to Remy's kitchen.

"Who is it?" I ask.

"It's the landlord. Are you decent?"

I open the door. "Not everyone answers the door half-naked, you know."

"Too bad, isn't it?" he says. "Anyway, I just thought I'd invite my new tenants up for some pizza. It'll be here any minute."

"God, yes!" George practically shouts and rushes past us. "I'm starving!"

Remy jumps back to let her through. "The lady knows what she wants!"

"Only when it comes to food," I explain, which elicits a hearty laugh.

"You know what, Holly?"

"What?"

"You're kinda funny."

"Thanks for noticing."

"You coming?" George shouts from the top of the stairs.

chapter 13

A Woman's Work

George shuffles out of her room, rubbing her eyes. Her curls are piled up in a loose topknot and she's wearing her fuzzy bunny slippers.

"Who the hell's calling us so early?"

"I just put a pot of coffee on. It'll be ready in a minute."

She stares at me blankly as I hang up the phone.

"Isn't it great, finally having our own stuff here?"

The movers had taken their sweet time (apparently, their truck broke down somewhere near Lincoln, Nebraska). Remy had been kind enough to lend us a few blankets and an old sleeping bag, but still—we'd been sleeping on the floor for a week. One more night of that and I would have been forced to blow our weekly budget on a two-hour massage at the nicest hotel I could find.

"Holly—it's 7:00 a.m. What's going on?"

"Didn't it feel good, sleeping in a real bed?"

"I don't have a real bed," she grumbles and flops down into a chair, curling up under the throw. "It's just your old futon."

"Oh, I'm sorry, princess! Should I order you a new mattress set?"

She gives me the finger.

"That was Remy. He wanted to know when we'd be upstairs," I say quickly, keeping my eyes on the floor.

"Upstairs for what?" she yawns.

"To start."

"To start what?"

"Work, silly!"

She sits up. "What?"

"Oh, didn't I tell you?"

"No, Holly, you didn't tell me anything. What's going on? Tell me right now!"

"I was pretty sure I'd mentioned it..."

"Holly..."

"Well, our rent is sort of, um, *subsidized*."

"I *knew* there was a catch," she moans. "I just *knew* it."

"Are you sure I never told you? Because I can't believe it would slip my—"

"Nope!" George begins rubbing her temples frantically. "You never mentioned it! Not a word of it!"

"Well, it's been so crazy the past few weeks."

"For heaven's sake—just spit it out!"

"Okay, okay. It's not such a big deal, really. But we sort of have to, um...help out around the house. In exchange for the cheap rent."

"What do you mean? We have to work for Remy?"

"In a manner of speaking, yes. The deal was, we get to settle in, see the sights a bit, then start lending a hand here and there. It's quite fair, actually. At least, *I* think it is."

"Pour me a cup of coffee immediately and put a bagel in the toaster," she barks, knowing I'll be glad to oblige under the circumstances. "God, Holly. Couldn't you find any place that didn't require manual labor as part of the lease?"

"Sure," I say, getting up. "But I thought this would be our best bet—our cash will last us a whole lot longer, which means we can be pickier about what jobs we take. That's a *good* thing, isn't it? And for what we wanted to spend, we would've had to go *waaay* out of the city. And what's the point of moving to San Francisco and then not getting to enjoy it because we're stuck somewhere in the middle of suburbia?"

"Aren't all the rich guys out there, anyway? In the Valley?"

"Maybe, but I thought we'd probably have an easier time finding jobs here. And you know me, G. I'm *very* sensitive to my environment. Living someplace that offends me aesthetically could interfere with all kinds of stuff—my health, my sleep, my mood, not to mention my writing. How am I supposed to write living in a box with parquetry flooring and a window overlooking the highway or some strip mall?"

"Still, I'm just saying…"

"If you want to move, I suppose we *could* settle for a really shitty part of town…" I am more than willing to play the danger card here. Preying on George's vulnerability and innate fear of strange men will virtually guarantee her compliance. "I just didn't think that was the best option. For *either* of us. And certainly your mothers wouldn't approve, and we couldn't really lie to them about something like that, since they know the city pretty well and it wouldn't be right, anyway. Look, George, call me crazy but I don't want to feel threatened or nervous walking home at night. Alone. In the dark. With sex-starved weirdos everywhere and winos limping out of alleyways and—"

"Okay, already! I get it! We're not moving into the *Thriller* video!" She folds her arms on her chest defiantly. "But you should have told me…"

"I just wanted us to be comfortable and safe, so this place seemed like the best bet. Especially since I had to figure this all out on my own, from over two thousand miles away."

"I suppose…"

"Trust me. This is the only way we'll be able to afford a neighborhood like this. I did my research, you know—apartments around here start at, like, eighteen hundred dollars minimum, and that's for *one* bedroom. So we were *very* fortunate to get it. Remy told me he had dozens of other tenants interested in the place."

"Okay, Holly. Give it a rest," she says. "Just wondering, though…how is that *we* got so lucky if Remy had so many other people interested in the place?"

"It was a very extensive application process. He liked my essay best, I guess."

George practically chokes on her bagel. "Essay? He made you write an essay?"

"Yes."

"That guy's a real character," she says. "I'm getting the sense he has a really twisted sense of humor."

"He sure does. But I think he's probably more lonely than anything. He doesn't seem to have too many friends."

Over the course of the past week, Remy Wakefield has subjected us to all sorts of nonsense, from dragging us to the vet for Fleabiscuit's deworming to attending a town council meeting about zoning bylaws. Not that I minded—we didn't have much else to do besides sit around and wait for our furniture and phone line, anyway. Plus, it was a lot more fun than looking for jobs, something we were more than happy to put off our first week here. I suppose we could have squeezed in a little more sightseeing, but I was happy just to explore the neighborhood and hang around with Remy. True, his early-morning drilling and hammering woke us up almost every day, which was infuriating, but…

George snaps her fingers in my face. "Hello? Earth to Holly! Come in, Holly!"

I slap her hand away.

"You have a *whopping* crush on him. It's *so* obvious."

"Like you don't." I laugh.

"I don't. He's gay, remember?"

"Yeah right. That's why he has a stack of *Maxim*s in the can upstairs."

"I saw a few *Vanity Fair*s, too," she reminds me. "And one *Men's Health*. So don't get your hopes up."

"So? That doesn't prove anything."

"It proves he's bi at the very least."

I throw a pillow at her.

"Hey! Watch it!"

"Get dressed," I say. "I told him we'd be upstairs in half an hour."

I suppose I do have a teensy tiny crush. But where's the harm in that?

"So I take it you finally told her?" Remy asks when we finally make it upstairs. He's standing in the kitchen, coffee mug in hand, and wearing what George and I call his uniform—the same pair of torn jeans, scuffed work boots and a plaid shirt.

George glares at us. "Conspiring against me. Very nice."

"Hey, don't blame me!" he says. "I was under the impression you'd *both* agreed to this when I rented you the place. Your little friend here told me to keep quiet about it."

"That's enough, Remy," I say quickly, to preempt any further protest from George. "So what exactly do we have to do?"

He takes a step back and gives us the once-over. We're both basically still wearing our pajamas—sweatpants and T-shirts. I wasn't about to get all dressed up to hammer in a few nails, no matter how cute the taskmaster. George is wearing lipstick, but I think it's still from last night. (I had a two-for-one coupon for Subway that had been burning a hole in my pocket all week.)

Remy shakes his head and sighs. "Since I'm assuming neither of you brought steel-toe shoes, I'll start you on light duty today. I'm also assuming you can both count and work a measuring tape, so—"

"Hold on a sec," George says. "Before we start, I'd like to know exactly what this little arrangement involves. If you don't mind."

"You're my slaves until you find jobs. Then, we'll see how much you can get done evenings and weekends."

She points her finger at me. "This is ridiculous."

"I can raise your rent, if you prefer," Remy offers, stepping in between us. "I figure the going rate for a renovated two-bedroom in this neighborhood runs somewhere about twenty-two hundred, plus utilities."

George skulks over to the window and stares out at the brambles and junk in the backyard.

"I don't think that would be very fair to my dad," I say to her. "We owe it to him to give this a shot."

"So the old man's floating you, huh?" Remy asks.

"None of your business. George, come on—it'll be fun!"

He goes over to her and puts his hands on her shoulders from behind. "Yeah, George—come on! It'll be fun! I guarantee you by the time I'm done with you here you'll both know a thing or two about carpentry. And if you're good, I may even let you wear my tool belt…."

She turns to face him. "Really?"

"Yup."

She sneaks a look at me out of the corner of her eye. "Okay. But if I get hurt, or hate it, I'm quitting."

"Not an option. But let's get started, anyway," he smiles and walks over to some sort of power tool on a workbench. "This, ladies, is the finest table saw money can buy…."

"You're right," George whispers to me as she passed. "He's not gay."

"How do you know?"

"I felt it."

I haven't checked my e-mail in ten days. Surely, there would be tons.

Hmmm…

Three. Just three?

Two were from Zoe and the other was from…my mom? (Well, wonders never cease!) Thank heaven for Zoe, at least. Seeing her name in my in-box confirms that I'm not a complete loser, and that I do indeed have more than one friend in this world.

To: hollyhastings@hotmail.com
From: zoewatts@doggietails.com
Subject: Miss you…
you there? howzit going? the city? the apartment? the book-writing? the men?

To: hollyhastings@hotmail.com
From: zoewatts@doggietails.com
Subject: Still miss you…
ahem. I said, you *there*?

To: zoewatts@doggietails.com
From: hollyhastings@hotmail.com
Subject: re: Still miss you…
hi, zoe! sorry I haven't written you back, but my dsl line won't be in till next week. the landlord lives upstairs and was kind enough to offer me the use of his computer in the meantime to check messages. how are things in philly? how's your dad? asher? puppy primping? I want to hear everything!

all's well on the western front. apartment's great, city's great, tho george and I have hardly had time to see the sights. you were right—the apartment is a sweet deal, even with the manual labor. We're working our asses off for this landlord guy. speaking of landlords, mine's a complete hottie! Pretty nice, too, tho a tad sassy for my taste. anyway, he's nice to look at. his name's remy. can you beat that? george has a camera phone, so I'll try and snap a secret pic and send it.

as for the business side of things, nothing really to report. we've both applied for a few jobs we saw in the paper but no word yet. And as for the REAL reason we're here, we haven't had a chance to meet any men, let alone men of means, since we're currently knee-deep in spackle and sandpaper. but fear not— a dot-com millionaire will be mine before the year is out! then the whole story will be coming soon to a bookstore near you! love to asher and the dogs,

h

And now for the painful part...

To: hollyhastings@hotmail.com
From: louisehastings@buffalonet.com
Subject: Hi Honey
Dear Holly,
How are you, dear? I am fine. I have been very busy planning my trip to Miami. I am leaving in less than two weeks. Aunt Deb has decided to come with me, so we will drive down in her car together. We are going to stop along the way and do some sightseeing. I do not know how long I will be gone but it could be quite a while. I am very excited and not at all concerned about your father. I am also taking a salsa class. It turns out I am quite a good dancer!
I will bring my laptop with me so I can follow the auctions. These collectibles don't buy themselves you know! So the best way

to reach me while I'm away is by e-mail. My freemail address is lustylou2@yahoo.com. Do you know what freemail is Holly? It means you can get your e-mail anywhere. Not just from home. Isn't that wonderful. E-mailing is very practical and I wouldn't want you to spend any more of your father's retirement money on long-distance calls from your cell phone. I hear from Cole that you've been calling him there quite a bit. You better have a good rate plan. I assume you still don't have a regular phone number or you would have given it to me by now.

I love you,

Mom

p.s. Hope you're having fun in San Francisco!

p.p.s. Have you found a job yet? You should hurry up and do that.

Nice. Very nice.

To: louisehastings@buffalonet.com
From: hollyhastings@hotmail.com
Subject: re: Hi Honey

dearest mother,

sorry—I guess I forgot to call you with my phone #. why don't you just get it from cole, since he seems to be on top of everything back there. i'm really glad to hear that things are going so well for you. it sounds like you're very busy and that's great. even though you're not worried about dad, I am and that's why I've been calling him a lot. I swore to myself before I left that I wouldn't get involved but let me remind you that this separation is VERY difficult for him (even though he won't admit it) so please try and be sensitive. he's the one being left behind in all this, so i'm just trying to make sure he's okay. i'm very happy and excited for you about your trip. taking aunt deb along is a great idea. I bet she hasn't had a real vacation in 10 years. please drive safely and rest if you get tired. don't

be a hero! I promise i'll try and be better about keeping in touch, if you do too. I will call you before you leave.
give flipper a big hug and a kiss from me!
love, holly
p.s. hope you have a good time on your road trip!
p.p.s. children of divorce are more likely to divorce themselves.

Just as I send it off, another message comes through. Maybe I'm not a loser after all! Maybe people back home really are missing me…

To: hollyhastings@hotmail.com
From: s7s#g(*&juU2798d38@yyl.net
Subject: R Cheep V!aG*Ra Will Make Your C*&K Hard!

I press delete without reading it. If it had been an "Increase Yer B*r&st Size In 14 Dayz Garanteeed!!" ad…well, that would be another story.

Upstairs, we're finally making some progress, but you wouldn't know it from the way Remy carries on about being behind schedule. Why he even bothers with a schedule is beyond me. It's not like he has anything else to do, though George and I certainly do—we want to see more of the city, take a cable-car tour, find real jobs so that we can be released from servitude. Alas, we're stuck working from nine to four every single day for a guy with sawdust on the brain (and we were supposed to be *happy* about it, because he wanted to start at eight!). Remy is still nice to look at, don't get me wrong, but a girl cannot live on proximity to cuteness alone.

During one of our designated thirty-minute lunch breaks, I finally gather up the courage to ask Remy something I'd been wondering since George had brought it to my attention two weeks earlier.

"Can I ask you something?"

"Sure, Holly."

"I'm curious. Why exactly did you choose us to live here?"

"Whaddya mean?"

"What was it about my application?"

"Oh. You mean why did I pick you out of the countless more qualified renters with better credit ratings and higher incomes?"

"Yeah, that's exactly what I mean."

"Sorry," he says and reaches out to tousle my hair. It's the first time he's actually touched me—the first time *any* guy has touched me since Mateo the golf pro—and I can tell exactly what George meant that day when she said he wasn't gay. "I liked what you said in your personal statement."

"I still can't believe you made everyone write a *personal statement!*" George says.

"And five hundred and fifty true or false questions," I add.

"No!" George squeals and falls to her side, laughing.

"What's so funny about that?" he asks, chuckling himself. "How else was I supposed to weed out the maniacs and losers?"

"I take it you were a psych major in college, Remy?"

"English actually. I minored in psych. And so what if I did, smartass? There's no law that says a guy can't put the Minnesota Multiphasic Personality Inventory to practical everyday use in his own life."

I reach over to grab another slice of pizza from the box. "Is that what that was? I sure am glad I passed, then."

"You didn't," he said. "But you were close enough."

"If I'm so nuts, why bother with me?"

"To make things interesting, I guess. 'They sicken of the calm, who knew the storm…'"

I swat him on the arm, now that we're on touching terms.

"If you want to feel my biceps, girly, just ask!"

George pretends to get up. "I could leave you two alone, if you'd like…."

"No, please, stay," he says.

"I'd smack you again, Remy, but I wouldn't want you to take it the wrong way."

"And what way would you have me take it?"

I try to think of a witty comeback, but can't. The story of my life. "Seriously. Why did you choose us?"

"You," George clarifies. "He chose *you*. I had nothing to do with it."

Remy puts his beer down and leans back. "It's no big deal. I guess I sort of liked what you said about wanting to be a writer. So I wanted to give you a chance. You seemed very…sincere. And odd. But in a quaint way."

"Quaint? You think I'm quaint?"

"She's not quaint," George says. "Not at all."

He nods. "Yeah, well, I know that now, don't I?"

"Thanks, guys."

"Enough chitchat, ladies! Back to work. These walls aren't going to put up themselves!"

George groans. "My job interview's at three and I really, *really* want this one. I'm already feeling a little queasy, so couldn't I just skip out now? I need to get ready."

"That doesn't take two hours." Remy extends his hand for her to take.

I suppose he could tell she needed some incentive, and it isn't like he doesn't know just how damn cute he is.

"So what about you?" I say to Remy later that afternoon. "You know an awful lot about me but I hardly know a thing about you."

With George out of the house, we're alone together for the first time, though I doubt he's as aware of that fact as I am.

"You know plenty about me, Holly."

"Not really. I know that you're from San Diego, and that you're probably not a very good soccer player. But that's hardly scratching the surface, I'm sure…"

He laughs. "What do you wanna know? And don't ask me if I'm gay!"

I think for a moment. "How can you afford this house if you don't have a job?"

"I had a job when I bought it."

"Did you get fired? What did you do?"

"I didn't get fired. I've *never* been fired. Although I bet you have…."

"But we're talking about you, now."

He puts down his hammer and cracks every one of his knuckles, plus his neck. Revolting, without a doubt, yet somehow strangely charming at the same time.

"Okay, for your information, I did have a job. I owned my own company."

"What kind of company?"

"What do you think? A start-up. In San Jose. My partner bought me out in '99."

"That was years ago. You haven't been sitting on your ass since then, I hope."

"Funny! But no, not exactly. I bought the house right away as a sort of forced savings. You should have seen it! It was a *complete* disaster! But I knew it would be a good investment in the long run and that I'd always have a roof over my head. Anyway, then I worked with my cousin for a bit, then I traveled until I was afraid I'd run out of money and have nothing left for the house."

"Are you sorry you sold your business?"

"Are you nuts? I was a genius to get out when I did, or else I'd probably be living in a refrigerator box under the Bridge. As it was, I lost a ton in the market."

"And so now all you want to do with your life is fix up an old house?"

"You got it!" His gray eyes twinkle impishly, as if he thinks he's being as bad as he could possibly be.

"So let me guess—once it's all done, you're planning to flip it for a huge profit. Very original. I suppose you could probably get double what you paid for it."

He shrugs. "Don't know. Don't care. I just want to live in it."

"But you'll need a job eventually," I say.

"Eventually," he agrees, and goes back to hammering. "But this is where I am for now. And don't think I don't see what you're doing over there...."

I'd been sanding the same patch of old paint off an antique railing post for half an hour to avoid my next task, which is considerably more taxing: installing it. George and I have both suffered severe fingernail trauma on multiple occasions. In spite of our clumsiness, though, the first floor is really beginning to take shape. We have almost all of the framing up and yesterday, George even started working on one of the walls. Unfortunately, once Remy noticed that she'd accidentally put holes through the panels in about ten different places, he tore it all down and made her start over. Still, real progress is being made.

"What about you?" he asks. "How long do you think you'll be able to go without a job?"

"Don't pressure me—I just started looking! Something will come up."

"I bet you'd be happier just writing."

"Of course I would," I say. "But I've got to make a living in the meantime. Someone's got to keep a roof over your head!"

He laughs loudly and goes back over to the dwindling pile of two-by-fours, shaking his head.

★ ★ ★

"I got it!" George shouts from our living room. "Holly! I got it!"

I run out of my room. "Are you serious? Really?!"

Her first interview and she nailed it! This was quite literally her dream job—assistant editor at a little boutique publishing house specializing in, of all things, women's fantasy and sci-fi.

"I can't believe it! It's too good to be true!"

"No it's not, G—you totally deserve it. This job was *made* for you! When do you start?"

"Monday!"

"That's in three days!"

"They were looking for someone ASAP. God, I'm *so* relieved. I was beginning to get calluses. See?" She shows me her palms. "Three weeks of manual labor and I'm already a mess…."

"Yeah, yeah, princess."

"I am just *sooo* psyched!"

She jumps up and down for a while, spins around a few times, calls her moms with the good news, then eventually collapses onto the couch with a bag of Baked Lays.

"You know what else this means, by the way?"

I shake my head. "We'll have more money?"

"Guess again."

"What?"

She leans in close. "It means that as of Monday, you and Mr. Wakefield will be working up there every day, side by side, *all alone*…."

"Shut up! You are such a child!"

"Aw, you want him, Holly. You *know* you do!"

"I do not! He's such a jock. I wouldn't go near him if you paid me."

"Yeah, right!"

"I'm serious. He's so totally full of himself."

She raises a doubtful eyebrow.

"Okay, so he's not a *complete* idiot, but he's definitely not relationship material. He has way too much of that too-cute-for-his-own-good-frat-boy thing going on. I don't trust it. And he's beyond immature."

George snorts in disbelief. "This coming from the woman who sought comfort in the arms of Jean-Jean, a guy who sleeps with a baseball hat on and carries a picture of his bong collection in his wallet."

"Ack!" I shriek and throw a pillow at her. "I told you never to speak his name aloud!"

"Fine. We'll see… But I have a feeling about you two."

"Me and *Bicycle Boy*?"

"No, you idiot! You and *Remy*. If you think you can convince me for one second that you don't badly want—and I mean *badly* want—the hot-bodied, quick-witted stud boy English-Major-From-Stanford who quotes Dorothy Parker and loves Kentucky Fried Chicken, then you must have me confused with somebody who doesn't know you very well."

I shrug. "What you're picking up on is a fact that I admit freely—I could use a little male attention. We both could. But I'll remind you that we did not uproot our lives and come all the way out here to have casual flings with the unemployed."

"Uh, I don't think he's doing too badly if he owns a house like this."

"Yeah, but he probably has a million dollar mortgage, too."

"You don't have to convince me. I'm not the one with the crush on the boy upstairs."

"You really hit the nail on the head, there, G—Remy's a boy. And tempting though he may be, I need a man. A *wealthy* man."

"Still, I wouldn't kick him out of bed for eating crackers…and I'm doing low-carb now!"

"Those chips working for you, then?"

"They're low-fat!"

I roll my eyes. "And therein lies the problem."

"One woman's potato is another woman's pain," she sighs, licking the salt from her fingers.

I steal the bag away from her. "You know, George, now that you mention it, we've wasted just about enough time screwing around here. Tonight, we're going out to celebrate your new job!"

"Yay!"

"And we'll also begin our *real* work, what we came out here for in the first place…."

"I'll shower first!" she yells, jumping up. "But don't you dare finish those chips before I get back!"

chapter 14

The Ides of March

Judging from the glowing three-page tribute in my trusty copy of *The Hipster's Guide to San Francisco*, the South of Market area sounded like a promising place to meet straight young men of means. At least for now. The bulk of my research actually suggested that we'd be best off heading down to Silicon Valley itself—the string of towns southeast of the city that are home to the world's largest conglomeration of high-tech companies—but first, I figured we might as well explore the options in our own backyard.

"It's nice just to be out of that damn house for a change," George says as we get off the bus at the corner of Folsom and 11th Street.

"Tell me about it! I feel like I've almost forgotten where we are!"

The financial district's glass-and-stone towers loom to the northeast. Were it not for the unmistakable point of the

Transamerica Pyramid reminding us otherwise, in the purplish twilight, it could almost be Manhattan.

And then a streetcar clangs faintly in the distance.

Nope! This is definitely not New York!

The realization courses through my veins like pure adrenaline.

"We should have done this the day we got here!" I link my arm through George's and we begin to walk. Here is exactly what I'd been hoping for—sleek thirtysomethings dressed in black, trendy nightclubs and restaurants housed in converted warehouses, beautiful people streaming in and out of beautiful cars. We read the names of the places as we pass. *The Public, Caliente, Butter, Wish, Loft 11…*

"Look—that one doesn't even *have* a name!" George marvels through chattering teeth as we walk by one particularly steely spot fronted with mirrored glass windows. The velvet rope outside suggests it might be busy later, although now there's no crowd to hold back. Just a beefy bouncer in a leather coat talking on a phone by the door.

"Sure it has a name. 808."

"That's the *address,*" she explains.

I stop and give her a long, hard stare. "George, remind me—when was the last time you were out of Buffalo before we came here?"

"Florida! With you!"

"Before that."

"I dunno," she shrugs. "Probably three years ago. I went to Saranac Lake with my moms, remember?"

"What about the city?"

"What city?"

"New York!"

"Oh! Not since high school, I guess."

I grab her arm and pull her back toward the restaurant. "Then this'll be perfect."

The bouncer smiles at us and pushes open the glass door. Inside, it's actually quite busy, and the welcome heat of bodies in motion mingles with the aromas of food being prepared. A mirrored, circular bar in the center of the space overflows with patrons, many of whom are *definitely* dating material. Aside from a few hanging chrome lanterns, the room's light is provided by a ring of connected backlit aquariums set into the wall.

"Hello, ladies." A gorgeous hostess with shiny black hair pulled into a tight ponytail teeters in front of us in thigh-high stiletto boots. "Will you be eating or drinking with us this evening?"

"Both," I say.

She grabs a couple of menus and leads us to a dark booth at the back. "The coat check is over there, if you like."

"I think we've found Nemo," George giggles after she's left. "And get a load of that guy!"

An enormous angelfish—bright yellow and flat as a pancake—drifts slowly past our faces and on to the booth beside ours.

"He'd be delicious pan-seared with a little sesame oil and lemongrass."

"First things first!" she says, pulling my menu away. "Drinks!"

"Okay. How about Manhattans tonight? A tribute to home."

"I was thinking something a little girlier, but okay," she says. "As long as you don't mind peeling me up off the floor when we're done."

"We're here to celebrate—you can get as drunk as you like, because starting Monday…you're a working girl!"

She groans. "Suddenly, I'm not so sure I want a real job. Is it too late to change my mind?"

"Uh, yes!"

"But I've never worked in an office before."

"I know. But it has its advantages. As soon as you get your first paycheck, by the way, we're taking you shopping. You can't wear that one suit every day."

Her face blanches. "Oh shit! I hadn't even thought about that! I need an entire work wardrobe!"

"Relax! That's the best part of having a real job."

"For you, maybe. You have the same body as the mannequins in the store."

"Minus the tits," I correct her.

"Whatever. But I look stumpy in suits."

"Well, maybe you won't have to wear a suit. It's probably not quite so formal out here, anyway, so I'm sure business casual will be fine. Just take note of what everyone else seems to be wearing and we'll figure it out."

"I better lose some weight before then," she says and opens her menu. "Oooh—but I bet the seafood risotto is good here. Should I have that? No, I probably shouldn't. Should I? No. But it's probably *sooo* good. God, but I've been so bad lately…."

"Go for it George. You deserve it. It'll be a nice change from pizza with a cardboard crust."

She nods, glad for permission to continue with her eating rampage. Pizza, and occasionally Chinese takeout, is pretty much all we've eaten since we arrived. More often than not, it was courtesy of Remy, so we were in no position to complain, although for an unemployed bum, we couldn't help but notice that he sure blew a lot of money on takeout and beer.

After three delightful rounds of cocktails, the food arrives. Who knows if it's any good, all I know is we're having a *really* great time. After vanilla-bean crème brûlées, we move over to the bar and even meet a couple of cute guys (at least, I *think* they're cute). Nothing really comes of it, though George and I definitely seize the opportunity to flex our flirting muscles.

It's freezing out by the time we finally leave, and I'm in high heels (another of San Francisco's many good points—the end of February, and no winter boots!), so we splurge for a cab home. We fall asleep as the car lurches down Market Street, and the driver has to wake us up when we get home. George throws up her very expensive dinner in the bushes on our way inside, but she definitely had a blast, anyway. We both did.

I curl up under my blanket and try to keep the room from spinning by counting sheep. Just as I'm about to drift off, it strikes me how for the first time in as long as I can remember, I am on my own and feeling good about it—no boyfriend, no job, no *therapist,* even! I'm blithely stepping on sidewalk cracks and forgetting to check the oven at night. It has been ages since I've recited my relaxation mantra or knocked on wood or blessed myself three times after sneezing. The other day, I walked straight past Deepak Chopra signing his new book at Barnes & Noble and went right to the fiction section instead.

So far, this city is good. *Very* good.

Of course, it doesn't take too long for that bubble to burst. I should have known better than to think purely happy thoughts. For those of us who live in the real world, the conscious realization that things are going well should also set off a little warning bell somewhere in the back of your mind: *Heads up, girl! Trouble's a-comin'!*

And trouble—this time, in the form of absolute mortification—is exactly where I find myself not two weeks later, standing in Remy's bedroom, completely unprepared for what has just happened.

He read my e-mail?

My cheeks burn with shame as he stands in front of me, laughing.

"…and I can't *believe* that you guys came all the way out here to find rich husbands! That's so…so…*evil.* I only took one women's studies class, but man—that has *got* to be wrong. *So* wrong!"

"How *dare* you read my private correspondence!" I gasp.

Not much of a defense, but it was all that came to mind in the horror of the moment.

"Hey, it's not like I went looking for it! I was just trying to check my Hotmail account but I got yours instead. You must have forgotten to log off. Genius move. Not that I have to justify any of this to *you,* since it is *my* computer, after all. And to think—I was nice enough to let you use it. Had I known you were going to pollute it with this…this…*filth!*" He waves his arm dramatically in the direction of the screen. "I certainly wouldn't have allowed it!"

I know Remy is joking, but I'm in no mood for it.

"Well, if I'd known you were going to invade my privacy so…so *egregiously,* I wouldn't have bothered! I would have waited for my own to arrive!"

"So *egregiously?* Ha! Are you gonna put that word in your book?"

"You…you *suck!*" I shout.

"Maybe," he snickers. "But now I know you think I'm, like, *totally* cute. Actually…I believe the term you used was 'complete hottie.' You know, you might want to consider writing for *Tiger Beat* instead."

God. Oh, God.

"Don't be embarrassed, Holly. I *am* cute. What can I say?"

He is enjoying this way too much, so I try to hit him where it will hurt. "You are possibly the most egotistical, arrogant, *amoral* piece of—"

"Amoral? I don't think so. Egotistical, maybe. Arrogant, most definitely. But I've done nothing wrong—my intentions were pure! It's my house, my computer, which means finders keepers." He grins triumphantly and takes a swig of his beer.

Despite his adorably messy hair and chiseled cheekbones, Remy Wakefield is suddenly very, very ugly. Outrage wells up inside me, and I seriously consider slapping him across his smug, perfect face.

Instead, I decide to take the high road. "Finders keepers? *Finders keepers?* What are you, in grade three?"

"You're just embarrassed!"

"Of course I am, because you've taken it all out of context and it seems so bad. But it's not like that!"

"It isn't?"

"No! But I'm too frazzled to justify it to you right now. Not that I have to!"

He stifles a laugh.

I spin around and stomp out of his room, desperate to get away from him.

But Remy follows me down the stairs. "By the way, your big plan sucks. If you'd moved out here a few years ago, before the tech crash, then maybe…but now? Most of those rich guys you're looking for have gone the way of the dodo, my friend. And I should know—I was one of them!"

"My private life is none of your business. I'm not discussing this with you anymore!"

I pray that he is wrong. He has to be. But I suddenly wish I'd read the business section of the *Bugle* once in a while, instead of getting all my news from *Entertainment Tonight*.

"Come on, now. Don't shoot the messenger."

"I feel like *strangling* the messenger."

"Your information is just a little out of date. But it was like the freaking Gold Rush out here in the nineties! Women were coming in droves from all over the world, trying to stake their claims!"

"How nice for you."

"I had to beat them off with a stick…."

"I'm sure you did plenty of beating off."

He smiles and looks off into the distance. "We were lighting our Cubans with hundred-dollar bills…."

"As much as I'm enjoying this little trip down memory lane, Remy, I'd really prefer it if you'd just shut the fuck up right now."

"Whatever," he says, shaking his head as he walks off toward the kitchen.

"And for your information," I shout after him, "Finders keepers doesn't apply to stuff sent through cyberspace! That's international territory, governed by international law!"

"Whatever, again!" he shouts back at me without turning around.

I sit down on the floor and concentrate on regaining my composure. What an ass. I consider calling Asher to find out if I have a case against him. Surely, the A.C.L.U. would have something to say about such a blatant invasion of a tenant's privacy. A lawsuit might be the best approach.

Remy comes stomping back from the kitchen, shaking a finger at me. "But for *your* information, what I find in *my* house is mine. *That's* the law. And if I wanted, I could kick you out on your butt if the contents of your correspondence offend me."

"Offend *you?!*"

"Yes, me! It's sexual harassment, and I won't be subjected to it in my own home!"

"That's *ridiculous!*"

"No, it's not! Did you ever stop to think that maybe *you've* made *me* feel like a piece of meat? Like an object? Like something pretty to be toyed with, used for his resources, then thrown away? On behalf of all men, I'm offended!"

He's making fun of me, but still, I want to kill him. Sarcasm doesn't go over well unless it's a two-way street.

"I could just as easily sue you, Remy. Under the California Labor Code. You've been…umm…unfairly profiting from our labor and blackmailing us with an illegal lease agreement! Without proper compensation or insurance for your workers, I should add, and your flagrant disregard for workplace safety codes is surely grounds for action! What if George or I tripped over one of those thingies over there and couldn't work?"

He laughs. "It wouldn't matter 'cause you don't have a real job!"

"My point exactly! Because I spend all my time slaving away here for you instead of looking for one. Which suits you just fine, doesn't it?!"

"Yeah, Holly. 'Cause being trapped with you in this house redoing all the work you mess up is exactly what I've wanted to do for the past month. It's already March 15, and I'm weeks behind schedule!"

That hits me. Hard.

I'd sort of assumed that he *liked* spending time with me, that he enjoyed my company, as I did his, but I guess I was wrong. And I thought I'd been doing good work, too, especially these past couple of weeks with just me and him. I bury my face in my hands and begin to cry. I honestly didn't mean to, but sometimes tears have a life of their own.

"Shit," he says. "No—no—don't cry. *Please* don't cry. I didn't mean to… I was just teasing…."

I look up and sniff. "*Et tu,* Remy?"

His features register a strange mix of fear and sympathy.

"Please, Holly. I'm sorry…"

But I jump up as fast as I can and run downstairs.

When George comes home from work that night, she finds me in a crumpled mess on the couch, surrounded by Kleenex and an empty box of Twinkies.

I tell her what has happened and she shakes her head. "That

snarky bastard. You need to get away from him," she says. "Find a job."

"I'm trying, George. I read the paper every day and have, like, twenty job search sites bookmarked. I check them every night." What I really need is a job with health insurance, so I can get my ass back into therapy. God, I miss therapy.

"I know you do, sweetie," she says, pushing my bangs out of my eyes. She's been at Venus Books for only two weeks, and is already loving it. She only wants the same for me. "Just keep at it. Something will come up. And in the meantime, don't you go back up there till you feel ready. I don't think he's going to be bugging you for a while."

"I just can't believe it got so ugly. We'd been getting along so well."

"I know. It's okay."

"I'm so mortified. He read all that stuff…."

"Forget about that—just concentrate on finding a job."

I nod and try to smile.

"Or we could start looking for another place, if you like."

"No, no. We'll never find anything better than this."

"Still…"

"It wasn't really that bad. I'm just totally humiliated right now. Everything will be fine once we make up."

"If you say so."

To give my wounded pride a chance to recover, I decide to avoid Remy for precisely four days. In the meantime, I put my free time to good use for a change and blitz the job thing. I apply for positions I wouldn't normally consider, including one horrid-sounding retail gig at a suburban electronics superstore and one equally frightening prospect that involves commission-based fund-raising for a "grassroots environmental initiative." I also put myself on the lists at three temp agencies. Anything to get out of the house and make a few bucks.

When I finally head upstairs to make peace, Remy is so sincerely apologetic (and so damn cute) that I catch myself secretly wishing I won't get any of the jobs I've been so busy applying for. Which in turn leads to a bit of a lightbulb moment—I realize that before the whole Ides of March incident, I hadn't really been trying all that hard to find a job because I was enjoying hanging out with Remy so much.

But all that is over now. That much is evident the moment I start back upstairs. Remy, being a gentleman at heart, tells me I don't have to work with him anymore if I don't want to, but I tell him a deal's a deal, and I am nothing if not true to my word. We both apologize for taking cheap shots; we agree things got a bit silly. He tries to convince me he didn't really think I was a bad worker, that he only said that because I accused him of being amoral. I explain that I'd been overly sensitive and that I don't normally cry like a baby when things don't go my way, just that I was mad at myself for forgetting to sign out of Hotmail.

Despite clearing the bad air between us, things aren't the same as before. For days, Remy seems to tread on eggshells around me. And every time we make eye contact, all the embarrassment I felt comes flooding back.

Exactly why this man's impression of me matters so much, I can't say. For some reason, he makes me doubt myself, the whole plan, everything. I know I have nothing to be ashamed of—it's just as easy to love a rich man as a poor man, after all, and becoming the successful writer I've always dreamed I could be is possible now that I have something bankable to write about—but Remy's disapproval bothers me more than I care to admit.

I reason that what I'm really feeling isn't so much shame as disappointment that things have changed between us. I'd been enjoying my crush on him immensely, but now I can tell that the dynamics of our relationship have been altered by the things we said. (Once that toothpaste leaves the tube, you can never get it to go back in.) It isn't only that he knows I'm attracted to him, while I have no idea how he feels about me; that, I can get over. I'm sure it came as no great surprise to him, anyway—Remy knows damn well how good-looking he is! What bothers me more is the possibility that he now sees me as something I'm not, or at least some things I like to think I'm not—shallow, ill-informed, weepy.

After a week or so of working together side by side again, the tension dissipates, as I knew it would. But things are definitely different. I can feel it.

"Hello? Holly?"

"Yes?"

"Hi! It's Vale."

"Who?"

"Vale! Jeez—I guess I didn't make as much of an impression as I thought! It was a few weeks ago…on Folsom Street."

I put my hand over the mouthpiece and whisper to George, "Who's Vale?"

She shrugs.

"Oh, hi!" I say. "Nice to hear from you."

"I've been meaning to call you, but I've been away on business and just got back into town a few days ago. But I'm glad to hear you gave me the right number, at least! You and your friend George were, uh, pretty happy…and, well…I wasn't sure if you'd even remember us."

The guys from the bar that night?

"Yeah, we were just blowing off a little steam. Long week, you know?"

"Sure, sure. I know what that's about…." He pauses.

"Hello?"

"Yeah, still here. So…my friend Quentin and I were wondering, maybe you and George would like to double date sometime?"

"You mean we didn't frighten you off with that whole drunken desperation thing?"

George, who is glued to my side listening in by that point, gives me a good smack in the arm.

"Is that what that was?" he chuckles. "Well, we don't scare too easily. And your friend left quite an impression on Quentin."

"She did?"

"Not too many girls who say they can tie a maraschino cherry stem into a knot with their tongue actually have the goods to back it up."

"I can do that?" George mouths to me.

I nod. "She's got a lot going on, that's for sure. What about me, though? I must have made some sort of impression too, or else you wouldn't be calling."

"Of course you did! While a simple man like Quentin might be impressed by parlor tricks, I myself am partial to a more sophisticated woman…a woman who has a lot going on under the surface."

"I did my Lucille Ball impression, didn't I?"

"Yup! Like I said, we don't scare easily." He laughs again and I try to remember what he looked like, but all that pops into my mind is a featureless blur and a striped blue tie. His voice is cute, though—gravelly, like he smokes two packs a day, although I doubt he does. It seems like nobody out here smokes.

"Well, that's good, I guess, because girls from Buffalo are very, very scary," I say, and George smacks me again.

"Stop it," I whisper to her. "It's working."

"Okay, then. So how about next Saturday? We'll take you out and show you the town."

George nods frantically.

"That works for us."

★ ★ ★

Just when I am about to consider putting my new skill-set to good use and apply for a job as a construction worker or, worse, contact the *San Francisco Chronicle* to see if they happen to have any openings for freelance obituarists, I get a call for an interview.

Despite our cheap rent and George's much-welcome new paycheck, things are getting a little tight. This city is plenty more expensive than Buffalo (our daily lattes cost twice what they did at home, and even the homeless people flip you off if you proffer anything less than a five). George and I are also both quite possibly on the verge of scurvy—weeks of two-for-one pizza and onion bagels from Starbucks have left us soft and slightly disoriented. Scary, yes. I know. But I don't want to call my dad and tell him we've burned through his first check in less than two months, when I'd been hoping it would last us three. So landing this job is important—our health *and* our pride depends on it.

I fluff my hair, do a quick breath check and push the buzzer. A little brass plaque next to the door reads ENCYCLO-PEDIA GIGANTICA. The hallway is dark and dingy; the neighborhood, not so hot. My heart sank with disappointment when I saw the building, one of those late-sixties architectural missteps that resembles rusty turquoise graph paper from the outside and feels like a rabbit's warren on the inside.

"Who is it?" a voice crackles through the intercom.

"Holly Hastings. I have an 11:15 interview."

More crackling.

"Okay. Hold on."

Encyclopedia Gigantica? Sounds vaguely pornographic… Come to think of it, the directory in the lobby seemed to have more than its share of "So-and-So Productions" and that top-heavy platinum blonde outside sure did look a little sketchy….

The door opens slowly, and the receptionist who welcomes me inside sets my mind at ease immediately; if *she* were in the adult film business, then the objectification of the fairer sex on celluloid has become more of an equal-opportunity venture than I had realized. Kitty, as she introduces herself, though friendly, is eighty if she's a day, and not much to look at, with horn-rimmed glasses and a nearly hairless, liver-spotted head and a neck that sticks out from her shoulders at nearly a right angle.

"Nice shoes," she says as she leads me into the empty waiting area. "My daughter will be with you shortly."

A family business. How nice.

Three minutes later Kitty reappears in the doorway. "Holly Hastings?"

"Yes?" I say, when it appears she's genuinely wondering who I am.

She curls a gnarled finger at me. "This way."

I follow her down the hallway into a small office, where a pleasant-looking woman in her late forties stands up to shake my hand.

"Hi! I'm Cinda Jarvis."

"Holly Hastings. Nice to meet you."

"Thanks, Mom, that'll be all," she says as she shoos Kitty out and closes the door behind her. "Please, Holly, sit down! Shall we begin?"

Half an hour later, I am back outside, gainfully employed as the proofreader for "a thrilling new line of hardback educational compendiums for nine- to thirteen-year-olds," as my new boss put it so happily, adding, "Trimmed in faux gold leaf!"

I already have the vague sense that the Encyclopedias Gigantica are probably not going to be quite the thrill Cinda Jarvis thinks they are, but they're her dream, and her enthusiasm was heartening. From what I could tell from our interview, she'd quit her job as a schoolteacher and bet the farm on this venture, which all depended on a publisher and national distributor picking up the line and marketing it door-to-door one day. First, though, she needed a product to sell, and that was where I came in—to verify, fact-check and proofread the prototypes she was writing. Two volumes, *A* and *Z*.

I call George at work to tell her the news, which I suppose is good. She confirms exactly what I'd been thinking.

"It can't be worse than writing obituaries or putting up drywall."

"I know. But it's the kind of work that's going to make it hard to write at night, not that I've been doing that, anyway, but still. Proofing gives me a serious headache. I used to do it at the *Bugle* sometimes…."

"Which is why you got the job! Because they could tell you're going to be great at it! You have the experience, the discipline, the—"

"George," I interrupt. "I don't need a pep talk. I know I can do this. It's just going to be so *boring*. And it's a contract position, which means no health insurance."

"Boring isn't necessarily bad. Boring's the new not broke! And if you need a therapist, just call Dr. Ben and Dr. Jerry."

I giggle. "But I didn't tell you the worst of it."

"What?"

"It smelled like tuna fish there. It was kind of a gross place."

"It smells like lilacs and jasmine here," she says dreamily. "Chloe says that fresh-cut flowers increase employee productivity. And even if they don't, they sure are nice to have around, aren't they? She comes in with big bunches of them every Monday and replaces them even before they start to wilt."

"That's very helpful, George. Thank you."

"Sorry," she laughs. Her boss sounds like an amazing person, and I've heard quite a bit of "Chloe says this" and "Chloe says that" since George started there.

I suppose the tables have turned.

While I'd spent years honing my skills in the antiseptic but largely inoffensive environment of the *Bugle,* George had been paying her dues ringing up Isaac Asimov books in a musty turn-of-the-century shop with rodents scrambling behind the walls. She's a talented and thoughtful writer, and I know she's going to make a great editor. At last, someone she respects—someone she can learn something from—has taken her under her wing. To say that I was really, truly happy for her would be an understatement. She deserves it more than anyone I know.

Yet, once again, here I am complaining to her about the faint odor of failure in my life.

"You're right, G. I'm going to make the best of it."

"Of course you are," she says. "And you can keep looking for something better. But in the meantime, you'll have a nice, steady paycheck. And we could use the money, honey!"

"The money's not so good. Less than I was making at the *Bugle…*"

"It's okay! My salary's pretty respectable, if I do say so myself, and besides—we're DINKs now! We'll shop till we drop!"

"DINKs?"

"Double Income, No Kids!"

"Oh my God, George—you're a yuppie! I never thought I'd see the day when you were excited to go shopping."

"I know! There were pigs flying by our window this morning!"

"I guess I must have missed that…."

"Sorry, Holly—I gotta go. Chloe needs me!"

chapter 15

First Dates and Second Honeymoons

The three stacks of laser copy sitting on my desk are each about six inches taller than the Webster's Unabridged English Dictionary right beside them.

Aardvark *(Orycteropus afer)*
Class: *Mammalia*
Order: *Tubulidentata*
Family: *Orycteropodidae*
Genus: *Orycteropus*
Species: *afer*

You really do learn something new every day.

The aardvark is a nocturnal, narrow-snouted mammalian insectivore native to sub-Saharan Africa.

Wow.

Early Dutch settlers in South Africa gave the animal its comic-sounding name, which means "earth pig."

Double wow.

Aardvarks love to eat ants and termites. They use their strong front legs to dig their prey out of their nests. Long, sticky tongues allow hungry aardvarks to consume vast amounts of insects each night, often tens of thousands at a time.

I glance at the clock on my desk. 9:15 a.m. Although Kitty's station is around the corner and down the hall from my office, I can hear her snoring.

Though similar to South American anteaters and Australian bandicoots, aardvarks are in fact distinct from those animals, mostly due to their unusual dentition.

We'll see about that. I click to connect to the Internet….
And click again…
And again…
I pick up the phone and dial Cinda's extension.
"Hello?"
"Hi, it's Holly."
"Holly! You settling in okay? Did my mother show you where the coffee machine is?"
"Yes, she did. Thank you."
"We also have tea. Earl Grey, I believe."
"I know. Thanks."
"If you prefer something else, like Orange Pekoe or Darjeeling, just let her know and she can pop over to the Safeway and fetch some."

"No, Earl Grey is fine."

"Oh—and did you notice I put a nice fresh box of red pens in your drawer? I figure you'll be going through a lot of them!"

"Yeah, I saw those. Thanks. Actually, what I wanted to ask you was—"

"And there's a new package of Post-its in there, too. The medium-size ones. I know they're handy to have around in case you want to remind yourself of something, like when you need to check something later. Or you can write *me* a quick little note and stick it right there on the copy, in case you want to point something out to *me.* That way, later on, when I go through the changes you've made and input them onto my master copy…"

Is she actually trying to explain how Post-its work? "I know, Cinda. Thanks. But, um, the reason I'm calling is that I seem to be having trouble getting online. The connection isn't working."

"Oh! Well, I suppose that's because I'm on now. I'm *obsessed* with online Boggle! I can't get enough of it!"

"Oh. So, you mean I don't have my own connection?"

"No, silly! We all *share* a line. What they charge for just one is a crime, don't you think? Plus there was the extra phone line I had to spring for, so I decided this would be best."

"Uh, okay. So how should I…check things, then?"

"Well, there's the dictionary."

"Yes, but for fact-checking I naturally assumed I would have access…"

"Hmmm. Since it's just the three of us here, and my mother's not quite up to speed yet with this whole Internet thing, you and I could just work out some sort of system when you need to use it. Mind you, it's probably best you don't get too dependent on it anyway, since it's dial-up service. I understand that means it's very slow. But I'm used to it, so I don't mind!"

Dial-up? What's next—a teletype machine? I pull open my desk drawer and check to make sure the red pens don't require ink cartridges.

"Also, there's a Public Library not too far from here," she continues. "Do you have a MUNI pass? The 44 stops just outside and it'll take you right there."

"Oh."

Cinda must sense my disappointment (which I'm not trying too hard to hide) so she begins extolling the virtues of simpler times.

"Since this whole Internet thing started, I feel libraries are horribly underused, don't you?"

"I guess so."

"It's a modern tragedy," she sighs. "But you'll see—the kids will come back to them one day. In the meantime, it's a great time for encyclopedias!"

I suspect she's unaware that there is more to the Internet than online Boggle. "So you're saying I can work at the library?"

"Well, the membership is free and it's a nice bright space, so I think it would be just fine if you needed to do that from time to time. That's where I do most of my research, too. Oh, wait a second, now—there might be a charge to laminate the card when you join. But I'll tell you what—you just bring me a receipt and I'll reimburse you!" she offers brightly.

Working on my own there could definitely have its advantages. "Okay. Thanks, Cinda."

I hang up and flip through to the last page of the first stack of copy.

Adler, Alfred (1870–1937). *In the annals of psychology, Alfred Adler was a giant. His ground-breaking work alongside Sigmund Freud marked him as one of the founding fathers of psychoanalysis, although he later broke from Freud and put forth his own school*

of individual psychology. His most important contributions to the field were his theories on dream analysis, archetypes and synchronicity.
Adler was born in 1870 in Venice to a successful grain merchant…

Oh my God. Not only was she confusing Adler's contributions with Jung's, but if I remember my *Lives of the Shrinks* correctly, the guy was from Vienna, not Venice. This was going to take months. Years, maybe.

All of a sudden, I miss Sandeep terribly. My old Ayurvedic mental health practitioner is just the person I need to inspire me. The value of extreme monotony was one of his favorite refrains; indeed, his entire program of meditation, chanting, diet and yoga revolved around it.

I scour my brain for my Calming and Focusing mantra….
Umbumbum? Bumbledybum? Umbalabumbum? That was it! Umbalabumbum… Umbalabumbum… Umbalabumbum…Umbalabumbum…

Around lunchtime, my phone rings.

"Hello?"

"Hi, Holly. I'm off the Internet, if you need it."

"Okay. Thanks."

An hour and a half later, after six grueling reboots and countless minutes spent watching aardvark pictures upload onto a twelve-inch monitor that possibly dates back to the Reagan years, I have finally confirmed that the toothsome earth pig does indeed have unusual dentition.

"It's official!" I scribble on a Post-it. *"This job sucks."*

I peel it off the pad and stick it to the last page of the third stack of copy, right next to the final line:

Alas, the Spanish conquistadors carried with them more than just a devastating smallpox epidemic—their greed for gold had all but destroyed the mighty Aztec civilization by the early 1500s.

Then I say a silent prayer, hoping never to see that Post-it again.

George and I decide it would be best if we meet Quentin and Vale somewhere nice and public, just in case they're deranged psychos. Vale half-jokingly suggests Fisherman's Wharf—he knows we've been in San Francisco for more than two months and haven't actually managed to get down there yet (mostly because Remy ranted and raved about how locals never go there). At first we were reluctant to admit that we wanted to go, but our mysterious suitors promised they would protect us from the crowds of nasty tourists.

We meet at Pier 39, out by the sea lions. As soon as I see our dates, I realize of course that I do remember them. Vale is wearing a navy blue peacoat and jeans that look like they've been ironed, but he's cuteish in a preppy sort of way—clean-shaven, short dark hair, collared shirt. He reminds me a bit of a young Warren Beatty (or, since I've never actually seen Warren Beatty in anything besides *Dick Tracy,* what I imagine he must have looked like in his younger and hotter days).

George gives Quentin the once-over and partially relaxes. Her guy is almost bordering on handsome, with a straight, narrow nose; a strong, square jaw and dark blond hair just long enough to suggest he probably doesn't have an office job.

After the usual awkward fifteen-minute getting-to-know-you conversation, during which we learn absolutely nothing about each other (though it's mercifully eased by the fact that there are four of us), we begin to walk.

"So, what do you guys have planned for us today?" I ask. "Something good, I hope."

Vale takes four tickets out of his pockets and flashes them at us. "There's nothing like Alcatraz in the springtime!"

"Great!" George says.

"It was my idea," Quentin says and takes a tentative step toward her. "But it can get wicked cold and windy on the boat out… We might have to use bahdy heat to keep wahm."

George quickly retreats. "Or…we could just sit inside."

Vale shakes his head and laughs.

"But then we wouldn't get to see the sea lions!" Quentin says. "They fahllow the boat."

"We'll take our chances," I say. "Maybe on the way back."

"Awesome!" Quentin turns to give a high-five to Vale, who reluctantly accepts.

"Don't mind him," Vale tells us. "He just really likes sea lions."

"I'm sure," George says. I can tell by her reluctance to make eye contact with me that she isn't quite sure yet about this Quentin character, and neither am I. His looks are in the plus column, but the Boston drawl is over-the-top and the jury is still out on his personality.

As we walk around, I try to get as much background information as I can without being impolite.

"So how do you guys know each other?"

"He's my brother-in-law," Vale says.

"Oh. So which one of you's married?" George asks, her eyes narrowing.

They laugh.

"Neither of us," Quentin says. "Our sisters are married."

"Legally, now, too!" Vale adds.

George perks up immediately. "Hey! My mothers are married!"

"Oh yeah?"

"Yup," she says proudly.

Vale nods his approval. "Second generation—that carries a lot of weight in this city, you know."

"Really?"

"Well, I guess it sort of depends on what circles you run in, but generally, yeah. It's pretty cool."

"Hmmm." George has never considered herself cool for any reason, least of all because she is, as she puts it, "Sapphic progeny." "I'm the only person I know whose parents are both gay, I think…. Holly and I know one guy back home whose dad came out, but that was, like, after he'd already been married for twenty years."

"My sistah has a friend who's third-generation lesbian," Quentin says. "It's like some sort of dyke dynasty over there or something."

Vale nods. "They're virtually royalty in the Castro."

We walk a few blocks west, over to the heart of the action. It's the first really nice Saturday of spring and the Wharf is thrumming with tourists and buskers and street vendors.

"Mmmm… What smells so good?" George asks.

"Bread baking, I think," Quentin says, glad for an excuse to talk to her. "We have time for a quick bite, if you like."

"Sounds good to me."

"Me, too! Come on…" Vale leads us through the long lineups of people ordering chowder and fried seafood at various concessions. "The best place is this way."

Despite the crowds and midday heat, we manage to snag a table with an umbrella just off the street. Vale and Quentin go off and return a few minutes later with four giant bread bowls full of soup, four lemonades and a huge box of fried shrimp.

"You eat the bowl?" George marvels.

"Yeah, but the soup's the best paht," Quentin instructs her. "And I'm from Bahston, so I know good chowdah!"

"Is he for real with that?" I ask Vale as discreetly as I can.

"Yeah," he whispers back. "His family moved here when he was ten. But he plays up the accent around girls. Don't ask me why."

George tears off a big chunk of her bowl and tastes it. "Sourdough!"

Quentin's eyes widen. He's clearly taking some sort of carnal pleasure in her appetite.

"George never met a carbohydrate she didn't like," I explain.

"Yeah, well when was the last time *you* ate a vegetable, Holly? And Caesar salad doesn't count."

"Do potato chips count?"

"No!"

"Tortilla chips?"

"No!"

"Popcorn? Come on—you gotta give me that one!"

"As you can tell, Holly has never met a partially hydrogenated snack food she didn't like," George says to the guys. "At least I *try* and eat a balanced diet."

"Well, whatevah you're doing, it's working!" Quentin drawls while he leans back in his chair, straining to get a glimpse of George's rump.

"I'm sitting on it. You'll have to wait till I get up if you want a good look."

"I'm looking forward to it," he answers with a grin.

She rolls her eyes as dramatically as she can, but I can tell she's flattered. And she definitely feels comfortable enough with the compliment to reach over for another shrimp.

Vale nudges me. "Is it just me or do I hear the pitter-patter of little feet?"

"Could be…they've definitely got some sort of weird chemistry happening."

George flushes bright pink and shoots me an I'll-kill-you-later look.

"Huh?" Quentin says.

"Never mind," I say. "Isn't the boat leaving soon?"

Vale checks his watch (which I can't help but notice is a Rolex). "Shit! We better go!"

The Alcatraz tour was excruciatingly long, so when we finally return four hours later, we are all hungry again. Vale suggests a great place he knows in North Beach "with pasta to die for." The owner is an old friend of his from high school and she sends us over cannoli and tiramisu for dessert. Everything is wonderful, of course, and even after spending the entire day together, we all still have plenty to talk about.

Afterwards, we stroll around the neighbourhood until dark. Just as the crumbling bookstores close for the night, the bars are opening, and music and laughter spill out onto the streets. Vale reaches for my hand as we walk down Grant Avenue to Green, where we stop in for a cappuccino at an offbeat little café. It's no Mulberry Street, but San Francisco's Little Italy definitely has its charms.

While Quentin and George debate whether or not *the* Al Capone had ever really taken a shit in the toilet we've seen in his cell, Vale and I talk about our jobs and families and friends. Okay, so maybe it's him doing all of the talking, but I'm definitely interested. On our way back to the car, he redeems himself by paying me one of the nicest compliments I've ever received: "Holly," he says, "I think you have the most soulful eyes I've ever seen."

If you're trying to woo a skinny white girl from Buffalo, telling her she has soulful eyes is like shooting fish in a barrel. I'm sure Vale Spencer knows that, but it's nice to hear anyway…especially since sex isn't on the menu, and I'm sure he knows that, too.

Since the guys definitely aren't psychos, we gladly accept a lift home. Before they drop us off, we make plans to see each other again the following weekend—separately, this time—after Vale returns from a business trip to Chicago. We do the kiss-on-the-cheek thing (double dates are not the right forum for anything involving open mouths) and wave goodbye as they drive off.

"Well, that was easy," she exhales, evidently surprised that things had gone so well. I'm pretty shocked, too. Both Quentin and Vale are excellent prospects for the future, just as we'd hoped.

"I know!"

"Maybe a little too easy…"

"Don't be so pessimistic."

"You're right, you're right," she says. "I'm sorry. They *did* seem okay, didn't they?"

"I think so."

"And cute!"

"I know! And they're…" Dare I say it?

"Rich!" George squeals and begins jumping up and down.

"Oh my God, they are, aren't they?"

She nods. "Let's walk around the block, 'kay? I can't go in yet—I need to deconstruct."

"Okay. So did Quentin tell you what he does? I didn't hear him mention it."

"Actually, he's a…what did he call it?…an adventure capitalist? Something like that."

"A *venture* capitalist? No way! That's good, George. Really good! That means he goes around investing his money making *more* money! I wonder how he ended up doing that?"

"Oh, I know—he told me! He used to be a gardener at some big company's head office and he got all these stock options and sold them at just the right moment."

"You're kidding. What company?"

"I don't remember."

"It hardly matters."

"Well, his car sure was nice," she says. "Small backseat, though."

"Oh, yeah," I agree. "Jaguar convertibles suck when it comes to leg room!"

She giggles. "Good thing my legs are short."

"He's *perfect* for you!"

We shriek and jump around again, until a strange look crosses George's face.

"Hold on, Holly. Let's get real for a second, here. I wouldn't say Quentin is *perfect*. He's a bit of an idiot, to tell you the truth. Your guy's better. He's got personality."

"Naw, ya think?"

"Could be…"

Vale does seem to have it all—he isn't hard to look at (by the end of the night, I'd decided he's definitely cute enough to be attracted to), nice (he offered to rub my ankle after I twisted it on a prison sewer grate) and wealthy (a bankruptcy lawyer with an Ivy League degree—"the only kind of lawyer to be, these days!" he'd joked).

Every instinct I have is screaming this is all way too good to be true. Come to think of it, the entire date seemed, well, choreographed, like they'd done it a thousand times before. And Vale was smooth. There's no doubt about it. But is that a reason not to trust him?

Though all the research firmly supports my Two-Thirds Theory of millionaire dating—hold out for looks, personality *and* bank account, and you might as well throw in the towel—perhaps Vale is one of the rare exceptions. Hard to say for sure, but I'm willing to stick around long enough to find out. My instincts are notoriously off when it comes to men, anyway, so maybe I'm wrong and he *isn't* too good to be true!

"Vale seems pretty well-rounded, I'll give you that. But Quentin might be one of those diamonds in the rough. Get past the boorish exterior and I bet you'll find he's a total pussycat. A real sweetheart."

"Really?"

"Sure."

"Well, he does seem to like me."

"A very important quality in a boyfriend."

"I've never had a normal boyfriend," she sighs. "It would be so great… They *are* boyfriend material, aren't they Holly?"

"Yes, George."

"Because they obviously weren't only after…you know… or else they would have just taken us out and gotten us drunk somewhere, right?"

"Right…although maybe that wouldn't have been so bad!"

By the time George stops laughing, we're back in front of our house.

"We should have moved here years ago, Holly. I love it. I'm *loving* this. All of it!"

"Well, our apartment does rock," I say.

"I've never felt so much like a real person before. It's so…*exciting*."

"What do you mean? You were a real person back in Buffalo."

"I know, but I feel like I'm actually contributing something out here."

"Your job *is* pretty amazing…."

"Yeah, but not only that. I feel like a real *Cosmo* girl." She twirls around so that her skirt flies out.

"Hey—I've been telling you you're fabulous for years. You should have listened to me."

"I even lost six pounds!"

"Really?"

"Yeah!"

"How do you know? We don't have a scale."

"I put a quarter into one of those machines. There was

one in the bathroom at the Pier today. And that's with clothes on and *after* I ate that huge chowder thing!"

"That's amazing, G!"

Just as we're about to go inside, Remy steps out onto the porch with a garbage bag. When he sees us, a huge grin spreads across his face.

"You look like the cat that ate the canary," he says to me.

"Maybe I did."

"Ah! So tell me—what have my two favorite little gold-digging hussies been up to all day? Staking out the Yacht Club? Slinking around the men's section at Neiman Marcus?"

George gives him the finger. "You coming?" she asks me.

"In a sec."

"Suit yourself." She shrugs and goes inside.

"That wasn't very nice, you know," I tell him.

"I know, I know. My bad. But I can't help it—you guys are just so teasable."

"I'm glad you're enjoying it."

He puts the bag down and begins picking up dried leaves off the porch. "I called before to see if you wanted to come up for dinner, but you weren't home."

"Not that it's any of your business, but we were on a date."

"That's nice."

"With two *really* great guys."

"You don't say."

"Yup."

I can't think of anything else to add, so I head for our door.

"Haven't seen too much of you lately," he calls out after me.

"Now that I have a real job, I suppose you're missing me terribly."

"It is a bit lonely. I'll admit it. But without you around to distract me, I've been getting a lot done. It's only been a week and I've already finished the mantel."

I stop in my tracks. "Really?" Remy had been particularly

worried about the mantel, since the woodwork was original to the house and had to be very carefully removed when the fireplace guys came to fix the masonry and reline it.

"Everything's back up and it looks great. You wanna come in and see?"

I hesitate. George is waiting and we still have so much to talk about. "Uh, no, I don't think so. Not tonight."

"Tomorrow, maybe?"

"Maybe."

Truthfully, I'm planning to wait by the phone for Vale to call. Is there any better way to spend a Sunday than basking in the afterglow of a wonderful date?

"I'll be around if you change your mind," he says and heads back inside.

"I'm really beginning not to like that guy," George says after I've closed the door behind me. "His attitude is completely offensive."

"Oh, he's not so bad. All that stuff is just an act."

"Yeah, well, I'm not impressed. And you shouldn't be either."

"Remy's just lonely, I think."

To: hollyhastings@hotmail.com
From: lustylou2@yahoo.com
Subject: Guess what?
Dear Holly,
I am having a lot of fun in Miami. We are staying in South Beach at a not that bad hotel just off Ocean Avenue. Deb found a cockroach in her bed but we are very happy to be here. Thankfully it was dead. Everyone here is very beautiful and all the buildings look like ice cream.

The manager at the Seaquarium granted me a private audience with Flipper. The only problem was that I found the aquarium to be a little filthy. I made a donation and now I feel better. I also have an autographed picture that I will frame. I also suppose that seeing this dolphin in person makes me realize that he is just a dolphin. But I am just a woman, so there! We are the same.

Also just to tell you that your father was waiting for me at the hotel. He had a dozen roses that he paid too much for, but this is a very expensive area and all the flower shops are run by fancy men who overcharge. Your father bought Deb a plane ticket home and a ticket for her car on the train. She has to go back to work on Tuesday and Uncle Herbie needs her, but I have decided to retire. As you know personally, your father is now very loose with money and I have decided that this is okay because what are we waiting for, anyway? So we bought a Winnebago. The one we got is called a Minnie Winnie. It has air conditioning, a kitchen with a convection oven and all kinds of luxuries. I refused to buy used since you never know who was there before you with the toilet. By the way the toilet uses special chemicals. It's like a second honeymoon.

There is a TV collectibles show in Baton Rouge which is in Louisiana on April 17 then one in Little Rock which is in Arkansas in the beginning of May. Deb is shipping part of my collection to me when she gets home. There is a very big market for this sort of thing in the South and your father agrees that if we want to get serious we should start with other shows too like *Gilligan's Island* and *Green Acres*. Maybe we will do crime shows too like *Mission: Impossible* and *Get Smart* because your father likes those. One day these things will be worth a lot of money and then they will be for you and your brothers, but maybe not Bradley. Olivia says he is doing very well for himself now in Detroit with his store but nobody tells me anything.

Love, Mom

To: lustylou2@yahoo.com
From: hollyhastings@hotmail.com
Subject: re: Guess what?
Call me! Call me! Call me!

I hear nothing from either of them for three weeks, and now this? I grab the phone and dial my parents' house. (Why neither of them has a cell phone is beyond me, especially now that my mom is so technically active.)

"Mom! Dad! It's me! I just got your e-mail, and I want you to call me as soon as you get this message! I am *soooo* happy and so relieved and so excited about all this…so, uh, call me, okay? Bye!"

I hang up and immediately call Cole.

"Cole?"

"Hey, Holly. Whazzup?"

"Did you hear from Mom and Dad?"

"Yeah."

"So?"

"So what?"

"Tell me!"

"They've gone crazy. Big surprise."

"It's not crazy, it's great! My faith in marriage is restored! All is right with the world again! Mom loves Dad and Dad loves Mom!"

"I guess," he snorts.

"Oh, for heaven's sake, put Olivia on!"

"'Livia! Take the phone!"

My sister-in-law is far more excited about the whole thing.

"Isn't it romantic?" she gushes.

"Totally!"

"I gotta tell ya, I did *not* think your old man had it in him. He just woke up one day and said, 'Kids—I'm taking a trip. I'm going to get her. Make sure you check the house every two days and don't let the mail pile up.' So I called Uncle Herbie to ask him if Deb left the name of the hotel where they were staying and Larry flew out that afternoon."

"When was this?"

"Last Thursday."

"And nobody told me?!"

"Your dad wanted to keep it quiet in case things didn't work out. I bet it's just about the craziest, most impulsive thing the guy has ever done in his life."

"Olivia—he hasn't even been out-of-state since the '80s!"

"Wow. You know, you had a lot to do with this, sweetie."

"Me? How?"

"You inspired him! I'm sure of it! People around here tend to forget they actually do have some control over their destinies."

"He just loves her, and he didn't want to lose her."

"Yeah. And I suppose when your wife leaves you for a fish, it's a real wake-up call."

"Flipper's a marine mammal," I correct her.

"Whatever he is, I'm just glad he was no match for your dad."

Isn't is funny how when you're the one who's gone, you kind of expect everything to stay the same at home? Especially if the reason you left in the first place was because it felt like nothing was ever happening there. But life goes on, I suppose. Things change. Even in Buffalo.

chapter 16

One Hump or Two?

I have an hour to kill before Vale picks me up for George's big book-launch party. It's her first major event and she begged us to come, just in case nobody showed up and the promising young author was left, humiliated, to read to an audience of carefully arranged chairs.

"There'll be free food and drinks…" George promised when she sensed my reluctance.

I am more than a little bit envious of any up-and-coming writer who isn't, well, me. A fabulous book launch in a trendy new club attended by all sorts of critics and authors and publishing professionals might only reinforce my burgeoning feelings of inadequacy and compound my writer's block even further. On the other hand, maybe it will spur me to action, which is why I agreed to go.

Yes, my book—if you can call it that—is an absolute mess. I have three jumbled notebooks overflowing with disjointed ideas; a huge collection of pithy quotes from imaginary husband-hunters (last names changed to protect their "anonymity"); and an appendix featuring a state-by-state directory of relevant specialty dating services, although the accompanying list of online matchmakers promising financially fruitful unions will probably be out-of-date by the time I finish the first chapter, anyway. The only main text that is even remotely first-draft quality is half a chapter entitled *"Shake Your Moneymakers,"* a guide to making your assets work for you (everyone loves a makeover!).

Instead of writing while I wait for Vale, which is what I should do, I call Remy to see if he wants to come downstairs. We really haven't seen much of him in the past month or so, since things have been going so well with Vale and Quentin. Truth be told, the man's life is an absolute mystery to me. He doesn't seem to have many friends, I've never known his family to visit and he spends all his time hunting down mysterious things like antique ceiling tin and cast-iron finials. The one and only time I opened a dialogue on the subject and asked him if he was lonely without George and me around anymore, he decided to raise our rent by $150. It was part of our original deal, but still—just when I start to feel bad for the guy, he always goes and does something annoying.

Remy comes in without knocking, of course, grabs a bag of pretzels out of the pantry and a beer out of the fridge, then makes himself comfortable on the couch.

"Do you mind at least taking your shoes off?"

"It's my house."

"Well, I pay rent here so it's *my* couch and *my* apartment," I say, and push his feet down.

"Semantics. So how's work?"

"All right. Boring as hell, actually."

"Monotony can be cathartic…." He taps his temple. "Especially for people with mental problems."

"Thanks, Remy. That's a super thing to say."

"I just mean that sort of boring, repetitious work has its advantages. Like manual labor. It can purge your pain."

"Like when I read *Ulysses*. I thought I was going to die, but when I finally got through it I felt like I'd climbed Mount Everest. Nobody can ever take it away from me."

He laughs. "I thought you went to community college."

"I did, you snob. They do teach James Joyce at schools other than Stanford, you know."

"Yeah, but did you understand it?"

"Enough to know that that's virtually impossible. And that I didn't want to read *The Odyssey.*"

"Fair enough. So, this job of yours—is it a permanent thing?"

"More of a temp job, I guess. I'm on contract right now, which means no benefits, of course."

"That sucks. Why'd they do that?"

"I just have two volumes to proof…then if a buyer likes the prototypes and picks up the line, I'll get hired full-time, along with a whole team of in-house copy editors and fact-checkers and freelance writers. Right now, it's just me and the boss, and she's writing the bloody things herself."

"What? She's writing a whole set of encyclopedias?"

"Just *A* and *Z* for now."

"Still, they're like thousands of pages each."

"I know—it'll take me months just to get through the first volume."

"But only one writer? It seems a little one-sided, don't you think?"

"Budget constraints. What can you do?"

Encyclopedia Gigantica is definitely a labor of love for Cinda Jarvis. She hired me right around the time she finished Volume A, four years after she started it, working nights and weekends. By the time she finishes Z—which she figures will take her another six or seven months, full-time—the idea is that I'll be all caught up with the proofing and doing the pages as she finishes them.

"It's ridiculous."

"I know. I looked up her main competition, *World Book,* and—"

"I loved those! My parents got me a set for my tenth birthday! They were trimmed in gold and every year I got an annual update…."

"Why, you're just a big nerd in stud's clothing, aren't you?"

He raises his eyebrows and gives me a wide grin. "So…I'm a stud, huh?!"

"And a legend in your own mind… Anyway, World Book has something like four thousand writers, experts in every field, contributing exhaustively researched articles, so of course it's absurd to try and write one yourself, but what am I supposed to do? Tell my boss she's insane? I need the job."

"You could help. Offer to write Z."

"I have my own book to write."

"Ah yes. The Great American Romance. And how's that been going?"

"Don't ask!"

"I just did."

Remy stops stuffing pretzels into his face and waits for me to answer. Annoying though he is, he really does seem to care. Since I know a guy like him could never be attracted to a plain Jane like me, I can only assume that he isn't interested in getting me into bed, which in turn is proof of his sincerity. I miss his friendship, I realize. And I've been neglecting him.

"Sorry," I say. "Slowly. It's going very slowly."

"Why don't you just write a proposal first? I don't think

publishers expect to see a complete manuscript when you're trying to sell non-fiction."

"Really?" Why didn't I think of that? A proposal is a brilliant idea!

"I'm pretty sure, yeah."

"Wait a second… How do *you* know so much about publishing?"

"My wife wrote two books."

I practically choke on my gum. "You're *married?* I can't believe you never told me, you ass! So tell me… Where is the lucky Mrs. Wakefield?"

"Not so lucky, actually."

"Oh?"

"God, I have to stop doing that," he mumbles to himself. "I'm sorry, Holly. My *late* wife. I meant my late wife."

Remy's a widower?

It's probably the last thing in the entire world I expected him to say.

"You can't be a widower—you're too young! Aren't you? I mean…how old are you?"

He looks up at me quizzically.

Shit. "I'm sorry… Obviously, there's no age limit for, uh, that sort of thing…." I fumble. "I don't know what to say… I mean, I'm sorry. Obviously I'm very sorry. God, Remy. I really don't know what to say. I was, uh, born with my foot in my mouth."

"Don't get yourself in a snit, Holly. It's fine. Most people just say 'I'm sorry,' or 'My God! What a tragedy!' or something like that."

"I'm *really* sorry, Remy."

"Don't worry about it."

"I never know what to say at times like these."

"Neither do I," he smiles.

I smile back. What else could I do?

Vale is already on his way to pick me up, but I don't really feel much like going to a party anymore. "Do you want me to stay here with you?"

"It's okay, Holly! Thanks, but I'm okay. It was five years ago. I'm over it."

"Really?"

"Well, no, I'm not *over* it, over it. But I've accepted it. I'm moving on."

"Do you mind if I ask…"

"How she died?"

I nod, painfully uncomfortable, yet unable to contain my curiosity.

"Breast cancer. It ran in her family. Her mother and two of her great-aunts died of it."

"How awful."

"She had it when I married her. We knew she didn't have long."

"Wow," I say quietly. "You must have really loved her."

"Yeah…" He laughs nervously, uncomfortable himself now. "Don't get the wrong idea, though. I'm no saint. And neither was she. *She?* What's the matter with me? I mean, Sylvia. Her name was Sylvia."

"Why didn't you tell me, Remy? I suppose it's not really my business, but…"

"But you're my friend. We're friends, and…" He shrugs. "I hate telling people. Because of this. This *weirdness* afterward. I hate it."

"I can definitely understand that."

"I don't want you to feel bad for me."

"I don't," I lie.

"Good, because most people treat me like a baby for a while after they hear. It's like, I'm a widower, not a leper, you know?"

"Of course."

"Okay!" he cracks his knuckles and gets up to leave.

"Why don't you stay for a bit?"

"Naw. Your sugar daddy's coming and I wouldn't want to hold you two lovebirds up. Have a good time tonight!"

"You sure?"

"Yup. I'm taking the pretzels, though."

"I figured you would."

He's halfway to the door when he turns around. "Oh—I almost forgot!"

"What?"

"I'm thirty-four."

"That's it? You look almost old enough to be my father."

"Old enough to be your big brother, maybe," he winks.

"Get out of here!"

George's book launch is painful, though she's never looked better, glowing with excitement and showing off her ten-pound weight loss with a sexy new outfit. After what seems like an eternity, she introduces the writer, who obliges us with a short reading from her novel, *Surrogate Moon*. From what I can tell, it's about a race of sterile humanoids on some distant planet who, too smart for their own good, devise a way for their females to mate with carnivorous plants.

I sit between Quentin and Vale. Vale keeps nodding off, and Quentin snickers loudly when the writer finally comes to the end of a violent five-minute passage describing the pod-babies' first attempt at breast-feeding. A few rows in front of us, George is on the edge of her seat, utterly enthralled. I try to pay attention, I really do, but my mind keeps drifting back to Sylvia. I wonder what she looked like, if she was smart, if she suffered. It occurs to me that I hadn't even asked Remy what kind of books she wrote. How could I have been so rude?

As promised, cocktails and hors d'oeuvres follow the reading. I eat and drink as much as I can, while Vale and Quentin try not to look bored out of their skulls. The crowd of ex-cited well-wishers around the writer do inspire enough envy in me to take Remy's advice—I vow to write a partial man-uscript and an outline of my research, along with a kick-ass query letter, and send it off to every publisher I can find that might possibly be interested.

A couple weeks after the reading, Vale calls from work to tell me his business trip scheduled for the weekend has been cancelled. He invites me over to his place for "dinner and whatever."

It's going to be The Night.

It probably would have happened sooner, if Vale wasn't always away in L.A. or Chicago or San Diego, or if he didn't work such ridiculously long hours. (I've accepted that dat-ing someone successful requires certain sacrifices on my part, especially while he's in his prime income-earning years.) What this all boils down to, practically speaking, is that we've been seeing each other for about five weeks and have done most of our courting over the phone. Aside from our first kiss—which I secretly suspected he'd penciled in, and which happened in the car he'd hired to take him to the airport then deliver me back home—the only time we'd even fooled around was one night at his place, but things didn't get too heavy because he had to be at work by five the next morn-ing, when business opens on the East Coast.

Despite his physical unavailability, Vale is really good at calling. Once, when he was in L.A., we got drunk together and had phone sex (my first time, but I got the sense he'd done it before). Usually, though, our conversations are much more mundane. At the end of each day, he likes to tell me exactly what he's done—almost a minute-by-minute play-by-play. Ninety-seven percent of the time I have no idea what he's even talking about, but it seems to be something he needs to do. At the end of these conversations, he politely asks about my day, and so I recap what I learned about absinthe or acetaminophen or whatever. Not that I'm complaining, because it certainly helps me fall asleep.

Anyway, all this is to say I'm ready. Since tomorrow also happens to be my birthday—May 10, the same day as Sid Vicious *and* Bono—I take a good chunk of my paycheck for the week and go out and buy some really sexy lingerie at La Perla, which specializes in small but wealthy chests in need of professional help. I consider the $110 Classic Push-Up Bra in black lace (and $75 matching thong) an investment in our relationship. Damn if I'm not going to make *my* assets work for *me.*

While Vale reheats the dinner his caterer had prepared for us that afternoon, he cracks open a bottle of Château Something that is way too good for somebody with my unrefined palate to be drinking. We make it about halfway through the first course—stuffed dates with goat cheese and pistachios—before we're in his bedroom, tearing off each other's clothes. Well, technically the only thing that got torn was the condom wrapper; the clothes were actually unbuttoned, folded and neatly put aside.

Before I know it, it's over.

It was…

Great!

Or rather, it was good. Solidly good!

Decent. More like decent…

Better than Jean-Jean, anyway.

Well…maybe not.

But at least it wasn't physically painful or anything. Which made it better than a trip to the dentist, though not quite as much fun as visiting the gynecologist. (At least with the gyno, you know you don't have to go back for another year and can enjoy the satisfaction of an unpleasant chore ticked off your list of things to do.)

And another thing…someone else's face kept popping into my mind at the most intimate moments. At first, I tried to push him away. What the hell was he doing there anyway? Afterwards, though, I realize that my fantasy visitor provided the only bright spots in an otherwise subpar eighty or ninety seconds. So I welcome my subconscious desires into the forefront of my mind and fall asleep thinking of plaid shirts and work boots, the smell of sawdust in my nostrils.

The light streaming in through the floor-to-ceiling windows wakes me early. I lie there for a while, trying to get my thoughts and stomach in order. The better the wine, the worse the hangover.

When I return from the bathroom, Vale is awake. I slip back into bed and snuggle up next to him.

"Happy birthday, Holly," he whispers. "Twenty-nine looks good on you."

"Thanks."

"I have something for you." He leans over me and opens the night table drawer. "And don't say 'You shouldn't have!'"

Why on earth would I say that? A girl has the right to expect a little something from her man on her birthday, doesn't she?

"Uh, okay."

He passes me a small turquoise box. Tiffany & Co. Not ring-size, but definitely jewelry.

"Wow! Thank you, Vale. But where's the card?"

He props himself up on an elbow. "Just open it, smart-ass!"

Slowly, I untie the bow and flip open the lid. Inside, on a blue velvet pillow, two diamond studs sparkle wildly. Two *large* diamond studs.

"Wow!" I say. "For me?"

"Of course, for you! I noticed the ones you always wear are pretty small and thought you might like an upgrade. Was I right?"

"Uh, yeah! Of course…"

I never thought of my earrings as small. They're the only diamonds I own, willed to me by my dad's mother, so to me they're pretty great. I'd cried tears of relief when I found the stud I thought I'd lost while packing up my apartment in Buffalo.

"Try them on for me!"

I walk over to the mirror and remove my earrings, then take the new ones out of the box.

Vale comes up behind me and kisses my neck. "They're screw-backs, so you won't lose them. And you might have to up your insurance. These puppies are three quarters of a carat each! Here, let me help you…." He pulls my hair back.

I slide the diamonds into my ears, screw on the backs and stare at myself. A skinny girl with a plain face, wearing an expensive bra and earrings that cost more than all the jewelry her mother has ever owned.

"Gorgeous," he breathes.

I turn to face him. "Thank you Vale. They're beautiful."

"I knew you'd like 'em. Happy birthday." He gives me a quick kiss, then goes to put his pants on. "I have to make a phone call to Chicago. It shouldn't take more than an hour, an hour and a half, tops…."

"But it's Sunday!"

"I know, hun. And while others are resting, I'm billing four hundred ninety-five an hour."

"Okay," I sigh.

"Why don't you take a nap? You must be tired…we didn't get much sleep!"

"Maybe…"

"Come on—it's your special day and you deserve to be lazy."

"I guess."

"That's my girl!" He smiles and pads off. I hear the door to his office close.

I put my old earrings into the Tiffany's box and slip them into my purse. "Better not forget these…"

Instead of going back to bed, I take a good, long soak in Vale's enormous bathtub—set on a raised podium next to a window with views on the Bay—and think about the night before. *Mediocre, at best.* The stuffed dates, on the other hand…now *those* were something special.

I get dressed, grab my purse and knock on the door to Vale's office. It's been over an hour, and by the look on his face when I walk in, I can tell he isn't anywhere near to being finished.

"Hang on a sec," he says into the receiver and puts whomever he was talking to on hold. "Don't tell me you're leaving, hun!"

"Yeah, sorry. I forgot I had lunch plans with George. She wants to take me out for my birthday."

He makes a pouty face.

"Will I see you this week?"

"Things are all fucked up in Chicago. Looks like I'm going to have to go out there after all. But I'll call you…."

"All right."

"Come here and give me a kiss, birthday girl…"

I go over and give him one. On the cheek.

I have no idea if George is even going to be home, so I'm delighted to find her seated at the kitchen table with a cup of tea, talking on the phone. She hangs up quickly when she sees me and comes over to give me a huge hug.

"Happy birthday!"

"Thanks."

"So how was last night? Dish! Immediately!"

I smile and sit down. "It was okay."

"Okay? Just okay? I want details! Tell me everything!"

"It was fine." She stands there, staring at me. I want to cry, but instead I ask, "So what about you and Quentin? When's that going to happen?"

"I dunno," she shrugs. "I'm not ready yet."

"Not ready? You haven't had sex in over six months! What are you waiting for?"

She exhales dramatically. "I'm not like you, Holly. I don't *need* it. I won't *die* without it. I'm like a…a sex camel. I can go for long periods without any male contact, provided I store up in advance. And the professor and I…I mean Stuart and me…we had that long weekend together right before we broke up. So I think I'm just gonna coast on that for a while. But I want to hear more about you and Vale, okay? So was it any good?"

I'm having enough trouble lying to myself about it, and I'm certainly not in the mood to be convincing someone else it was great when it hadn't been. "Let me get this straight—you're waiting with Quentin because you stocked up on nookie half a year ago? It doesn't make any sense. What's really going on?"

George's face turns bright red. "For God's sake, Holly! I don't want to talk about it!" She stomps off to her room and slams the door.

Is there trouble in paradise?

Vale has mentioned on more than one occasion that his brother-in-law is still completely smitten with her, so I naturally assumed that things were fine, though I realize I haven't heard it from the horse's mouth in quite some time. George has been working really long hours and we haven't had much of a chance to talk lately. On the weekends, she usually comes home after I've gone to bed (since my boyfriend has been off saving the insolvent masses, I've been renting a lot of movies and catching up on sleep). A few weekends ago, when we'd all gone out together—dinner and the latest John Grisham adaptation, which Vale had snorted through condescendingly—they were lovey-dovey enough, although in retrospect maybe Quentin was holding up his end a little better.

I knock on her door. "George? Can I come in?"

A faint "Yeah," followed by sniffles.

She's half buried under her giant quilt, her face turned toward the wall.

"You okay? Because I have a really good joke about you being a sex camel and it would be a shame to waste it."

"Joke?"

"I was going to ask if you were of the one-hump or two-hump kind…"

Instead of the laugh I'd been hoping for, she wails, rolls over, and begins crying again. "Two humps, Holly! That's the problem! Two humps!"

"Come on, it can't be as bad as all that."

"I'm so sorry!" she sobs. "I don't mean to be such a basket case. But I've been feeling a little…a little fragile lately."

I sit down on her bed and pull the covers back. "Why?"

"Oh, Holly. I don't know what to do and I can't take it anymore. I'm *racked* with guilt…."

"Is everything okay?"

"Yes… No… I don't know! It's just guy stuff. Do they suffer like we do? Do they?"

"Highly unlikely."

"And I've been putting off telling you because I thought you'd be upset. It was going to be so much fun, me and Quentin and you and Vale, just like we'd talked about. And now you and Vale are totally together and, well, I don't know what to do…."

"Spit it out already, will you?"

"Well… I met someone." She peeks back to catch my reaction.

"You met someone?"

"Un-huh."

"Someone not Quentin, someone?"

"Un-huh."

"Who?"

"Max."

"Max?"

"Un-huh."

"Max who?"

"Max Levine."

I wait for her to explain, but she doesn't. She just lays there with her eyes closed.

"For God's sake, George. I'm going to need a little more information."

"He's Chloe's son."

"Chloe, your boss Chloe?"

"Un-huh."

"Wow."

"I know."

"Does she know?"

"No."

"I see. So…this is bad because you think she'll be pissed?"

She nods. "That's part of it. They don't get along very well at all. What if she finds out and fires me? What if I can't find another job? What if it doesn't work out with me and Max and I throw away the best job I'll ever have in my entire life?"

"Slow down, George. First things first. Who is this guy? Does he even like you, or is this some sort of unrequited lust thing?"

"No—it's the real thing, all right. I met him at Fran's book launch. He was the cute guy with curly brown hair and glasses sitting in the second row."

"There were a lot of people there. Did you introduce us?"

"No. I only started talking to him after you guys left."

"If he doesn't get along with his mother, why was he even there?"

"His therapist suggested they do things together. It's complicated."

"Oh. So what happened? You started talking and…"

"We hit it off, like, *completely*. Then everyone was leaving so he asked me over to his place—"

"You went to some strange guy's apartment you don't know?"

"Well, I know his mother, so I figured it would be okay."

"And…"

"And we stayed up all night talking."

"And…"

"And we didn't do it that night, if that's what you're asking. We haven't yet. But it was so magical and we kissed and talked and I don't think I've ever gotten along so well with anyone in my whole life! He's *exactly* right for me—he's cute, smart and *soooo* funny and sensitive to women's issues and not gross or vulgar or a slimy kisser at all. Can you believe it?"

My silence must speak volumes.

"But he's not rich…" she continues. "He's a musician. A struggling musician."

"Oh." *Of course he is.*

"He was in this really great band for a while, but it didn't work out. He played me their demo!"

"Yeah?"

"He plays banjo."

"Banjo. He plays banjo."

"*Electric* banjo, actually. I know it sounds kinda weird, Holly, but he's *amazing*. And he's pretty confident that once he gets another group together, it won't be long before he lands a serious record deal. His sound is, like, *totally* original…. It's sort of this new folksy, half-funk kinda thing with some bluegrass influence, obviously, as well as—"

"George!" I snap. "Focus!"

"What?"

"I can't believe you went over there when you already have a boyfriend. What about Quentin?"

"I dumped him. The next day."

"What? You did?"

"There was no spark, Holly. What can I say? I'm a romantic—I want it all."

"But how come you didn't tell me?" I hate being out of the loop. It makes me feel neglected *and* neglectful.

"I've hardly seen you!"

"Yeah, but still—this is the kind of thing you make time for. God, I can't believe Vale didn't tell me."

"I doubt he even knows. Quentin left town the next day. He said he needed to get away."

"Yeah, but you should have at least waited to see if things work out with Max! What if he turns out be an ass and now you've let a good thing go with Quentin?"

"He's not an ass, Holly," she says defensively.

"How do you know?"

"Well, you'll see when you meet him."

But I don't want to meet him. I want Quentin and George and Vale and me to live happily ever after together, just like we'd planned. It doesn't sound like Vale and this Max person will have anything in common, leaving Vale and me…on our own? The thought isn't quite as appealing, especially now that I know he has backne.

Maybe I'm getting ahead of myself, but is it so wrong to want to go through it all with my best friend? Engagements, registering for china, bridal showers, weddings, *baby* showers, tummy tucks…

"So let me get this straight. You dumped a really nice

guy… A *rich* guy who's totally into you…for a banjo player you hardly know who has issues with his mother?"

My words didn't seem cruel until I hear them out loud, and they hang in the air longer than I would have liked.

George stares at me sadly and shrugs. "When you put it like that…yes, I suppose I did."

What the hell is the matter with me?

"Wait, G…that didn't come out right. I don't mean to sound so completely awful. It's not about the money. I know that. If you like this Max guy, then that's the most important thing."

"Really?"

"Of course really. I'm an asshole for implying otherwise. I have no idea why I said that. Maybe I'm just a little freaked out today. The last twenty-four hours have been…strange."

"Oh, Holly—thank you! I was *so* terrified to tell you! I didn't want you to be mad." She crawls out from under the covers and hugs me. "I really, *really* like him. He's amazing. You'll see…"

She'd been scared to tell me, and who could blame her? I am a gold-digging hussy, just like Remy said. Did my best friend actually think I was going to stand in the way of her and the love of her life? If so, I need to do some serious soul-searching and some major behavioral editing.

Maybe this is the reason I'm having so much trouble writing my book. The idea is great, which makes it sellable, and I think I've more than justified the evil-sounding premise—hell, I'm even *living* it these days—but the words just aren't coming. Is the problem that I don't believe a single word of it myself? Maybe I want what George has, or at least what she thinks she has—the sincere belief that in this crazy, unromantic and impossibly random universe, she's somehow managed to smash right into her one true soul mate.

Who am I kidding? Of *course* I want that. We all do.

But that also means my big Plan is dead in the water; putting finger to keyboard, utter hypocrisy. No matter! I can secretly embrace the paradigm shift, provided I am able to fake it long enough to write my book and sell it to a publisher. A classic example of fictional non-fiction. Once the royalties begin pouring in, I'll turn my attention to my true life's work: *Finding Your Soul Mate: A Realist's Guide to the Romance of a Lifetime.* It might not be as lucrative an endeavor, but it would be the truth.

I squeeze George's hand to reassure her. "I'm behind you one hundred percent, G. I'm even a little jealous...."

"Jealous? Why? You've got Vale and he's got it all!"

I make a face. "I'm not sure. Last night was a bit...I don't know...weird?"

Understanding dawns. "Jesus, would you listen to me? I'm such a jerk! Here I am on *your* birthday, making such a big deal out of my own stupid problems. Let me take you out for lunch and you'll tell me all about it!"

"You don't have to, G."

"Don't be silly! I feel a million times better now that you know and we've got some serious catching up to do... Hey! What are those?"

"What are what?"

"Those! In your ears!"

chapter 17

All Maxed Out

When it came to choosing love or money, George certainly made it look easy.

Since my relationship is obviously in a delicate place (read: deteriorating rapidly), George tries her hardest not to act like a moony love-struck teenager around me, but it's no use—Max is on her mind twenty-four/seven. She's head-over-heels in love. That he lives over his father's new wife's ex-husband's garage doesn't seem to bother her, and for that I admire her.

So George is floating on air, nearly impossible to have a normal conversation with. If it were anyone other than her, it would be extremely annoying, but because George is as sincere as she is silly, I can't help but be nearly as excited as she is.

Especially once I meet Max.

He is one of the oddest people I've ever encountered, in

a charming sort of way. After weeks of stories about Max and His Crazy Life ("Max met the Dalai Lama on the bus!" and "Max kicked his pot habit by going to live with the Amish!"), I'd sort of pictured him as one of those on-the-verge-of-homeless types, his trusty bongos (or banjo, in this case) strapped to his back with a frayed bit of rope and wrapped in a dirty Navajo horse blanket.

I am quite relieved when he walks into Starbucks wearing a crisp white T-shirt and jeans, and smelling not of patchouli oil or cigarettes but fabric softener. Better than that, Max Levine completely endears himself to me by proving he virtually worships my best friend.

It seems that for every Incredible Max tale I've heard, he has at least one "Isn't George Great?" story to share. He tells each one like we're sitting around a campfire, complete with sound effects and wild gesticulations. George rolls her eyes on cue, but she is obviously loving every minute of it. His enthusiasm, though a little over-the-top, seems completely heartfelt.

He's also somewhat of a miracle worker in that he's somehow managed to mend the rift between her and her mothers. Max had actually called them up one day and introduced himself over the phone, with, I imagine, George quivering in fear in the background.

"How on earth did you pull that off?" I ask him.

"I just imagined what it's like to be in their shoes. They're two thousand miles away from their only child. It can't be easy on them. So basically, I just explained that we're all on the same page when it comes to Georgie and that I have her best interest at heart. They also needed to hear that although she may have left for the wrong reasons..."

"*George!* You told him?"

She shrugs. "I couldn't help it."

"Don't worry, Holly. Your secret's safe with me."

"Please don't hate me, Max."

"I don't."

"It sounds a lot worse than it really is…"

"Hey, it's not for me to judge. From what Georgie's told me about you, I'm sure you'll come around in your own time. In the meantime, you just walk your own path and see where it takes you. It's cool, okay? Don't worry about it. Anyway, the mothers were actually quite open to the idea of Georgie stretching her wings a little. It's only natural."

"And it didn't hurt that he's Jewish and under forty-five," George adds. "And socially conscious, not to mention polite and sweet and—"

"Good manners go a long way in the Perlman-MacNeill household," I say. "Good call."

"Actually, I think it was the Nancy Drew bit that really sold them on me."

"Huh?"

He leans across the table. "Do you know who George is named after?"

"No."

"George Fayne!"

"Who?" I say.

George blushes. "Nancy Drew's sidekick. I always assumed I was named for my great-uncle George…you know, the only one from my mom's side who came to my Bat Mitzvah. But Max says Jews only name after dead people, and Uncle George isn't dead. So he asked them if George Fayne had anything to do with it…."

He nods excitedly. "George Fayne is a lesbian *icon.*"

"There was a lesbian character in *Nancy Drew?*" I ask skeptically. "Weren't those books from the forties and fifties?"

"She wasn't out, or anything, but the signs were clearly there—she was 'athletic,' she had close-cropped hair and was always described as a 'boyish girl.'"

"Wow! I had no idea!"

George giggles. "Neither did I! And you'd think they would have told me... But I love that you knew that, sweetie," she says and kisses him on the cheek. "He's so well-read, isn't he?"

After a twenty-minute account of their recent Sunday-afternoon trip to Muir Woods that Max made sound like the parting of the Red Sea, he excuses himself to go to the bathroom. In the time it takes her boyfriend to void a Grande mochachino latte with soy milk, George brings me up to speed on something that has been a lot longer in the making: She finally had an orgasm. (I mean, not flying solo.)

I'm sold. How could I not be?

They're perfection.

Vale and I, on the other hand, are not perfection. We're more like confusion. Some days, I still really enjoy his company; others, not so much. And dating him is easy—he's out of town so often that I can't be absolutely positive I *don't* like him. In the meantime, I've decided to be open-minded and give our relationship a chance to grow into whatever it is destined to become.

With George otherwise occupied and no therapist in my life for a change, I need someone to talk to. Although Zoe and I still e-mail almost every day, the last time we really spoke was about two weeks ago. I'd planned to get her opinion on things then, but she wasn't feeling well and had to go throw up (I assumed she was pregnant, but was too superstitious to ask—less than three months along was way early). Olivia and I also chat regularly, although it just isn't the same as face-to-face relationship dissection with a good friend.

As luck would have it, I know a good listener who also happens to be nice to look at. Oddly enough, Remy makes for a pretty decent stand-in when it comes to girl talk. He also brings the male perspective to the table, which is crucial if I ever hope to decipher Vale's hot-and-cold behavior toward me.

Since we both hate eating alone, I often go upstairs soon after getting home from work. Like me, Remy is a shitty cook, but to make up for it, he has the widest selection of delivery and take-out menus I've ever seen.

"I saw your friend this morning on her way to work. She seemed pretty happy with herself," he says as he bites into a roast beef sub with the works. "She even gave me a kiss hello."

"I think she's really in love."

"Ah."

"You have mustard on your shirt."

"I like it there," he says without looking down. "So what about you? Have you and your Legal Eagle said the L-word yet?"

I smile. For some reason, I like that Remy never calls Vale by his name, though he knows perfectly well what it is. Instead, it's always "The Ambulance Chaser" or "His Honor" or "Barrister Bill." They're the kind of little jabs I always let go, probably for fear he'll stop.

"Not exactly. I'm still trying to decide if he even likes me or not."

"Poor baby. I had no idea." He picks up the remote and flips on the TV. Remy isn't about to let girl talk get in the way of a Giants-Padres game.

"To be honest, Vale's kind of withdrawn, so I'm having a little trouble figuring out exactly how he feels about me. And what his intentions are."

"What do you mean? Like you think he's stepping out on you or something?"

"No, no. I don't get the sense he's being unfaithful."

"Yeah, 'cuz girls can always tell," he snickers.

Technically, he's right. For all I know, Vale has girlfriends in three different time zones.

"Seriously, Remy."

"Fine. So what is it, then?"

I shrug. "I just sort of wonder sometimes why he's even with me."

"Hopefully because he likes you."

"He doesn't really know me. Like, I haven't even told him I'm writing a book."

"Maybe because he'd find your subject matter unpleasant?"

I kick him. That logistical stumbling block has always plagued me. Originally, I imagined I would finish writing the book *after* snagging a wealthy guy so that I could benefit from my own experience, quit my job and have the credibility I needed to get published, but how would my moneyed mate react to the news that he started out as mere fodder for my master plan? Even if I could somehow manage to write it in secret, getting those first copies would be extremely awkward.

Would I be able to convince him that despite my dubious initial intentions, I really did love him too? (Which I would, of course, with all my heart.) Probably not, which was yet another reason to write a different book altogether. Even if I faked it, treated it like fiction or satire instead of a serious how-to guide, a book like *How to Marry a Millionaire (And Still Love Yourself in the Morning!)* could be offensive to future prospects. On the other hand, *Finding Your Soul Mate: A Realist's Guide to the Romance of a Lifetime* might scare them all away.

"I figured I'd say it was a self-help thing. But I still haven't found the right moment to bring it up."

"And why is that?"

"Because we're always talking about him and his stuff?"

"You tell me."

"To be fair, I guess it's not all him. Maybe it's because we're just not totally comfortable with each other yet, so I don't really open up to him, you know?"

"Or maybe it's more of a physical thing," he suggests, sneaking a quick glance at me.

"Well, when he's around, the sex is great."

"Yeah. Okay. Sure it is."

"You didn't buy that?"

"Not for a second."

I exhale as dramatically as I can. There's no point in lying. "Okay, you win. The truth is, even when he's around, and we have the chance to be…you know…*alone*…it's always me that initiates it. God, I can't believe I'm admitting this to you."

"Why?" He turns away from the TV, suddenly very interested in the conversation. "I can girl-talk with the best of 'em."

"Oh yeah?"

"Of course. I'm not the chump you think I am—I know the difference between pads and tampons."

"Only because you were married. Otherwise you'd have no idea."

"Not true," he says, and begins chuckling. "My brother stuck a tampon up his ass once on a dare!"

"Too much information, Remy…"

He can't stop laughing. "Cost me fifty bucks! But it was so fuckin' funny…*totally* worth it!"

"Ahem…"

"Sorry. Guess you had to be there…. So let's recap. Your boyfriend sucks in bed… I could have told you that, by the way. The instant I saw him."

They met only once, for about three-and-a-half seconds while Vale was waiting for me to come outside.

"How would you know?"

"Any guy who drives a *yellow* automatic Audi TT is

overcompensating for something. That much I can tell you for sure."

"He's not short, if that's what you mean!"

"Actually, that's not what I meant…."

"Remy, I'm not going to discuss my boyfriend's penis with you. No matter how much you may want to."

"Dearie, the last thing I want to talk about is your counsel's endowment. I just thought I'd point out that his shortcomings may be part of the—"

"He doesn't have any shortcomings!"

"Okay, so if it's not him, then it must be you. Are you admitting you're no good in the sack?"

"I refuse to talk to you about this."

"Aw, come on…"

"A lady doesn't reveal her bedroom secrets."

"Unmarried ladies aren't supposed to have bedroom secrets."

"And I'm sure you were a virgin when you got married."

"At least I was in love with my first. I bet you weren't."

"I'll bet *you* that you only thought you were…."

He nodded. "Okay, you win. Mrs. Robinson and I weren't meant to be."

"Was she really an older woman?" I ask, completely intrigued.

"A gentleman doesn't reveal his bedroom secrets."

"You are so full of shit."

"Yeah, but you like me this way. So while we're on the subject, tell me—does size really matter?"

"I can never tell if you're being serious or not."

"I'm as serious as a heart attack. And I only ask because I'm beginning to feel bad for your poor Johnnie Cochran…it seems he can't fill out his briefs."

"The real reason, in case you're interested, is that I just don't think we click."

It's a relief to say it out loud to someone. And because it's true, it doesn't feel like I'm betraying Vale at all.

"Hmmm…no chemistry, huh? Do you think it's because…oh, I don't know…you're *dating him for the wrong reasons?*"

"Despite what you may think you know about me, I would never date somebody I don't like or respect. And I really do like Vale most of the time. He's very smart and he can be really funny. I just don't know him that well. And…"

"And what?"

"What if it's because he's just not attracted to me? That's sort of what I've been thinking… But I'm hoping maybe that'll come in time, you know?"

"You're right. Sparks can be dangerous, anyway. Who needs 'em?"

Does he really believe that?

"I suppose…but they also keep you warm at night."

"An electric blanket will keep you warm at night, too. And I'm sure you'll be able to afford a *really* nice one if you stick it out with your barrister."

"Are you trying to make a point?"

"Just playing devil's advocate."

"I don't need an advocate. I need somebody who'll tell it to me like it is. George has been so preoccupied with Max and her job and her boss and her mothers…I don't know. I just have no idea what to do."

"Sorry. I'll be serious."

"If I tell you something, promise you won't make fun of me?" I ask.

"Of course."

"Well, Vale's sort of like my first real boyfriend in a long time. So I don't have a lot of experience. I don't think I know what a grown-up relationship's supposed to feel like, so I can't tell if this is a good one or a bad one."

He answers without skipping a beat. "Holly, if you were in a good relationship, you'd know it. But if you're spending all your time worrying if it's right instead of *knowing* it is, then, well, it simply isn't…and there's not a damn thing you can do about it. I say kick him to the curb, girlfriend."

"Well, you're right about one thing for sure."

"What's that?"

"You really can girl-talk with the best of 'em. Thanks."

"Dr. Phil ain't got nothing on me."

Over a lunch of cheeseburgers and Caesar salads at our new diner—halfway between Venus Books and the world headquarters of Encyclopedia Gigantica—George fidgets in her seat. She can barely concentrate on my incredibly riveting story about how Kitty fell asleep standing up while making the coffee.

"Something on your mind, George? You seem a little distracted."

"No…"

"But…"

"No buts. Well, maybe one but."

"What but?"

She sighs. "Forgive me, but I'm nervous."

"What now?"

"I have something to tell you."

The last time George had "something to tell me," it was pretty big.

"Should I be scared? You're not dumping Max are you?"

She looks at me like I've just suggested she set her own hair on fire.

"*God,* no! Why would I do that, silly?"

"Are you in a family way?"

"Huh?"

"Pregnant. Are you pregnant?"

"What? No! It's nothing like that. This is a good thing. I think."

"So shoot."

"Okay. So, um, Max thinks… I mean, we've decided *together,* that we should get our own place. Just me and him… so, I guess we're, like, moving in together."

She eyes me suspiciously, waiting for my head to explode. I'll admit that my heart dropped into my gut for a second, but otherwise, I feel fine. A little numb, maybe…

"Wow, G. That's—"

"Look, Holly," she interrupts, presumably to preempt any negative fallout. "I know what you're thinking…that we've only been together for a couple of months and this is a big step and all that. But he needs me, and I need him. I *love* him. I really do. And I want to be with him as much as I can."

I get up and give her a huge hug. "Don't worry George. It's fine! This is great news. It's incredibly exciting and wonderful and romantic in every possible way. I'm really *really* happy for you."

She hugs me back as tightly as she can. "Thanks for faking it, Holly. It means a lot to me."

"I'm not faking it! You know I really like Max…"

"But…"

"No buts."

"Come on."

"Okay… The but is just that I love you, too. That's all. So I'm going to miss you."

"I'm going to miss you more. But you don't have to say it like that. Because this doesn't mean our adventure's over."

"I know, I know. Don't worry about me, George. I've always wanted to live alone. And I'm sure Remy will give me a break on the rent if I agree to help him out upstairs on weekends. He could use the help."

I pray that he does. Remy could get triple what he was

charging us. It's easy to see how tempting it would be for him to just kick me out and get it over with. God, what would I do then? Shuffle off to Buffalo? Heaven knows that's the last thing I want. But that's how expensive San Francisco is. Unless, of course, I choose to move in with half a dozen roommates in some crappy part of town. After living the good life in Remy's basement, that would take some serious sacrifice. Maybe I'll have time to find a better job. I *definitely* can't ask my dad for any more money.

"So when's this all going to happen?"

"Fourth of July weekend's crazy for movers, so we couldn't get a truck till the 14th."

"That's in three weeks!"

She shrugs. "I know it's kinda last minute, but Max's friend knows this guy who's getting rid of this awesome place in the Haight that's supercheap because it used to be a hostel or something and you have to share a bathroom with your neighbor."

"That's really gross."

"I know," she giggles. "But Max said we could get a chamber pot and put it behind a screen. Like in the old days."

"The old days means fifty years ago, George. Not five hundred years ago."

"Max also said he'll pee off the balcony when the weather's nice."

"I guess the weather won't be so nice for the people down below…."

"Oh, don't be ridiculous. There's nothing under the balcony but a Dumpster from Ming Palace."

"Well, that's a relief! Wow, George—this place just keeps getting better and better! By the way, I'm sure you won't have *any* bugs…'cause I've heard that cockroaches don't really like Chinese food all that much…"

"Shut up!" she laughs. "You're making it sound bad!"

"Bad? Not bad. Just in violation of about twenty different health and safety codes. I think private bathrooms are pretty much a guaranteed right, these days, in case you're interested."

"I know, but I think it's okay that they're shared because technically the place is still considered a hotel or something, even though there's no front desk or room service or anything like that. It's mostly long-term boarders. Oh! And there's this one old lady who's been living there, like, forever, and Max said his friend told him she used to know Kerouac or one of those guys and once he came over and..."

George drones on and on but I don't hear a word. I am slightly preoccupied with crunching the numbers, and figuring out how I can ask Remy to reduce my rent by half and still make it sound like I'd be doing him the favor.

My happiness for George and her good news slowly morphs into self-pity over the course of a lonely, boring afternoon spent researching Antarctica. There's no other way to look at it: While it was all good for my best friend, the whole thing kind of sucked for me. On the bus ride home, I catch myself silently cursing the teenagers making out across the aisle. Was the entire world in love except for me?

When Vale finally calls to say goodnight from Chicago (and tell me all about why he's having trouble converting a Chapter 11 proceeding for a limited liability company to a Chapter 7), I can barely keep it together.

"So she's moving in with her boyfriend. What's the big deal?"

"Everything's changing."

"So?"

"So, I don't know... It's weird for me. I feel like I'm being left behind. I like Max. I really do. But they're so...intense. Sometimes I just wish she and Quentin would have stayed together. Don't you? It would have been so much fun..."

"I guess."

"Does he miss her?"

"Who?"

"Quentin! Does he miss George?"

Somewhere along the way, I started to feel sorry for the guy. I imagined him pining away for her in his big empty loft, dejected and alone, maybe even turning to alcohol to dull the pain....

"God, I don't know! Quentin's a big boy, Holly. And believe me, it's not like he has any trouble getting laid, so I highly doubt he's sitting around boo-hooing over your friend."

Hmmm...was that the stirring of passions I heard?

"Vale, that's not the point. He really liked her!" I would defend Quentin to the death if it meant provoking an emotional outburst from my boyfriend, just to see if it was even possible.

"Yeah, he liked her. So what? He'll find someone else. Jeez. Why are you being such a girl about this, anyway?"

"What's that supposed to mean?" Screw Quentin—now it's getting personal!

"It means get over it, already! You seem to care an awful lot about George's love life. Don't you just want her to be happy?"

"Of course I do," I snap. "But I thought the four of us were going to be, I don't know, together."

"Who the fuck cares about them? You have me."

That prospect must have struck a subconscious chord somewhere deep within me because I start bawling uncontrollably.

"Holly! For God's sake, pull yourself together!"

"No! It's our anniversary and I can cry if I want to."

"What?"

"It's June 25th. We've been together for three months."

While I sob, I pictured him rolling his eyes in his posh suite at The Drake, leaning over for another scoop of caviar and pouring himself a glass of champagne. Doesn't he care that I'm upset? Breaking down isn't something I do all that often, so I when I do, I expect a little more than total indifference from the person who's supposed to be there for me no matter what. If the tables were turned and he was upset, wouldn't I do everything I could to help him feel better?

"Are you done?" he asks when I pause to catch my breath.

"No."

"Aw, quit being a baby. Why don't you go out and have a few drinks somewhere."

I sniff. "Because I have no one to go with."

"So go with your landlord. Whatsisname."

"He's probably asleep," I sniff. "It's past midnight here. Hey, why are you calling me so late? Did you go out or something?"

"Aha! So *technically* it's not our anniversary anymore. Which means you should stop crying, then."

"Don't lawyer me, Vale. I'm in no mood for it." I can't help but notice he didn't answer my question.

"I'm going to hang up now."

"No! Please don't…"

"I can't talk to you when you're like this. And I don't respond well to manipulation."

What the hell is that supposed to mean? "I'm not manipulating you. I just don't want to be alone."

"Call me in the morning when you're back to yourself."

That man is cold as ice, and I can feel the chill from two thousand miles away.

chapter 18

An Indecent Proposal

I considered our anniversary phone call our first fight, though it didn't seem to phase Vale at all. He told me it was fine and then refused to discuss it further. "Let's just pretend it never happened," he said the next day. I got the sense he thought of me as some daffy chick, prone to the pull of the tides or my period or whatever forces of nature happened to be at work that minute. His attitude never came off as nasty or overtly sexist or anything like that, but I couldn't shake the feeling that he'd already made up his mind about me, or maybe women in general, and decided we were something he would just have to live with.

The night he returns from Chicago, he makes dinner reservations for us at Julius' Castle, a landmark restaurant perched on Telegraph Hill, directly beneath San Francisco's largest stone phallus, Coit Tower. The place is known for being extremely romantic, cheesy even, with amazing views of the ocean, crystal chandeliers and wood-paneled walls, all designed to draw your attention away from the mediocre food. Maybe it's Vale's way of apologizing. I'm kind of hoping it will give me a chance to see if our relationship is salvageable. I've decided that if there is really nothing going on between us, I will take Remy's advice and move on. It's too early in the game for me to resign myself to a life without sparks (or even the faintest wisp of smoke).

So here we sit, Vale and I, for two-and-a-half hours, and eat while the sun sets. I start with the shrimp cocktail and then have the New York strip; Vale orders the *foie gras* and the rack of lamb. True to form, the meat is tough, though not as tough as the conversation that accompanies dessert.

"Vale, can I ask you something?"

"Don't tell me you want another piece of cheesecake!"

"Very funny," I say, though I seriously consider the offer.

"I don't know how you stay so thin, Holly. It's amazing."

"Actually, that's sort of what I wanted to talk to you about tonight…."

"Oh?"

I take a deep breath, attempt a smile and brace myself.

"This is kind of hard, okay, so I'm just gonna say it fast. Vale…are you attracted to me? I mean, do you think I'm sexy? At all? To you, I mean. Am I hot to you? God, that sounded so raunchy…basically, what I want to know is whether or not you find me even remotely attractive."

Admittedly, it wasn't quite the smooth phrasing I'd come up with during rehearsals, but the bottle of Bordeaux that made the food go down so much easier must also have dulled my capacity for eloquence.

His brow furrows. "What do you mean? Of *course* you're hot." No eye contact, excessive throat clearing and a nervous chuckle.

If there were a Richter scale of enthusiasm for possible

responses to that question, I'd give Vale's weak rumble a two-point-five.

"So…then why don't we ever fool around?"

He takes his napkin off his lap and places it on the table. "Actually Holly, there's something I need to talk to you about, too."

"Oh?"

Damn it! He's breaking up with me before I can break up with him!

Is that fair? Can he do that? My utter lack of experience in these things makes it all so confusing. All I know is that I'd prefer to remember this breakup as *my* choice, both for posterity's sake and to reduce the risk of regret. Did being preemptively dumped change all that?

"Holly, I need you to know that I care about you tremendously. You're intelligent but you're also sensitive, which despite what you may think is a quality I admire. It really is. Plus, you're creative and funny and sharp, not to mention extremely attractive and—"

"Uhh, let's not go overboard…"

"Please. Let me finish." He grabs my hand and holds it tightly. "Look. You've obviously already tuned in to the fact that something's going on, and you're right. I'm afraid I haven't been completely honest with you…."

"What?" My heart is pounding so loudly I'm afraid I won't be able to hear what he has to say.

He stares into me with his big brown eyes and begins…

"When my big sister came out to my parents, she was only eighteen years old. My dad disowned her on the spot. My mother sent one of the maids upstairs to pack Courtney's suitcase and sneak a few hundreds into one of her pockets.

"That was more than twenty years ago. My parents have never looked back, never changed their minds. Not once have they wavered in their dedication to their hatred of her.

They see Courtney's lifestyle as a choice, as an affront to them, an attack on their values, somehow. I'm the only one in my entire family who still speaks to my sister, despite their initial efforts to make sure that didn't happen."

"Well, thank heaven for that, at least."

"Let me finish. For years, they threw out the letters she sent to me, the birthday cards, the Christmas presents. One day, a letter got through, I don't know how, and I realized what they'd been doing. Obviously I didn't want to cut her out of my life…I still loved her and by then I was old enough to make up my own mind. But I love my parents, too, which is something Courtney still has trouble with. Anyway…eventually we all grew into an understanding—my sister pretends my parents are dead, my parents pretend that she's dead, and I don't try to convince any of them otherwise…."

"How awful," I murmur. "How do you deal with it?"

"I don't know. I just do. You see, Holly, the thing is…it's about money. My family's money. My great-grandfather did very well for himself in various businesses back East, and he invested it wisely, mostly in real estate, and so did my grand-father. So, basically, what I'm trying to say is, they're wealthy, my parents. *Quite* wealthy, in fact. I am also. And I want things to stay that way."

"I can understand that. So what's the problem?"

"The problem is… I'm gay, too."

He pauses, waiting for me to say something, but I don't.

"Obviously, I'd be disinherited if they knew. So I tried like crazy to change, pretend it wasn't true. But it is true and there's nothing I can do about it. At first I was extremely de-pressed, suicidal even. After high school, I deferred my col-lege acceptance and went to live with Courtney for a while. I told my parents I was going to Europe and they bought it. Can you believe that? I suppose they never got too involved in the details of my life, as long as I did what they wanted, you know? Anyway, my sister tried to help me come to terms with my sexuality. Not at all an easy thing to do, by the way. But by the time I finished law school and I'd been on my own for a few years, I realized that I wouldn't want to change even if I could—I'm happy the way I am, more or less. So I came up with a plan…and I'd like you to be a part of it."

I stare at him blankly, still unable to speak. All I can think of is Remy's snarky but vague reference to my boyfriend's "shortcomings." Being gay would definitely qualify in that category in this case.

"First of all, I need to apologize for having deceived you these past few months. Oh, and I also want you to know, in case it isn't obvious, that I never cheated on you. With anyone. I'm not *that* much of an asshole…." He laughs nervously, waiting for me to concur. When I don't, he simply clears his throat and continues. "Of course, I don't want you to get the wrong impression from all this and assume I haven't enjoyed the time we've spent together. I think we get along pretty well, don't you?… No?… Not ready to go there yet? Okay, I can respect that. I'll just get to the point then…so where was I?"

The fog begins to lift and I realize I'm still holding his hand. I pull it away.

"Wait! Before you say anything, let me lay it all out for you! What I'm proposing is a mutually beneficial arrangement, with just a few strings attached. But they're good strings—courtship, engagement, marriage and, of course, children. A life together as close friends. You would be free to pursue discreet extramarital relationships, as would I. Eventually, if the arrangement no longer suited us, we could divorce. Everybody will get what they want—my parents can go on thinking I'm the son they want me to be, we'll be able to give our kids the best of everything and you'll have the freedom to do things you never even dreamed of. And if it doesn't work out in the long run, there would obviously be an ample settlement in it for you in exchange for your discretion and years of…"

"Years of service?" I offer.

"Well, no, that's not how I would put it."

"How would you put it, then?"

"Years of marriage…years of love."

"Love?"

"Come on, Holly…" He reaches for my hand again. "Be my Grace."

"I don't want a Will. I want a *real* husband. Come to think of it, these days I don't know if I even want that."

"I've worked it out for you, Holly. The pros far outweigh the cons. That much I can virtually guarantee."

The whole thing sounds a little too well rehearsed.

"Am I the first one you've…how should I put this…proposed to?"

He exhales deeply. "Holly, I said I was going to be completely honest with you from now on, so the answer is no. You're not the first. There was one other woman, last year. But it didn't work out."

"Well, I'm not surprised, Vale! What you're suggesting is a bit…a bit…"

"Holly, *please* just think about it. It doesn't have to be such a big deal! It's just a different sort of life. Not bad, just different. You could have kids, lovers, fabulous clothes… You could even pick out your own engagement ring! My mother knows Fred Leighton personally."

The waiter approaches to ask if we want coffee, but Vale shoos him away.

"You can't just pretend the last three months didn't happen! You seduced me under false pretenses…."

"I did not! I…uh…*enjoyed* it."

"I thought you were going to be honest with me."

"Okay, okay. Just remember that your motives were far from perfect, too, Holly. But since you laid it on the line when you told me about that Moneyed Mates dating service thing you did, knowing full well that most men would hate you for that, I'll be equally forthright—"

"Wait a sec…how do you know about that?" I ask. "I never told you about Moneyed Mates!"

"Yes, you did. That night at 808. But I was never quite sure if you remembered telling me. We were sitting at the bar and—"

"808?"

"That aquarium restaurant in SoMa…the night we met. Since you were so drunk you didn't even remember me when I called to ask you out the next week, now I'm thinking you probably also forgot you'd been a little indiscreet in regards to your gold-digging endeavors."

Vale knew I was hunting for a guy with money this whole time? Throughout our entire relationship?

"I… I don't know what to say… I'm so embarrassed."

As the past three months come into focus, every insecurity I've ever had careens through my mind like a runaway train. Vale was the one, not I, who thought he'd struck gold the night I opened my big, fat Manhattan-guzzling mouth. I suddenly see myself through his eyes…superficial to the point of transparence, financially motivated in the extreme, unencumbered by the kind of moral values that would make a better woman slap him and run, and to top it all off, desperately single and ready to put an end to it all with a diabolical plan of my own! Vale must have seen in me a kindred spirit, a female alter ego, a perfect partner in matrimonial perversion. No wonder he called me and courted me so aggressively— I was his *dream* girl. How stunned he must be that I didn't accept his silver-tongued proposal the instant he uttered it!

"Come on, Holly. Was what I did really so wrong? Is what I want really so bad?"

I shake my head in an attempt to clear it. "Vale, even if you think you've found someone who might agree with you, you can't just go around being the gay Don Juan, proposing marriage to anyone who looks at your Rolex with goo-goo eyes! Some woman's gonna kill you one day!"

"Is it my fault my family's proof of the genetic basis of homosexuality?"

"Are you saying there are more of you? One of your parents?"

He snorts and gulps down the rest of his port. "Distinctly unlikely. Must be a recessive gene somewhere."

"You're probably right, but remember that you and your sister *were* raised in exactly the same environment by the same people...so maybe it's partly nurture as well as nature after all."

"There wasn't a lot of nurturing going on in my house, Holly. It isn't exactly a quality I would ascribe to either of my parents. But I do think you and my mother would get along really well, by the way. You should meet her...."

"*Meet her?* I don't want to meet her! I want to *smack* her...for, like, a *thousand* different reasons! Vale, forget it!"

Crestfallen, he leans back and starts slowly rubbing his temples. "I'm under so much pressure to marry... I don't know what I'm going to do."

He's so sad, so pathetic. My outrage melts into pity, and my pity into empathy. Here is someone who's even more confused than I am, no matter how together he appears to be.

"God, you really are a mess."

He nods, unable to look at me.

"While I'm not condoning any of...of *this*...I guess I am the teensiest bit flattered that you consider me suitable heir-producing material. And you're right about one thing, at least—I *do* think we get along well. You're a good guy, Vale.

But you seriously need to figure some stuff out if you wanna get happy."

"Or find the right girl."

"Uhhh…yeah. Maybe, I guess. But as for me, well, I just don't think I'm the right girl. I don't have a strong enough stomach for decades of deception."

Or do I?

Briefly, ever so briefly, I consider it.

For here I am, poised on the brink of success. This is my chance to put The Plan into motion, my chance to achieve everything I've ever dreamed of, just like he said. Or, I could turn around and walk the other way, possibly giving up my one and only kick at the can. But what if it *did* work? Vale's Plan may not be traditional, but then again, neither was mine. Who's to say it couldn't work out? *Maybe I should ask him for some time to think about it….*

The clink of champagne glasses from somewhere behind us gathers my wandering thoughts and leads them back to the face of the man sitting across from me. It's a face I know well, but it's also the face of a stranger.

"…but are you one hundred percent sure, Holly? Have you *really* thought about what this would mean for you? Every success imaginable, every *excess* imaginable…all of it awaits if you just say *yes!*"

"I know," I sigh. "I know."

An inkling of hope puts some of the fire back in his eyes. Vale grabs my hand again. "Have you ever shopped the Ginza in Tokyo? Been on safari in the Serengeti? Bought your parents a Bentley?"

No, no and no.

But…is what Vale offering me really success? More likely, it's the worst kind of failure, all wrapped up in a pretty blue box with a big, fat bow. The kind of success that spoils once it's been sitting out in the sun for a while.

"I can see it for you, Holly…" Vale's normally staid expression begins to twist, revealing a curious grin I've never seen, and his fair complexion is overcome by an angry purpling "I'm offering a life of unmitigated luxury."

Vale stares me square in the eyes, and I meet his gaze dead-on.

Might this be my True Defining Moment?

All I know for sure, in this instant, is that the more seriously I consider accepting Vale's offer, the more disgusted I become with myself, and the less I want to be a person who would live her life like that. Even if I ask for some time to think about it and walk out of here in limbo, I'd hate myself for it, and I'd never be granted a do-over. My entire body hums with the certainty that I was meant for greater things than what Vale Spencer had to offer.

And this growing visceral reaction within me leads me to a thought, and then to another, and then another, and another, until I arrive at a thought I've never thought before: that maybe there *is* something I want more than a moneyed mate, more than a bestseller, more than bigger boobs or a bigger byline. More, even, than a plain old boyfriend.

Peace.

I want peace. Quiet in my own mind. Release from the burden of worrying all of the time about all of these things, these instruments of self-torture and yardsticks of failure that have shadowed me as far back as I can remember. For the longest while, I believed that rejecting my need for them outright, denying them, was the only way to be free of them. More recently, I decided that achieving them one by one was the way to go about it. Now I see that letting them go with a smile is the only way I'll ever be happy. And that's what I really want. To be *happy*.

Isn't that all anybody wants?

"So, Holly? Will you at least think about it?"

With an evil grin of my own, I squeeze his hand. "I guess you don't know me as well as you think, Vale. I want no part in this. Any of it."

Now it's he who pulls his hand away from mine. "A fortune lands at your feet and you step over it to get to the unemployment line?"

"Why do you care so much about the money, Vale? Aren't you rich enough already? Wouldn't you rather be free from pretending you're someone you're not?"

"I know exactly who I am, Holly. Make no mistake about that. And I also know exactly what I want. Being a lawyer will never afford me the kind of life I need to have, the kind of legacy I need to leave for my children. It's like…the difference between flying first-class and owning the plane."

"Seems to me a better legacy for your kids than a private jet would be a father they knew loved their mother. Or, better yet, a father who loved their other father."

He smiles. "It's complicated."

"It always is."

"So this is goodbye, then?"

"Yup," I say, getting up quickly while the adrenaline is still pounding through my veins. "Good luck, Vale."

On my way out, I pay the bill.

The house is dark when I walk through the door. George is out again, probably staying at Max's place, so I call Remy. I gather up the strength to tell him what happened—that he was right about Vale, of course; that I'd been a fool—but I get his machine.

I leave a short message and hang up.

A second later, the phone rings.

"Remy?"

"Hi, Holly."

"Asher? Is that you?"

"Yeah—"

"God, I'm so glad you called. How are you?" I so need a friend and his voice is like music to my ears.

"Not so good. Zoe's dad died."

chapter 19

Back to Buffalo

My old bedroom doesn't look quite the same as it did six months ago. Granted, I hadn't actually lived in it for almost ten years, but I've always enjoyed knowing my room's there, just as I left it the day I moved out during my second year at Erie. Time waits for no woman, I suppose.

My mother, in her zeal for change, had torn down all my posters and taken my bulletin boards off the wall. My once-beloved stuffed animals had been rounded up and summarily dumped at Goodwill. The contents of my closet? Boxed and put in the basement. Even my old-fashioned gumball machine was gone (it didn't work—I'd once tried to turn it into a fish tank by waterproofing all the cracks and moving parts with a glue-gun—but was that any reason to put it out with the trash? I think not.)

Greeting me instead are built-in glass display cases (locked!) crammed full with an impossibly odd assortment of sixties'

TV memorabilia. Auction catalogues and photographs of garish figurines and old lunch boxes cover my desk. Against one wall, stacks of cardboard boxes overflow with foam packing peanuts; against another, empty prefab shelving. God only knows what she has planned for that. *Bonanza* trading cards? Gilligan's coconuts? Mister Ed's riding tack?

It's amazing how much shit she's managed to amass in such a short time, and if I weren't so shell-shocked already, I probably would be extremely weirded out, not to mention angry. Heaven forbid she move a single football trophy or model plane from one of my brothers' rooms, but my entire pre-adult life? No problem—we'll just get rid of it!

"I changed the sheets," my mother says by way of apology as my dad places my suitcase at the foot of my bed.

"Thanks, I guess."

"What time's the funeral?"

"Umm…tomorrow at 11:30, I think."

"I'll check the paper and find out for sure. Your dad and I are going to come, too."

"Yeah? That would be nice. I'm sure Zoe will appreciate it."

"I always liked that Douglas Watts," she says. "He certainly had his plate full raising those girls alone. He struck me as a very decent man." My dad nods in agreement, though I can't remember them ever having met face-to-face. "Imagine? Beating the cancer only to slip in the bathtub like that. It just goes to show, when it's your time, it's your time, and there's not a whole helluva lot you or I or the good Lord can do about it."

"I suppose."

"Oh, and did I tell you? Cole's having a Fourth of July barbecue on Sunday. And then we're off again on Monday."

"This Monday? Where?"

"A show in Atlantic City. Peter Tork is speaking."

"Who?" I mouth to my dad.

"He's one of the Monkees, dear," he whispers.

"I can hear you, Larry. You're standing three feet away from me. I don't expect you to know this, Holly, but if Peter Tork signs the *TV Guide* I recently acquired from the week the show first aired, it just might fetch us a pretty penny in Anaheim this fall."

"Anaheim?"

"Big collectibles show," my dad says loudly in her direction.

"Not just big. The biggest! Frankly, Larry, to say the N.A.C.'s annual event is just big is an *insult* to the participants who travel there from all over the *world*—"

"Watch it, Louise, or we're going to start cutting back on some of your budget and redirecting it to our portfolio like we talked about. So don't push me!"

"You're right. I'm...I'm very sorry, dear," my mother stammers, then blushes.

"It's okay," he says and kisses her on the cheek. "Just remember we have to keep things in perspective."

It's by far the longest conversation I've seen them have in years, and the first public display of affection *ever*. Obviously, they're completely insane, but it seems to be working for them.

"Okaaay...so, um, you guys are leaving when? Tuesday, right? I took the whole week off so I'm going to stay until Saturday, if that's okay."

"You'll have to show her how to work the alarm, Larry."

"Don't worry about that now."

"I'm just saying, is all." She checks and then rechecks the lock on a case.

My dad's eyes meet mine and he smiles. He clears his throat. "Leave that alone for now, would you Louise?"

"Fine." She turns her attention to me instead. "Holly, you look drawn. You want a cup of tea?"

"No thanks. It was a long flight. I'm just going to try and get some sleep."

I had a Gravol and four bloody Marys on the plane (part of my plan to eat more vegetables), so even though it's only 11:30 East Coast time, I can barely keep my eyes open. All I want is to sleep for ten hours, get through tomorrow and spend the rest of my time in Buffalo doing whatever I can to make things easier for Zoe.

It doesn't take long for my subconscious demons to wake me. The wisp of a dream escapes into the darkness as I rub the sleep out of my eyes and squint at the time— 2:13 a.m.

By 3:00 a.m. I've counted a thousand sheep and named all my therapists in alphabetical order. By four, I've named all the neighbors on my block, which unexpectedly brings back the dream that had awoken me....

Rena Helmdry was a take-no-shit kind of girl who lived across the street from me growing up and whom I envied desperately because her parents were never home and because she was allowed to smoke in her room.

Anyway, Rena's older brother Rob had an impressive collection of true-crime books which I never tired of reading. In one of them was this incredibly haunting photograph of Marilyn Monroe, dead, and laid out on a slab in the morgue. Just like that. Her eyes were closed, she had a strange double chin, and her face was dark and discolored. You could hardly tell that it was her.

What fascinated me about the picture was how surreal it was. I found it amazing that they just sort of stuck her in a drawer, probably next to some homeless drunk or stroke victim. Like who she was didn't matter anymore because she was dead. And you'd think that if anybody could look good in an autopsy photo, it would be her. But she didn't. Not at all.

At the moment of her death—nine years and two husbands after she filmed *How to Marry a Millionaire*—Marilyn Monroe also had dark roots. Presumably, the very different person she used to be was trying to get out and she'd finally tired of fighting her.

I dreamed that instead of just lying there on that table, Marilyn sat up and walked away.

The next night, I wake up at around the same time. I attribute it to too much coffee at Zoe's house after the funeral. But the next night, the same thing happens (was it all that food at Cole and Olivia's barbecue?). And then again the night after. If a dream is to blame, it's a mystery to me, because I can't remember a thing. All I know for sure is that sleeping in my old room is becoming harder each night.

The fourth night, I decide to get up. My parents left for Atlantic City this morning, so I don't have to worry about waking anyone. I creep out of bed and go downstairs to the kitchen. It's only 11:30 on the West Coast, so I take the cordless phone back up to my room, crawl under the covers and dial in the dark.

"Remy?"

"Holly?"

"Yeah."

"Hi!"

"You weren't sleeping, were you? I mean, I'm sorry if I woke you…"

"Nah, you know me. What's up? Isn't it a little late there?"

"I couldn't sleep…. Is it okay that I called you?"

He laughs as if it were a ridiculous question. "Of course. I was hoping I'd hear from you."

"Really?"

"Yes, really! So how are you?"

"Okay, I guess. I don't know. It feels kind of strange here. I don't know why."

"Going home is always a weird buzz. Especially under unpleasant circumstances."

"This is the first time I've ever been away from Buffalo long enough to make it weird to be back, I suppose."

"How was the funeral?"

"Awful. I feel like…like death is all around me."

"That's because it is."

"I used to write obituaries and it never got to me."

"Professional distance, probably. It's different when it's someone you care about."

"Still, every day I was reminded that people die. But it never seemed as random and senseless as it does to me now."

"Heart attacks, lung cancer, falling safes, plane crashes… don't bother trying to make any sense of it. Something's going to get each and every one of us, whether they find a cure for cancer or not. A great man once said, 'All we have to decide is what to do with the time that is given us.'"

"Gandalf the Grey. *Fellowship of the Ring.*"

"Man, I love that you know that."

"Remember who my best friend is. I've seen *Lord of the Rings* at least 10 times. When *Return of the King* came out, George made me go with her to the back-to-back screening of all three."

"12 hours well spent. A faithful adaptation."

"Don't tell me you've read the books because I won't believe you," I say. "Nobody's read them and everybody lies about it."

"Okay. But I did. In junior high. I was really into Middle Earth." He's quiet for a second and then adds, "I was a bit of a nerd."

"Middle Earth," I sigh. "That's the beauty of fantasy. There's this wonderful sense of order and justice and in the end, good things happen to good people while the bad guys get ripped apart by orks and tossed into the abyss."

"You're saying Zoe's dad didn't deserve to die?"

"Exactly."

"Well, nobody deserves to die, Holly, but it's kind of unavoidable."

"And what are we supposed to do until then? Pretend that's not true?"

"Live your life, I guess. Put one foot in front of the other. Follow your nose and see where it leads you. And when you're ready, your destiny will reveal itself to you."

Hmm. Destiny? "So it's all about fate."

"Not exactly," he says, then pauses for a few seconds. "I believe in choices. But I also believe there comes at least one time in your life when all the choices you've made converge to either haunt you or heal you. Where you go from there is up to you."

"Ah yes. A True Defining Moment. So what's yours?"

"I don't know if I've had one yet. You?"

"Leaving Buffalo, maybe." Turning down Vale, definitely.

Remy and I continue to talk for nearly an hour—about everything and nothing and the funeral and Zoe's pregnancy (finally confirmed) and the irony of life and death…. It's one of those weird middle-of-the-night conversations where the next morning you may not believe or even remember what you said, but it's comforting just to talk to him. As we're about to hang up Remy reminds me that life goes on.

"No matter how outraged we are that it possibly could," he adds.

I think about Sylvia and wonder if somebody said something similar to Remy after she died. "But it's hard to have faith when you don't have…"

"Faith?"

I laugh, because that was exactly what I meant although it sounds completely absurd.

"Do you want me to tell you a story?"

"Okay."

"I've never told anybody this, so you better appreciate it."

"I will."

"All right. So after Sylvia died, things were rough. To be expected, obviously. So I kind of just let things settle for a while. Let her being gone sink in, you know? We knew it was coming, so we said what we needed to say to each other, but still, it hit me pretty hard. After a few months, I realized I needed to move, get out of that house. So I was packing shit up for the movers, cleaning out the garage, actually, and I found a beach ball that she'd blown up the summer before…."

"Remy, you don't have to tell me this if you don't want to." The last thing I want is for him (or me) to feel uncomfortable.

"No, it's okay… So I find this ball. A beach ball with *her* breath in it…." He hesitates. "It was like…like striking oil. Like pirates' treasure and Christmas and winning the lottery all at the same time. Better, even. So after I moved, every now and then, when I really, really missed her, I'd go downstairs and get it and open that little plastic plug and…and suck the tiniest bit of air out."

My chest tightens. As usual, I have no idea what to say.

"What happened once the air was gone?" Best to stick to the facts.

"Nothing. It was just gone. That was it."

"So…what did you do?"

"I dealt with it."

Hot tears roll down my cheeks and onto the pillow.

I realize now that I love him. I love Remy Wakefield.

Instead of leaving on Saturday, I change my ticket to go back to San Francisco early. Zoe has insisted that I not stick around on her account, even though Asher had to go back to work. She's staying behind with her sisters for another week or two to get her dad's things in order and finish with everything. Packing up their childhood home is something she and her sisters need to do together, she says, without husbands or friends or boyfriends around to distract them. Truthfully, I can't wait to get home.

chapter 20

Some Like It Hot

The U-Haul rolls away with George and her two Ikea bookcases, a closet's worth of new clothes and the only thing her mothers had agreed to send her from Buffalo: Her signed life-size cutout of Lieutenant Uhura. (I told my mom about it recently and even e-mailed her a picture, thinking she might be interested in making an offer, but she coolly informed me that *Star Trek* memorabilia was an entire industry unto itself and ridiculously overpriced, to boot.)

I wave after her like an idiot while Remy snickers behind me.

"Do you mind? I'm trying to have a moment here."

"Somehow I don't think this is the last time you'll be seeing each other."

"We're having lunch tomorrow, for your information, but that doesn't mean this isn't the end of an era—my little girl is leaving home. I can't help but be a little nostalgic."

He sighs and pulls up the bottom of his T-shirt to wipe his forehead. "Come inside. It's disgusting out here."

Only if you promise to do that again.

"Hello? Earth to Holly?"

"I'm fine. I think I'll just sit and cool off on the porch for a while."

"Cool off? Are you *insane?* It's ninety degrees in the shade!"

Ahh. Summertime in San Francisco. Probably quite nice, if it wasn't for the garbage strike.

"Suit yourself. But I'm going in—there's a six-pack in the fridge calling my name…."

"A six-pack?"

An hour later, Remy and I are lying on his bed for all the wrong reasons—because it's beneath the only ceiling fan in the house. Air-conditioning for the Wakefield manor isn't on the agenda until next summer.

"I'm a charity case," I tell him as he passes me another beer. "I know that. But I do have my pride, and I don't want to feel like I owe you for every little thing. Or feel guilty if you see me come home with a new pair of shoes or something. Because I'd rather move out than deal with that. *Capiche?*"

We're discussing the details of our new arrangement. I am simultaneously dreading it and looking forward to it at the same time. It's basically the same deal as when George and I first moved in, only in exchange for the cheap rent, now I will be working full-time *and* helping Remy with the renovations every spare moment I have. So I'll be exhausted and permanently sweaty on the one hand, but I'll also be able to enjoy the pleasure of his company almost every day. (Maybe, just maybe, Remy will even work shirtless! Oh, the possibilities…)

"For the tenth time, Holly, you don't have any pride. But

that's besides the point. And technically, you're not a charity case, either. It's not like I'm doing you the biggest favor in the world, you know—you'll be my *employee*. I'm even thinking I might write you off as a tax deduction."

"Aw, I bet you say that to all the girls."

"Nope—just you. And if it makes you feel any better, I'm going to put your rent back up the second you get a raise."

"…or when pigs fly."

"Whichever comes first. Or you might sell your book. Then I'd be asking you for a loan!"

I sit up. "I'll pay you back, Remy, I promise. I already owe my dad thousands of dollars, but I'll move you right to the top of my list of creditors…."

"I didn't mean it like that. This isn't a loan. It's just a re-version clause in our lease. And frankly, having you stay makes more sense for me…the thought of having to find a new tenant right now is a complete nightmare."

"And here I thought you enjoyed my company."

"Not so much. So quit slacking off and grab a paint-brush…."

"Forget it!" I say. "It's way too hot for fumes."

"Fine. First thing tomorrow, though."

"I don't get Sundays off?"

"Ha! You would never respect me as a boss if I agreed to that. Don't try and take advantage of me just because we're friends."

"So…we're friends?"

Oh, God. Did I really just say that?

The combination of heat and alcohol has me playing fast and loose with my heart. Since Buffalo, once I realized how I felt about him, I've resolved not to discuss our relationship or even allude to it, since I figure I'll probably say something so lame and obvious that he'll figure out I'm in love with him, an incredibly humiliating prospect from which no good can possibly come. Yes, the thought of him letting me down easy is about a thousand times worse than lusting after him in secret for all eternity.

"Of course we're friends! Why? You'd prefer we were enemies?"

"No," I laugh. "But I'm glad you think so, too. I've always believed that men and women *can* be friends without...you know."

Okay, now I'm *really* pushing it. If he even remotely senses I'm trying to see if he likes me, I will shrivel up and die. But somehow I can't help myself. It's like watching a car wreck, only I am the sadomasochistic lunatic behind the wheel.

"So, men and women can be friends, huh?"

"Sure. As long as there's no chemistry. Like me and Asher. He's one of my best friends. Always will be. But only because there was never anything, you know, going on between us."

"Can I tell you something, then? As a friend?"

"Sure."

Please, please, please don't break my heart...

"What I want to say is this..."

He pauses and looks into my eyes.

"*What,* Remy?"

"Holly, what I want to say is...grab a paintbrush. Seriously. The kitchen still needs another coat. Oh, and make sure you cover the counters—I just put 'em in. If you spill so much as a drop...let's just say it won't be pretty. I'm going to take a nap...."

"Not a chance! Friends don't let friends drink and paint. And while we're on the subject, would you mind going downstairs and getting me another beer? I want a cold one."

"Forget it!"

"Come on, be a gentleman."

"You've had enough, m'lady..."

He's right. One more beer and I'll be professing my love in song.

"...and speaking of gentlemen, or whatever passes for gentlemen these days, how's your attorney doing? Did he miss you while you were away?"

Great. Just what I want to talk about. Remy still doesn't know about my delightful marriage proposal. I left town two days later and was mortified at the thought of admitting it to anyone besides George. Nor was I in any rush to broadcast the fact that my sex appeal apparently extends only to desperate bicycle messengers and gay men. Not exactly the kind of image I want to project to a guy who is out of my league to begin with.

Then again, since courtship obviously isn't on the menu for us, friendship is the next best thing. I might as well get used to it. And friends are supposed to tell each other things. Remy trusted me enough to open up to me about Sylvia, after all, so why should I keep anything from him, no matter how embarrassing? He's a good listener, he obviously has some insight into people, and maybe it would be good to get a guy's perspective on the whole horrible experience...

But before I can answer Remy's question, tell him all about Vale and what had happened, the doorbell rings. He rolls off the end of the mattress and walks over to the window. "It's the guy for the plumbing estimate. He wasn't supposed to be here till four. Probably can't wait to tell me how much two hundred feet of copper pipe is gonna cost me." He shakes his head in disgust. "These guys are no fools! They *know* I have to do copper....Damn city! They won't approve anything else in these old places even though PVC is just as good and..."

I manage to peel myself off the mattress and follow him downstairs while his rant branches out into the corruption of municipal politics, the evils of contractors in general, why plumbers and electricians in particular are the bane of his existence, and so on and so forth.

I'll admit it—what he's saying isn't overly interesting; his tirades rarely are. But there's something about the *way* he blabs on and on about whatever happens to be bothering him or inspiring him or distracting him at the moment that I find totally attractive. It's proof that he's a passionate man.

"…and get this—the last plumber who came out here pulled up in a Hummer. A fucking *Hummer!* Can you believe that? Plumbers, man. I tell ya…"

"Remy?"

"Yeah?"

"I'm going down to my place. I think it might be half a degree cooler in the basement."

"Sure. Come up later? We'll do pizza or something."

"Okay. Good luck with the plumber."

He shoots me an as-if look and goes to answer the door.

Downstairs, everything looks exactly the same (of course it does—all the furniture is mine!) but just knowing George's room is empty makes my heart ache. I sit down at the kitchen table with a pile of mail. Phone bill, cable bill, another "No Thanks" letter from a publisher…

Frankly, I'm impressed by how quick and efficient the publishers have been at stuffing my S.A.S.E.s with the bad news; it had taken far less time than I expected for the rejections to start rolling in. At first, I was a little disheartened. The more I thought about it, though, the more certain I became that I was meant to write an entirely different book, anyway.

The real problem with the mail that has piled up while I was away is the bills. Without George's half of everything, even with reduced rent, it actually looks like I might be going broke in the not-too-distant future. When I notice the interest charge on my Visa bill, I briefly consider calling Vale and setting a date for the wedding. Being a writer-philan-thropist with a gay husband would surely be better than this!

I get out the calculator and crunch some numbers. For one very dark moment—even darker than the moment I considered calling Vale—I think about moving home, living with my parents while I get back on my feet. But then I remember my room and how sleeping there had literally been one long nightmare. Philadelphia is a better option. It's a lot less expensive than San Francisco, and a fresh start might do me some good. But damn it, I like it here. And leaving every time things get hard is a pattern I can't afford to develop, both because of short-term moving costs and the even greater expense long-term therapy might incur.

Fortunately, I don't have to decide anything just yet. I take a long, cool shower and flop down onto my bed. I'm not generally a napper, but the heat and the beer soon lull me away to a better place….

When I wake, it's already dark, but still hot as hell. I throw on some shorts and a tank top (there's no point in hiding it from him anymore—I am a 34 A on a good day and bras for me are obviously strictly ornamental). I drag myself up the back stairs and into the kitchen.

Remy is on the phone with his mother. He must have just taken a shower because his hair is wet and his T-shirt is clean. Since he hasn't gotten around to buying an actual table and chairs, he's sitting on the newly installed granite countertop, his legs dangling over the side. I try not to stare at his bulging quads as I push past him on my way to the fridge.

While I poke around and try to find something to eat, he discusses with his mother at length her concerns about his grandmother and her sciatica, someone named Helen's up-coming cataract surgery and his father's plans to build a new toolshed. After a great deal of eye-rolling and promising to go home to San Diego for a visit during Labor Day weekend, he finally manages to hang up.

"Sorry. The older she gets, the harder it is to get off the phone with her. She goes on and on, repeating the same things over and over. I can only assume she doesn't know she's doing it. My father must have the patience of Job."

I love that he's nice to his mother. "It's okay. You're a mama's boy. You don't have to apologize."

"Don't push me, woman."

"Forget that. I'm starving." I hop up beside him onto the counter. "Ah—cool on the backside. Good idea."

He reaches across my lap for the stack of dog-eared delivery menus. Even though I've definitely slept off my beer buzz, having his skin so close to mine leaves me a little woozy.

"Pizza or Chinese?"

Our eyes meet.

"Both!"

Over yet another delightful meal from Chang's Italian Gardens, I tell him all about what happened with Vale. Had I known the crashing and burning of my personal life made such fabulous dinner conversation, I might have told him sooner. I think Remy pretty much guesses where the story is going once I get to Vale's less-than-convincing response to my big "Am I Sexy?" question, because he can barely contain his laughter from that point on. Granted, I embellish the good parts a little, adding a horrified gasp or a dramatic sob here and there, so that the whole thing actually ends up sounding a hell of a lot funnier than it seemed to me at the time. I should have known the only thing Remy would enjoy more than being right about my boyfriend being so wrong was listening to a blow-by-blow account of me learning it for myself. Who could blame him? I'd definitely failed to see the signs.

"So…not quite the proposal you'd imagined, huh?"

"I imagined the Fred Leighton part, all right…"

"Who?"

"He's a jeweler…never mind."

"Just chalk it up to experience and move on. That's my advice."

"I just can't believe how willing I was to deceive myself for something…something I don't even *want!* I can totally see that now, by the way, in case you were thinking of making fun of me some more."

"Don't worry, I won't. You've suffered enough."

"Thanks. And to make matters worse, this whole thing has really done a number on my self-esteem!"

"Yeah… I've been kinda wondering about that. Why are you so down on yourself? Don't you think you deserve a decent guy?"

"Of course I do," I sigh, and attempt to condense the past ten years of my social life into two or three sentences. "But I don't exactly have the best luck with men. My only real boyfriend, this guy Jim, was a real loser. And that was, like, a *decade* ago, anyway, so I guess being single for so long… well, after a while, you just begin to think it's not the guys, but you. I mean, me. Oh, you know what I mean… But I am picky. Or I was, anyway. Too picky. So I guess it *is* the guys, too…"

"Whoa. Hold up—you didn't get *any* play between Jim and Vale? Nothing? Wow. That *is* a long time. Was it…intentional?"

Great. Now he thinks I'm one of those born-again virgins. "For heaven's sake, Remy. I'm not a *complete* nerd. Of course I've had, uh, some action. There were a few short-term things, just nothing serious…"

He scratches his head. "Nope. Don't buy it."

"Excuse me?"

"It takes more than one putz and a dry spell here and there to inflict the kind of psychological damage and self-sabotage you seem to labor beneath."

"You really like to think you know it all, don't you? Okay, Mr. Minor in Psychology. Fine. You wanna know my dirty little secret?"

"I don't know. Do I?"

"It all goes back to when I was twelve…"

"Cripes…is this gonna be another one of those tragic first-kiss stories?"

"Do you want to hear it or not?"

"Sorry. Go on."

"There was this guy…and *yes*—he was the first guy I ever kissed. It was awful. I almost bit his tongue off and there was all this blood and so of course he had to go and tell everyone I was a hermaphrodite and that's why I had no boobs and, well, high school pretty much got worse from there."

"Okay, that's pretty bad," he chuckles.

"Suffice it to say I'm pretty sure that's what made me so self-conscious about my chest."

His eyes go right to where my boobs should be. "Your chest? What's wrong with your chest?"

"Oh, shut up. So now you understand why this whole Vale-being-gay thing has thrown me for such a loop…."

"I don't get it. What does one have to do with the other?"

"Maybe the only reason Vale liked me to begin with or chose me or whatever…it's because I'm flat! Otherwise, he wouldn't be able to keep it up long enough for us to make babies, see? I bet he was pretending I was Brad Pitt while we were—"

"Hold it," he interrupted, shaking his head in disbelief. "That is so wrong on so many levels, I don't even know where to begin."

"Really?"

"First of all, Brad Pitt definitely has bigger pecs than you."

"I appreciate the sentiment, Remy, but that doesn't make me feel any better."

"Okay, fine. What I mean is…let me see…how should I put this? Well, to quote another great man, 'Anything bigger than a handful, you're risking a sprained thumb.'"

"Anthony Michael Hall," I sigh. *"Weird Science."*

"Damn, you're good."

"You just don't understand what it's like, being permanently self-conscious, feeling like you're being judged all the time for something that's totally beyond your control. This is a breast-centric, world, Remy—you can't deny it. Even my brothers called me Wall-y Holly! It's a world where Hooters is the hottest restaurant in town, where women torture themselves to look like magazine covers. I'm so damn tired of it…. We pay men to surgically insert silicone volleyballs into our chests and we spend a trillion dollars on miracle diets and then we eat ourselves into oblivion to numb the pain of failing to be perfect! It's…it's infuriating! And if you *somehow* manage to evolve beyond it all…well, just when you think you've accepted yourself, love yourself for the way you are, a gay guy comes along to play on your insecurities and pretend to love you and then wants to hire you to be his wife!"

"By 'you,' you don't actually mean me, do you?"

I manage a weak laugh, but my eyes are filling with tears. "Sorry to rant. I just don't want to be controlled by these superficial things anymore. I resent all the time and energy I've wasted on them."

"Look, Holly. I do understand what you're saying. It sucks being liked—or disliked—for the wrong reasons, whether they're perceived or real. I *do* know what that feels like. Who the hell doesn't? But half the time it's all in your own head, anyway. Like, everyone has something they *think* weighs them down, whether it's a flat chest or an empty bank account or the brain of a rocket scientist trapped in a supermodel's body. You just have to surround yourself with people who like you fine the way you are and not get too worked up about the ones who don't."

"In theory, sure. But it's hard to not let these kinds of things affect you. And even though you know how much it hurts, it's also hard not to judge other people in exactly the same way they judge you."

"Of course it's hard. Most people can't do it. That's why the world is overrun with assholes and idiots. But at least you're trying."

"I was an asshole, too," I murmur.

Can I blame Vale for offering me exactly what I wanted? I never really liked him all that much and I was willing to be with him, anyway, and *not* just for the sake of "research." I now understood what Jill saw in Boyfriend—a chance to not be alone. Vale's proposal was a twisted variation on that theme. Was it fair to hold him or anyone else to a higher standard than I held myself?

"You sure were," he agrees. "But there's hope for you yet."

"So what's your hideous flaw, Mr. Perfect?"

"Hmmm…I don't know…maybe my calves? They're a little smaller than I'd like. But are you gonna throw the babe out with the bathwater?" He flexes them for my benefit and flashes me his best smile.

"You're right. They're hideous. And your bottom teeth are crooked, too."

"Yes, but they give me character."

"I just feel like I've spent a lot of time, too much time, wishing I were rich, wishing I were beautiful, you know? It's a waste of energy. I'm ready to let it all go."

"You are beautiful. You must know that."

"I know I'm *okay*. But I'm not exactly drop-dead gorgeous…."

He turns my chin toward him. "Yes, you are. Well, maybe not to *everyone*...but so what? You are to me."

"What's that supposed to mean?"

"Are you serious?"

Oooh!

Before I can think of something ridiculous to say that will ruin everything, he leans in and kisses me. And before it's over, I know that if I had to choose one moment to live over and over again for the rest of my life, this would be it.

He pulls away and smiles.

"Wow," I say.

"Wow," he agrees.

"My heart..."

He puts his hand on my chest. "I feel it."

"Wow," I say again.

"You said that already."

"I guess I don't know what else to say."

"Say you'll come upstairs with me."

"Uh, okay."

He hops down from the counter and turns to face me, putting his hands on my hips. "Are you sure you want to?"

"Uh, yeah. I mean yes. Yes, I want to..."

He kisses me again and I try my best to kiss him back like I mean it (the first time, I think I was a little stunned, so it probably wasn't my best work). I open my eyes for a second, just to make sure I'm not dreaming.

The kitchen glows and I definitely feel like I'm in a dream sequence...or is it the subtle recessed lighting we installed together earlier this week? In the corner, near the door to the backyard, is the tile cutter I almost sliced my finger off with last month. I remove my hand from the back of Remy's neck and hold it up to check for the scar. It's still there, angry and pink, despite weeks of slathering it with vitamin E.

Nope! Definitely not dreaming.

I slide off the edge of the counter and press up against him, wrapping my arms around his waist. We kiss some more, just standing there, until at last I completely forget myself and there's nothing in my mind but the kissing. Which is quickly becoming quite a bit more than just kissing....

"So…"

"Yeah."

He leads me through the dining room, past the walls we'd put up, into the living room, where we'd argued about the height of a chair rail, then up the stairs I'd sanded and stained and varnished and then *re*sanded and *re*stained and *re*varnished because the color was half a shade off. The second floor is a mess; not much has changed since I first saw it six months earlier. Aside from the bathroom, there's only one room with walls…but it's the best room of all. The *only* room that matters. Remy's bedroom.

I walk up to the window while he goes over to the bed and sits down. I have no idea what time it is, but the moon is high and it lights up the room.

"Did you ever notice the trim on the house across the street?" I ask.

"Yes."

"I like it."

"So do I. What's your point?"

"No point."

"Then come over here."

"Okay," I say. But I can't move. Remy is so gorgeous to begin with that in the moonlight he appears almost divine. The perfect angles of his face, his lonely gray eyes, the straight lines of his nose and chin and cheeks take me aback every single time I see him, and tonight is no different, except that I am on the verge of seeing the rest of him as well. *What on earth could this heavenly creature possibly want with me?* But my cheeks still burn from his stubble, and there he sits, waiting for me to join him.

"What's the matter?"

"Nothing."

"We don't have to rush."

I breathe out my fear and try to be as honest as I can. "If this is a…a pity thing, Remy, then I don't want it."

He flops back dramatically onto the mattress. "Watch it, Holly. Or I might change my mind."

"Don't do me any favors," I say and turn back to the window.

He sighs. "I didn't mean it like that. I was just teasing. You know you'd be the one doing me the honor."

"No…"

"Of course!" He gets up off the bed and comes over to the window. "You're a beautiful creature. I've been pining for you for months. I was just waiting for you to be single again so I could make my move. And the second you told me, I did!"

"Yeah, right."

He shakes his head. "Why won't you believe me?"

"I…I don't know."

"Have I ever given you a reason not to trust me?"

"No."

"Well, then why stop believing me now?"

I glance over at the bed. "Hmm…could it be…?"

"Okay, I'll admit that I'm more than a little, uh, ready, right now, but I'm not the kind of guy who'd trick a girl into the sack by lying to her. That said, I sure as hell ain't gonna *beg* you either…"

Him beg me? I giggle at the mere thought of it.

"You're killing me, Holly. You're fucking killing me."

"Okay, okay," I say and kiss him quickly. *Broken heart be damned—this guy is worth the risk.* "But can I ask you something first?"

"Sure."

"Will this be the first time for you since…"

He looks at me uneasily, not quite sure what I mean.

"Since, you know…your wife?"

"*God,* no!"

"Oh. Okay. Of course…"

He must have guessed that I am blushing, because he touches my cheek with the back of his hand. "I mean, I don't exactly sleep around, but I've had some action. Sorry to disappoint you."

"I'm not disappointed. I've just never seen you with anybody, that's all."

"So you've been keeping track of my comings and goings?"

"Maybe a little," I admit. "You're surprised?"

"Not really. You're pretty easy to read. I knew you wanted me the second we met." He moves back over to the bed and lies down, and this time, I follow him. "Am I right?"

"Yeah."

"See?" He smiles and begins kissing my neck. "I'm irresistible…"

"So, I guess you wanted me right away, too, then?"

"No."

"Hey!"

"Don't worry—it didn't take too long. You can't deny there's some pretty good sexual tension between us."

"Well, yeah. But I just assumed it was one-sided."

He kisses me again, and thankfully I'm already lying down because I surely would have swooned.

"It doesn't feel like that if it's only one-sided."

"Oh. Okay."

"Holly…"

"Yes, Remy?"

"Can we stop talking now?"

I nod my head and smile.

chapter 21

Alone in the Wilderness of Despair

For an entire week, I avoid Remy like the plague. I tell no one, not even George, what has happened between us. I know I'm in love—in love for the first time!—but I also know that I'd better get over it before I make the mistake of thinking it will end well. Do I regret sleeping with him? Of course not. It was the best night of my life. I do regret getting my hopes up, though, since I am now in the unenviable position of having to deprogram myself and move on.

In case you're thinking, there she goes again—letting her dark side, her melodrama, ruin a perfectly good thing, let me set you straight: During the delicious three-and-a-half hours between first contact and when the bubble finally burst, I believed Remy Wakefield and I actually had a chance. More than that, even… I was thinking he was my *soul mate,* an appellation not to be invoked lightly, least of all by a studied cynic like me. We fit together perfectly, no doubt about it, and there was chemistry, passion and connection to burn. So what if he's hot and I'm not? Big deal. I'll get over it. So what if he's unfocused and immature? I'm just as self-deprecating and neurotic. We'd complement each other's weaknesses and thrive on each other's strengths.

What *was* a big deal was the one thing we couldn't move forward without. The one thing I didn't realize I should have been worried about all along….

Timing.

As in, I'm too late. *Way* too late.

All these years of singlehood, I've been worried about finding the right guy. I just never imagined how important the *when* would be, once the *who* was taken care of. Luckily, I didn't see it until after Remy and I had slept together and it was staring me right in the face, so I didn't miss out on the night I will surely treasure fondly as the highlight of my sex life. Thank heaven for small mercies, I suppose.

It had come out of left field, while my defenses were down. Remy and I were eating leftover chow mein in bed, sharing one pair of chopsticks and making a complete mess.

"Not a bad way to work up an appetite," he said.

I smiled. "Just another lame Saturday night with the landlord."

"I guess neither of us has much of a social life."

"Nope."

"Don't think this gets you out of our arrangement, by the way. You start painting tomorrow at seven."

I kicked him beneath the covers. "I don't think so!"

"Well, maybe we could work something out in exchange for letting you sleep in a bit…"

"Isn't that sexual harassment?"

"If you're lucky!" He rolled over to grab the glass of water beside the bed. "You gonna report me?"

Over Remy's heart, in the pale light coming in from the hallway, I noticed the outline of something very small, maybe the size of a quarter. *A birthmark? A rash? A third nipple?*

"What's that on your chest?" I asked, just as I realized what it was.

He froze.

It was a tattoo—a tattoo of a beach ball. With a single name written beneath it.

Sylvia

The crush of disappointment descended on me like a pall, squeezing every trace of joy from my newly opening heart in a fraction of an instant.

It wasn't me that he loved. It was her.

It would *always* be her. And so she would be with us always, existing as a part of him. In ink, least of all.

This would never work.

During sleepless nights, I try to figure out exactly what happened, what Remy's motivations were, and whether or not he was even aware of them. What I came up with was pretty simple.

Sex. He wanted sex.

At one point, I half wonder whether one of my brothers had got wind that I liked Remy, called him up and bet him how long it would take him to get my knickers off. Maybe they even had a little pool going back home. Fortunately, though, Mike and Bradley didn't even know he existed, so it couldn't possibly be their fault.

For a few days, I just chalk it up to the heat. In the city, the heat can make people crazy. Especially lonely people. It had made me crazy enough to believe that Remy really liked me, and almost crazy enough to think I could compete with a ghost.

Yes, the simple fact is that Remy, like all guys, probably just wanted to get laid. He saw me as an easy target—tragically and recently single, living far away from friends and family— and he went for it. He could be forgiven for that. On the other hand, his flattery seemed so sincere. The oldest trick in the book. He hadn't had a girl up there since we'd moved in, or at least none that I knew of.

He was horny. I was easy. Case closed.

Not that he was a jerk about it or anything like that. He called me the next day, and the day after that. He even came downstairs a few times, but I made sure to keep the door locked and just pretended I wasn't home.

The last thing I wanted was for him to have to lie and give me some lame excuse about why it—*we*—could never happen again, why it was probably best that we leave it as a one-time thing. It would be humiliating. Having him think I expected more from him than a one-night stand would be far worse than pining away privately. For now, I still love him; that much is out of my hands. What I *can* control is the way I deal with it. Hopefully, in time, my feelings for Remy will melt away into harmless memories, of a kind pleasant enough to look back on and smile, without the rankle of regret and hurt and shame that still tortures me when I think about Jim. I should have seen the signs then, but I didn't. I should have seen the signs with Vale, but I didn't. This time, with Remy, I would. No excuses.

So until I can figure out what to say to him and gather up the courage to face him, I have to make sure I don't completely lose my mind. More than anything, I need a distraction…a way to let the immediacy of the hurt dissipate a little so that I'll be able to vanquish it completely once I'm ready to revisit it....

I'll focus my attention on my work! And I mean my *real* work, not the encyclopedia stuff (turns out researching acorns and the Acropolis isn't as cathartic as I'd hoped). I'm a writer; of that much I'm certain. I just need to self-actualize a little. So rejections be damned! The idea of marrying for money is so totally behind me that I honestly couldn't care less if not a single publisher was interested. Besides, the prospect of faking my way through an entire book about something so false is beyond unappealing.

Instead, I will rework the entire thing, start anew! Re-opening myself to the idea of having a true soul mate—one who hasn't already found and lost his—will coincide with my new writing project: the process of finding one. It will be unironic, nonsatirical, nonfiction. It will be truthful. It will be therapeutic. And I will be proud to let any prospective life partner know exactly what I'm writing about. If it scares him off, then he isn't the one for me, anyway.

chapter 22

Attempted Love Suicide

In one of those cruel twists of fate, a letter comes just as I'm putting the finishing touches on my new book proposal. Not expecting much, I drop my purse and keys on the kitchen table and sit down to tear open the last of the envelopes I had stamped and addressed myself with so much optimism nearly three months earlier.

Dear Ms. Hastings,
Thank you for your recent submission to MacLaughlin Binch. We would be very interested in seeing a full manuscript for *How to Marry a Millionaire (And Still Love Yourself in the Morning!)* Please contact us at your earliest convenience so that we can discuss this project with you in greater detail.
Sincerely,
Grace Lee
Senior Acquisitions Editor
Nonfiction Division
MacLaughlin Binch, New York

Shit.

Seventeen rejection letters and now this. I'm in desperate need of a cash influx, and therefore in no mood to be putting my money where my mouth is, since my mouth has in fact very recently been boasting far and wide how I wouldn't write that book now if they paid me.

I am weary to the bone. Is a little mental peace and quiet too much to ask for? After a quick slice of leftover pizza, I run a bubble bath, peel off my work clothes, and slip into the tub. A good long soak will help me figure out what to do, or at the very least, help me forget myself for a while.

Only once my toes and fingertips are good and wrinkly do I get out. The air in my apartment is mercifully cool (I'd finally splurged on an air conditioner—buy now, pay later!). I flip on the TV, grab one of the giant chocolate bars I'd hidden in the back of the pantry for just such an occasion, and install myself on the couch. Inspired by back-to-back episodes of *Extreme Makeover,* I paint my toes bright pink and give myself a facial. I drink half a bottle of wine, too….

The muffled shouts of someone pounding at the back door interrupts my dozing.

"Holly, I know you're in there! This is ridiculous, already!"

No sense in putting it off any longer.

I stretch, lower the volume on the TV and go over to let him in.

"Remy," I say as coolly as I can. "What a pleasant surprise. I just got home a little while ago. Would you like to come—"

He raises an eyebrow at me, then pushes past me into the living room.

"It's been two weeks! Why the hell are you avoiding me?"

I feign innocence. "Why, I haven't the faintest idea what you're talking about! I'm sorry if I haven't had a chance to return your calls yet, but I've just been so busy. You know how it is. So…how have you been?" I shut the door and follow him.

"You really are an idiot," he says, grabbing me by the arm as I walk by. "It's almost frightening. What's the matter with you?"

My ice-princess act melts away the second he touches me. "I didn't want this to get all weird, and now look…."

"You're the one who's made it weird! What's your problem?"

I struggle to twist out of his grasp. "Remy…just leave me alone. Please just leave me alone."

He lets go and steps back. "I don't understand."

My pulse quickens. I glance at the clock hanging in the kitchen—it has been fifteen days, seven hours and twenty-two…make that twenty-three minutes since I last looked into his twinkling gray eyes. I guess I'm not quite over him yet.

"I don't want to be mean, but has it occurred to you that maybe I'm trying not to lead you on? That I don't want to give you the wrong idea about us?"

The hint of a smile crossed his lips. "Wait a sec…" He shakes his head and folds his arms across his chest. "Are you going to stand here in front of me and try and convince me that…that *you* used *me?*"

What an ego! I bet the guy has never been on the receiving end of a breakup in his entire life. "Why? Is that so hard to believe?"

"Uh…yeah. It is."

There's obviously something seriously wrong with my wiring, because the egotistical jackass thing makes me like him even more. *Steady, Holly, steady…*

"Look, Remy. What we had was…wonderful. But let's be honest with ourselves and each other before we say things we don't mean…."

Let him down easy before he could let me down easy— that's the plan. Because even if he's up for a fling, I know my heart would never survive when we crashed and burned, as we surely would. Having a ghost as the other woman…how could I compete?

"What things?"

"What I'm saying is, let's just be smart and not go somewhere with this that neither of us really wants to be."

"Yeah right." He stifles a laugh. "If you think I believe that…"

"Well, aren't we cocky today!"

"Holly, there isn't a single thing about me that you don't like. And I know it, okay? So you can drop the act. You know, I preferred it when you told me how you really felt, like before we—"

"Fine, Remy! You're right! As usual, you're right! I just wanted to make this easier for the both of us, but what the hell—I'm going to be completely honest, okay? I was trying to give you a way to save face! But if you'd rather come down here and make it harder on *me* with some line about us being better as friends, or how things got a little out of control, or how maybe once in a while we can do the C.S.B.F. thing, or how you're gay, or involved with someone else, or just an asshole, or afraid of commitment, or shipping out in the morning, or…or…"

"Okay, okay! I'd say that covers just about every excuse I could possibly have…at least I think it does. What's C.S.B.F?"

"Casual sex between…oh, never mind. Would you please just listen to me? I'm trying to do the right thing here and give you an out. I'd take it if I were you. Then we might be able to salvage our friendship. Because you're right—I do like you, Remy. A lot."

I stare at the floor and try not to cry.

"So why won't you even give me a chance to say what I want to say?"

"Because I don't want to hear it."

"Are you sure?"

I nod.

"Fine. See if I care," he says and stomps out, slamming the door behind him.

"Oh yeah?!" I shout as loudly as I can. "Well, guess what? There *is* something I don't like about you—your cat! I *hate* cats. *Especially* Fleabiscuit!"

I run back into my room and collapse in tears.

It takes about five minutes for me to rue every single word that has come out of my mouth. No matter how many times I replay it in my mind, the outcome is always the same: I am the fool. Sure, I've accomplished my goal—Remy no longer has any say in what happens between us, and I haven't allowed myself to become one of those silly, needy women who wear their hearts on their sleeve. Women like that are the ones who end up alone or, worse still, in really bad relationships, aren't they? Sure they are. And I'm not about to let that happen to me. *I'm* the one in control here....

But then why do I feel like such crap?

No matter how hard I fight against opening my mind to the truth, a new awareness slowly asserts itself. Remy Wakefield isn't an asshole or a jerk; he isn't a Jim or a Vale. He's an honest, decent man who never gave me any reason not to trust him. Maybe the reason I feel so bad is because once again, I've let my head win out over my heart. Do I really want to be one of those people? Not on your life. Not anymore. And besides, who am I to usurp the natural order of things? Relationships are like living beings, with lifespans of their own. To let this one simply play itself out without me cutting it off at the knees was probably the wiser choice. I'm sure I hadn't done a very good job of hiding how I felt anyway, and Remy isn't an idiot. The proverbial shark was circling the lifeboat and my blood was in the water, only instead of trying to stay alive as long as possible, I'd jumped in feet-first.

It's love suicide.

"Having your heart broken by someone else can't be worse than doing it to yourself."

I sit up. The blue glow from the TV backlights a perfect silhouette in the doorway. "Remy?"

How long he's been standing there, watching me sob into my pillow in the dark, I have no idea. But I'm thankful that he is.

"Are you done?"

"Yeah," I sniff.

He walks over to the bed and sits down beside me. "I'm not a game-player, Holly. What you see is what you get with me. So I've decided not to let you pull this crap, which I'm chalking up to the fact that the only two relationships you've ever had ended like a plane crash."

I nod.

"I was going to come back down here and tell you what's been on my mind, but since it seems like you've already decided that for me, I thought I'd let you go first. Tell me the truth. And you better get it right this time, because this is it. So, go ahead—I'm listening."

"The truth?" I sigh. "The truth about how I feel? I've been trying to figure that out for two weeks…actually, a lot longer than that. The truth is, I have no idea what the truth is anymore. I don't think I ever did! I'm so confused about everything these days…how about I just tell you what I'm thinking right now, okay?"

"Okay."

I wipe my nose and sit up. "Okay… So, um, first of all, I'm sorry that I ignored you. I shouldn't have done that. But the more I thought about that night, you know, what happened between us…the more I was afraid that it was just…just too good to be true, I guess. I didn't know what to say to you."

"How about 'Hi, Remy, you're the best I ever had. Thanks a million!'"

I smile weakly. "No…it's more complicated than that and you know it. I'm just going to say this as plainly as I can, even at the risk of supersizing your already inflated ego…."

"What?" He grins, like he already knows what I'm going to say.

"We can dance around the issue as much as you want, but you know it and I know it—you're out of my league."

"Am I?"

"Yes. Or rather, I'm out of yours. That's part of why it could never work."

"What could never work?"

"God, why do you have to make me say it? Us! You and me—*we* could never work. Couples that are equally attractive have the best shot at happiness. It's a fact… Not that you're even thinking we could *be* a couple, I know, but—"

"Exactly where do you get this shit, Holly?"

"It's basic social psychology."

"Well, I took plenty of psych classes and I wasn't aware of that particular law being written in stone. Wait…is this some sort of weird girly trick to get me to say you're beautiful? Because that's *really* pathetic…."

I shrug. If there's any hope of me letting my guard down with Remy for good, then I'm going to need to hear him convince me over and over again how wrong I am about everything. "You can say what you want. But I know the truth. You could never be attracted to me."

"Hold on… I'm confused. Did you think I was faking it or something?"

"I know how the male body works, Remy. I mean you

could, technically, be attracted to me for brief periods of time, I suppose, to suit your physical needs, just like Vale could, but in the long run? I doubt it…and I don't want to spend any more time feeling like crap about myself, or being self-conscious or any of that because, frankly, I'm over it. I'm looking for a soul mate now and I'm not ashamed to admit it!"

"What happened to hunting millionaires and…how did you put it? Oh, yeah—'actualizing financial freedom'?"

"*That?* I told you from the beginning—it was all just for the book." I wink, just to throw him off a little. "I never actually planned to marry one and throw my entire life away, along with any chance at happiness or love. God. As if!"

He scratches his head. "Okay, Holly. Fine. You've been, uh, sort-of honest, and I appreciate it. So now I'm going to do the same."

"Okay."

I steel myself for the worst.

"First of all…you have a killer body."

"*What?* What's that supposed to mean? You could learn to live with me as long as I put a *bag* over my head?"

He laughs. "Sorry! It was the first thing that came to mind because, in case you forget yourself, you're sitting here in your bra and underwear. And with all that stuff on your face…"

My hand darts up to my cheek and I pull it away—my fingertips glow green.

"Oh my God!" I laugh, amazed that I'd forgotten. "I am such an idiot! It's a mud mask—I was giving myself a facial to feel better, and I was eating all this chocolate and wine and—"

"A mud mask, huh? Well, I've seen what's underneath it, and it ain't too bad, either. Love those freckles, by the way. Did I ever tell you that my brother thinks you look a bit like whatsername?… that actress, you know, the one who shop-lifted…"

I grab some Kleenex from the box beside the bed and begin wiping off what I can. "My sheets! What a mess. Do you think it'll come out?… Wait a sec… What did you say? About your brother?"

"I, uh, e-mailed him a picture of you. From when we were trying out my new digital camera, remember?"

How could I forget? My eyes were red in all of them. Remy said I looked like the devil in coveralls. *But why would he send his brother a picture of me?*

I open my mouth to ask…

"Because I wanted him to see the girl I like."

"Oh."

He reaches for my hand, even though it's covered in mud. "I'm not emotionally unavailable, Holly. I don't have a girl-friend. I'm not moving away. I'm not gay or bisexual or crazy or deceitful or any of the other things you seem to enjoy imagining. What I am is here…and it's not too late."

I hug him and try not to cry.

"What's the matter? Isn't this a good thing?"

"I want to believe you, Remy. I really do. But I don't think you know your own heart well enough to be able to offer it to me."

He pulls away from me. "What? Why would you say that?"

"Because we have bad timing. Because of Sylvia, and how you still feel about her. Because you've already had the love of your life. And that's what I'm looking for—the love of mine. A soul mate. *My* soul mate."

He stares at me sadly. "I can't undo the past, Holly. And I wouldn't want to."

"I understand that. It's a part of who you are…" I touch his chest, just over his heart.

"Ohhh…so *that's* what this is about!? My beach ball?"

"Yeah. Your beach ball."

"I got it because that's what I needed to do at the time. I

was…afraid I'd forget. Now I know that I never will, with or without the tattoo."

"I don't know if I can compete with that, Remy. As much as I'm tempted to…"

For a change, he doesn't have such a quick answer. He just sort of sits there.

"I'm sorry. I don't mean to upset you, but it's been on my mind…."

"Don't be sorry, Holly. I guess I haven't thought much about what it must be like for you. I can understand how it probably seems hard or weird or whatever. And you're right—I *will* always love Sylvia. I guess all I can say is that it was like, I don't know, another lifetime. That's how I look at it. I died when she died, only I was born again. So, yeah, she's gone. But I'm still here, even though some days it's not easy."

"And no one should ever ask you or even expect you to get over her. But you also have to understand that I want to be with someone who thinks of me as their first choice, not an experiment in moving on. I think I'd always feel like I was in her shadow."

"You know, you cast a pretty tall shadow yourself."

I link my fingers through his and squeeze. "Thanks. That's very sweet."

"I'm not trying to be sweet! I just want you to see how losing my wife five years ago doesn't mean I should be single forever. I'm not ruined, I'm just a widower. Yes, it's weird. I know. I get it. But so what? Deal with it! I've been through counseling and I think I've invested enough in the whole process to be sufficiently aware of my own motivations and limitations and I know that I'm not looking for a replacement for Sylvia or anything sad or pathetic like that. I just want what everybody else wants—to hook up with the right person. For the occasional conversation and lots and lots of sex! But if you feel like you can't deal with me or my big scary past because of your own trust or self-esteem issues or whatever, then you only have yourself to blame. So thanks, but I think I *do* know my own heart, Holly. It may be bruised, but it's still beating. Oh—and in case you were wondering, you have plenty of shitty baggage yourself."

He leans back against the headboard and folds his arms over his chest, pleased with himself for having figured it out yet again and tied it all up in a neat little package. I have to hand it to him, though. The guy knows exactly who he is.

Maybe, just maybe, Remy really is ready to move on.

"You've been to therapy? Wow! I must say that I'm quite impressed. So tell me—which school do you prefer? Being an anxiety-prone phobic with a tinge of O.C.D., I'm a fan of the behaviorists, myself, although I can't say that I've ever really committed wholeheartedly to a true course of psychoanalysis…."

"Holly!"

"I'm just teasing! I hear you, Remy. I *get* it. And you're right, of course, as usual. But how do I know you're not going to flake out on me some day?"

"Technically, you don't. But so what?"

"But what if every time I see the beach ball, I'm re-minded—"

"Tough shit. It's a part of me. And so is Fleabiscuit, by the way. The cat stays in the picture!"

I must have pouted unintentionally.

"Come here. Closer… Okay. Now listen carefully, be-cause this is as much commitment as you're going to get from me for now, and I reserve the right to deny having said it. But since you obviously have such a *huge* problem with this whole beach ball thing, I will say this. Just because I already have one tattoo doesn't mean there isn't room for a new one some day, provided the right woman inspires me."

My heart leaps. "Really? You'd get a 'Holly' tattoo?"

"Actually, I was thinking maybe one that says 'Mom.'"

"Very funny."

"Who's joking?"

"But…"

"But what, my little nut job?"

"But the spot over your heart is taken."

"My pecs are huge. There's still lots of room…. Oh, for God's sake! I'm laying it on the line here, Holly! What more do you want? Are you trying to get me to say that I love you? Because I won't!"

"That's not what I meant!" I hit him with a pillow.

"There's green stuff on my shirt now. Thanks." He smacks me back with the pillow. Hard.

"Watch it—I'm feeling very fragile."

"Too fragile for this?" he asks, and kisses me on the cheek. Mud mask and all.

"No. That's fine."

"What about this?" He kisses me on the mouth.

"I guess that's okay, too."

The guy is irresistible; there's no sense in fighting it any longer. As George would say, "Resistance is futile." It's a line some creepy *Star Trek* aliens gave to their terrified prey before assimilating them into robots, which is not unlike how I feel at the moment—in the grips of something much bigger than me, and about to be changed forever. But in a good way, of course.

"Hey, I have an idea! Maybe if you stare at my chest for long enough, you'll become desensitized…."

He starts to take off his T-shirt, but I stop him. The last thing I need is his body clouding my judgment.

"Actually, I think part of the problem is that I feel like I don't know anything about your old life. Maybe that's why I find it so threatening. So…do you think you could tell me about it?"

"Uh…does this mean we're not having sex now?"

I wipe a smear of mud off his cheek with my thumb. "Yes, Remy. It does."

"Fine," he sighs. "Are you sure you want to hear this stuff?"

"Yes, if you don't mind telling me."

"Of course not. I suppose it'll do me some good, too."

And so he tells me all about her.

Maybe the rarest love of all, grand enough and certain enough to survive anything life can throw at two people, isn't really so rare. My mother and father have it. Cole and Olivia have it. Asher and Zoe do, too. George and Max? Quite likely. I have no idea if Remy and Sylvia had it, but I hope so for his sake, and for hers.

If true love is the child of chance, destiny makes not one bit of difference. I know from watching the people around me that it isn't always pretty or perfect, that it isn't always called true love, that sometimes it's just called commitment. But I also know that often it works, and when it works, it lasts, and when it lasts you can count on it. And *that's* what counts, doesn't it? Soul mates, high-school sweethearts, arranged marriages, second marriages, no marriage at all, two men, two women, three of each, May-December romances, mail-order brides, shotgun weddings, Moneyed Mates, on-line lovers…what does it matter? As long as it's working for you, it's true love.

As for me, who's to say if I deserve to find true love or any love, or whether it's something a person can deserve at all. More likely, it all hinges on the willingness to receive it—a concept that takes some getting used to. Remy brings out the best in me, makes me like myself, and want to be a better person. I'd be a fool to hold out on a technicality or two. I love him, whether he loved someone else before me or not, whether he's gorgeous or not, whether *I'm* gorgeous or not, whether he has a tattoo of a beach ball on his chest or a sprig of holly on his butt.

Because waiting for the One is hard enough without holding out for the Only.

epilogue

My Soul Mate Next Door

George slides into the booth precisely at noon. Although she moved out three weeks ago, it feels like I see her now more than ever.

"So, I finally told her!" she says as she looks over the menu. "Did I get the chef's salad last time or the Hunter salad? I can't remember. One had olives and the other had those little oranges...."

"I have no idea, G. Told who what?"

"Chloe! About me and Max!"

"Oh! So how did she take it?"

"She was surprised, all right! But she likes me, you know, so she warmed up to the idea pretty quickly. I told her the entire story, pointing out how it was kind of her fault we hooked up in the first place because she made him go to that launch party the night we met. At the end I just said, 'Look, Chloe, I love your son and he loves me. Please don't fire me!'

She thought that was pretty funny. God, I can't believe I was so worried!"

"Wait—where was Max?"

"He thought it would be better if he wasn't there. She's a very domineering woman. He's still working through it with his therapist, but he's just not ready for a confrontation yet." She rolls her eyes and spits her gum out into a napkin. "The funny thing is, it was Chloe who insisted he go see someone to begin with. It was supposed to be career counseling at first, but then he started getting into all these deeper issues…you know how it is. Anyway, I'm surprised she's still paying for it, frankly, considering they haven't spoken in months."

"What is it with all these West Coast men and their mothers?"

She waves me off. "Oh, all the good ones have a thing with their mothers. Strong women raise sons who respect them, sometimes a little too much. It's mostly a positive quality, though—they treat women well and they usually know how to do the right thing. Guilt is a powerful motivator. Believe me, I know."

"Well, at least you guys are out of the closet now. Maybe you can help them reconcile, now that it's officially your business."

"Oh, I will. After what he did for me and my moms, I'm definitely planning a little revenge intervention. I invited her over for dinner next week. Max doesn't know yet, but…"

George shares every detail of the menu she's planned, along with an exhaustive history of Max's relationship with Chloe so that I understand exactly how momentous an event it will be. It isn't until the waitress sets the cheesecake down in front of me that I can finally get a word in edgewise.

"By the way, I got a request for a full," I tell her.

"What? When?"

"Last Monday."

"And you didn't tell me?"

"I'm telling you now. But it doesn't matter anyway because I'm not going to do it."

Her big eyes grow even bigger with surprise. "Excuse me? Did I just hear you say that you're turning down the chance to write your book? The book that was going to make you rich and famous? The book that was going to turn you into the writer you've always wanted to be? The book that's actually the *reason* we're sitting here in this diner a million miles from Buffalo? Are you kidding me?! Why on *earth*…"

"Take it easy, G! I'm just changing my idea."

"Oh. To what?"

"Promise you won't laugh, okay?"

"Okay, fine. To what?"

"Finding true love."

"Oh, Holly. Are you serious?"

"Yeah. I've made up my mind."

She smiles warmly. "So you're going to trade a millionaire for a soul mate, huh?"

"Yup. I've already got the main research down."

"You do?"

"I sure do. And I even have a working title—*The Soul Mate Next Door: Seeing the Love in Front of Your Face.*

"Well, that sounds nice. Too bad no cute guys live next door, huh?"

I push soggy strawberries around on my plate (fruit can ruin a perfectly good piece of cheesecake if you're not careful) and wait for a better reaction.

"Are you going to eat those?" she asks, picking them off one by one. "Berries are the preferred fruit option for Phase Two of the South Beach Diet, you know."

"Even when they're covered with sugar and jelly?"

She sticks her tongue out at me. It's bright red. "Well, you don't have to follow it exactly."

"So do you like my title?" I ask her.

"Sure. *The Soul Mate Next Door.* Sounds good. Didn't I say so?"

I smile, and she stares at me, confused, until it dawns on her what I'm really saying.

"*Oh! My! God! Remy?* You mean Remy?"

"Yes."

She actually gets up out of her seat and begins to jump up and down. "I knew it! He was so mean and nasty to you it *had* to be love. And you guys were *so* totally all over each other from day one! It was like, get a room already!"

"We were?"

"Weren't you?"

"Come to think of it, I guess we were," I marvel.

Being in a relationship with Remy is something simultaneously strange and perfect. By the end of September, seeing him outside of our house doesn't feel odd anymore. Now, when we walk down the street holding hands, having girls stare at him, then at me, then back at him is something I've grown to enjoy.

At first, he would meet me every day in the park near my office, where we would talk or make out under a tree. (I took the longest lunches I could without having Cinda think I'd walked off the job.) But now that the honeymoon's over, we usually just go eat at the Burger King down the street. It doesn't sound romantic, because it isn't really, but it suits me fine, anyway, since it was there that he first told me he loved me over a Double Whopper with Cheese. Just like that.

That was a good day. The best, actually.

And every day since then, I continue to be amazed by what a difference a year makes. The hard part is the first step. After that, things will just sort of fall into place if you let them. As for that pot of gold at the end of the rainbow, it isn't love,

even though that's what I happened to have found there, too.
Nor is it an engagement ring, or a book contract, or Flipper's autograph, or breast implants, or even the gold itself.
The reward is simply the peace that comes from leaving the
doom and gloom behind. A chance to enjoy the process of
becoming who you are. Getting happy. And to think—sometimes all it takes to make such an amazing thing happen is
an ill-conceived plan, a plane ticket or two and a huge leap
of faith.

Today is shaping up to be another good day.

At precisely 2:18 in the afternoon, something wonderful
occurs: I finally reach the end of Volume A, the first of the
two prototypes Cinda will need to land a commission for a
full set of encyclopedias and, possibly, make a long-standing
dream come true. But right beside the last line of the entry
on the ancient Aztecs, I see something—the Post-it I remember praying I'd never lay eyes on again: *"It's official! This job sucks."*

This job still sucks. That much is true. But now I can see
that it sucks in a good way. I know more about Aardvarks
and AIDS and the Antebellum South and Saint Thomas Acquinas than I ever thought possible. And as long as I stick to
the schedule, Cinda doesn't mind if I work on my own
book when the inspiration strikes.

I pick up the phone.

"Cinda? I'm ready for it!"

Within seconds, she's at my door bearing a huge stack
of copy.

"Here it is!" she says proudly.

I motion for her to come over and she deposits the pages
on my desk.

With a deep breath, I look down at the first word on the
first page.

"Zaire." I say aloud.

"A beautiful country. At least, it looks that way to me."

"What about Zagreb?"

"I'll put it in with Croatia."

"Can you do that?"

"I can do whatever I want. It's my encyclopedia!"

"Fair enough."

She turns to leave, but changes her mind and comes around the desk to give me a hug instead. "We're halfway there, Holly! In a few months, *Z* will be done. Can you believe it? Gosh, I better start learning that Quark program. I don't think we have the budget to keep that freelance layout person after all, so it looks like you and I are going to be the new art department. We'll design *Z* on our own! Sound good?"

"Sounds great."

Her enthusiasm is contagious.

I search through the many zippered compartments of my bag, feeling around for something I know must still be there—something I haven't seen in a really long time—but my purse is like a graveyard for every bit of paper ever issued to me.

At last, I find the tattered square folded up inside the receipt for a golf lesson at the Ritz-Carlton Golf Resort in Naples ($140 an hour! What was I thinking?). I open it up carefully and begin to read...

Hastings, Holly. 1975–2060. Passed away of chronic liver disease on Friday, December 31, 2060, alone again on New Year's Eve, since she didn't have a date, and hadn't in many, many years. She was 85....

I take a fresh red pen out of the box in my drawer and begin to make some changes.